Butt-dialing the Billionaire

BILLIONAIRES OF MANHATTAN

ANNIKA MARTIN

v000010112022ff2p

For my book family. I'm so glad I found you.

One

Jaxon

Paris

My parents' man of business, Barclay, waits for me in the dayroom, clutching his hat in his hands so tightly he's liable to crush it. "I took the first flight from Heathrow. My condolences, Mr. Henningsly."

"I should offer you the condolences," I say. "You knew them better than I did." The man probably talked to them every day, carrying out their directives and updating them on their empire.

I haven't talked to them in years.

And I never will again now.

"Nevertheless, Mr. Henningsly," Barclay says. "Very good."

Nevertheless and *very good* are phrases staff members use when dealing with me. Verbal blank screens, able to deflect anything. I sometimes think there was a memo: "If you're not sure what to say to the terrible son, *very good* will work in most circumstances. Otherwise, try *nevertheless*."

This man has used both now, a mark of his extreme unhappiness about having to work with me now.

No doubt he wishes I'd been the one to land a plane at the bottom of the Channel. Most people would prefer me dead—after suffering a bit, preferably. Made to feel sorry for how I am and all that.

For the record, I'm not sorry for how I am.

Still holding his hat, he follows me down blindingly polished marble floors. "Two of the finest people I've ever met."

I can understand him saying that sort of thing in public. My parents put a lot of work into their smoke-and-mirrors image and fooled most everybody who's anybody. Such a close colleague of my parents would know what they were. I don't appreciate being lied to and treated as a fool.

We continue down another endless hallway. I'm hoping the police, the aviation people, and the rest of the officials are gone. In the twenty-four hours since my parents died, it's been an endless parade of officials in and out of their Paris residence.

My residence now. One of them, anyway.

We're in the redundantly named Mansion Room, with high ceilings traced in gilt moldings and a roaring fireplace the size of a minivan. The window has a view of the elaborate gates that surround the place, topped with gold spikes and fleur-de-lis as if it's the official residence of the President of France himself. Those gates were creaking open and closed all through the night last night, operated by a nervous young security guard who quickly embraced my suggestion to oil them.

"*Very good, sir. Very good!*" he said, nearly melting with terror. As though I might rip his head off if he didn't comply.

The officials have indeed left. It's only my cousin Charley, along with my manservant, Arnold. Arnold has been with me my whole life; he's seventy now—a sporty and hale seventy with a thick pelt of white hair.

"Security cleared the paparazzi from the entire block," Arnold says.

I nod. My parents always did have effective security.

"Doing okay?" Charley asks, maybe mistaking my somber mood for grief.

"It's been a long night," I say simply.

Barclay stands there regarding me warily, still squeezing his hat.

"Is there something else?" I ask.

"So sorry to trouble you further...at such a difficult time."

"What is it?"

"A request, Mr. Henningsly. It's...the business. The board hopes you'll deliver a few optimistic words of reassurance to the troops."

"They want optimistic reassurance out of me?" I say. "God help them."

He blinks, unsure how to answer. Then, "Nevertheless, Mr. Henningsly, there are a great number of companies, investment houses, individual stockholders, and various entities across the globe under the umbrella of Wycliff Inc. that need to know that they can count on you to continue the tradition of stability and wisdom in terms of leadership, et cetera. People need to hear that you intend to keep an even keel. People are worried, you know..."

It's me they're worried about, but Barclay doesn't want to say it.

"The death of your parents has thrown a number of entities into panic," he continues. "There's the stock to consider, valuations in jeopardy..."

"Let's get rid of it, then. Dump the whole thing."

Barclay looks alarmed. Even my cousin Charley looks surprised.

"It's a bloated empire built on deceit and corporate espionage," I say. "While I suppose I can get behind that, Wycliff has that whole do-gooder image. If I'm going to run a predatory and underhanded international corporation, I wouldn't want it to have a fake good façade. It's just not me. I have a reputation to think about, you know."

"You can't just dump it all," Barclay says.

"According to the rules of the trust, I can," I say.

"Hundreds of thousands of people will lose their jobs," Barclay says. "It would spark a sell-off. Share prices would plummet. Employees' retirement accounts could be decimated. People across the globe would be affected. The markets themselves—"

"And I care about that why?" I ask.

Charley glares at me from his perch on a green velvet chair. The white porcelain cup in his hand gleams almost as brightly as his blond hair.

When you're me, you tend to deal with a lot of glares, and you get to know them the way grizzled old sailors get to know the wind. There's the garden variety what-an-asshole-I'm-in-shock style glare, the hate-you glare, and of course, the want-to-kill-you glare, which tends to be the most amusing of all, especially when people really put their hearts into it.

Charley has perfected the I-expected-better-of-you glare, a grand and well-practiced glare of his. "Hundreds of thousands of people, Jaxon! For once can't you do the right thing?"

I fix my shirt cuffs. "I'd prefer not to if it can at all be avoided."

Charley deepens his glare.

I give him a smile.

Barclay straightens. "You care because if you keep their business running as is, at least for the near future, it would be infinitely more wealth for you. As opposed to a sudden dump the day after this…this tragedy."

"I already have more wealth than I want," I say. "I need nothing from my parents."

Arnold pipes up now. "But Jaxon, if you had *infinitely more* wealth, you could more easily destroy your enemies."

"I'm comfortable with my current ability to destroy my enemies," I say.

"But with vastly more wealth, you could destroy them with impunity," Arnold points out.

I finish with my shirt cuffs. "Well, when you put it that way...I do love impunity."

"You'll do it, then?" Barclay asks.

I sigh wearily. "Fine."

"Excellent, sir," Barclay says. "We've got your father's PR man working on the address. We've got businesses across the globe synchronized to hear you read it. We'll set up in the third-floor great room. A few minutes and you'll be on your way. We'll have you deliver it at lunchtime, which will be morning in the US and dinnertime in Asia."

Barclay and Arnold head off, presumably to set up the third-floor great room, leaving Charley and me alone.

"Oh, Jaxon," Charley says, placidly sipping his tea.

Most people hang around me for the proximity to wealth or the notoriety of being linked to Villain Number One, as pronounced by the Eurozone tabloids not to mention each and every fan of the Formula One racing world. As the good-natured son of a branch of the family easily as wealthy as mine, though, god knows why Charley hangs around. Obligation, I suppose. An unhealthy fixation on family togetherness. Tradition. We were sent on a lot of countryside errands as boys.

"Well then," Charley says, setting aside his teacup. "I suppose I'll get back to the guest wing." He's looking at me expectantly. That's Charley, always expecting more.

"You won't stay for late lunch?" I say. "A bit of sushi, maybe?"

Charley straightens, examining my face for signs of how to take this. "Really?"

"I'm thinking we could eat it off the backs of softly weeping virgins," I add.

"Oh, Jaxon," he says. "You keep pushing me away, but you're

family. And I happen to know that it's hard to deal with this sort of thing alone. I had my sisters when my parents died."

"Is this where I cry on your shoulder?" I ask him. "You do recall the part about them being monsters."

"No man is an island, Jaxon. Or at least, he shouldn't be," he adds.

"What's wrong with being an island? Islands are great. Especially the ones that are rich in resources with nice weather and little places you can have a drink in, and you never have to deal with people's bullshit."

"I'll come back for moral support on the company-wide address," he says.

"Please don't." I sink into an incredibly uncomfortable couch.

"Someday you're going to be sorry for playing the villain all the time, Jaxon. Someday reporters will get sick of hearing you say scathing things about royals and socialites and even your frenemies won't come to your parties anymore."

I sigh. "Don't be ridiculous; frenemies have to come to my parties. It's practically in the job description."

"You got unlucky in the family department, Jaxon, but I'm here," Charley says.

"Oh, I don't know about unlucky," I say. "Having the family I did saved me a great deal of delusion about human nature."

Charley presses his lips together, a sign that he has something more to say. It'll be something about Jenny, my old nanny. He's dying to bring her up. Kind, sweet, loving Jenny who ran off in the middle of the night.

He won't dare—not with the way I'm glowering at him now.

Two

Jaxon

Two hours later we're in the third-floor great room, the storied post from which my father commanded his business empire. There's a desk set up with state-of-the-art broadcasting equipment.

I eye his very kingly chair. It's bad enough that I'm reading a speech his PR guy wrote in order to calm the empire he built. No way will I sit in his chair. Too on the nose. "That chair. No. Get one from the dining room."

Servants scramble.

Charley has taken the easy chair by the roaring fireplace. "Did nobody tell Uncle Cliff about the newfangled invention known as Zoom?" Charley asks.

"He would have no use for Zoom," I say. "That would require showing his face and seeing and hearing others."

"Ouch," Charley says, wearing his usual good-natured grin.

A PR guy hands me a sheet of paper. "The address, Mr. Henningsly."

I skim it. Frown. "*We must not despair but rather soldier on toward a brighter future*?" I read. "Who am I, Churchill?"

"This is the style your father preferred. People admired him deeply," the PR man assures me, a subtle dig.

I stare down at the words, remembering self-important, high-handed proclamations like this addressed at me. Part of his fake image of goodness everybody fell for. It made me feel crazy growing up, everybody admiring my father when I knew the truth. Even Charley didn't get it.

"This is bullshit," I say.

"This is the style they are used to," Barclay says. "It's what the circumstance requires."

"If you're not going to do it right, why bother?" Charley says.

"Five minutes of your time," Barclay says. "You keep the stock price nice and high for when you choose to sell."

"Yes, I understand the concept," I say.

"It's good you're doing this," Charley says. "Reaching out a helping hand."

"Don't pretend I'm something I'm not," I growl, adjusting the microphone, hating myself for doing this.

Three

Jada

"Twenty minutes!" somebody calls out.

"We got this," I say.

Rockabilly seamstress extraordinaire, Renata, pushes a pin into her wrist-held pincushion before pinning a quick dart into the fabric, careful not to poke Size Ten Tina. Tina is every Manhattan design house's most beloved fit model thanks to her awesome proportions, standing-still abilities, and gossip skills. You never want to stick her.

We've been here since five in the morning, racing to adjust our two-piece women's run wear sample. Things have to get out to the factory for quoting ASAP or we'll blow our chance with Target.

Renata calls out some numbers and I get on the tablet, adjusting the pattern.

We would've had this done days ago if it weren't for Bert Johnston, our horrible new CEO, who forgot to pass along some key information we were waiting on.

Bert was installed by the giant faceless corporation that bought our company last winter. He knows nothing about the garment industry, and he fired a lot of our best people.

Rising to the post of senior designer here has long been a dream of mine, but I wanted to earn it from hard work, not from my beloved mentors getting fired.

Dave from accounts comes out with a selection of energy bars from the vending machine. Dave has a talismanic belief in the power of energy bars, and he so wants to help. Everybody in the design department knows how important this thing is.

"I'll eat when I'm dead," I whisper, fingers flying over the screen.

"You two are killing it!" Dave says. "Savage."

Renata snorts. Dave is so sweet. Everybody here is. We're a family, and nothing Bert does will take that away from us.

Unless he succeeds in destroying the company. Sometimes it seems like that's his goal. But why would you deliberately sabotage the place you were hired to oversee?

Renata ties a quick knot. "Good?"

I take a look. "Good."

"On it." Lacey changes the material allocations.

Furious murmurs and texts suddenly ripple through the office.

"No way," Renata says.

"No, no, no, no!" I whisper.

"Bert alert," Dave says in a low voice, beelining back to his desk. Bert alert means Bert's been spotted heading down the hall. People scramble to look busy like birds fluttering frantically in front of an oncoming tidal wave. If Bert thinks you're not working, you'll get a demerit. If you get three demerits, you're fired—no unemployment, no insurance, no nothing.

Bert's been like a man on a mission, handing out demerits.

"Conference room!" Bert barks as he bursts through the door. "Mandatory, all-company call. Now."

Lacey goes up to Bert, clutching her notebook, looking terrified all the way to the roots of her purple hair. "W-what is this about?"

"A new generation of the Eadsburg von Henningslys is taking over Wycliff, and there's an important introductory address," Bert says, broad cheeks glowing pale pink under the stark lighting. He is a big man, an ex-football player with a crew cut and intensely scrubbed-looking pink cheeks, almost porcelain-looking in certain lighting.

"Um... Who are the Eadsburg von Henningslys?" Lacey asks.

I wince. I know what Lacey's doing—she's trying to stall Bert, trying to give us time to finish up and hand the package off to the bike courier who's currently waiting down on the street.

"The family that owns the Wycliff corporation? SportyGoCo's parent company? AKA your employer?" Bert barks, in a tone designed to suggest she's the biggest fool ever.

"A new generation?" Lacey asks, playing dumb.

"The son's stepping up. Some kind of Euro race car driver." Bert claps his hands. "Come on, people, get in there."

Design team members scurry past, hoping to avoid Bert's wrath.

It's here that Bert turns his attention to Renata and me. "This isn't optional."

I keep working. "We're just wrapping up this package. Fifteen minutes. This is our bread-and-butter line for—"

"Not optional," he interrupts. "Demerits for anybody who's not there in two."

"Can we finish this up in the conference room while we listen to the address? If we don't make the cutoff, we'll lose all of this work."

"And whose fault is that?" Bert demands.

It's like he's daring me to say *yours*. "Staff only." He turns to Size Ten Tina. "Out."

Tina gives me a sympathetic look and heads off to change. I choke back my tears. A sure-thing Target slot: Gone.

"Sorry," Renata whispers to me, standing. She can't afford another demerit—she already has two.

So do I.

There's a mocking light in Bert's eyes. "Thirty seconds."

Devastated, I grab my phone and follow the rest of the staff into the conference room.

Months of work. My first flagship design.

Crashed.

The full design department—all two dozen of us—are assembled around the conference room table, dead silent, expressions grim.

Bert looks on smugly, a vampire feeding off of our low morale, then heads off, presumably to make sure the rest of the departments are being prevented from doing anything productive.

Whispering starts up at the far end and I can distinctly hear the words *gotta get out of here* and *fuck this.*

SportyGoCo was the best place to work before the Wycliff-pocalypse.

There's a rumor that if our sales numbers don't rise in a matter of weeks, they're closing the company.

The speakerphone crackles. We've heard these addresses before—they're ridiculous and buffoonish. Some old guy who loves the sound of his voice, and you're supposed to be grateful, I suppose.

"We've built this place and we can save it. We're a family," I say.

No response. People just look defeated.

My heart twists. This group here saved my ass more times than I can think, especially when I first came to the city, naïve and bewildered. And when it became clear I'd never earn an actual living as an actress, they helped me channel my passion for fun clothes into a career.

Aside from Bert, any one of these people would give me the shirt straight off their backs, and I'd give them mine.

Or more like I'd make one that's even better, full of sequins and sparkles, and give them that.

"A new generation taking over," I say. "Maybe it's good news. Maybe the younger generation will make things better."

"Yeah, it worked great in North Korea," Shondrella says. "Oh wait, umm..."

"A European racecar driver billionaire," Lacey mumbles to our side of the table. "Like, seriously?"

"It doesn't matter who runs that thing," Renata says. "These sorts of people own so many companies, they can't even name them all. Nothing will change."

"And we still have Unicorn Wonderbag," I point out. "We'll get to work on Wonderbag, and everything will turn around."

The speakerphone crackles. A man comes to announce there will be an announcement. He talks about what a good thing it is to have a steady hand in times of turbulence.

"Which turbulence?" somebody grumbles. "There are so many turbulences."

"Who can keep track?" somebody else jokes.

The voice on the speaker talks about the company history, and finally introduces Jaxon Harcourt Eadsburg von Henningsly. The five-part name gets an eyeroll.

Jaxon Harcourt Eadsburg von Henningsly, our fearless new leader, begins to speak in a beautiful baritone voice. Too bad the things that this beautiful voice says are every bit as pompous and ridiculous as every other speech from the billionaire Wycliff owners, or as we call our parent company: the "why not jump off a cliff?" owners.

My heart sinks as the son spouts phrases like, "soldier on in the face of adversity" and "do not despair but rather square your shoulders in the direction of the future."

Back when the evil, faceless Wycliff corporation first took over and started up these ridiculous addresses, people would make finger-pointing-down-the-throat gestures and self-stabbing motions.

And I would look at them scoldingly, because I'm the senior person now, the mom of the design department.

Now they don't even bother to make the gestures. That's how deeply everybody's spirit is crushed.

In real life, I'm not that professional or mom-like. At home with my girlfriends, I can be silly, but one thing doesn't change and that's my work ethic. I always like to be achieving, whether it's making videos of our apartment building or doing a bit part in one of my friends' weekend plays or making food or saving this company—and my fashion design career.

Professionalism is a muscle that anybody can build—that's what I always say. Act as if. Right? But I always make sure to wear one sparkly thing, like a pin or a belt or a shoe ornament.

Jaxon Whatever-von-Henningsly drones on about how he'll continue the leadership that we've grown to respect and admire.

I can feel morale plummeting like a thousand anvils off a thousand Road Runner cliffs. Another obnoxious out-of-touch owner a universe away.

Cringe.

They said this son was European, but he definitely has an American accent. Is that what rich people do? Live in different places? I would never up and move like that. A person needs roots. They need their people.

On he drones, "We shall turn our gazes toward a productive future, full of pride and promise and joint prosperity."

It's so outrageous, considering they're destroying this company.

Shondrella makes a half-hearted self-stab. Her self-stab says, why even bother with a self-stab? Shondrella's going on four decades in the design business, and she says she's never seen a design house go downhill so fast.

"Continuing the exemplary leadership..."

I catch Lacey's eyes. She's exhausted. She looks like she's going to cry. She has the most to lose of anybody here.

All at once, I've had enough. I've hit my limit.

I don't know what possesses me, but I start to mouth along, pretending to say the words that the pompous son is saying.

"Soldier on through thick and thin," I mouth along to the speakerphone—badly. I clap on a dorky expression.

Lacey snorts and claps a hand over her mouth.

Actual laughter. It's music to my ears. When did I last hear laughter at SportyGoCo?

I mouth along some more, and suddenly everyone is laughing. I'm sure it's a shock to them—it's so unlike me to show my fun side at work.

Still. I haven't heard laughter in this office for too long. It's like the life and camaraderie are rushing back into people. I glance over at the closed door. Well, what's the harm in a little bit of morale-boosting silliness to take the edge off of today's devastating Target debacle?

The son drones on.

I stick my pointer finger up into the air and rock my head from side to side. It's stupid, but who cares! The speech is stupid! I'm making a face; I'm flapping my jaw.

People are laughing. Shondrella is practically rolling on the floor.

It's almost sad when the fancy-pants owner ends his fancy-pants conference call.

The team is still looking at me, wanting more. So I keep it going, outright impersonating the guy now, saying all the rich-person things I can think of. "What's more, as reward for you to soldier on, I shall send each and every office a jar of Grey Poupon mustard!" I'm fully channeling my inner actress now, right down to the baritone.

"Please square your shoulders and wash away adversity as I wash my teeth with my silver toothbrush!" I've added a foofy accent. The son has a nice voice, but the dad had an upper-crust accent, and the accent is funnier.

"Please do not despair," I continue. "I shall indeed hire the worst people to oversee you and even that won't stop you from your awesomeness." I look all around. "Wait, where is my Grey Poupon? I'm a billionaire, I must have my Grey Poupon!"

It's so dorky, but people are laughing their heads off. Dave is lying faceup on the conference table.

I rack my brain, trying to think of more rich-person things to say. "Please bring me my silver and diamond-studded nose hair device. I shall lead this company through thick and thin, but not without my nose hair device!"

Renata hits me in the shoulder. "What is that, even?"

I have no idea, but that isn't stopping me. "Quiet, peasant!"

She hits me again—hard. She does this rockabilly roller derby on the weekends and has more strength than she knows.

"Quick, fetch the servants, I now need some smelling salts. Where is my cravat? Where is my Foppish Ascot?"

I can literally feel the togetherness in the laughter. I can feel the love, the camaraderie. This is why we stayed. We are a family.

"If I cannot drive my Foppish Ascot 3000 in the NASCAR race, I will truly despair!" I continue.

"What's a Foppish Ascot 3000?" Lacey asks.

"It's a race car," I emote. "That I shall drive to joint prosperity."

Right then a voice breaks through the speakerphone. "What the hell?"

We all freeze.

The voice is Jaxon Harcourt Eadsburg von Henningsly.

"I don't know," somebody on the owner's end says.

"Shit!" Dave whisper-yells as he lunges for the table and stabs the speakerphone buttons.

Four

JAXON

THE PR PEOPLE are overjoyed with the speech; everybody is—even Arnold and Charley.

Barclay looks on approvingly, thinking, perhaps, that the bad seed son has decided to change his ways and pretend to be good.

Because you never want to show you care, I stare down at my phone, scrolling a lot of nothing, but really, I'd like to put an ice pick through my ears. One for each ear, preferably continuing on into whatever part of my brain remembers things. Or maybe a good old-fashioned frontal lobotomy would do the trick.

It's that Türenbourg lawn photograph all over again.

One moment of weakness. I shouldn't have agreed to it—not any of it. Letting myself get boxed in like this.

It's then that the feed fires back up with a series of clicks and an overseas-sounding ring. Voices blare out over the speaker.

Specifically, a woman's voice.

"Please square your shoulders and wash away adversity as I wash my teeth with my silver toothbrush!"

Barclay's looking around the room, confused.

The voice goes on about Grey Poupon. Is somebody making a comedy routine out of the speech?

The voice has an accent now, going on and on.

"Quick, bring the servants, I shall need some smelling salts. Where is my cravat? Where is my Foppish Ascot? If I cannot drive my Foppish Ascot 3000 in the NASCAR race, I will truly despair!"

"What the hell?" I say.

"I don't know what's happening." Barclay's stabbing buttons on the phone as the voice goes on. It's almost an out-of-body experience. "Seems to be a phone number in the US."

Arnold simply unplugs the whole system.

Dead quiet.

People stare at me, waiting to see what I'll do. People are always staring at me, wondering what terrible thing I'll do.

Finally. I'm feeling like myself again.

Arnold tries a tentative smile. "A bit of joviality," he tries.

Barclay waves away the mocking voices. "The call was a great success. I'm already getting messages and texts congratulating and thanking you."

I'm shown said texts and messages, and it appears that the whole world loved the speech.

Except for the Grey Poupon woman.

Charley stands. "I, for one, am ready for a cocktail."

"Me too," I say.

"As for whoever that was, naturally, that person will be ferreted out and fired," Barclay says.

"No need. I'll handle it," I say.

Everybody stares at me, dumbfounded.

"What?" Charley says.

"Find out who it is. I'll take it from there," I say.

"What do you mean?" Barclay asks.

"I mean, identify the person and tell me who it is," I say. "And I'll take the punishment from there."

Charley looks baffled. "What are you going to do?"

"Whatever I damn well please," I say casually.

"No doubt that it was clear insubordination," Barclay says nervously. "Misguided if not deeply insulting, no doubt about that. But to go to such lengths to personally fire her—"

"I didn't say I'd fire her," I say.

Barclay looks relieved.

"I said I'd punish her. I may have her drawn and quartered. Maybe strung up by her thumbs. And there's always a piranha pool. There are many ways to destroy a person. Get me a name, Barclay." I head out the door.

Charley catches up to me. "Come on," he says.

I give him a look and keep on.

"You get the name, and then what? You're not really going to destroy this poor woman?"

"Why not?" I say. "My schedule's clear."

"It's not enough that everyone on the continent hates you? You have to go pick fights with the Americans, too? Listen to yourself, Jaxon. Going after this woman would be despicable!"

"You don't have to sell me on it, Charley, I've already decided to go."

He snorts. "You're grieving, Jaxon. Petty distractions like this won't make your grief hurt less."

"Considering my grief over this is zero, can you hurt less than zero?" I ask him. "Would a negative number of hurting be the same as pleasure? Anyway, dragging my family's name through the mud has always been one of my favorite pastimes. I can't take an axe to Wycliff just yet, but this works."

"Think what you're doing. Can't you just say, 'Who cares about this random snarky person? I'm gonna live my own life.'"

"And the fun in that would be what, exactly?"

His mouth forms into a grim line.

Five

Jada

I'm cowering in my cubicle across from Renata. "What was I thinking!" I say. "Whaaaaat..."

"Stop it," Renata says, fixing her polka-dot hairband over her jet-black hair. "No way will Bert get it out of anyone. What happens in the conference room, stays in the conference room."

I sink lower in my seat, typing out my email to the factory explaining that it's going out late and begging them to consider rushing the Target quote. No way will they say yes, but I have to try.

"It'll drive him buggy," Renata says. "It'll be fun and entertaining to see him fume."

"Unless he fires all of us."

"You heard Lacey. No way will he know it's this department."

"He'll suspect," I say. "It's very design department to do that."

"Or marketing," she reminds me, and then she cringes. "Except marketing has snitches and we don't. But hey! Let him suspect. Anyway, you work too hard. It was fun to see your silly side."

"My silly side has no place at work, especially now that I'm senior designer. Just watch, though. I'm not taking any more stupid risks. I'm going to be a million percent professional from here on out."

"You are professional."

What Renata doesn't realize is that when you're tiny and blonde, you need to be twice as professional as your coworkers if you want people to take you seriously. "A million percent professional. No more screwing around."

"Everyone knows this place would fall apart without you. Most people in your shoes would have taken the job with your friend's style storefronts. They would've left without looking back."

"You wouldn't have."

"For a merchandising job like that? Are you kidding? You know, you are supposed to abandon a sinking ship. It's what they recommend."

"I'll never abandon it," I say, firing off the email.

"Bert alert," Dave mumbles as he walks by.

I grab his wrist, stopping him in his tracks. "Lacey's in the break room."

"On it."

Lacey's horrible fatigue drives her to need a late-afternoon nap. The doctors say there's nothing wrong with her, but we know different, and we work together to give her rest breaks.

"Here's the deal," Bert says, standing up at the front of the room, all angry pink cheeks under his salt-and-pepper crew cut. "We know it was somebody in this department. Each and every one of you will be fired for insubordination if I don't get the name of the person who did it."

I hide my phone under my desk and text Renata.

Jada: I have to come forward.

Renata: He's bluffing.
He has to be.

Jada: What if he isn't?

Renata: DO NOT.

SHONDRELLA STANDS. She's an elegant fifty-something fashion industry veteran with a streak of white down the front of her jet-black hair and connections all over the city. "Can you give us a few more details? I'm not really sure what you're talking about."

Bert eyes her suspiciously. "After the company address, there was an accidental callback where people were heard making fun of Mr. Von Henningsly, yucking it up after the call ended. I assure you, he is not amused. He has personally asked for information." Bert looks at his watch. "You have precisely one minute to give up a name or I start cleaning house."

My heart pounds. I have to do it. I feel Renata's eyes on me, her famous warning scowl. Don't you dare—that's what the scowl says.

"Was this recorded?" Shondrella asks. "If we could hear the recording, maybe we could ID the voices."

Freaking brilliant of Shondrella to try and see if they have a recording.

"Thirty seconds," Bert says.

A text under my desk.

RENATA: NOOOOOOOOOOO

I STAND. I have to confess.

Bert frowns at me. "Jada?"

Lacey strolls up next to me, casually sets her phone down on my desk, and taps a long pink fingernail onto the screen. I glance down to see a text from Bruce in shipping.

Bruce: He's telling every department he knows it's them. TOTAL BLUFF.

"JADA?" Bert barks.

I swallow. "Why would we stay after the call and goof off when we had that two-piece to finish?"

Bert comes up to me. "Is this insubordination? Is that what this is?"

I straighten up. "Just pointing it out..."

He stares at my eyes for an uncomfortably long time, and I stare right back, all confused and concerned. Did he know I was about to confess? Sometimes I feel like he has evil psychic abilities. "We'll keep our ears open," I chirp.

"You'll keep your ears open, will you?" he says.

I give him a polite smile. "Yup."

"Nobody?" Bert looks around.

There's more silence.

"Last chance." He settles his gaze on Lacey, who looks like she just woke up. With her two demerits and her health issues, she's vulnerable, and he knows it. Anybody who helps me out, of course, would be rewarded.

Lacey shakes her head.

"What do you think would happen if I sent the recording to a lab for voice analysis? Am I going to find out it was somebody in this department? Am I going to find out that you all know exactly who it is and are refusing to tell?" He strolls across the room, staring as he goes. "You'd best hope not." He pauses to let that sink in, then he leaves.

"There is no way he's got a recording," somebody mumbles. People agree. No way.

"Even if he does," Renata says. "A hundred women work here. He'd voice print us all? Puhlllease."

"God, I'm so sorry!" I sink into my seat. "I am going to be all business from now on. So serious!"

"Dude, it was worth it!" Dave says.

"Yeah, seeing Bert freak?" Shondrella says. "Priceless."

"The family," Renata says in her *Godfather* impression. "You come for one of us, you come for us all."

"That's not a thing anybody ever said in *The Godfather*," Dave says.

"Maybe it should've been," Renata says. "Anyway, it's a thing in our family."

Six

Jaxon

Four Weeks Later: London

Workers scurry around, packing up my parents' London residence. Charley's sprawled out on a priceless couch he's thinking of taking for one of his residences. Arnold comes in with a large, framed photo.

"Christie's," I say.

"Jaxon, no!" Charley says. "It's the first signed print. Iconic Danbery. And look how happy you are!"

I glower at the photo that fooled the world, taken by a celebrity photog my parents hired at great expense. Mom and Dad and me on a picnic blanket, the three of us smiling out at the world. The richest little richie-rich boy with his doting parents, the splendidly groomed grounds of our Türenbourg castle unfolding in the background.

Totally fake.

Arnold comes in with an original oil painting of my parents in their prime.

"Christie's," I say.

"If nothing else, keep it for your kids," Charley tries.

"As if I would inflict the Von Henningsly bullshit on another generation."

"Mark my words, you'll want a family someday."

I point. "Christie's."

Charley still believes in the fairy tale. His entire family does, a fact that I witnessed over the many Christmases I spent there. Always laughing and clinging to each other and creating their own traditions. They'd put an old Dolly Parton doll on the top of the tree and then do this whole dance to the song "We are the Champions." They always watch scary movies on Christmas Day, huddled together. The ridiculous lore and traditions they developed over the years seemed to create this illusion of togetherness that they cling to.

Who can blame them? You're born alone and you die alone. It's not an easy truth to face.

Charley sighs and leans on a nearby wall, watching Arnold place the portrait to be crated for auction. "Congrats on getting the share prices back up, by the way," he says. "That pompous speechwriter, though."

"Never again," I say. "Shoot me if I sound like my father ever again."

"Will you be selling Wycliff now?"

"Eventually. I still have to destroy the butt-dialer."

"What?" Charley pushes off the wall, straightening up. "I thought you dropped that whole sordid thing."

"Of course not. Management hasn't been able to identify the offender, so I'll be taking the investigation into my own hands. I'll take a position there under an assumed identity and find the perpetrator myself."

Charley blinks at me, confused. "A position?"

"A position at the company," I explain. "As in *job*. If you want a thing done right, you have to do it yourself, it seems. I'm having

Soto arrange it." Mr. Soto is my business guy. My parents' guy, Barclay, quit soon after the conference call.

"That's madness," Charley says. "You can't take a job."

"Why not?" I say.

He stares at me as though he can't get his mind around the question. "Forget the company. Come out to my villa, Jaxon. You can clear your head there. The sudden loss of both one's parents is huge, whether you'll admit it or not."

"Soto lined me up with a position already. Office-gopher-slash-delivery assistant. I'll be undercover." I grin. "What do you think?"

"You're not thinking straight," Charley says. "You don't know how an office works. You have no actual skills. You've never held a job in your life."

"That's not true," I protest. "I've had a job."

"Motorsport is different from a job," he says.

"What do you mean? I built a team and showed up at a specific time to do a specific task."

People thought I didn't have the discipline to become a driver for a Formula One team. I was too unruly, too hotheaded, not disciplined enough for the long hours on the track and in the gym, but I proved them wrong.

"You got booted out for fighting," Charley reminds me.

"Gundrun deserved it," I say.

"A lot of people deserve it. You go to some office and you're gonna find a lot of people who deserve to be hit. You might even end up with a boss who deserves to be taken down a peg or two, but guess what? You'll have to sit there and smile. No brawling allowed. You won't last a day."

"So little faith. When I set my mind on something, I typically do it," I say.

"An office worker? People aren't stupid, Jaxon..."

"I'm not going there to work. I'll socialize with people until I get my answer."

"And what if somebody recognizes you? Your picture is everywhere. Americans have tabloids too, you know."

"I'm not the sort of person that American tabloids track. American tabloids are all movie stars and British royals, not minor continental celebs. They probably think the Grand Prix is a bike race."

"Formula One racing is growing in popularity over there."

"Well, they weren't paying attention ten years ago," I say. "I'm a historical figure. I'm Herbert Plumer."

"People still share the clip of the fight."

"They're not looking at my face, they're looking at a brilliant and well-deserved left hook."

"You lived in Manhattan on and off. You still know people."

"I haven't been back since I was twelve. You're not talking me out of this."

"New York is an international city. You can't tell me it's not international. Get one person who's spent any time in Monte Carlo nightclubs, and you'll have a pack of paparazzi on your ass."

This gets me thinking. The next time Arnold comes by, I instruct him to send for somebody who can change my looks.

"Not what I was imagining," Charley drawls unhappily.

A theatrical costumer named Bev shows up a few hours later. She suggests a new haircut with a center part.

"I want a disguise, not a new style, I'm an American who works at a wage job." I search American hair fashions, and soon find myself on a website called Sav-R-Mart fashion fails. "Here we go. This." I point at a picture. "Give me this."

"No, Jaxon!" Charley says.

"This is not a current hairstyle," she says nervously. "Gelled spikes with frosted tips hasn't been popular since the nineties."

"Perfect. You'll give me the hair. I want those tinted rectangular glasses and the short-sleeved shirt, too. What is this shirt? Men actually wear this?"

Arnold's back with another heirloom I don't want. He peers at the screen. "Is it a Hawaiian shirt?"

Bev looks, too. "No. Hawaiian shirts have flowers. I would call this a 1990s party boy shirt."

I take a closer look. It's a neon-blue button up shirt with lots of pink and yellow triangles and squiggly lines on it.

"Get me some shirts like that."

Staff is dispatched to shops. I take a seat and instruct Bev to begin.

With trembling hands, she drapes a cape over my shoulders and then pauses, looking upset.

"What is it?" I demand.

"Bleaching the ends of your hair, Mr. Henningsly...I don't recommend it."

"All the better. Do it," I say.

"I just want you to know, I am advising against it."

"Are we going to start anytime this century?"

An hour later, the hairstyle is complete. Bev steps back, looking uncertain. "I'm sorry, this is what you asked for," she says.

Charley is just laughing. "Help! I'm having NSYNC flashbacks!"

Bev hands me a mirror. I look like a different person—almost. "I love it."

Bev grins, surprised.

"It's not enough, though. You make up people for the theater. Do you have fake scars or something to try on?"

"Can I suggest you try on a different bizarre and disturbing obsession?" Charley says.

"We can give you something more." Bev roots around in her cases, sounding braver now. "A disguise has two parts—what you cover and what you offer up as a distraction. This might be a little extreme, but if you truly don't want to be recognized, you have to give them something else to look at." She extracts a black thing the diameter of a pencil eraser and affixes it to my cheek. "There we go.

It's a stage mole, designed to be seen from the audience." She steps back. "It's a lot."

Charley is just shaking his head. "It's too much!"

"But it does draw the eye and give his face a different character."

"It's not realistic at all!" Charley says. "Nobody has a mole like that!"

"You're right—nobody has a mole like that. It's a stage mole. It's not designed to be realistic, but people will accept it," Bev says. "People are a lot more focused on themselves and schooling their own reactions than you might realize. And if they focus on the mole, it'll be to make stories to explain it."

"Like why he didn't remove it," Charley says. "Most people would remove it."

I hold up the mirror. It's huge and extreme, but I find I like it. "I wouldn't remove it," I growl.

"Of course you wouldn't," Charley says. "You'd give it a name and put it up for knighthood."

The rest of the accessories have been delivered by now, and I try on the whole ensemble—the glasses from two decades ago, the obnoxiously bright shirt. I fluff up the hairstyle that everybody seems to hate.

"Yet somehow these things aren't ruining your looks," Charley complains. "They should ruin your looks more."

"I don't give a shit about my look. I don't want to be bothered, that's all. Let's give it a spin." I grab my phone and head downstairs, girding myself as I usually do when I go outside, ready for people to get in my face or try to get a quote or a picture. Or if I'm in a hat and sunglasses, for people to recognize it as a disguise and try to penetrate it with varying degrees of success.

I walk the block without being noticed. Some people stare at my mole and then look away. Some glance over me briefly and carry on. I don't know if it's the hair or the glasses or the shirt or the mole, or maybe it's the whole thing, but people are avoiding my eyes. I've never experienced anything like it.

It's as if...I'm invisible.

I stroll around the block, reveling in it.

"I love it," I say when I get back.

Seven

Jaxon

New York City

SportyGoCo occupies the top three floors of a decrepit building in an unremarkable part of the Garment District. They apparently design and market sportswear to be sold in large stores. After a number of moderately successful years, their fortunes have plummeted precipitously.

God knows why my parents bought the place, though it's far more likely that they didn't know that they had. It's hard to tell how much interaction they had with Wycliff Inc. beyond my dad using them as a captive audience for self-important speeches.

I report into the human resources office where a man named Derek has packets and forms for me to fill out with my new name —Jack Smith. He smiles at me but mostly keeps his eyes on the forms and the packets as a way of not staring at my mole.

Fucking brilliant.

He leads me up to the design department, my new home base, but they'll share me with shipping, he informs me.

Perfect. Whoever tried and failed to identify the source of the butt-dial put the design department at the top of their suspect list along with shipping; this way, I'll have interaction with both.

I can't imagine this taking more than a day or two. People always give me what I want.

I'm told the CEO himself will bring me a binder. With that, I'm left at the design department, which is a large room with garish lighting and rows upon rows of cubicles like a movie set.

A woman with dark hair and a 1940s-looking outfit introduces herself as Renata and leads me back, saying things about the department that I'm not listening to, because the whole place is a sea of cubicles. People actually sit in cubicles? I thought that was just in movies.

The soundtrack is like a movie too, what with the low murmur of voices and the clatter of keyboards punctuated by soft beeps. Is this actually real?

Renata pauses to introduce me to a petite blonde woman with doll-like features and pencils stuck willy-nilly into her messy bun. "This is Jada. She's our senior designer."

Jada assesses me with a piercing gaze, spine erect, making the most of her short stature. Whereas Renata and the HR guy struggled awkwardly not to stare at my mole, Jada looks me clear in the eyes, as if to size me up. "Glad to have you here, Jack," she says. "We've been so short-staffed—thank goodness they sent someone to help."

I snort. "*Someone to help* might be overstating things."

"Hah," Renata says. "You'll totally be helpful, I know it."

"No, wait, I want to know what that means." Jada fixes me with a big frown. "*Might* be overstating it? Are you not here to help?"

I fix her with a lighthearted smile. *So I've met the resident humorless control freak,* I think.

"Not if I can avoid it," I say.

Jada's delicious frown deepens to a moue of disgust. I should try to move on and meet the rest of the people, but I'm unable. It's almost a physical impossibility. She is exactly the kind of person I cannot stand, and she can't stand me, and it's delightful.

I answer her frown with an even bigger smile, and her annoyance is a thing to behold.

"Great. Just what we need." She takes a seat and goes back to it, tapping angrily.

"Oh, come on, I think you're a big joker, Jack," Renata says loudly.

Jada grumbles and keeps typing. Jada's obviously not the butt-dialer, but Renata might be.

"Come on, then." Renata leads me back to a cubicle a bit behind Jada's and futzes with a computer from another decade. "I'm logging you into the intranet. Your username is your name with no spaces and your password is password, no caps." She steps aside and looks at me expectantly. "Home sweet home."

"This is where I sit?" I ask.

"Where else?"

"An actual cubicle," I say.

Renata laughs. "Only the best here at SportyGoCo!"

"Guys!" Jada twists around and says something about an alert or being alert; that one short, sharp command has the entire office hushed up. That is some serious buzzkill control freak power right there.

"Look alert!" Renata tells me before settling into her own cubicle across the row.

Jada gives me an intense stare, then twists back around to her monitor.

It's here I notice that a head of short dark hair has appeared at the far end, but that's all I can see thanks to the fact that I'm in a *cubicle* of all things. The head approaches. Soon there's a pair of beady eyes and strangely shiny cheeks.

Yet another office buzzkill—that's clear right away.

My handler, Renata, pipes up. "This is Jack Smith, our new

office-gopher-slash-delivery assistant. We've just been settling him in. Jack, this is your new boss, Bert Johnston, CEO of SportyGoCo."

Bert glares at me and my mole in the most annoyed way possible, as if it is actively offending him. There truly is no end to the delight of my new mole.

"Apparently somebody from corporate saw fit to transfer you here, Mr. Smith, not that we have the need or the want, but here you are." He slams down a three-ring binder. "Company Code of Conduct. I advise you to study it well. And if you take a look at the home folder on your desktop, you'll find a PDF with the orientation materials and a link to the training video. I suggest you start there."

He stares at me, seeming to wait for me to do something. "Got it," I say.

Still he waits. "Any day now, Mr. Smith."

Does he want me to look at these things now? I turn to the screen and identify the PDF in question and open it up, shocked to see that the thing is over 200 pages long. He points at a link on the screen. I open the video; it has a runtime of over an hour.

Is this some kind of a joke? Who reads things this long? Or watches things that long? Bert stands there still.

"Well? Have you prepared an executive summary?" I ask.

Bert looks at me incredulously. "Excuse me?"

"An executive summary. A shortened version that you would prepare with just the highlights for me to peruse," I explain.

"What do you think this is?" he barks. "No, I did not prepare an executive summary for you. You will read through this entire package. You will watch the video on a speed of one point zero. Is this understood?"

I stare at him, torn between laughing and firing him. But it comes to me that neither of these are good choices if I want to conceal my identity long enough to unmask the butt-dialer.

"Understood?" he demands once again.

"Oh, very much so," I say, trying not to grin. It's hard with him so upset. This man is actually yelling at me. People do this?

"It's not optional."

"I can see that," I say.

Bert scrutinizes me as if he's waiting for something more. It's excruciating, not so much in terms of pain, but just that I am allergic to authority figures and already this job has given me two of them—Control Freak Barbie and now this guy.

What now? What is he waiting for?

"Uh, that'll be all, then," I say with a wave. "You're dismissed." This is what I habitually say when I want people to get out of my face, but I know it's the wrong thing even before the gasp goes up from the sea of cubicles, even before Bert's cheeks turn an alarming shade of deep pink.

"Excuse me?" Bert thunders.

This is the wrong time to smile, but I can't help it. He's so angry! Charley was right. Blending into an office is no easy matter.

Bert stabs the finger onto the three-ring binder. "In the rules and regs binder, Mr. Smith, you will learn about demerits. If you get three demerits, you will be fired. The insubordination that you just demonstrated has earned you one demerit."

"You just gave me a *demerit*?" Is it possible he's joking? I've never had a boss, unless you count my father, though that usually ended in fists flying between us and me on the ground. Until I got into my teens, at any rate.

"And you'll find yourself with yet another demerit if you don't wipe that smile off your face," he says.

"Wipe the smile off my face?" People say that?

"And there's demerit number two. Are you going to go for three?"

I look past where Bert stands, over at Renata and Jada, who are both twisted around, staring, horrified.

It occurs to me here that this Bert really might be able to fire me, after all the work that Soto did to get me in here without letting anybody know who I am.

"Well, let's get reading, then," I say, and with an almost superhuman effort, I suck in my lips, point my face at the computer, and pretend to read the PDF.

Bert stands there a while longer, maybe sensing that I'm not actually reading it, sensing, perhaps, that the only thing stopping me from another demerit is the flesh-piercing pressure of my teeth on my in-turned lips.

Finally he walks off.

"Okay, then!" I say once he's gone. "That guy's a real asshole!"

The blazing eyes of Workaholic, Control Freak Barbie appear over my cubicle wall. "Do you *want* to get fired?"

I give her a smile that I know will annoy her. "Not at the moment, no."

Jada comes to my cubicle doorway, as it were, and looms over me, all five foot two of her. "If you're here to disrupt things, please just leave now. We need this department to function at peak efficiency."

"An executive summary is efficient. That's why they make them." I say this all very casually, but my pulse is racing and I'm feeling strangely energized.

"Except you're not an executive, are you? You're a delivery assistant and office gopher who we desperately need help from, and you nearly got yourself fired on your first day."

My pulse races. I'm having trouble processing the experience of somebody bossing me. First Bert and now Jada.

"I mean... 'You're dismissed'?" she continues. "What's wrong with you?"

"What's wrong with me...it's a pretty long list, to be honest," I say. "The specifics would vary depending on who you talk to."

Jada's scowl heats up. "Excuse me?"

I cross my legs and adopt a relaxed posture, but really, I didn't expect this experience to be so enlivening. "The nature of the things wrong with me would definitely vary from person to person as well, but I'm sure there'd be overlap."

"You think you're funny?"

God, those hot, frowning lips. She's nobody I'd ever be with, but it doesn't matter—the hot frown is getting me deep down. It's just how fiery she is with all of that bossy control mania. I want to stir and stir and stir those embers until they go full flame, and then I'd bask in her heat.

"Of course, wrong has its advantages," I find myself saying. "There are scenarios where, it could be argued, the wronger, the better. If you know what I mean." I lower my voice to a deeper register. "And I think you do."

Jada's color rises, and somehow, she's even more delicious. "Oh. My. God. I'm gonna pretend you didn't say that. We are struggling for our lives here and they send us Don Juan the Entitled Delivery Driver?"

"Don Juan the Entitled Delivery Driver?"

"That's right."

A nickname. "I like it."

Her nostrils flare. "Whatever!" She storms back to her cubicle and sits. I stay at my cubicle, fighting the impulse to go after her.

Don Juan the Entitled Delivery Driver.

Renata shakes her head and gets back to work.

I read through the boring PDF. Clearly I do need some pointers if I'm going to blend in long enough to unmask the butt-dialer, but what I really want to do is go over to Jada's cubicle and be Don Juan the Entitled Delivery Driver some more.

Ten minutes later, a figure looms at my side. I look up to see a young guy with slicked-back hair and a laid-back vibe that reminds me of the surfer boys along the French Riviera.

He introduces himself as Dave, eyes roving over my spiky, blond-tipped hair, glasses, and mole. He looks stunned for a moment, and then he waves a hand between us. "Dude, this whole thing you have going on. This whole presentation. It's savage." He keeps waving his hand between us. "Savage."

"Thank you," I say.

"The whole look, the attitude, the presentation," Dave adds. "You keep on doing you." With that he walks off, leaving me wondering what kind of place I've stepped into.

Eight

Jada

Renata comes up to me at the fabric cutting table.

"Whatever, huh?" she says.

I sigh. "We needed another designer, not some office gopher who's just gonna disrupt things."

"Right?" she says. "And what's up with the nineties hair?"

"Maybe he doesn't know better," I say, glancing over at his cubicle, mysteriously agitated. It's more than the disruption he causes. His entire persona is somehow agitating—it's his insolent attitude, his ridiculous personal style.

"Maybe he's from somewhere really backwards," Renata says. "And the nineties only just got there. Who's gonna break it to him about Kurt Cobain?"

I inspect a swatch. "According to his file, the last place he worked was upstate. A shipping company of some sort, but who knows where he's actually from. His accent is...not East Coast. Kind of generic."

Renata tosses it onto the pile. "Seriously, though, who goes to the store and says, yes, these are the glasses for me? Yes, a neon-patterned button shirt is the style I'm going with? And who in modern times does not remove a giant mole? Maybe it's a religious thing."

"That guy is *not* religious," I say. "He's way too defiant."

"Maybe they don't have proper medical services where he's from. Not that the mole ruins his looks," Renata says. "That's the killer of it all. The mole says, look at me, I'm on this face, but even I, in all my moleness, can't stop the hotness."

"Oh, that's what the mole says? You got some Baileys in that coffee?"

"Don't you agree? That he's so hot? In spite of it all?" Renata presses. "He pulls it off."

"His annoying personality counteracts all hotness. Any and all possible hotness."

"Also, 'that'll be all'?" she says. "'You're dismissed'? This is what he says to the CEO?"

"It's as if he has no normal social skills whatsoever." I put a swatch in the maybe pile. "Train him on the system. We need to get him up and running. At least getting him filing. Surely he can do that. He can still be an asset to the team."

"We'll see about that," Renata says.

I glare over at him. He seems to be doing something on his phone. I've worked with guys like him all my life, guys who put in minimal effort and get twice the credit, while I work twice as hard and get pegged as the blonde bimbo.

"I'm serious. He's here, and he's gonna be an asset. I'm gonna make him an asset. He needs to understand how much we need him. Maybe that'll help."

"The man got two demerits in two minutes. I'm thinking he's a lost cause."

"No such thing as a lost cause," I say. "That's what he wants us to think so we let him off the hook, but he is going to be sorely disappointed. And make sure he appreciates the company culture.

The only way we get through this is as a tight team. He could be a help to us; we just don't know."

"Oh my god. You think he's hot, too."

I pull a pencil out of my hair and draw a line on the fabric. "No, I'm thinking everyone can be a contributing member of this team, even if you're arrogant and backwards and a sexual harasser and have no clue how to act."

"Fine," Renata says. "I'll train him on the system and find out where he worked before, and then you wanna know what else I'm gonna do? Makeover. I'm gonna give him a makeover. I know a Tom Hardy in the rough when I see one and I'm gonna bring it all out, and then maybe I'll reap the rewards."

I frown. "Why not just let him be? This is the personal style he's chosen."

"But he could actually look good."

"What would the world be if you homogenized everyone?"

"I'm not gonna homogenize him, I'm gonna hotify him," Renata says.

It doesn't sit right with me. I want to argue with her, but what do I care?

Nine

Jaxon

Renata's showing me the ways of the office computer, specifically that thing called the company intranet, which she explains as a mini-internet just for them. Could Renata be the butt-dialer? She has a certain mischievous attitude. If it's not her, she knows who it was.

"You didn't have an intranet at your old job?" she asks. "Where again did you work before?"

"I was a driver in different places," I say, wishing I'd reviewed the information Soto gave me about my supposed background.

"Like where? What was the last place?"

I shrug. "Türenbourg?"

"Is that a shipping company?"

"It's a small principality in Central Europe," I say.

"But you're American..."

"Yes, I am," I say. "I attended school here as a child, but we spent most of our time overseas, mostly Türenbourg."

Jada's carrying a bunch of fabric and paper toward one of the giant tables in the work area that stretches up and down the side of the space. She's so petite, but she has this big presence that makes it hard to look away when she's in the room.

Renata narrows her eyes at me. "Weird. We thought you had a job doing deliveries upstate."

"I've driven all over," I say as Jada sets down the fabric. She has a certain magnetism. How is it that such a killjoy is wrapped in so much hotness? It's not right.

Renata's asking me more questions.

"Excuse me?" I say.

"So you grew up mostly in Europe, then," she repeats. "In a small, relatively unknown European country."

"It's known to those of us who live there," I say.

"Oh, of course!" she exclaims, nodding. "I didn't mean that to be insulting. I think I've heard of it. It's just not one of the main ones!"

Jada stops to talk to Dave. She smiles at him and leans in. I frown. Office romance?

"Is it very rural?"

"What?" I ask, turning back to Renata.

"Türenbourg," Renata says.

"Very," I say. "One of the most rural on the continent. Many of the buildings there date back to the medieval times."

"Really!" she says.

I sigh, thinking about the ridiculous castle my parents spent a fortune on to make themselves feel royal. "Decrepit piles of old stones barely fit for human habitation, if you ask me. Crumbling walls, leaky ceilings." I shake my head. All those millions they poured into the place, and the servants still had to pull out a bucket or two whenever it rained. "Swarms of plague-infested rats would be right at home in those old places, let's just say."

Renata looks concerned. "That's terrible!" She bites her lip. "Your home at least had heating and cooling, I'd imagine."

things like personnel decisions. Can't you avoid getting demerits? Is the job difficult?"

"More like annoying. You told people I worked upstate?"

"In Buffalo. Did you not read the email?"

"No," I say.

Soto tells me that he'll send it around again, and we click off.

PEOPLE ARE EATING their lunches at their desks. Some leave the office briefly, only to return with sandwiches wrapped in paper marked with the word "Subway." Others heat cups of things in what seems to be a small microwave that they keep in a sad little room called the break room, a windowless space full of plastic furniture, dirty appliances, and tall, glass-fronted display cases all combining to create the most disturbing dining ambience this side of the Rothenburg Medieval Torture Museum.

It's no wonder they take the stuff to their desks.

I slow as I pass by Jada's desk. She has a sandwich encased in a clear triangular plastic shell. Is this what people carry their lunches to work in? It seems odd. Like something from a science fiction movie.

Jada looks up. Her eyes have a gem-like depth and clarity to them. They're hazel—light brown around the pupil and green toward the outer edge. "Can I help you?"

"Got your lunch, I see," I say.

"Yes. Chicken club," she says.

"Mine's coming soon. Delivery," I say. A few people had pizzas delivered, so Italian delivery will be right on point for this office. I'm finally starting to get the hang of things.

"Good for you."

Some perverse need to nettle her some more keeps me rooted to the ground. "I understand we have thirty-five minutes," I say.

She looks up. Jada doesn't gape at my mole and nervously look away like everyone else, and she doesn't stare maniacally at my pupils or at my nose like Varsha does. No, Jada looks into my eyes in a normal, relaxed way, treating me like a human and all that.

She really is insufferable.

"Don't get your hopes up," she says. "If you want to get out of here anywhere near on time, you'll eat while you work."

"We're supposed to get out at five," I say.

She snorts. "Good luck with that."

"But it says so at the top of the PDF," I say. "Five o'clock. Quitting time."

She gives me this look, as though she can't decide if I'm joking. "You think you'll get out of here at five?"

"I'm planning on it."

"If you still have things to do, you'll have to finish them."

"I'll finish the next day," I say.

"What if we send you to Ship2Speed with a package and you're still in line at five? You can't discard it. If you're out on a local delivery, you can't just abandon the truck."

"Certainly not," I say. "I'd pull to the side first. Don Juan the Entitled Delivery Driver would never leave the truck blocking traffic."

She sniffs, unimpressed. "You're so full of shit. And you're not leaving at five."

"We'll see."

"You aren't."

I run my finger over the strip of plastic at the top edge of one of the three carpeted cubicle walls that surround her laminated desk and I lower my voice to a rumble. "I dare you to give me a delivery at four fifty."

Her lips part and it's everything. "Oh my god, what is up with you?" she demands.

"What?"

"Are you trying to act like an incompetent jerk so we don't ask you to do things? Or are you actually that guy?"

Ten

Jaxon

Arnold opens the door and takes my coat as I step out of the elevator of La Manche House, my family's Upper West Side residence. "They've delivered the weight room equipment, sir, and we've already put it up top. I've been assembling the furnishings to sell in the second-floor day room, but you'll need to make a few decisions on the more prominent pieces."

"All the stuff from when I lived here goes," I say.

"Nevertheless," Arnold says. "A few things need your review, and Chef's got fresh-caught tuna. Is six good?"

"Seven. I want to get in a workout."

"Very good, sir." He hesitates. "And did you get the answer you wanted? Regarding the caller?"

"Not yet, but I will."

I head up to the top floor, a former ballroom. I recall it as cold and cavernous, but it's smaller than I remembered. I instructed Arnold to have the window coverings removed from the windows, so it's quite sunny now.

I peel off my mole, scrub my face, and change into my workout gear.

Arnold appears while I'm doing squats. "So you'll be going back, then? To your...new job?"

"Yup." I grab the jump rope and start jumping. "They don't want to break ranks and give me the answer I need. But they will."

Arnold looks baffled. "You worked the job all day?"

I keep jumping, whipping it under my feet. "Today was mostly training. Tomorrow I'll have duties. There'll be deliveries, I imagine. Somebody mentioned filing."

Arnold nods. "And the people accepted you as a fellow employee?"

"Why not? But the Papaggio delivery? That was all wrong."

"I tried to warn you—"

"Yeah, yeah, yeah. It's fine. It was funny, actually. They thought it was a joke, and the senior designer, Jada..." I grin. *Do you not take anything seriously?* "She'd like to have a word with you. She found it to be a very cruel trick."

"Oh, no," Arnold says.

"She's so serious. She's not the butt-dialer, but she's so intense about rules and the team and pulling together. You've never met such a little Joan of Arc—the shining warrior, fighting the good fight with pencils stuck in her bun." I grab a towel and wipe my face. "She keeps looking at my eyes when she talks to me instead of staring at the mole or averting her gaze, treating me with respect and dignity. God, people can be so fucking irritating."

"Is this truly the best use of your time, sir?"

What is this? The day of everybody in the universe questioning me? I give him a stern look.

"All of this focus on a workplace issue...your parents only just died..."

I snort and throw the towel over my shoulder, which is more than that comment deserves. "I'm going to need to bring a lunch like other people bring. The people like to bring their lunches in molded plastic containers with specific labels. I don't know where they get them, but I'll be needing one for tomorrow." I grab my phone, text Arnold the photo I discreetly shot of Jada's sandwich packaging, and then my minute break is over, and I start up the jump rope again.

Arnold furrows his brow at his phone. "Are you sure..."

"Of course I'm sure. Bringing the same sort of food as they bring will show them I'm one of the gang. It's like a rugby jersey. Once they see me wearing the team jersey, they'll pass me the ball."

"Yes, Mr. Henningsly."

I keep hopping. "Do you know a computer program called Excel?"

"I do indeed, Mr. Henningsly."

"You'll teach it to me after dinner."

"It's a bit complex, sir."

"I need to know it," I say.

"Very good, sir."

~

EXCEL CONTINUES TO BE MADDENING. It seems to have a mind of its own, and you have to create an elaborate formula just to ask it to do something. "Who designed this, Satan himself?" I complain.

Midway through the torture, Arnold gets an email from the tech team. They've enlarged the label image of Jada's sandwich and figured out where to get one—at the airport. A courier has been dispatched.

"Do you have a preference between egg salad and barbeque chicken?"

I frown. The airport seems a bit of an odd place to shop. It's not as if these people are going to the airport for their sandwiches.

They must have another source for them. "The chicken, I suppose."

"Very good, sir."

Eleven

Jaxon

There are always a number of urgent if not hyperventilating texts, emails, and voicemails regarding the Wycliff empire, as well as the various holdings I inherited, my social calendar, and random publicity matters. I ignore them all in favor of completing tasks from Varsha's "gopher list," a scrawled list of mostly restocking and delivery activities. She drew what I assume is a gopher up top and handed it over, seeming to marshal every bit of willpower to gaze at my nose and not my theatrical mole.

After I complete the tasks on the list, my overlords down in shipping have me run a few things across town, and suddenly it's lunch.

Jada stops by my desk with a bag of microwave popcorn. "Half a day with no demerits! Call the papers!"

Is Control Freak Barbie joking with me, now?

"Can you believe it?" I tease.

"Will you be getting lunch delivered by Papaggio again? That would probably do it."

I produce the insulated bag that Arnold sent me with. "I brought a lunch from home."

She tilts her head like she can't figure me out. She probably has a perfectly ordered and arranged world where everything makes sense. "Do you live near here?"

I lean back and cross my legs. "I'm staying at a place on West Seventy-sixth Street."

"Wow. Nice."

"Oh, it's nothing special, trust me," I say, wishing I hadn't divulged this bit of information. "Where do you live?" I decide here to unpack my lunch as a demonstration of my regular guy status.

"A building on West Forty-fifth and Ninth—it's the Times Square side of Hell's Kitchen. It's a cool place. Well, not amazing on a physical level, but a lot of my best friends live there. I had a roommate, a dancer, but she moved in with a guy, and this tiny studio opened up on the top floor and I grabbed it, even though it's way too expensive for me...somehow I swing it, but—" She falls silent as soon as I pull out my sandwich. "What is that?"

"Barbeque chicken." I open the plastic shell.

"You brought that from *home*?" she asks.

"It came out of a lunch bag from home, did it not? Is there some rule in the PDF about it? Because I honestly can't be bothered to read that whole thing."

She blinks dramatically. "Are you being funny right now?"

I frown. I'm used to being the amused one, not the amusing one. I give her a stern look. She's just a poor girl with pencils in her bun—why do I care what she thinks?

Usually a hard look is enough to back people off, but not Jada. Also, what the hell is so funny, anyway? It's exactly the brand of sandwich she had.

"That is your bag lunch from home," she clarifies.

"Obviously."

"But it's a *vending machine sandwich*."

What the hell is a vending machine sandwich? It doesn't matter. I sit up straight, giving her the lordly look that usually wilts people. "This is the sandwich," I bite out, "that I brought from home."

Jada's eyes glow with stunned amusement, which I find I like less than simple amusement. "Who would pack a vending machine sandwich in a bag lunch from home? Oh my god, did your friend Arnold tell you to do this? Tell me the truth, did Arnold give this to you?"

"I told him what I wanted, and he got it for me."

"Okay, maybe you asked your friend Arnold for a sandwich to bring, but he got it in a machine, Jack. He's playing a joke on you, and it's not even a funny joke. He got it in a machine."

Dave comes by wearing a winter hat. "Got what in the machine?"

"That's the sandwich Jack brought as his bag lunch," Jada says. "He brought a vending machine sandwich from home."

"Dude! You brought a vending machine sandwich from home?" Dave puts his fists on either side of his head and then spreads his fingers, making an explosion sound. "That is so *meta*, dude! Fucking meta!"

Jada frowns at the sandwich. "Arnold is not a good friend to you. You need to understand that." She returns to her desk.

"Hey, Jack, you don't have to eat at your desk," Dave says. "Come on."

I want to stay—I'm feeling unfinished with Jada, but I remind myself I'm here to ferret out the butt-dialer.

I follow Dave into the gloomy break room. It's here that I notice what I thought were display cases are machines that sell sandwiches like mine, along with other food items. These apparently are the vending machines.

"So meta," Dave says, feeding a bill into a slot. He pushes a button and a bag of pretzels falls down. He bends down and takes it from a small door, then moves to another machine, this one for soft drinks. "You ever try this?" he asks, sitting down and ripping open the bag. "Pepsi with Snyder's Pretzels. It can't be Coke, though. The sugariness of the Pepsi contrasts with the salty." He takes a bit and a swig. "Mmm. Otherwise," he adds with his mouth still full, "I'm gonna recommend Cheez-Its and Cherry Coke. Savage flavor bomb. Savage."

I spread a paper napkin on my lap. "Thanks for the tip."

"Don't mind Jada. She can be intense, and she works like a maniac, but I guess we should be thankful. This department wouldn't function without her."

I nod, wishing people would stop talking about Jada. It's like this whole place is the Jada show where you can't stop thinking about her, even when she's not around.

"Sounds like somebody needs to get a life outside of work," I say.

"And whatever you do, don't insult this place. She'll go ballistic," Dave warns. "This place is everything to her. Don't get me wrong, I don't want this place shuttering, either, but Jada would shoot herself out of a canon in a flaming barrel if it kept this place open longer."

I sit next to him. "Why bother? It's just a job that doesn't produce much beyond misery for people in cubicles, as far as I can tell."

Dave nearly chokes on a pretzel. "Do not, I repeat, *do not* say that in front of Jada."

I make a note to repeat exactly that in front of Jada. I can't wait. She'll get that frown and stare pretty daggers at me.

"Promise," Dave says. "Oh, also—" He holds up the pretzel bag. "These pretzels with the saltwater taffies that Varsha keeps in a bowl at reception? Killer combo. Her family has a saltwater taffy shop in Atlantic City, and she brings them for us special."

"So what's your job here exactly?" I ask.

"Accounts receivable and payable." Dave pulls out a Tupperware of something that might be gazpacho. "Billing specific to the design department. It's just a stepping stone while I go to night school. I'm working to be a CPA. A good CPA is worth their weight in gold."

"So...three million and some?"

"Excuse me?"

"You weigh what, one sixty? A pound of gold is twenty thousand. Last I knew."

"Huh." Dave stirs his cold soup. "I suppose that's a good fact to know. Strange but good."

"A stepping stone to where?" I ask, pulling the bread off my sandwich and looking inside. There is no way I'll be eating this sandwich.

Dave takes off his hat and sets it aside. Everybody here seems to have the same clumsily knit hat in the same shade of royal blue with a big pom pom on the top.

Dave tells me about his dream job. He's speeding up his plans due to "Wycliff-pocalypse," as he calls it. He promptly launches into a lot of bad Bert stories, which gives me the perfect segue.

"I hear there was a butt-dial incident during a company call. And Bert was livid..."

"That was hilarious. Just...wow." He tosses a wrapper into the garbage. "You would've loved it. I mean, the guy deserved it. Some pompous jackalope who never worked a day in his life telling us how to feel."

"And somebody was...making fun of the guy?"

Dave snorts. "It was savage. You would've loved it."

"I love it," I assure him. "Who was it?"

Dave turns to look at me now. "I'd tell you if I could, but then I'd have to kill you. And then people would kill me." He snorts. "Bert was pissed, though!"

I give him my best conspiratorial smile, the conspiratorial smile that has pried bits of gossip from tight-lipped royals and coaxed the primmest of socialites into outrageous misbehavior. "Now I have to know."

"Dude," he says. "I can't."

"Just between us," I say. "Renata?" I try. "Shondrella?"

"There was a pact." He shakes his head. "I can't." Like he's powerless over the whole thing.

"I won't tell," I say.

"We said it wouldn't leave the room," Dave says.

I can't believe how intent everybody is to uphold this ridiculous pact. "I'm so curious now. Come on now," I say breezily. "Don't be boring!"

"Sorry."

I study his face, shocked. I'm used to people falling all over themselves to anticipate my needs and desires, to give me what I want before I can even ask.

Now suddenly I'm in this opposite world where these people are withholding information for no other reason than their little pact.

Never mind.

Nobody keeps secrets from me for long.

Twelve

JADA

THE NEXT MORNING, Jack leans casually on the wall in front of Varsha's desk like he's some bored prince on a yachting holiday, chatting away with her.

He's wearing yet another oversized 1990s button-up shirt. This one is bright yellow with blue and black triangles and circles all over it. Still, you can tell he has a muscular build under there—entirely due to genetics, no doubt, considering that this guy is the laziest assclown I've ever had the misfortune of meeting.

He'd have lovely black hair if he hadn't messed it up with those bleached tips. His brows are dark and harsh—the kind you'd imagine on a villain. They add this alluring intensity to his gaze. Especially when he bothers to remove his itty-bitty shaded rectangular glasses that he possibly time-traveled to steal from the face of Leonardo DiCaprio circa 1995.

Where does he shop that he's getting those things? Why did nobody stop him? Of course it perfectly goes with his personality.

Why be pleasing to the eye when he could be trolling people with his weirdly squandered hotness potential?

And then there are the things he can't mess up. His nose, for example, is on the large side, roughly sculpted in a good way that goes with his cheekbones and strong jaw. His lips are expressive—very "there" lips.

He looks over and catches my eye. He tips his head down and peers at me over his glasses, gaze glittering under those villain eyebrows.

A rush of feeling arrows to my core and I look away, because I can't even. His eyes are golden brown like burnt butter, with thick lashes, of course. Offensively thick. You could expect nothing less from Jack Smith, entitled delivery driver.

I grit my teeth. I told him to look busy—why is he bothering Varsha? The man has the worst work ethic I've ever witnessed, though I do have to admit that he completes his delivery duties with shocking speed.

But other than that, the worst!

Renata told me that he attended school here as a child, but mostly grew up in an impoverished, rural Türenbourgian village where they lived in decrepit homes without proper heating. "All goat carts and rat-infested stone rooms, from the sound of it," she said. "Very backwards, like medieval!"

She also thinks he lied on his resume, which is increasingly easy to believe. The possibility that his only work experience is from a rustic village on the other side of the world explains his ignorance of basic office operations and his bewilderment about things like bag lunches, which that asshole Arnold took such advantage of.

Maybe Jack is from humble circumstances, but for Arnold to order white-glove meal service for his clueless friend on his first day at work? And then the next day he gets him to pack a vending machine sandwich for his bagged lunch? What a psycho!

It's my guess this Arnold character is well-off—that Upper

West Side place is probably his. A bored rich bro with no conscience.

Tragic poverty would also explain Lacey's report that Jack nearly keeled over in shock when he saw her drinking from a water fountain out in the hall. "Is that...tap water?" he'd asked, horrified.

"I explained it was perfectly safe, but the way he acted, you'd think it contained bubonic plague spores," Lacey had whispered to Renata and me afterwards. "Has the man never seen a person drink out of a water fountain?"

"Maybe their water back home is full of bacteria from unsanitary farming practices," Renata had said. "Maybe he doesn't understand that it's safe to drink the water here in America."

"I told him it was safe, and he wouldn't believe me," Lacey said.

I look back up. Jack smiles at me. I frown. He shouldn't be goofing off with Varsha—he's liable to get another demerit, and worse, he might get her one, too. Jack is mostly useless, but Varsha isn't.

He seems amused that I'm frowning, judging from the width of his smile.

It's not his fault that his parents raised him in a village where he acquired all of the office skills of a rabbit, but he needs to at least try to be a decent employee.

He leans in and says something to Varsha. She smiles, enchanted.

Dave told me that Jack was curious about the butt-dial incident. It's *so* Jack to zero in on the exact thing he needs to leave alone. God, is that what they're talking about? Is he quizzing Varsha?

I can't stand it. I head over.

"Sorry, Jada," Varsha says, ducking back to her duties.

Jack is unbothered, as usual.

"If you'd put half of the energy that you expend screwing

around into your work duties, you might actually help us around here."

"But what fun would that be?"

"It would be fun for those of us who give a shit about the company," I snap.

"But I'm Don Juan the Entitled Delivery Driver."

"You need to stop distracting people, and if you don't have anything to do, you need to ask us how you can help. And at the very least, you need to look busy when Bert comes through."

He makes an exaggerated concerned face that is a hundred percent fake.

"Fine. It's your funeral." I head back to my desk. God, why am I bothering with him? Why should I care if he gets fired?

Naturally, he follows me. "Big bad Bert."

"That's right." I sit down.

"I hear he's irate over some hilarious butt-dial incident. Some pompous jerk getting the piss taken out of him."

"Give it up," I say.

"What?"

"Nobody's gonna tell you who it was." I give him my own pretty smile. "Nobody."

He looks caught out for a moment, then quickly recovers. "Is that a challenge?"

"It's not a challenge; it's a fact."

"Mmmm," he rumbles. "I think it's a challenge."

"For real, Jack, don't be a child! You're so shit at looking busy. Bert would love nothing more than to fire you."

"Why would he hire a person only to fire them?"

"Because he's dedicated his life to destroying this place and ruining morale." I wake up my screen, showing that I'm getting to work. *Hint hint.*

Jack comes around and leans on my interior cubicle wall. A hint of a smile plays on his full lips, causing his cheekbones to be more defined, more model-like even. Apparently his sexy charisma is the only thing about him willing to work overtime.

"I can see that Bert's an asshole," he says, "but why set out to destroy the company he's running? Presumably the man wants to keep his position."

"Well, I'm telling you that's how it is."

"But it doesn't make sense."

"Not everything that's true is going to make sense to you. I mean, you packed a vending machine sandwich in your lunch the other day, so..."

"It's the sandwich I requested," he says, doubling down.

Right then I have this rush of compassion for him. He still doesn't understand why it was weird.

"Look, Jack, this was a great place before it got bought, before Bert came. And sometimes it's frustrating to me that you'll never know how good it was, and what a privilege it was to work here, even a year ago."

I tell him about the good people who fled, leaving me with the work of three senior designers. I tell him about our fun celebrations. Our camaraderie. I don't know why I'm so invested in Jack's positive opinion of SportyGoCo in general and our scrappy department in particular, but I really am.

"It's just a job," he says.

"Excuse me?"

His warm eyes twinkle. "Just a job that doesn't produce much beyond misery for people in cubicles, as far as I can tell."

My jaw drops.

"Maybe it should be shut down," he says.

"Oh my god! Screw you, because you know what? People here love this company. We care about each other and pull for each other. We're a family, and family is worth fighting for."

"Is it, though?"

"Excuse me? Is family worth fighting for? That's what you're asking? Yes, it is."

"Not so sure about that," he says.

"What? You don't think family is worth fighting for? Or do you mean you don't think *this* family is worth fighting for?"

"A little of both, I suppose."

My mouth goes dry. I barely have words. "So this family? Just not worth it?"

He shrugs.

People are starting to look in our direction. Ughhh, why do I let this guy get to me?

I take a deep breath. "I'm gonna give you a pass because you've only been here for a little while and I get that life has given you some hard knocks. But this is your family now, too."

He sighs wearily, as though he hates the very concept of family.

"Look around you, Jack. Every one of these people here would drop everything they're doing if you needed them. Maybe things seem bleak here at the moment, and it's not exactly a living wage for Manhattan, but we're gonna come out the other side together." I'm picking up steam, here. I once read a study that showed that if a teacher treats struggling students like they're top of the class, those students do better. This might be a good strategy with Jack. "You may not realize it, but people have noticed what a fast delivery guy you are. You are already a valuable member of this family—did you know that? You're part of a tight, loyal, hardworking family who will always pull for each other, no matter what."

"A tight, loyal, hardworking family who will always pull for each other, no matter what?" he asks.

"Yes!" I say.

"Hmmm." He drapes an arm over the cubicle wall and gazes wearily at the ceiling, a position that causes his shirt to draw tight over his muscular shoulder. "No, thanks."

I straighten. "Excuse me?"

"The family thing. Hard pass."

Outrage courses through me. God, why am I even paying

attention to him? I lean in. "Sorry, but you don't have a choice. You're here, therefore, you're part of our family. We'll pull for you whether you like it or not."

"You'll pull for me?" He wipes an invisible speck from his shirt. "Please don't."

"Too bad," I say, heart racing. "I'm gonna guess that people were unkind to you at your previous places of work—if in fact there were any—and they may not have had fair employment laws, but you're gonna find out it's different here. It's your first week, so you get a pass."

He leans in, all burnt-butter eyes and villainous brows. "I don't want a pass."

"Too bad! You get a pass, Jack."

"I reject it," he says.

"You can't reject a pass. I've given it already."

"I've tossed it away," he says.

"Sorry," I say, leaning in. Just a couple more inches and I'd be feeling the coarse brush of his thick five-o-clock shadow on my face. "Once given, a pass cannot be tossed."

"I believe it can."

"Get a room," Shondrella says, gliding by.

"More like a padded cell," I call after her. "If I have to hear any more out of this one." I take my seat with a huff.

"This one's returning to his cubicle," he says.

"Good." I sit, feeling wild. What was I working on?

He's back. He sets his chin on my cubicle wall. "What's more, *this one* is going to unmask the butt-dialer."

"Why do you want to know so badly?" I demand.

He smiles his stupidly pretty smile. "At this very moment? Because you don't want me to."

"Knock yourself out." I stand, and one of my bun pencils slides out and clatters to the floor. "There was a pact before you came, and we honor our pacts. There's nothing you can do about it. Not one. Little. Thing."

"I'll get it out of somebody."

I smile. "No, you won't."

"Won't I?"

I lean in. "I'll see to it that you don't."

He kneels down, scoops up the pencil, and rises back to his usual infuriating height. "I'll find the weakest link—you know I will."

He settles gentle fingers onto the top of my hair as he slides the pencil into my bun. He leans in close and whispers, "And I will mercilessly exploit that link. *Mercilessly.*"

He strolls off, leaving me standing there, seething. I yank out the pencil and sit back down.

I'm letting him get to me. Worse, I may as well have created an engraved invitation for him to make it his life's mission to unmask me as the butt-dialer.

I tell myself he's not the type to tell Bert—I've never met a man with more aversion to authority figures. But he'll find a way to lord it over me if he could. If I was a sweater, he'd probably think he could unravel me.

I watch him over at the copy machine. *You think you can unravel me? Think again, party-shirt peacock.*

Thirteen

Jaxon

I'm discreetly texting with Arnold, sending him some delivery stuff to collate onto a central Excel sheet. Naturally, he's taking his own sweet time with it. I find this almost as annoying as the fact that nearly the entire office gang is gathered across the room by the windows.

The cool kids all gathered by the windows, I suppose you could say, or at least the pathetically struggling office worker version of the cool kids, which isn't all that cool.

As a man who's rather vigorously hated, you'd think I'm used to being excluded from things, but in fact, it's the opposite. People constantly invite me to their gatherings. My presence adds a note of controversy if not notoriety, a way to spice up an otherwise sure-to-be-boring event. I rarely show up, but I'm always invited.

Not that I care about being excluded from whatever idiotic display it is I'm seeing here. Some sort of meeting that seems to be led by our resident spitfire, pencil-bun Joan of Arc herself, Jada Herberger.

They chat excitedly in hushed tones; it's quite the work family hoedown.

I focus back on the text, ignoring them. Ignoring her.

We honor our pacts and there's nothing you can do about it. Not one. Little. Thing.

Jada has no idea who she's dealing with. She and her mighty little attitude and perky posture and perfect little nose. She thinks she can stop me?

Jada looks happy and radiant, and she seems to be complimenting somebody, lovingly cooing over them.

I grit my teeth. Whoever could be the unlucky recipient of such an outpouring of love from buzzkill Jada?

Not that I care to be part of it. It'll be a one-on-one thing when I find and break the weak link that I know to be here. It's not as if people divulge secrets when there's a group listening. Once I get the identity, I'll determine next steps after that.

Somebody from shipping is suddenly in my face. "Do you have the stock level update?"

"Working on it," I growl.

He looks at my computer screen where a blue circle bounces around on a field of black. "When do you think you'll have it?"

Whenever my valet-slash-personal assistant finishes it—that's the real answer, but I don't need to be Workaday Wally to know it's not the one to give. "You'll get it when you get it," I say.

"What does that mean?" he asks.

"Soon," I say, watching the group. Who the hell is Jada so lovey-dovey over? Not that it matters.

"Pleistocene era soon or today soon?" he pursues.

I grit my teeth. Life is so much easier when you can dismiss people, like clicking the X on an annoying pop-up window. "You'll know when it happens," I inform him.

He mumbles something and walks off.

Finally I can't stand it anymore. I stroll over to see what the fuss is.

Dave grins. "Have you met Keith yet?"

A snarl rises up from my chest unbidden. "Keith?"

"You'd remember if you met Keith," Dave assures me. "Let Jack see."

People shift around. Jada and Shondrella the fiftysomething fashionista are kneeling on either side of a dead cactus—if you can call it that. It's more like a spindly, spiny six-foot-high husk that used to be a cactus. Shondrella is poking at the dirt with a toothpick.

"Keith the Cactus," Jada says, beaming at the thing. "We found him next to a dumpster down on the street and we've been trying to rehabilitate him in this sunny window. He's totally getting better!"

Is this some sort of joke? It's obvious the thing is dead. "A garbage cactus," I say.

"Rescue cactus," Jada says. "He has his own Instagram—Keith the Rescue Cactus." She puts on a baby voice and points at one of the protrusions. "Look at his little arm. He was all alone in the world, and nobody cared about him, but we're saving him."

"Not from the looks of it," I say.

She glares at me, lips pursed into a luscious little rosebud of admonition. "Luckily you're not the be-all and end-all of cactus knowledge."

"It doesn't take a be-all and end-all of cactus knowledge to see that it's dead."

"You're just saying that because you didn't see how he was before," Jada says. "We worked together to research food and pooled our money to get a light meter, and he's responding—see? Come here." Lacey shows me a smooth patch of green the size of a thumbprint. "This was all brown before. He's getting better."

"You probably just rubbed off some dirt," I say.

"No, man, we're helping him," Dave says.

I'm still eyeing Jada. "Rhymes with *bossed jaws*."

Jada looks confused, then she works it out. Her glare flares, connecting right to my groin. "No cause is ever lost."

I don't know why I should be so irritated by the fact that this woman's ridiculously fierce loyalty extends all the way to a plant from the garbage.

"It doesn't matter what you think, does it? Everybody can see he's getting better."

"Dude," Dave says. "He's bouncing back. But you can't tell Bert. Bert can never know about Keith. As far as Bert is concerned, Keith is just some sad office plant that we never think about."

"Wait, what? Bert thinks it's a sad office plant?" I tease, but people aren't listening. As if they haven't irritated me enough, they're now literally breaking into song.

"Go *Keeeeeith*, go *Keeeeeeeith*, go *Keeeeeeith*."

They're moving their hands around, singing like the fucking Von Trapps, or Charley's family, singing Queen songs around the Christmas tree.

It's so sweet, so saccharine, it hurts my teeth.

It hurts my entire soul.

Fourteen

Jada

The next day, I head down the back hallway to storage and receiving to check for the package of zipper samples that supposedly arrived, and what do I see? Way down at the end of tall rows of shelving, there's Jack, playing wastebasket basketball with Nate from accounts receivable.

Nate is usually a diligent worker, but Jack has managed to corrupt even him.

They don't see me—that's how into it they are. Two grown men throwing wadded-up paper at a trash can they've put on a high shelf, all grunts and jump shots—a full-on testosterone-fest.

I should tell them to get back to work—I really should.

Nate makes a shot and immediately looks at Jack, who tips up his head in a kind of reverse nod, showing his approval.

Nate smiles widely.

I roll my eyes.

Nate's a workout machine, a man who moves boldly and heavily, with arms so muscular that they don't hang flush to his body.

Jack, on the other hand, has got leopard-like grace; he shoots and pivots loosely, but he jumps with explosive power.

Nate makes a long-distance shot. He's acting nonchalant about it, but I'm sure he's thrilled to impress Jack, to move deeper into Jack's rare and special orbit.

It's like Jack's entire life goal is to be as distracting as possible to SportyGoCo workers. He is the worst—he really is. In the fable of the ant and the grasshopper, he's the ultimate grasshopper.

I despise grasshoppers.

Nate gets another reverse nod, and you can see him preen. How can Nate allow himself to be enchanted by this man?

And Jack. He thinks he's so hot. The way he struts, you'd think he's the most eligible bachelor on the planet.

I shake my head hotly, remembering his words. *Of course, wrong has its advantages. There are scenarios where, it could be argued, the wronger, the better. If you know what I mean, and I think you do.*

If my Jersey galpal, Mia, had been there when Jack said that, she'd have kicked him in the balls— *Wrong like this, you mean?*

He would've deserved it.

The wronger, the better...if you know what I mean...and I think you do.

Who wouldn't? And yes, wrong things can be sexy—it doesn't take a rocket scientist to know that. And outrageously wrong things can be outrageously sexy.

I watch him shoot, thinking about wrong things. Things that would be offensive in real life, but sexy in sex.

Jack, of course, would be an expert in that, being such an all-around offensive man. He probably has whiteboards at home full of advanced mathematical formulas on how to increase his offensiveness.

But we're in a workplace, I remind myself. Here in the workplace, wrong is not at all sexy.

He grunts, blocking Nate's shot, all fancy footwork.

Not sexy.

Naturally, he would want to make sure all womankind is aware that he would deliver on wrongness and forbiddenness. He may as well walk around with a sandwich board sign. *Ladies, whatever wrong thing you're thinking? I will deliver.*

So annoying.

He does this spin-jump and a wad of crumpled paper arcs into the air and lands in the wastebasket.

As if he feels me watching, he turns to eye me playfully with those burnt-butter eyes that probably melt other women.

Nate gets an alarmed look. "Gotta get back." He beelines up the row of boxes, not meeting my gaze.

Naturally Jack has no problem getting caught goofing off. He smiles. You can tell when it's a genuine smile because the dimple on his left cheek fires away. It's a lopsided dimple smile that he has. "Want to play?"

Does he think he can corrupt me as easily as he's corrupted Nate? "No, I don't want to play."

"Why not?" he asks.

"Why not? Because this is a sinking ship," I say. "A sinking ship where we're fighting for our lives."

Jack Smith, insolent king of leisure and corruption, continues to smile. "All the more reason to play." He picks up a crumpled paper and shoots, giving it a little jump.

"Deliveries in the dock," I say. "You should get to them one of these days." I don't know this for sure, but there always seem to be deliveries ready to go out.

He grabs a stool, ignoring my directive. God, what would it be like to not care about anything? To have all of that powerful charisma and use it almost exclusively for ill? He seems indifferent even to being fired. What kind of upbringing makes a man act like this?

"To be so useless and so entitled at the same time!" I marvel.

"I aim to please."

"Also, Chris from shipping has been complaining that you were an asshole to him," I say. "He wanted a report, and you wouldn't give him a straight answer about when you'd get it."

"He was being insufferable." Jack climbs up the ladder and grabs the wastebasket off the top shelf.

"*You* were being insufferable," I say. "He asked you for something, and you treated him like he was ruining your spa day. You're here to support these people."

He climbs down, looking amused. "So Chris is my boss now?"

"In a way, we're all your boss. You're here to help when we request it," I say. "But more to the point, the desperate situation we're in is our boss. We're all trying to work together to save this place that we love. You can't act put out when somebody requests something. Maybe you've been in places where you weren't valued, but we value you and we really do need you."

He looks concerned. Am I actually getting through to him?

"You don't want people to think you don't care," I add.

He puts the wastebasket back in the corner, sets aside the stool, then turns to me with a thoughtful look. "People will think I don't *care*?"

"Yes."

"Well then..." He gets this solemn look. "They would be right."

I narrow my eyes. "Oh-em-gee, sooooooo hilarious."

"I thought it was."

I sniff in disdain. "How about you go do your deliveries? And make it snappy."

He saunters in my direction, which is also the direction of the door. I'm all lit up and angry and strangely electrified.

I cross my arms, facing him square on. I'm partly blocking the walkway out of here, and I don't care. He can turn and sidle around me. The sooner he realizes this is my house, the better.

He nears.

I stand my ground, face to face with his glittering gaze and villain eyebrows.

He stops in front of me and I breathe in his woodsy scent.

He says, "Aren't you going to ask me how my butt-dial investigation is going?"

I smile coolly. "I know how it's going, and I know how it'll end. Rhymes with *pilarious pabject pailure.*"

He looks surprised for a moment, and then he laughs. He didn't expect that out of me. He thinks I have no sense of humor. He thinks I have no teeth. He would be wrong.

He sidles around me like I wanted him to, but I didn't think it through.

I didn't think I'd be forcing him to brush against me, chest to shoulder. I didn't think there would be any kind of frisson of feeling—even through fabric. I didn't think how close his face would come to my cheek. I didn't think I'd feel his breath in my hair when he leans down and whispers, "The night is young."

Fifteen

Jada

I slam into work early the next day and hit the ground running—the zipper samples for our Unicorn Wonderbag design.

Unicorn Wonderbag is a secret, off-the-books project that Renata and I have been playing with for a while now, and then we got Shondrella on board. Shondrella knows the fashion industry in and out, and she was thrillingly enthusiastic. We're going to slip it into our spring/summer lineup when it's all worked out, specifically when it's too late for Bert to doom the project.

Being that it's October, spring/summer ordering is virtually here.

Unicorn Wonderbag can transform into three different modes, from elegant purse to sporty bag to shopping sack, and it can also be rolled up into a "unicorn horn" for travel. The design is bold, and there's an enamel unicorn zipper charm.

Dave says they're going to close the company if we don't get enough orders in this accounting period, and this bag is our silver bullet. We're pretty sure we can sell it to Target and maybe even Walmart.

It's not until almost lunchtime that I notice Jack hasn't punched in, even though he's been buzzing around, mostly doing stuff for the shipping guys.

When I see him up at reception with Varsha, I take the opportunity to stretch my legs and remind him of the rules. "You're supposed to punch in, Jack."

"Oh, right. I will."

Varsha's eyes widen. "You have to punch in! Otherwise, you're not technically here."

"Bert saw me," he says.

"That'll keep you from getting a demerit, but you won't get paid if you don't punch in," I say.

"I'm so touched that you care."

"Oh, I don't care," I say.

"Not even a little?"

"Not even a little. *We* should be paid for putting up with *you*."

Jack gives me a big smile-frown, then he strolls to his cubicle and settles in.

I head over right after him. He fires up the intranet and clicks the radio button to signify his arrival at work, then twists in his chair, all the better to address me annoyingly. "Happy?"

I pause over him. "Help me out with a decision tree here. Are you incompetent or just indifferent?"

He leans back in his chair and crosses his legs. "I'm extremely competent at certain things. Very competent."

Heat rises to my face. "I doubt that, party-shirt peacock."

He grins at the name. "Do you, though? I don't think you doubt it. I think you've been thinking about it—more than you want me to know."

"That's cute that you think that," I say casually. "And what, pray tell, have I been thinking? What is this '*it*' you think I've been pondering so hard? Please enlighten me with your sure-to-be-impressive revelation."

"To be honest, I think there are a lot of '*its*' that you've been pondering when it comes to me."

I shamble on a surprised face. "You don't say!" Deep down, I'm aware that I'm playing with fire, but I can't stop.

"Well," I say. "Let's hear one of them. Just for entertainment's sake."

"For one thing..." He looks over his shoulder.

I follow his gaze past the cutting tables, past the shelving systems that groan with binders of fabric samples and boxes of fixings, all the way over to a remote corner where there's a scuffed door that leads to a deep closet full of office supplies.

"The office supply closet," he says.

"Ah," I say. "And what about the office supply closet?"

"You keep thinking about us in there, that's what. You're imagining us in it. It's outrageous and just wrong. You are my boss, after all."

I snort. I should cut this off and get back to work, but I tell myself I need to know how far his arrogance goes. His arrogance is a phenomenon, an extra-annoying force of nature that must be tracked and monitored. "And whatever is it that I'm imagining?"

"Two words: hate fuck. Or is that one? I never really know."

"*That's* what you think I've been imagining?" This like it's so hilarious.

"All-out, no-holds-barred hate fuck. Or is it no *holes* barred?" he says. "I never know that, either."

My mind spins. "Guess it's too much trouble for your lazy ass to google such a thing," I manage.

"True, and also, why bother? A proper hate fuck would have no *holes* barred as well as no *holds* barred, don't you think?"

"Oh-ho-ho," I fake laugh.

He lowers his voice. "I'd hold you by your hair, that's a given. You know, a pretty little blonde bun isn't just for holding pencils anymore. Or maybe I'd undo the whole thing so I can pull it a little —or actually a lot. I'd pull it pretty hard, I have to warn you."

My mouth goes dry. "You have quite the overblown sense of yourself for somebody who is so incapable—"

"There a problem here?" Bert asks.

I straighten up. How did I not see Bert bumble into the design department? Was there a Bert alert I didn't hear? "No problem at all," I say.

Bert looks from Jack to me and back to Jack and then he walks off.

I turn to Jack. "You need to stop distracting me."

"I was distracting you? I'm sorry, am I the one who interrupted an important exchange that I was having with Varsha and then hounded me all the way to my desk, trying to get me into a lurid conversation?"

I give him an indignant stare and point at the supply closet. "In your dreams."

Sixteen

Jada

Renata is sewing a plastic molded zipper onto the Unicorn Wonderbag prototype. She flips it inside out and we assess it, first in the handbag mode, then in the sporty cross-body mode. We don't have to put it in shopping bag mode to know that the zipper isn't right.

"Size up?" she asks.

"Yup."

Renata starts ripping out the stitches and I unwrap the next size up from the zipper sample box. A smaller zipper will make it cheaper and more pleasingly compact when you collapse it into the unicorn horn, but the bag needs a substantial, quality feel, and a good zipper is a big part of that—more than most people realize.

Jack swans in after his deliveries and stops to talk to pretty Varsha.

"Oh, yay," I say. He's been bringing more normal bag lunches lately, sometimes really nice ones. Today he had a pressed Italian sandwich with arugula and roasted red pepper with a side of grapes and fancy cheeses, plus Pepsi and Cheez-Its from the vending machine.

Renata looks over. "You shouldn't let him get under your skin. He's probably just getting the gopher list."

"I'm not letting him get under my skin," I say. "Other than the fact that he's the worst employee I've ever seen or even heard of. How'd he even land this job?"

"Betcha anything his references are fake," she says. "He has no concept of office life."

"Or maybe his boss upstate heard he was thinking about moving here, so they gave him an amazing reference to help him get a job so that he'd leave," I say.

"I've heard of that for sure," she says.

Jack leans in, speaking to Varsha with an air of intensity and confidence.

"Or maybe his references were truly awful, and that's *why* Bert hired him. A few weeks upstate and the rest of his experience is in a real-life Renn fest."

"Like Bert planted somebody to distract and annoy you?" Renata asks.

"All of us," I say.

"Primarily you, though."

"No, he's objectively annoying," I say.

"Uh-huh," Renata says, tying a knot in the end of the thread.

Jack's assumed a relaxed and elegant attitude, leaning on the desk, which he probably feels is at a perfect height for showing off his supposedly muscular physique. He tips his head, perhaps imagining that even the garish office light is kissing his scruffy cheeks.

Is he saying supply closet things to her?

"Mister fucking Jack Smith," I spit. "The whole freaking world is a prop for him to peacock against, and no nineties outfit and certainly no weird mole is going to stop him. No, not Jack Smith." I wad up the wrapper and toss it into the recycling bin. "Looky there, Mr. Shitstyle Charisma, posing for one and all. What's that?

Oh, noooo, he loves his weird glasses and above all he loves to be as offensive as he possibly can."

I flatten out the new zipper with perhaps too much force.

"My manly-man body says come here, but my style choices scream maniac," I continue, "and I don't care about anything until I find out somebody else cares, and then I move heaven and earth to try and ruin it. And god forbid I'd be helpful. No, no, everything's a party and nothing matters, because I'm a big nineties peacock. *Wock-wock.*"

I look over to find Renata staring at me. "Did you just go into a fugue state?" she asks.

"Shut it." I turn back to Jack. "You know what the worst thing about him is?"

"No, but I bet you're about to tell me."

"He chooses to be awful, but he could be an amazing ally. He's competent when he puts his mind to something." I pause, pondering hard. "Maybe he needs to feel more a part of things. Not just in terms of office duties, but like he's in on the fun side of things. He wasn't here when it was good, but there's no reason he can't still get a glimpse of the good stuff and come to love being part of this family ."

"I don't know. The man is a lone wolf."

"Even lone wolves have packs," I say.

"Do they, though? Because where did the phrase come from?"

"What are you, a wolf expert now?" I say.

Renata puts her hands on her hips. "That'll be all, Jada. You're dismissed."

I snort. Ever since Jack said that to Bert, people have been saying that when they don't have a good reply to something. "No, you're dismissed!" I say.

"No, *you're* dismissed," she says.

Seventeen

Jaxon

I fly south for the weekend, working out at a local track and enjoying the ocean. Arnold teaches me more about Excel. I feel like I have a good deal of expertise by the time Monday rolls around. In fact, the minute I'm at my cubicle with some rare free time, I grab a personnel list and repurpose it to keep track of who in the office I've ruled out for being the butt-dialer. The women I've ruled out are coded red, those I'm iffy about are coded orange, and the ones who could be the butt-dialer are green.

Rockabilly Renata is an iffy orange; Lacey, the purple-haired project manager with health challenges, is green; fashionable Shondrella, industry expert and merchandiser, is green. Jada is ruby red, of course, being that she's all about following the rules.

Naturally, just as I'm getting into it, Jada stops by looking fresh and perky with her pencil bun and pink cheeks and doll features that are perfectly symmetrical, because everything about Jada works in diligent harmony—even her face.

She's wearing a maroon skirt with a matching maroon blazer

and a white shirt underneath, and you can see just a hint of lace where her bra grazes the fabric. Of course she'd wear white underwear. So Jada.

"Earth to Jack. Did you hear me?" she says. "I'm going on an offsite errand and I'm gonna need some lifting and logistics support."

"No, thanks," I say.

"Your job duties are not optional."

"What if I'm doing something for somebody else?"

"Are you?"

"Yup," I say.

"For who?"

"Myself."

Her gaze turns indignant, and this feeling of intense satisfaction shoots through me. "Work projects take about a zillion times precedence over your personal projects!"

"Agree to disagree," I say, barely concealing a smile.

"It's not up for debate!"

"I'm debating it right now," I tease. "So apparently it is up for debate."

"Come on, Jack," she says. "This'll be fun."

"I get it. You're trying to get me alone."

"Oh, yes, because lazy roustabouts in party-boy shirts are every girl's dream." She grabs her purse and returns to loom over me. "You're coming. This is part of your duties."

"You'll need to sweeten the deal a lot more if you think this is headed..." I tip my head at the supply closet.

She glares at me.

A few minutes later, we're walking down Thirty-Seventh Street.

"So this is a walking errand," I observe.

"Cookie run. There's a Cookie Madness up ahead," she says, waving at a barber through the window of a barbershop.

"We're getting *cookies*? This is your important errand?"

"Yup."

"So much for the pressing need for productivity," I say. "Back at the ol' sinking ship of an office."

"Getting cookies *is* about productivity. Cookies make us happy, and that's good for morale. It brightens up a Monday."

"That sounds suspiciously like what somebody says when they want a cookie."

"No, it's true!" she protests, because apparently there's nothing Workaholic Barbie hates more than the idea of doing something for pleasure. She gives a buck to an old woman sitting next to a shopping cart.

"Bless you, Jada!"

"Backatcha, Jory!"

I groan.

She continues on, unruffled. "A year ago when the place was good to work at, we'd have bagel Wednesdays, we'd have pizza parties when we hit goals, we'd have birthday celebrations. The new owners took away celebration funds in their quest to crush our spirits, but screw them, you know?"

I glance at her discreetly, surprised by this rebellious edge popping out because she's usually so earnest and dedicated. I like it. I like how resourceful she is, too. Kind of an operator, in a way.

"Treats are totally about productivity and keeping the family together. They're one and the same. Especially for the design and sales department, because we create and sell the products."

She picks up a fallen sandwich board sign outside a BBQ place and sets it right. A big man in a BBQ-stained apron comes out wiping his hands. "One of these days I'll get my nephew to fix that thing," he says.

"Well, if you fixed it, what the heck would we talk about?" Jada jokes, and she and the man have a good laugh, because apparently that's what passes for witty repartee here in the Garment District. She gives him a brilliant smile. The man smiles back, clearly enchanted with her.

"Otis, this is Jack, gopher and delivery assistant extraordinaire."

Otis pumps my hand and assures me of how lucky I am to be part of Jada's crew. Niceties are exchanged. We escape the clutches of Otis only to be accosted by a fruit seller who stops us and gives us each a Washington cherry and refuses to accept any other response than those being the best cherries in the world. When we comply, she's delighted because, "Jada knows cherries."

"Jesus Christ!" I say when we finally get rid of her. "What next? Are people going to break into song? Maybe the cast of *Mary Poppins* can rush into the street."

"What do you mean?" she asks.

"All these little interactions." Does she actually encourage this kind of thing? If there has been one thing I've enjoyed about being in disguise here in America, it's been my utter anonymity. Nobody pointing, nobody in my face trying to provoke me, nobody getting on me about the Gundrun brawl, no paparazzi.

"I've worked in this neighborhood for, like, eight years. You get to know people," she says, as if anybody who works in a neighborhood for eight years would be on a first-name basis with everybody and universally adored. Does she understand she can choose to ignore people? But she'd never do that. She actually likes people. Genuinely likes them.

"Wait." She crouches by one of those grates that trees grow out of, and then stands triumphant, waving something in her hand. As she nears, I see it's a fifty-dollar bill. "Look what I found!"

"Wow," I say.

She flattens it between two fingers as we walk, gazing at it like it's the portal to paradise. She did say her new apartment is beyond her budget. Will this make a dent in her living expenses?

I tamp down the strange ripple in my chest. "You're very excited," I observe.

"I just found fifty bucks! Found money is special. It's...a boon. Found money—well, you of all people should understand that."

"*Me* of all people? What does that mean?"

"Nothing," she says quickly.

"So does this go for *any* found money? Even a dime?"

"Even a dime," she says.

"That's a little pathetic."

"Oh, I'm sorry," she says. "Is my happiness bar set too low?"

"The highlight of your day was brushing some dirt off a dead cactus."

"It takes big things to make Mr. Jack Smith happy. Big, important things. World peace. Perfect harmony."

"Harmony," I groan.

"Oh, what? You hate harmony?"

"Yes, I hate harmony. I really do."

She snorts. "Isn't this getting old? A bit predictable? I get it. You're a growly loner. Alright already."

"Don't forget roustabout," I say, concentrating on the sidewalk, trying not to stare at her too much, but the chilly walk has put apples on her cheeks. She's wearing the style of knit winter hat that Dave and the others wear, with a crude insignia and a giant pom pom, and bits of blonde hair have escaped from the sides, framing her face, which is positively radiant with glee and goodwill.

"So what does it take? To make your day?" she asks.

I shrug, unsure how to answer that. "Winning, I suppose. Vindication. Crushing my enemies."

"Vindication? Crushing enemies? What are you, a Bond villain?"

"It also makes my day when people refrain from asking me to do errands they clearly don't need me on."

She snorts. "This found money means we have to buy something for ourselves that we wouldn't normally buy, and you're gonna help me do that."

"What about your rent?" I ask, not that I care, but she was just complaining about it, and even I know this is an expensive city for regular people.

"Are you kidding? This is a found windfall. It's energy. You have to spread it around and enjoy it. We have to treat ourselves to something splurgy that we wouldn't normally treat ourselves to."

"Mm-hmm," I say. The subset of splurgy things I'd like that I wouldn't normally treat myself to contains exactly zero items.

"I got it!" She turns around, walking backwards. Her eyes are a dazzling shade of green in the sun. "Have you ever had a Holey Icewich?"

"Is this something we should head back to the supply closet for?"

"No, it's build-your-own donut ice cream sandwiches."

I frown. "So it's a task and a disgusting-sounding snack?"

"That settles it, we're getting some. I'm buying us each an ice cream donut sandwich with this money, and then with the rest I'm gonna double our cookie order."

"You just found fifty bucks. If you need it, you should keep it," I say, feeling unaccountably annoyed. My fake Good Samaritan parents were buying yachts off the backs of these people, and here she is buying treats. No doubt she's being underpaid. I should look into the pay.

"You pass it on. What's the problem?"

"Any more of this sweetness and rainbows and my teeth are going to fall out, that's the problem."

"Human connection is as valuable as money, if not more so. I can't believe that would be a surprise to you of all people."

"Me of all people? Why do you keep saying that? What about me says I believe in bullshit?"

"Just forget it." We get in a line of people that stretches out of a hole-in-the-wall place with a red awning with rainbows and pink witches.

"Me of all people?" I ask.

"It's none of my business. And we have decisions to make.

Look." She points at a chalkboard menu. "Choose, or I'll choose for you."

"If you think this is going to stop me from my butt-dialer quest, think again."

"You're still on that?" she asks wearily.

"Why wouldn't I be?"

"Rhymes with *tossed haws*," she says.

After a ridiculous wait in line and an endless deliberation at the counter, we emerge with our concoctions. She has a cookie crumble donut with chocolate-covered pretzel ice cream and Oreo ice cream inside, with chocolate icing topped with M&Ms. She insisted I get the same thing, but with Fruit Loops on the top—"for the crunch factor." It's so her, all the sweetness and brightness and a little bit of the devil.

"What person in their right mind would eat this?"

"Us!" She leads me to a stoop—there's no walking and eating this kind of thing. We have a perfect view of orange-striped construction barricades guarding an expanse of rubble, creating a bottleneck and a congested street.

"I suppose this is about productivity, too."

"I'll do a working lunch and" —she gestures at me— "not a lot of lost productivity on your end."

"What? Ouch!" I protest.

She takes a bite then pauses, closing her eyes, fully given over to the experience. Her fine features are suffused with softness, and a sheen of sugary ice cream lights her plump lips. She looks perfectly serene. It's...arresting.

She takes another bite and groans. A new part of her plump lips is shiny now. "Mmmm," she says, just sitting there maddeningly, not eating any more, not doing anything. Just luxuriating.

It's here that it hits me: this is her pleasure face.

I can't look away, because I'm seized with this certainty that it's her orgasm face, too, and my mind crowds with annoying images of some faceless manbun dude fucking her. I try to erase the manbun dude, but I can't. They'd lie in bed together afterwards and talk about office productivity. Or how many pencils to fit in a bun. Other things to store in a bun. Chopsticks. Thumb drives. Found money. Ice cream sandwiches.

She opens her eyes and I force my attention down to the continent's most dubious confection. "I actually have to eat this?"

She gives me a stern look. "Yes!"

My mind is still churning on the very unappetizing Jada-fucking-a-manbun image. Not that I care. Jada can fuck whatever manbun she wants to, assuming she can spare the time from her precious SportyGoCo activities.

I look over and notice that there's a dab of chocolate just above her lip. The urge to swipe it is driving me mad. It's all I want to do.

"You have something..." I point at my lip.

Her pink tongue slides seductively over the spot. It does nothing to remove the chocolate, but it does everything to wind me up all the harder. Is everything she does maddening? Withholding information from me just for the hell of it. Forcing me on this errand. Being all taunting sweetness and light with a chocolate dab on her lip, perfectly positioned for maximum distraction.

"What?" she says.

"There's still chocolate."

She tongues it once again; once again, she fails to get it.

Before I can stop myself, I'm pressing my thumb to the upper edge of her perfect doll lip. It's soft and warm, and the electric sensation of our skin-to-skin contact skitters over my hand.

I bring my thumb to my lips and suck off the chocolate.

Her lips form into a scolding smile. "Well, that wasn't inappropriate," she says.

"Were you hoping for wildly inappropriate?" I ask, mouth dry.

"Yeah, you wish."

The noises of the city seem to recede into the distance.

I press my spoon into a corner of the confection in my lap, isolating a bite that's equal parts of everything. I give it a taste.

She's grinning like the Cheshire cat. "You like?"

I've had thousand-dollar entrees served in exquisite Mediterranean settings. I've had Michelin-starred meals and feast aboard super yachts. I've had opinions about them all.

But this. This is a messed-up thing I don't have a category for. I don't know if it's the fresh-baked warmth of the donut or the iciness of the ice cream or the easy crunch of the colorful cereal bits or the cacophony of the city or still the chocolate from her lip.

"I suppose it has wrongness that I like," I say.

"Treats taste best when found money bought them," she declares.

Not it, I think, staring down at the ridiculous concoction.

Our next stop is Cookie Madness. Her friend owns the string of stores, she tells me, and has swung her a running discount on day-old frosted cookies. "But today we're getting fresh, hand-picked ones."

"How wonderful," I whisper.

She puts a lot of thought into picking them out, consulting me here and there, like which shoe cookie looks yummiest, or which is the biggest rainbow cookie.

She's eking every last drop out of finding the money. It's beyond tedious. At one point she turns to me and asks if I have any hobbies.

"Driving," I say.

"No, come on. That's your job. I mean your hobby. Your passion."

"Driving is my hobby and my passion."

"Just driving around."

"Around and around," I say. "Nice and fast."

"You have no other passions? No other hopes for the future?"

I stifle a grin. Of course this would irritate Workaholic Barbie. "I hope in the future my time is spent driving."

"I guess that's...well, zen at least. Though I really think you could do more." She picks out a car cookie. "The red frosting one," she tells the person behind the counter. "That's the nicest."

She turns around and presents it to me in a little wax bag. "For you."

I take it. "And this is the errand you so desperately needed me for. This."

She grins, like that's so entertaining of me to say.

"People are gonna be excited that they're not getting random ones," she says on the way back. "People are gonna be grateful that you helped pick out the cookies."

"I barely helped. Who is the snake cookie for?" I ask on the way back, because she seems to have a person in mind for each cookie.

"The snake is for Marv, the security guard. He has a pet boa constrictor at his house. He brought it in one time. He's not technically part of the group, but Bert has really harassed him, and it would be terrible if he quit."

"Dare I ask who's getting the bomb?"

"Lacey. Because she likes to yarn bomb. It's like knit graffiti where you cover public surfaces with knit stuff. Though she hasn't been doing it much lately. It's all she can do to stay awake. You know not to go into Meeting Room A when the cloth shopping bag is hanging on the doorknob, right?" she asks. "It means she's napping."

"And you call me unproductive."

"For you, it's a choice; with Lacey, it's not. She has this horrible fatigue that no doctor can diagnose. She's one infraction away from being fired, which means she wouldn't get unemployment—she'd be destitute with no health care or safety net. I don't even know how she'd live. She's all alone in the world except for us."

"So she's been sleeping in there while you cover for her?" I ask incredulous.

"We can't let her get fired. She's begged for part-time hours while she deals with this, but Bert won't give her that. He'd prefer to fire her."

"So you cover for her. While she's napping."

"When she has a bad week, we split up her tasks among us."

"I didn't realize Lacey was such an operator," I tease.

"What's that supposed to mean?" Jada demands.

"You're doing her job and guarding her when she *sleeps*?"

"Oh my god. Are you serious? You think she's playing us?"

"You're doing her job while she sleeps," I say. "All signs point to—"

"Seriously, screw off with that!" Jada says, angry now—actually angry. Her sudden intensity surprises me.

"Okay," I say. "It's just, you know, napping at work while others do your job—"

"That is really rich coming from you, Mister Executive Summary!"

I hold up my hand in surrender.

"No, no, I'm sorry. It's just that she was such a dynamo before. This was a fun place to work with exciting things happening, and she and the former owners were this project management and brainstorming dream team. You have no idea how devastating this fatigue problem is for her. Especially when people question it, because the last thing she wants is to have to sit on her ass. She was a real ally to me, too."

I nod. I'm sure it was a blow—I've never seen somebody more into teamwork.

"Also, I have some expertise in the area of jerks taking advantage," she continues, "and that is not what's happening here."

I narrow my eyes, not liking this. Who would take advantage of Jada? "Expertise?" I repeat, wanting more. Maybe even names.

"In my past. It's no big. In fact, I'm glad for it. For the learning experience." She brightens up. "Do you have brothers or sisters?"

"No. Nor parents."

She turns to me with a pitying look. "You're...an orphan?"

"You say that like it's a bad thing," I say.

"I'm so sorry."

"Don't be," I say, yearning to get off this subject.

"What about...other relatives?"

"There's a cousin who may or may not be talking to me at this point. Hopefully the latter."

"But I'm sure that you have people. A found family."

"Nope."

"So wait—" She looks over at me so sadly, so balefully. "Just...nobody. You're alone in the world?"

"I like to think of it as unencumbered."

"What do you do on holidays?"

"Give thanks that I don't have to make a forced trip somewhere annoying and have people mad at me for not acting like I'm having fun."

She stares at me in disbelief. She probably loves holidays. She probably has a hot Santa's helper outfit. "And you're happy about that?"

"Ecstatic," I say.

"But what about people who love you and who you love? Maybe you don't have a birth family that you love, but we all need people."

"No, no, no, and no, thanks," I say. "I promise, I live a life that most people would envy."

"Driving and being alone."

I tap the tip of my nose.

She looks unconvinced. "Driving. That's the place where you feel the most happiness."

"That and the times in my life when I've punched men who richly deserved it. That gave me a great deal of happiness. Taking a smug smile off a man's face. Highly recommended."

"That's terrible!"

"It can be extremely pleasurable."

"Violence is never warranted," she says.

"Not even against Bert?" I ask. "Coming in here, ruining your hard work, hurting the people you love, terrorizing the office. Are you telling me you wouldn't enjoy seeing him get it right in the kisser? A nice big knuckle sandwich?"

"What is this, the 1920s?" she jokes.

"I'm not hearing a no. You wouldn't like to see somebody wipe that smile right off of his smug face?"

"It's wrong," she says.

"Oh, of course it's wrong. That's not the question. The question is, would you enjoy seeing it?"

"It doesn't matter if I'd enjoy seeing it. Violence never solves anything. We'll defeat Bert, and it'll be through the hard work of our family pulling together. And it's your family, too. You don't have to rely on your fists; you've got a family behind you now."

"No, thanks," I say.

"Too bad," she says. "We're your found family."

"Consider yourself unfound," I say.

"You are so funny." Her smile fills my chest with a lightness that's a little too close to cotton candy. "Sometimes I feel paranoid that Bert senses how we feel about Lacey, like he knows how vulnerable she is. I'm bracing for him to go after her."

Bert is a type of man I know well—cruel, petty, and power mad. I grew up under the thumb of exactly such a man. "You can't let a man like that sense vulnerability."

"You won't tell him about Lacey, right?"

"Hell no."

"Thank you," she says, beaming at me with this open-hearted gratitude that is just disturbing.

"Who am I to ruin a brilliant scam like what Lacey has going?" I add.

She snorts. "Shut it."

We continue walking, past an exercise place full of sweaty people on treadmills.

"Does Bert have any actual skills for his position? Is there anything he does well?"

"No. And if he was only shitty at his job, that would be fine, but he seems to go out of his way to ruin what we're doing, and we're not the only department he meddles in."

None of this adds up. Why would Wycliff hire somebody so awful? "Have you lodged a complaint?"

"Of course. They put this management company in charge when they bought us, and that's who hired Bert. We've provided examples, documentation. We complained when he first fired our top designers. These were people who were aggressively recruited by our old owners—people so sought after by our competitors, and Bert let them go for things like dress code stuff. The man works overtime to destroy the company."

"That doesn't make sense," I say.

"Just because it doesn't make sense, doesn't mean it isn't so."

"Usually it does mean that."

"Yeah, well, it's almost like you work overtime to make yourself disagreeable," she says.

"I don't have to work overtime to do that," I say.

"Har, har, har. True enough," she says.

Shondrella gets a shoe cookie. Dave gets a sunglasses cookie. Lacey nearly cries when she gets her bomb cookie. Dave is there, joking about the bomb cookie, trying to cheer her up. She says she's going to do the knit bombing again soon, talking with this look of grim determination I've seen on her face before—I'd imagined it to be simple humorlessness.

Is there no way for her to be moved to part time? And is it true that Bert is making things worse? Bert's a shitty person, no question, but is he that unfit as a leader? Or would this group hate anybody who wasn't their beloved former owners? The way they talk about the old owners, nobody would fill their shoes.

Right then, some fabric delivery comes. Dave takes over the

cookie delivery while Jada, Renata, and Shondrella slam into garment production mode.

Over the following days, I notice that that's how this office seems to operate; hurry up and wait followed by a frenzied period of work. I've noticed also that a lot of the hurry up and wait happens because Bert inserted himself into things, delaying or misplacing shipments, changing rules and specs. One time he even took a delivery up into his office, supposedly by mistake, but it seemed like an awfully strange mistake, and it sent the whole department into panic mode.

Bert needs to shape up. With a few tweaks, this place could be run better. Not that I care. I don't know shit about business, and the last thing I want to do is follow in my father's footsteps. But I do hate to see a group of hapless people tormented if I can at all avoid it.

Anyway, I came here to find the butt-dialer. Eyes on the prize.

And then I'll sell Wycliff to somebody who's actually good at business, and that'll be best for everybody.

Eighteen

Jada

Renata, Shondrella, and I arrive at work early in order to nab the fabric samples for Unicorn Wonderbag before Bert can see them and start asking questions.

And now it's crunch time.

We're at the back table putting pins and chalk lines on the new fabric. Shondrella's got paper and pencil and her calculator app open, working out how the print will hit, which will help us determine the finishing sizes and zipper sizes. We have to get the zipper sample order in by noon.

I haven't stopped thinking about the storage closet. Sometimes I look at Jack being all debonair with his villainy eyebrows and offensive nature, and I think about the wrong things in the closet.

Of course that's what he wants.

I haven't stopped thinking about our Monday cookie run, either. The way he pressed his thumb to my lip, slow and sexy, and the sizzle that shot through me. And then he slipped his thumb between his lips and sucked off the chocolate.

Was he trying to be madly sexy?

Because that's how it felt—sexy and wild and even a bit naughty. So much so, it made my vision blur.

And there's also how angry he seemed at the idea of jerks in my past taking advantage of me. I didn't say who those jerks were, but I feel like he wanted to know, and that he would've maybe even liked to punch them.

The adult me abhors the idea of violence. Violence is never superior to dialogue, to working things out, but the young girl all alone, caring for her mama without help from the men around her —that scared young girl completely without a champion—that young girl was thrilled with the idea.

"Look," Shondrella says, showing how well the print lines up with the pattern. "We can get three per yard." She whips out her calculator. Renata's already cutting.

Naturally, Bert chooses this moment to bumble in. Renata grabs a tracksuit reject from the box below and coolly drapes it over the Wonderbag stuff, and I'm praying to the big box fashion gods that he doesn't recognize it's so last season. If Bert gets involved with Unicorn Wonderbag, it'll never get off the ground and we'll never get enough orders to save the company.

Luckily, he keeps moving.

He stops at Jack's cubicle, and I wince, hoping he didn't catch Jack screwing around. But no, he seems to be telling him something. I strain to hear what they're saying over the clatter of keyboards and murmurs. I catch something about OSHA something. Was there trouble in shipping? What does it have to do with Jack?

I flatten the fabric on the board while Renata lines it up to the ruler.

Bert's done with Jack. He's on the move.

Our way.

Keep walking, keep walking, keep walking, I whisper-pray.

No deal. Bert's standing in front of the table, looking at the three of us pretending to do something nonsensical with a tracksuit from last year that we saved for fabric scraps.

"Jack's been picking stuff up from out at the warehouse space, but he doesn't have proper shoes," Bert says, eyeing Jack's Converse sneakers. "He's gonna need steel-toed work boots."

I nod with the minimum of eye contact, unsure what it has to do with us.

"I'm gonna have you take him out for regulation footwear, Jada."

I give him a stunned look. "What? Me?"

"Yes, you."

I look at Renata and Shondrella. Either of them would be more logical choices, being that I'm senior designer and all. Or Varsha, or Lacey, or literally anybody else. "We're trying to turn this around today," I say, hoping he doesn't look too closely and see our tracksuit full of holes.

"What is it?" Bert asks, perhaps sensing something new to wreck.

"Just a random measurement tweak," Renata says, bored.

"Well, this isn't an option," Bert says. "You're with Jack. Now."

"I can arrange to get my own shoes," Jack says, strolling up.

"Apparently not," Bert barks.

Renata says, "I could go. Or better yet, we could just give Jack the address!" she adds brightly. "Jack is amazing at finding addresses."

"Is this a no?" Bert asks. "Are we countermanding orders now?" He looks from one of us to the next, and when he comes to me, he gives me the faintest little smile. My heart drops, and I know plain as day that he's deliberately giving me offsite busywork. I want to cry.

"We got this," Renata says.

I give them a few last instructions. They assure me they have it.

Yes, they'll text with questions. Yes, they'll make the noon drop or die trying.

"YOU SEE how he's deliberately sabotaging us?" I say when we're predictably stuck in gridlock. "He wants me out of the office as much as possible because I keep things on track. Do you really need somebody to take you shoe shopping? You're incompetent, but not an imbecile."

"Well, that's hurtful," he says. "I clearly need to work on my imbecile skills."

"You're not even funny," I say. "Let's just do this and get back to the office. If we can be quick, I can still get back and help."

Traffic loosens up, and he does seem to be trying to make time, slipping into one lane and then the next, flowing through the Manhattan traffic with surprising skill. Especially considering his driving experience was upstate and before that—to hear Renata tell it—on rural European roads in a scenario that may or may not have involved goat carts.

His shifting movements are strong and precise, yet he's got this loose touch, like he's part of the machine. I've never seen a man concentrate so hard. It's very competence porn, which is a thing I wouldn't have imagined saying about Jack back when we first met. He seemed the opposite of competence porn with his blindingly bright print shirts and lazy, entitled attitude. Most guys I know try to act more capable than they are.

Not Jack. If anything, he acts less capable.

"What is the project?" he asks.

"You can't tell Bert."

He gives me a look. "Please," he growls. Something about the way he growls the word "please" warms me from the inside out. Jack's hot when he drives, and he's also hot when his assholey offensiveness is aimed at Bert.

I tell him about Unicorn Wonderbag, how we think it's the key to saving the business and keeping the orders up for this all-important accounting period. How desperately we're trying to hide it from Bert so he can't throw a monkey wrench into it. How we think we can get it into Target's and Walmart's spring lineups.

Jack seems interested. Is he actually taking an interest in the company now?

I find myself telling him personal stuff about Wonderbag, like how proud I am of it, and how I don't want to jinx it, and how I sometimes feel as if it's a magic design.

"Hence the name?" he says.

"Yeah," I say. "So I guess it's not that big a secret that I feel like that."

He's set his glasses on top of his head, like that'll help him drive more efficiently. The effect is intense, what with his eyes and hands and crazypants driving competence. I'm trying not to think about the supply closet with exactly zero success, because what would it be like, to be with a man like this? To give in to that strange dark pull of him?

"We're gonna get you back."

I stare out the window at the somber grays and browns of the buildings. "There's no use. It's deadlining in an hour. There's no way."

"I still don't understand it. Is he truly sabotaging the office?"

"Have we not been over this before?" I say.

"Seriously. Has he brought nothing in terms of skills? Zero?"

"Asked and answered," I say. "Less than zero!"

Jack looks thoughtful. "Well, maybe he *should* be fired." He looks over at me as if to gauge my reaction.

"Oh my god. Do we actually have your buy-in on Bert being a shit boss?"

"The man is making me get some sort of ridiculous boots to wear," he says.

"Oh my god," I snort. "The work boots? That's what put it over the top for you? It's all about you, isn't it?"

"What else would it be about?" he asks.

I'm laughing, even though, seriously, can he be more obnoxious? But I feel happy around him. Weirdly lighter.

"So that would be your wish? For him to be fired?" he asks, interrupting my thoughts.

"My most fervent wish."

He seems to contemplate this. "But what if he were instantly fired?" he asks. "Would there be a problem with having his position going unfilled?"

"No problem at all! He literally does more harm than good. Look what just happened. He could've sent anyone. Why not Dave? Dave's not busy today. Why not Varsha? Why send the senior designer?"

He takes a corner, flowing into what I would've guessed would be the worst lane but turns out to be the best lane. He gets through the traffic quickly but without being a dick about it. He navigates like a fish, flowing through a stream, one with the car, all competence-porn overload.

"Nice driving," I say. "You're actually helping for once."

"Better than listening to you moan any longer than necessary," he says, looking over at me.

I smile at him, and the strangest expression crosses his face before he looks away. I don't know if it's the competence porn of him driving, but god, the pull of him.

"Where did you learn to drive like this?" I ask.

"Roads."

"Roads where? They don't have this kind of traffic upstate, that much I know. Renata said you drove overseas. Where would that be?"

He looks back at me, seeming to assess me. "Türenbourg, for starters."

"The European country? That's one of the places you've lived, right?"

He nods.

"You drove in *Türenbourg*."

"Yup."

"Just…Türenbourg. That seems like a code word," I say. "Am I going to find out you're a driver for a notorious jewel heist gang or something?"

Jack looks over at me slyly and I can't help but smile. Maybe it's stupid, but right then, it's like we're the only two people on the planet somehow, and I think he feels it too.

"You just can't stop thinking about the supply closet, can you?" he asks.

"Yeah, but it has nothing to do with you. It's the yellow legal pads. Yellow legal pads drive me crazy!" I force my gaze forward, trying not to think about kissing him. Whatever the worst thing is, Jack figures it out and says it. It's quite the talent.

"There's a nice table in there," he continues. "The perfect height, if you know what I mean."

"Oh, please." My pulse speeds. "Are you in the habit of measuring tables?"

"A maestro knows his instruments."

I roll my eyes. "Oh, lord, who says that?" He's not the type of man I'd ever be with—ever.

If I saw Jack's profile on a dating app, I'd swipe left so fast. A delivery driver who hates the idea of family and teamwork and togetherness and holidays, whose hobby is to drive and annoy people, and his greatest ambition is to quit work at five on the dot. Oh my god, I'd crash the app with how fast I'd swipe left!

And I seriously doubt he's actually interested in me. It's probably more about the challenge of corrupting me, like he tries to corrupt Nate and Varsha and the rest of the gang. It's the one and only place he seems to expend effort. That and his butt-dialing investigation.

He pulls in front of Sadler's, a massive old-school shoe store in Brooklyn that caters exclusively to the trades and women who came of age in the 1970s. This is where they have the regulation stuff.

We get out of the truck and head down the walk. My phone pings right when we're coming up to the door. A text. It's a screenshot of the zipper sample order, submitted twenty minutes early.

I'm stunned. They finished it? Already? I text with Renata some more, to make sure they got all the elements right. They did.

"Wow," I say. I pocket my phone, gazing into the dusty display window, which contains work boots, loafers, ladies' heels, and several cobwebs—and not the fun Halloween décor kind.

"What's up?" Jack asks.

"They finished it."

He regards me for a second, then puts on a face of shock. "Without you controlling the outcome? Is that even possible? Can Workaholic Barbie actually take a break now?"

"Screw off," I say as we head in. "It's just...kind of shocking."

"Sometimes fewer cooks in the kitchen..."

"I know but it's my recipe." I text more questions and instructions. I can feel Jack's gaze on me. "I'm not a control freak." I look up and he's just laughing.

My phone pings. It's another piece of screenshot proof. I text back a smiley face and a thumbs-up and the word "nice" with many exclamation points.

"Don't you have boots to buy?"

"Yeah, but..." He gestures around him like he's waiting for something to happen.

"Let's find the boot section."

"Oh," he says.

I look around and locate a sign. "Occupational footwear, second floor."

"Right." He follows me up a set of creaky stairs onto a floor with rows upon rows of shelving, like a crusty old library, but instead of books, it's work shoes—white medical shoes, slip-resistant restaurant clogs, anti-fatigue slip-ons, waterproof utility boots, and more.

Jack stands there, seemingly mesmerized by the sheer volume of shoes and boots for sale.

I find the section with steel-toed boots and call him over. "What's your size?"

"How am I supposed to know? Maybe at some point the staff could rouse themselves to come out and trace my feet."

"Trace your *feet*?"

"That *is* the first part of the process," he says.

What is he talking about? What is this, the Middle Ages? "Just because the shipment got put to bed, it doesn't mean I just want to mess around now. What size?"

"I'm sure it's on file somewhere," he says.

"What do you mean, on file?" I say.

He looks caught out.

"Do you seriously not know your own shoe size?"

"Not offhand," he says almost indignantly.

I point at his sneakers. "What size are those?"

He looks down at them. I make him take them off. The size is worn away, of course.

"You suck at shopping more than the average man, even though that's not saying much." I grab a size twelve. "Sit down and hold this to the bottom of your shoe. See if it's close."

He complies.

He thinks people should trot out and trace his foot? Is it possible Renata's right, and he's just from the most backwards place possible? I thought Türenbourg was a sophisticated place, but tracing the foot? It's a pre-industrial mode of measurement.

"Too small," I say. "I'm thinking thirteen." I take the shoes back and grab a thirteen.

"Are you really supposed to be rooting around up there?" he asks.

"No, *you* are. But apparently your incompetence and entitled white maleness literally knows no bounds."

I throw the shoes at him, one after another. He catches them, laughing. He tries on a few pairs. We settle on a thirteen wide and bring them to the front. I check back into the office to make sure the package got picked up.

"Will that be all, sir?" the clerk asks him.

"Yes," he says. "I'll have these wrapped and sent around to the SportyGoCo offices. Jada, can you give him the address?"

I look up. "No, what? We're taking them."

"One hundred fifty-nine ninety-nine," the man says.

Jack stares at him like a deer in headlights. "I'll sign for them."

"You'll sign for them? This isn't a hotel, Jack! This is the step where you pay."

"Right. I didn't bring money, though."

"I'm sure they take credit cards or a payment app. You know, on your phone?"

"I didn't think to bring anything like that," he says.

"You have no money or credit cards and no payment app on your phone?"

"I didn't expect to go shopping," he says.

I pull my wallet out of my purse. I hand over a card. "Put it on here."

"No! *You* can't pay for it." He takes the card from my hand, horrified. "I won't have it—I won't."

"I don't know how they shop where you're from, but you actually have to pay for things here."

"I'll send for cash."

"You'll send for cash? What does that even mean? We have to get back," I say. "Pay me tomorrow."

"I can't have you buying me shoes. I'm sending for the money." He turns to the clerk. "We'll be back with the cash in under thirty minutes. Does that work?"

The clerk is fine with it. Jack heads out, texting.

"You're being silly," I say, following him out to the sunny sidewalk. "Have the money sent to the office if you want it that way."

"You aren't buying me shoes. I draw the line at that. Thirty minutes." He points to a small park. "We can sit there and wait."

He seems strangely troubled by the prospect of my loaning him money to buy shoes. Is this a European thing?

We sit on a bench. There are kids on a nearby swing set. Some older men play chess. A guy's doing a shell game near the fence for some unwitting tourists. Somebody's selling artisan ice cream sandwiches. "Yum," I say.

Jack follows the direction of my gaze and groans.

"So is that how they shop in the village where you're from? You pick things and they get sent to you?"

"It depends," he says vaguely.

"If you don't have any form of money on you, how did you even get to work?"

"I took a car."

"Like a Lyft?"

"A car."

"That's clarifying. And cash is being sent to you," I say.

"My...uh...friend Arnold's bringing it."

"Oh, god! Arnold? I get to meet Arnold? What a treat that will be," I say.

"Arnold's a good guy," Jack says.

"He sent you to work with a joke sandwich. After that ostentatious lunch. Who does that? Are you sure he'll even come through with the money? Because he seems like he lives to mess with you."

"Oh, he'll come through," Jack says.

My phone buzzes. More office business.

"I could win that game," he says when I click off.

"What game? The shell game? No, you can't. It's a trick."

"I've been watching."

"They always have a guy there pretending to lose easy ones to make onlookers feel confident."

"I'm telling you." Before I can stop him, he gets up and goes over. "What's the buy-in?"

"Five bucks," the guy says.

He plunks his phone down on the table. "One game, please."

"Jack, no!" I say. "You can't gamble your phone!"

"Can and am." He tips his glasses over his head and sits. The man grins and shows him the stone and then claps the cup back over it and shuffles them all around, hands lightning fast. He stops and looks up. Jack taps the end cup. The man frowns and lifts it. Relief floods through me as the man hands him a five.

"One more," Jack says. He wins that one, too, and heads over to the ice cream stand. "They have your favorite," he says, pointing to the cookie dough ice cream sandwich. "Right?"

"Yeah," I say.

"Two, please."

"Wow, thanks," I say as he hands mine over, impressed by the sweet gesture. It's weird, but welcome.

"Well, you can't bitch about being away from the office for too long if you've got one of these stuffed in your mouth."

I unwrap it. "You know what I think?" I ask.

"What?"

I take a bite and pause, enjoying the huge wad of cookie dough I got. "Mmmm," I say, closing my eyes and luxuriating in the unexpected bounty. I open my eyes and find him watching me closely.

"What?" he asks again.

"You act like this growly villain, but I think your bark is a lot worse than your bite."

"There's only one way to find out about my bite."

I sigh wearily. "Give it a rest."

We watch some kids swing from afar and wander back to the bench.

"How'd you know you'd win?" I ask. "You know that guy brought his A game when you put down your phone."

"It's part of being a good driver," he says. "You learn to soften your view and see everything at once. People who lose this game only focus on one thing. I see everything."

"Except in the office."

"I see plenty in that office," he says. "People can't keep things from me for long. As you'll soon discover."

"Dream on," I say, because of course he's talking about the butt-dialer here.

"I'll get it out of somebody," he says.

"That's rich coming from a man who doesn't know his own shoe size."

Just then, a sleek black town car pulls up. An older man with a thick pelt of white hair gets out. Jack waves and the man heads over.

"Is that Arnold?" I ask.

"Yeah."

I follow him, surprised. I suppose I expected more of a downtown financial-bro type.

"How much do you require, sir?"

"Two hundred," Jack says.

"Very good, sir." The man counts out a few twenties.

"Sir?" I say, coming up behind Jack. "Do you think that's funny? Mocking him like that?" I demand.

Arnold looks bewildered. "I'm sorry—"

"It's okay, Jada," Jack says. "Arnold, this is Jada. We work together."

"It's not okay," I say. "Listen, Arnold, Jack may not be as sophisticated and worldly as you are, and he may not understand how things work in contemporary society, but that doesn't give you the right to make jokes at his expense."

Arnold puts on a surprised face, as though he doesn't understand.

"I mean, sir? You think that's funny? Rolling up here in your limo and calling him sir? Jack can't help where he's from. My god, the man has never even been to a shoe store."

"It's okay," Jack says, like it's all so amusing.

"You shouldn't let him patronize you, Jack."

"Thank you, Arnold," Jack says. Arnold nods and returns to his limo.

"Calling you sir," I say. "He drives up in his posh car, like, who does he think he is? 'Very good, sir.' How obnoxious."

"He's not patronizing me or being obnoxious, I promise," he says, like it's so funny.

He goes over to the shell game table and gives the man a bill and then heads across the street to get the shoes while I text with Renata.

~

When I get back, I get a full report on the print-to-pattern sizing and zipper sample order. Apparently, they did everything just right. The project survived without me, which I only feel a little bit weird about.

Renata gives me a look that tells me there was a hitch. "What?" I demand.

"Bert came back around and seemed curious about what we were ordering zippers for," she says.

"No!" I gasp.

"It's fine," Renata says. "Shondrella gave him a big freaking zipper smokescreen."

"Good." I lean on the cubicle. "You were right about so much—Jack's friend Arnold? He really is a rich jackhole!"

"I knew it!" she says.

"I think that job experience was for sure made up." I tell her about the shopping trip. "He doesn't know his own shoe size."

Renata does a dramatic double take. "What?"

"He didn't know. He thinks they *trace* your *foot*. As if that's how shoe shopping is done."

Renata looks distressed. "Poor Jack."

"He was also totally bewildered by the number of shoes, as if he'd never been in a shoe store in his life!"

Renata frowns. "Maybe he's only ever had access to used shoes. Like a cartload of shoes gets pulled around and the people of the village try them on or something? A goat cart. And they all run out into the street when the goat cart comes."

"Renata, your image of Europe is just bizarre!" I say.

"You weren't there to hear him describe it. And Jack is out there trying so hard to find fashionable shoes, because he really does care—you can tell he's trying to be fashionable," Renata continues. "Putting together that outfit took some real work—that's how hard he tries to escape his goat cart roots."

"I think you just want him to have a goat cart in his life," I say. "Or maybe you want a goat cart."

"What about goat carts?" Shondrella says, coming up.

"It's the poor rural village Jack is from." Renata turns to me. "Is he from Türenbourg or did he just work there?"

"He worked and lived there, it sounds like," I say.

"Türenbourg is one of the wealthiest and most sophisticated places in Europe," Shondrella says.

"The US is one of the wealthiest nations on this continent and we still have pockets of truly desperate poverty."

"I suppose." Shondrella sounds unconvinced.

"I mean, tracing his foot? Like the town cobbler toddles out and traces people's feet? And they use the tracing to sew a bit of leather into crude footwear? Maybe that's why he's so arrogant and disagreeable—he's just trying to put a good face on things," Renata says.

"Hell no," I snort. "Jack is definitely not trying to put a good face on things. If anything, he enjoys putting a bad face on things. Jack hates being agreeable. He hates harmony."

But then I'm thinking about the shell game guy. The way he returned the money that he won.

"You know who else traces the foot?" Shondrella points out. "Bespoke shoemakers. Bezos, that's how he'd get shoes."

"Maybe that's it!" Renata laughs. "Jack has a bespoke shoemaker!"

We all laugh.

Renata looks over at Jack. "He has so much fashion potential, all completely squandered."

"Not all of it," I say, watching him move across the office like a panther. "He has very nice eyes when he takes off his glasses. Which, come to think of it, he did a couple of times." I frown. He took them off for driving, he took them off for the shell game. He seems to remove them when he reads. "I wonder if his prescription might be wrong, because he takes them off when he wants to do something important."

Renata watches him. "Maybe the glasses are secondhand, too. We so need to give him a makeover. I'd encourage him to get contacts, that's for sure."

Shondrella's watching him, too. "He'd look good in the right clothes. He really would."

"He'd look good in no clothes," Renata says.

"Let's cut this," I say. "If it's not okay for men to say this sort of thing about women in an office setting, it's not okay for women to say it about men."

"You're right," Shondrella says.

"Jada's just against the makeover," Renata says.

"I *am* against the makeover—very against it. You need to leave him be," I say with more emotion than I intend.

Nineteen

Jaxon

The design office window looks out onto West Thirty-seventh, and every day, starting around three in the afternoon, people start checking to see if Bert's green car is gone. Apparently he leaves early to beat the traffic, much to the relief of everybody in the design department. And the shipping department. And judging from the attitudes when I pick up and drop deliveries around the building, the photography, social media, merchandising, production, and styling departments, too.

I finish helping in shipping, and I'm back up at my cubicle just after Dave looks out there and sees Bert leaving, and the whole office seems to relax.

I hate business and have precisely zero interest in ever running a business, but even I can see that this is bad management. It's ridiculous.

"Party time!" Dave calls out.

Shondrella tosses a wadded-up piece of paper at him, then Lacey follows suit. "Get back to work!"

Dave, of course being the dude he is, beans Lacey and Shondrella right back.

Lacey's laughing, having a good day, and this stupidly makes me feel relieved, because, even though I'm still not a hundred percent convinced she's not playing everyone, it seems I've been infected by the Lacey drama, or the mass hypnosis she has us all under, that allows her to nap during the day.

"You guys," Jada scolds. "If anybody has free time, I could use more hands on unpacking the Mankomi hardware. And by the looks of it..."

"Keith has more green!" Dave says from the corner by the dead cactus. "You guys!"

"No way!" Renata says, rushing over.

Everybody's gathering around Keith except for me; I've opted to stay at my cubicle.

"I have a photograph from three days ago," Varsha says. She holds her phone up next to Keith's spindly middle section. People are discussing and comparing.

"He's way healthier," Dave assures everybody. "Way better."

Naturally, everybody agrees, because there's no mass hypnosis this gang doesn't go in for.

Jada's positively sparkling with happiness, as though a little green on Keith is the second coming, which is not a great advertisement for modern office life.

Somebody sticks a red bow on the side of Keith's pot. Pictures are taken—to post on Keith's famous Instagram, no doubt.

I groan, and Jada gazes over at me with her Barbie-perfect eyes, lids half-smudged with green sparkle eyeliner, because she'd find a million more important things to do than fix her makeup.

I fix my attention back on the screen where I'm reading the comment section on the Doha Grand Prix report.

Jada starts up the song-chant: "Go Keeeeeeith! Go Keeeeeeith!"

I look up to find her snapping her fingers, hands raised level with her ears, and she's gazing over at me, happily chanting, "Go Keeeeeeeeeith! Go Keeeeeeeith!"

It comes to me with some surprise that she thinks she's cracked the code of how to cause me maximum possible annoyance. And she's going for it.

Renata claps her hands. "Come on, Jack!"

I keep eyeing Jada. "I draw the line at singing songs to dead plants."

"Don't you listen to him, Keith!" Shondrella squeaks.

Jada keeps on. She's clearly enjoying herself.

I turn my attention to my screen, but it's impossible to concentrate. The cactus is dead, but the life thrumming through this office is quite stupidly alive.

"Dude," Dave calls out. "You have to at least look at him!"

"Don't have to look at a dead cactus to see the mass delusion happening here."

Jada laughs like I'm being a fun and entertaining member of the team. I am a lot of things, but "fun and entertaining" isn't one of them.

Jada has added a shimmy to the song. "Go Keeeeeeeeeith! Go Keeeeeith!"

Jada calls me arrogant but she's the arrogant one. She's arrogant if she thinks they can bring a dead cactus to life. She's arrogant if she thinks she can force everybody into this misguided family that she's styled through sheer force of will. Most of all, she's arrogant if she thinks she can keep me from obtaining the information I've set my sights on.

She wanders over, still singing and snapping her fingers. "Jack, come on!"

"For somebody who's so rabid about saving the company, you're spending a whole lot of time on a dead thing," I say.

She fixes me with her pretty smile. "The pleasure of seeing Keith come back to life will be almost as great as the pleasure of seeing your face when you realize we saved him. When you realize there is nothing this group can't do together."

"Uh-huh."

"And you'll be like, 'If only I hadn't been so standoffish and negative about Keith!' And one day when you find yourself all alone here in the office, you're going to go up to Keith and say, 'Keith, I'm so sorry I doubted you.' And you'll fall to your knees and say, 'Keith, please forgive me.' And I think a tear might just roll down your cheek."

"Oh, I'll do better than that. If by some unholy miracle that stalk of crust comes to life, I'll be like, 'Maybe this planet is more than a rolling ball of misery full of people whose destiny is pain and death.'"

She regards me unblinkingly for a few moments, and then she laughs, bell-like. "Oh, Jack! You actually are pretty damn funny sometimes!"

I narrow my eyes at her, heart pounding. "It's as if you've gleaned nothing at all from me."

She continues to beam at me, undeterred, and an incomprehensible sense of lightness flows through my chest. Like we're having fun or something. I don't know how to feel about it.

"Anyway, I'm busy with another project," I say. "And I think you know what that is."

She leans in here, lowering her voice. "You think anybody here is gonna betray this group?"

I can't help but smile now. "I'm counting on it."

She leans in—near enough that I can smell her coconut lilac shampoo—and forms two words with those lips. "Sauced maws." With that, she returns to the group, singing more tauntingly this time.

And I'm imagining hauling her little body right up to mine, taking those tempting lips in mine. The intensity of the urge is unlike me. I'm always in complete control. And god, this is Jada. We're oil and water, Jada and me. Still I'm thinking it. I'm so awash in the thoughts of it that I don't notice the hush that comes over the office in the next moment.

People are frozen, gaping at the door.

I follow their gazes to where Bert is standing.

"What's going on?" Bert barks.

"Stretch break," Shondrella tries. "It helps productivity."

Bert looks unconvinced. "Who's Keith?"

Renata smiles. "An Instagram personality."

I feel this tension well up in me, like what if Bert figures out how important Keith is to everybody and does something? Not that I care, but the wailing and gnashing of teeth would be unbearable.

People have drifted away, getting back to work. The sound of clicks and keyboards once again fills the air.

Bert heads to the large cutting table and sets down a package. "This came."

Jada drifts back there. "Ravaldi? We didn't order anything from Ravaldi."

"I had my assistant get a set of zipper samples couriered over," he says. "For the bag you're working on? I saw that a zipper sample order went out, and I think these would be better."

The clatter of keyboards quiets.

Jada looks pale. "Ravaldi zippers?"

It's clear that Bert's talking about Unicorn Wonderbag, the project Jada desperately wanted him not to know about.

"You sent out for a range of ten-inch zippers, but you overlooked the Ravaldi, and I've decided that any bag coming out of here should feature Ravaldi zippers."

"But...that's a luxury zipper. It'll increase the price by...fifty-fold."

"Sustainability is one of the initiatives of SportyGoCo, and Ravaldi uses reclaimed metals, which is better than plastic or non-reclaimed metals."

"But there are regular plastic and metal zippers in all of our stuff," Shondrella protests.

"Is that a no?"

Jada says, "The bag design we're playing with has tons of sustainability features that make up for all that."

Bert's attention turns to Jada with the harshness of a search-light, and a growl rises in my throat unbidden.

"Well, I wouldn't know about those features since I didn't see a one-sheet about it cross my desk, did I?" Bert pushes the zipper package to the middle of the table. "You'll produce that one-sheet straightaway, and this is the zipper brand I'm having you use. You'll price any bag you produce with the Ravaldi zipper."

Jada looks distraught.

Does that zipper truly raise the price by that much? Is it possible she was right all this time, and he really does want to throw a monkey wrench in things? It seems outrageous to put a luxury zipper into a bag destined for Target and Walmart—even I can figure that one out.

Bert ambles down the row of cubicles. The keyboards start up once again—furiously. He heads up the next row, and then ambles toward the window where Keith is.

And stops.

Maybe it's the bow on Keith's pot that draws his attention or maybe, like most bullies, he has a radar for vulnerabilities. He stares at Keith, with a frown that seems carved into the lower half of his face.

The computers, which have become like canaries in the Bert coal mine, have quieted once again.

"What the hell is this?" Bert barks. "There is to be nothing blocking this window."

Dave's right there. "Want me to move it?" He goes to stand by Keith.

My pulse pounds. I don't give a shit about Keith or this faux family, but bullies like Bert who live to torment the powerless? Those types of men are my weakness, let's just say.

Not my problem, I tell myself. *I'll fire him in the end,* I tell myself.

"Things like this should be in the break room," Bert says.

Dave says, "But there are no windows, um...though..."

"You don't want to put it in the break room?" Bert barks.

"No, of course I want to. I just..." Dave pushes the dead plant across the floor, careful not to let it tip. At six feet tall, Keith is too tall to pick up and carry—the thing would crunch into the ceiling.

I grit my teeth.

Bert follows Dave. It seems like he's going to do something more to Keith. I look over and see that Jada thinks so, too. The look of terror on her face hits something deep down inside me, and in a movement as natural as a flower turning to the sun, I stand up from my cubicle chair, rising up to my full height.

This is enough. It's just enough.

I can feel my vision change, zeroing in on Bert.

Bert stops and turns. "Something to add, Mr. Smith?"

The room seems to shrink. It's just him and me.

I have a lot to add, a hell of a lot, and none of it is in the English language. I step out of my cubicle. I want to get in his face. It'll be delicious. And if he wants to go, I will thank all the gods in the sky.

And I so hope he wants to go. I ball my fists. Energy seems to animate my arms. He needs to be hit—he just does.

But then I look down to find Jada watching me, horrified. She's shaking her head frantically, mouthing *no*.

That's when I come back to my senses.

The rest of the room starts filling in again. What am I doing? This isn't a racetrack or a paparazzi-filled sidewalk.

I remind myself that this is an office. With cubicles. And a dead plant.

I give Bert a smile through the heat I still feel in my face.

"Nothing to add at the moment," I say casually. I pull a pencil from my breast pocket and walk the few feet to the pencil sharpener that's bolted to the edge of a nearby table and I start sharpening.

I'm coming down.

I sharpen and sharpen. What am I doing, playing savior like that?

I nearly got fired just now, not to mention a massive potential lawsuit with a massive payout to this jackass. What's more, anybody who needs me as a savior is clearly beyond saving.

Not my people; not my family.

I know I need to stop sharpening the pencil—any more sharpening will be a threat. I go a little more. Just a small amount more of a threat. Then I stop.

When I look back up, he's still watching me. I make a show out of blowing the shavings off the pencil, and then I saunter back to my desk.

Bert needs to be fired. He's a shit CEO and a fucking annoyance.

I can't fire him on the spot—not only would it blow my cover, but I know enough to know that there's probably a protocol around it. Plus, if the people here realized it was me who fired him, they'd be so grateful, I'd probably end up needing to punch my own face to get right again.

"Let's get to work, folks," Bert barks, storming out.

"He really is a jackass," I say.

Jada comes up to me. "Were you just going to go up and say something to him?" she asks. "You can't say anything to him about Keith—you know that, right?"

"Oh don't worry, I was just going to get in his face," I say. "No words required."

"Wait, what? Get in his face?"

"Put my face in his. Followed by my fist, ideally. I find a good fist in the face does wonders."

She studies my eyes, unsure if I'm joking.

"It would be worth that last demerit, don't you think?"

Jada frowns. "So you don't give a shit about the company until there's an opportunity to punch someone?"

I shrug. "I'm a man of simple pleasures."

"And what about us?"

"What do you mean?" My gaze falls to her lips where I thumbed off the chocolate spot. Her lips are fucking gorgeous, and suddenly all I can think about is tasting them. I'd haul her hot little body against mine and kiss those perfectly shaped Barbie lips into slack-jawed pleasure. "Are you back to the storage closet?"

"Us. Our family. If you're fired?" she says. "We need you. We've never had somebody as fast at deliveries. You got up to speed on spreadsheets so fast. And people like having you around. You're an important part of the family."

"You really are screwed, then," I say.

She looks so sad suddenly.

Lacey walks up. "Keith can't survive in there," she says. "He needs light."

"Can't somebody just bring him home if you're all so worried?" I say.

"He's six feet tall," Jada says. "We had to bring him up diagonally in the freight elevator and almost broke him. Also, it's freezing out there! You can't bring a cactus outside in the cold!"

"It would shock him," Lacey says.

Jada slants a glare at me. I'd better not say anything about Keith being dead, that's what her glare says.

I smile.

Twenty

Jaxon

I walk in, toss my glasses on the counter, and peel the itchy mole off my face. "Get me Soto on the phone. I have some company business to discuss with him."

"Right away, sir?"

"Right away." I head through the bedroom to the closet to change into my workout clothes. I'm feeling a few rounds on the heavy bag coming on.

Arnold's still there when I come out from scrubbing my face.

"What is it?"

"I found a box of things you'll need to look at."

"Christie's, consignment, or garbage." I breeze past him. "Figure it out."

"This would need your input," he says.

"After Soto. I want to talk to him while it's still business hours somewhere on the planet."

I wrap up my hands, ready to go in. The hand wraps feel tight and snug, like my hands are packed dynamite. I don't warm up, I just go at the bag—no leisurely long-range jabs and crosses; just hard, close-quarter hooks and uppercuts.

Soto's call comes through just as I've gotten myself exhausted enough to start being sloppy. I put him on speaker and head to the far end of the workout space where massive windows overlook the park. "Who do I speak with about personnel changes at SportyGoCo? I need to have somebody fired."

"Did something happen?" he asks. "Have they seen through the disguise?"

"No, there's somebody whose face I never want to see again. Bert, the CEO. What do I need to do to get rid of him?"

"It might not be so easy," Soto says.

"I do own the company, do I not?" I say. "Don't worry, I have legit grounds. The man is an objectively terrible CEO. He seems to go out of his way to screw up viable projects and destroy morale. He needs to go."

"You want somebody fired because they're not doing a good job?" he asks.

"What's so strange about that?"

"Nothing. I'm pleased to see you taking an interest in the company."

"I'm not taking an interest in the company. I don't give a shit about the company. I'm taking an interest in never seeing this blowhard's face ever again. Get someone on it. I don't want him in work tomorrow."

"Well...here's the thing. SportyGoCo is run by a management company named Bloxburn who would have the power to make decisions."

I frown. Bloxburn. The name sounds familiar. I can remember my parents talking about it, always in furtive whispers. "But I'm the owner."

"I'm still trying to work it out, but as a management company, Bloxburn would have some sort of contract with Wycliff that would likely give them power over personnel decisions, in other words, hiring and firing. And it's not typically something you can simply override. A lot of these sorts of management companies, once you put them in place and work out the contract, they don't like to be second-guessed."

"I'm the owner, though," I say.

"I'm telling you there might be a signed contract."

"He's a terrible employee who deserves to be fired under any sets of laws."

"I can look into it, but..."

"No, don't look into it; make it happen. Get rid of the guy or cancel the contract."

"I'll see what I can do."

"Check in on the pay, too. I'm going to review the salaries and make some changes."

"You want to cut the pay?"

"I'm making changes. Who knows, maybe a few people will get raises."

Soto laughs at my seeming joke, and we click off.

I'm back at the heavy bag, doing Thai round kicks this time, lobbing my leg into the bag with wicked force.

I can feel Arnold hovering at the doorway. Eventually I tire and grab a towel. "What?"

"Did something happen to upset you, sir?" he asks.

"Nope. Just some personnel changes I want to make," I say. "What's this thing you found that I need to look at?"

Arnold hesitates. "Maybe later, after dinner."

"Meaning after I've got a nice meal and tumbler of scotch in my belly?" I am not loving the direction this is taking. "Show it to me now. Let's get it over with."

"No, really, this can wait."

"Now or never," I growl. If there's bad news, I want it.

Arnold peers at me unhappily. "It's some old letters," he says.

I toss the towel aside. Can this day get any more maudlin? "Let's see them."

Arnold observes me darkly for a few more moments and then, with obvious reluctance, he leads me to the lower level, through the great room, the den, and over to the library area. On the desk that was my father's stands a wooden box, like a large cigar box. There's a stack of envelopes next to it, mostly bright pastels—pale pink, light blue, mint green.

Even from where I'm standing in the doorway, I can make out the loopy scrawl of my longtime nanny, Jenny.

This strange haze comes over me, almost a buzzing in my ears. I'm awash with old feeling—not anger, but something else.

Jenny was with me from the time I was a toddler until I was ten. She and I used to write letters together, fighting for things. There was no cause Jenny didn't want to fight for. There was a time when I imagined she'd fight for me, but I imagined wrong.

For a moment, I think these are some of the letters we wrote together, but then I read what's written on the top envelope: Clifton Eadsburg von Henningsly. With the Türenbourg address crossed out, forwarded to the Manhattan address.

Clearly I should've had the meal and the scotch first.

"And why do I want to read whatever the hell she wrote to my father?" I ask with a breeziness I do not feel.

Some of the envelopes have been opened. Arnold grabs one and holds it out for me. "I took the liberty."

"I believe there are five fireplaces in this home capable of burning all kinds of things. That's the liberty you should've taken."

"Jaxon," he says in the voice that means business. The voice I couldn't ignore as a young boy. The voice I won't ignore now, because I need to see.

"Jesus Christ." I snatch the envelope, glaring at him. He looks old. He's been with me for the entirety of my life and sometimes I forget I've been most of his career.

I can't quite bring myself to look down at it. "Were they having an affair? Is that it?"

He shakes his head.

I pull out an envelope wrapped in a note. I unfurl the note and there it is, Jenny's loopy scrawl.

I don't care what you tell him for why I'm gone, but if only you could give him this, so that he knows I remembered, that I'm thinking of him. He's just a little boy, and it would mean the world to him. You can read it yourself—it's just the birthday wishes is all. I'm asking you as a father that you would make this day a little brighter for him.

I blink, not making sense out of this.

"She can't have it both ways. The woman left without warning—without so much as a goodbye—to go off to be with her rocker boyfriend. And suddenly she's all about making my day brighter?"

"Look inside," he says.

I open the card. It's got a picture of an elephant balancing on a cake that has a ten on it. My tenth birthday. The year she left.

Happy birthday, Jack. I'm so proud of you today and hope you are feeling so much love. I miss you like the dickens, and I'm so sorry I can't be with you, but I think of you always. Love, Nanny Jenny.

I toss it on the desk. "She left, Arnold. She made her choice."

"Are you sure it was her choice?"

I roll my eyes. Arnold always gave her the benefit of the doubt. He'd always say things like, "It never sat right with me," and "There's more to the story—there has to be."

"So this is what you were going to show me? Was there something else?"

"She broke your heart, I know that—"

"She was just a nanny."

"Jack."

I give him a glare—my own shut-up glare.

"This box is full of cards she sent to you. She never forgot. You should go see her. She splits her time between the city and the Catskills. See if she's in town. I could call her. I could call her tonight."

"Why would I go to see her? She was paid to be my nanny, and then she wasn't. Why would I look her up?"

"I never thought she left of her own accord, and this is further proof."

I scowl at the box, emotions churning in me like ocean waves.

"She loved you. And you loved her."

"Have dinner on the table at seven." I turn and head back to the gym.

Twenty-One

JADA

SHONDRELLA, Dave, and Renata gather around my desk with grave expressions. Lacey comes up behind them. "Did you tell her?"

"Tell her what?" I ask, alarmed. I'm thinking it's more stuff about the closure problem for Wonderbag. Now that Bert has specced a luxury zipper, we need a different closure.

"I have it cued up." Lacey joins the others, tablet in hand. "What's going on?"

Shondrella casts a worried glance at Jack's cubicle, which is empty due to another mandatory afternoon in shipping.

"It might not be anything," Dave says. "That dude probably has nine lives knowing him."

I straighten, alarmed. "Is Jack in trouble?"

"Kind of!" Shondrella says.

"What?" I ask, maybe too fervently.

Lacey winces. "I was looking up some pictures about this weird bump that I have on my arm, just worried that it might be cancerous, and look what I came across." She hands me her tablet, and there on the screen, in full-color photography, it's a mole that looks like Jack's.

"This is a cancerous mole?"

"It is the worst type of cancer there is," Shondrella says. "One of us has to say something to him."

"I'm sure he's gotten it checked out," I say. "It's not like it's in a place that he can't see!"

"This is Jack we're talking about," Renata says. "Does he strike you as somebody who's up on modern medicine?"

"The EU has affordable health care," I say. "I'm sure it was looked at."

"I have two words for you." Renata leans in.

"Stop it with the goat carts," I say.

"Somebody at least has to ask him if he's checked it out," she says.

They're all staring at me. "Why me?"

"You know him the best," Renata says.

"And you're our leader," Shondrella says.

I snort. "Some leader," I say. God, I sound like Jack.

"You're the mom of our family," Dave says. "But not like a mom. You're the cool older sister."

"Nice save," I say, scrolling through the disturbing pictures of moles that look like Jack's. "I don't know how I'm gonna bring this up to him."

"You'll find a way," Renata says.

~

I RUMINATE over the mole situation for the rest of the day. Jack doesn't do well with people being concerned about him. I try to think up jokey ways to bring it up, but at the same time, I want him to take it seriously.

If he hasn't gotten it checked out, he really, really needs to.

He rolls in at a few minutes to five and starts packing up his stuff. The shipping guys say he's being a big help down there. Apparently, he knows how to fix all kinds of trucks, and he can lift a surprising amount. I look at his muscular hands and think about his desire to get in Bert's face, which is guy code for starting a fight. Bert's got a good fifty pounds on Jack, but I think Jack has more muscle. Jack would kick his ass.

Not that I'd want it to come to that. We can win this struggle the right way.

I saunter over, cool and casual. "Five on the dot," I say. "God forbid you stay."

"I'm thinking the company truck can get me as far as Jersey City, at which point I'll abandon it."

I know he won't, but I don't say that. Jack always wants you to think the worst.

"Say," I say, tilting my head. "We're considering doing a skin cancer screening one of these days. Have you ever done one of those?"

"A screening?"

"A screening," I say. "Like moles and things. To make sure they're not cancerous."

He narrows his eyes. "You don't like my mole? Is that it?"

I shrug. "Have you ever gotten it checked out?"

"It's not cancer, don't worry. I would not do a screening."

"So you've never gotten it checked?"

He puts on his coat and shoves his phone in his pocket. "Nope."

"Then how do you know it's not cancer?" I ask.

"Because I do."

"You know this how? It's important, Jack."

"Are you proposing an exam of some sort? In the you-know-what closet?"

"Screw off, be serious!"

"I'm not worried about the mole."

"So you got it checked out already?"

"I haven't gotten it checked out, but it's not a problem."

"God, do you take nothing seriously?" I gust out, feeling angry. "Excuse us if we care about you."

"You're paid to tolerate me. There's a difference." It's so Jack to hate any idea of somebody caring.

"We're paid to tolerate each other *and* we care, and that's because we're family and there's nothing you can do about it. You're the black sheep who acts like he's not in the family, but he totally is."

His eyes shine in all of their burnt-butter, thick-lashed gorgeousness. "Families don't keep secrets from each other."

"Oh my god, you're still on the butt-dial? If only you would apply some of that energy toward your job, you might help us save this company."

"Unlikely. Your biggest departmental accomplishment is removing a dead plant from the trash."

I snort, enjoying myself in spite of his jackhole-ness. "Is somebody jealous of Keith?"

He sighs.

"Jealous of Keith," I tease. "The laziest and most unprofessional man on the planet, now jealous of a cactus. So sad."

His eyes flash and I have the stupidest urge to close the distance between us, to press my face to his neck or something. Supposedly we're co-workers. What is wrong with me?

"It's just a matter of time," he continues. "There are twenty-five or so people in this department. You think I can't crack one of them?"

I get in his face—frustrated, angry, and so alive. "You never will." I draw closer. I'm thinking about the way he wiped the chocolate off my lip. The feel of his thumb. Sure and warm and good. "Because everyone here knows it's wrong to break a pact. So sorry," I whisper, inappropriately close.

"But as we've established, wrong things can be so much fun."

My heart skips a beat. I should cut this off but I can't, or maybe I don't want to. I'm creeping up, closer and closer, the exact place I shouldn't be. "You think you're hot but you're not."

"I think I'm hot," he says. "And so do you. Look, we agree on something!"

Twenty-Two

JAXON

JADA SNORTS and leans in closer, the maddening coconut and lilac scent of her washing over me. “So full of yourself.”

She’s so excruciatingly proper and perfect, and god, all of her disdain for me. And her bossy ways and her taunts and her workaholic pencil bun. And all I want to do is kiss her. I came for the butt-dialer, but I can’t stop with Jada.

And I have so many questions about her. Like what drives her to work so hard? Does she have hobbies? Favorite shows? A life outside of work?

“The big, bad villain and all his wrongness,” she says.

I lower my voice to a deeper register. “What fun would it be without villains like me? There would be nobody to hate on, nobody to talk about. Nobody to imagine doing wrong and outrageous things within the supply closet. The pleasure of forbidden things.”

“Actually, I’m thinking about the pleasure of preventing you

"I'm sorry, whose phrase is it?" I grab her finger and the jolt of our contact rocks me. "Mine." I force myself to let her go.

"You don't own it!" Lacey protests. "It belongs to all of us now."

Jada has fallen uncharacteristically silent. She's looking over my shoulder. Everybody has fallen silent. Everybody is staring at the doorway. Bert must be back, I think.

Bert caught us screwing around—me and my two demerits.

I'm thinking I'll be fired, and I find that I don't want to be fired. I don't want to leave.

And then I turn, and something inside me collapses as I make sense of who I'm looking at.

It's been twenty-some years. Her dark hair has gray streaks and her face is thinner, more defined, more regal somehow, but she still has the same warm eyes.

Nanny Jenny.

I swallow.

"Jaxon?" she says with a faltering smile.

Like a ghost, I'm moving toward her—if nothing else, to get her out of the office. "What are you doing here?"

"I had to come see you. I needed to see you. I wanted to explain things."

"There's no need," I say in a calm voice, even as my belly twists around like a pretzel mobius.

"Of course there is," she says.

I look behind me. People are resuming their positions in their cubicles, trying to act like they're not paying attention, but we're right there in the office doorway, so of course they're paying attention. Varsha is typing away, also paying attention.

"Come on." I lead Jenny out of the office and down the hall toward the open-air space that's actually the rooftop of the neighboring building. I'm thankful nobody is out here at the picnic table or in the smoking corner. "Did Arnold call you? There really was no need."

"Of course there was a need! You never even got the cards." She's staring at the mole. I can tell she wants to ask about it. She blinks, thinking the better of it, I suppose. "You probably thought I abandoned you without a second thought, Jaxon, but that's not how it was. I never wanted to leave. I hated to!"

"Then why did you? Without so much as a goodbye," I say before I can stop myself, because supposedly I don't give a shit. I straighten up. "I understand that I was just a job to you, but it was bad form, that's all. It's customary to say goodbye." I manage all of this quite unemotionally.

"Arnold told me the whole story. How everybody said I'd run off to join a boyfriend in a band on a world tour or something like that."

I gaze out over the dirty facades of the buildings that line the street. It looks like a tunnel with no top from here.

"He told me how you'd refused to believe it. And then they agreed to put their private investigator on it to track me down to get you to stop worrying and that the PI confirmed the story of the boyfriend. But it was never true, Jaxon. They made you think I'd left without a second thought. But there was no boyfriend in a band."

My blood races. "I see."

"Jaxon," she says, and she waits until I look up to her, all the better to fix me with the gaze that I remember so well—frank, open, and loving. I'm flooded with the memories of how it was with her. She was always so honest with me, always interested in what I thought about things, though I'm sure I was insufferable. We'd have long conversations, Jenny and me. We were curious about the world together. She was sad when I felt sad, and it made me feel less alone in that empty Manhattan townhouse. Or the times when we got dumped off in Monaco. Or worse, the summers in Türenbourg, the small principality in Central Europe where they bought the drafty old castle.

"You probably don't remember Donnie, my twin brother," she

says. "He came by a few times when we were in town. He met us out at the zoo one time."

I nod. Of course I remember Donnie. I was fascinated by Jenny's family. I wanted to be in Jenny's family. I would've traded it for anything.

"When you were around nine, Donnie became extremely ill with a neurological condition that the doctors could never diagnose, but one thing that we did know is that he benefited from some very expensive medicine and the kind of twenty-four-seven care that I couldn't give him. One day your father came to me with an offer to pay for his treatment and round-the-clock nurses."

"That doesn't sound like Dad."

"It was severance pay for my resignation, effective immediately. On the condition that I had no more contact with you."

I turn to her. "Why?"

"Your father and I had a few confrontations," she says. "I never knew exactly what was happening between you and your parents, but it wasn't right, the way they treated you."

She'd confronted him? She'd stood up for me? My blood races. "They never could stand it when somebody saw through their philanthropist bullcrap," I say.

Jenny saw through it. Jenny knew. I thought I was the only one.

No wonder they dismissed her.

"You deserved better. You had such a big heart," she whispers.

I'm feeling unmoored, suddenly. She knew. She was with me. I'm a puddle of emotions. I need to reorganize myself, somehow. I open my mouth, thinking to back her off with something pithy and scathing, maybe even a simple "that was then; this is now," but the words don't come.

"Your heart was too big," she says. "That's why you had to cover it."

I finally get ahold of myself. "I was a child, Jenny. That isn't me anymore, and really, this is all pointless."

"You haven't changed either," she continues. "So headstrong and full of feeling. You were the most sensitive, passionate boy I had ever met, much as you tried to hide it."

"People grow up," I grumble.

She fixes me with that frank gaze. "I had to take the offer. Donnie would have ended up homeless or worse. He was my twin, and I couldn't turn my back on him. He was my heart. But you were my heart, too."

I nod, mouth dry.

"I wrote those cards because I wanted you to know that somebody was thinking about you out there. Somebody loved you. I loved being your nanny. I followed your career. Your parents kept me away, but I was always there. I was at one of your races—the one they held in Austin, Texas. They threatened to have me charged when they found out."

My pulse whooshes in my ears. She'd attended a race?

"I'm so sorry, Jaxon. And I'm so sorry that they died," she says.

"Well, you of all people should know what a non-tragedy that was," I manage.

"You never got a chance to come to terms with them. You never got a chance to make things right together. Don't pretend you didn't want that—all children do. When I heard the news, I wanted to reach out to you. It was the first time I could reach out to you without worrying what would happen to Donnie, but I'd never heard from you, not even as an adult. I assumed you didn't want contact with me. But then yesterday when Arnold called and told me the story, and that you'd never even gotten the cards I sent, I had to reach out to you."

I can't process any more of this Jenny tenderness. I'm a trapped animal, desperate for an exit from this conversation. "I need to get back," I say.

She looks toward the door. "It's nice to see you with your people. They obviously like and admire you—I could see from their faces, this found family of yours—"

"These people are not my family in any way, shape, or form. They barely know me."

"I know what I saw," she says. "The laughter. The affection they have for you is written all over their faces."

"Probably just gas."

"Oh, Jaxon." She furrows her brow, and she swallows down whatever bullshit she was going to say next. Instead, she reaches into her bag and pulls out a red envelope, just a bit larger than the kind you mail, tattered on the edges. "I wanted to give you this."

Warily I take the thing and peek inside. I only have to glimpse a corner to know that it's the famous Türenbourg lawn photo featuring my parents and me, all fake smiles. I hand it back. "No, thanks."

"Look closer."

"I know what it is."

"Look, Jaxon."

I slip it out of the envelope, surprised to discover it isn't the famous photo after all. It's one of the discarded shots. In this version, I'm staring somberly into the camera. For much of the session that day, I'd refused to fake smile. It was leverage, of sorts—a misguided attempt to keep my parents there, to keep us together. I didn't realize at that point that I was just a tool, a stepping stone. Eventually, my dad took me away for a talking-to that wasn't a talking-to, and when we returned, I had a fake smile on my face and a good deal of blood under my clothes. They flew out that night.

I'm staring at it for an inordinately long time, this artifact from a lost history. The print is lower quality, or maybe my eyes are blurring. To think Jenny was there all that time, in my corner.

"This is the authentic shot. You longing for something real. With a heart so big...don't let anybody tell you different."

If she thinks she's gonna get a hug, she needs to get her head examined, because I'm not the emotional chump she thinks I am. I'm Jaxon Eadsburg von Henningsly. Has she not been following the tabloids?

"I'm not that kid anymore." I slide it back into the envelope and hold it out to her with a shockingly steady hand.

She refuses to take it. "Keep it."

"I gotta get back to work. I'll walk you to the elevators."

She says, "I'm heading to the Catskills with my son, but when I return—"

So she has a son. Lucky for the son. I'm leading her down the hall, the route out of this madness. I'm focusing on the elevators.

"I know this is a lot—"

"I appreciate the visit." I stab the down arrow. The thing opens almost instantly.

She gets in and turns, looking loving and concerned. The doors can't close fast enough, but eventually they do.

I stand there in the empty hallway, face to face with my blurry reflection in brushed steel, holding that fucking red envelope. Why did she have to come?

It's too much, too late.

I attempt to steady myself. Who is she, really? Just a woman who got paid to boss me around when I was a kid. She doesn't know anything.

She kept the reject picture.

I turn to go back to the department and there's Jada coming out the door, heading down the hallway toward me, concern all over her face.

More concern. It's the last thing I need.

"Are you okay?" she asks.

"Why wouldn't I be?"

"You looked stricken when that woman showed up. You still look—"

"Stricken?" I give her a fake smile. It's one of my best, designed to cover how hard I'm reeling from Jenny's pointless yet disturbing visit.

Jada comes to me. She reaches out and takes hold of my arm. Her hand is a hot brand on my arm and the ground seems to tilt.

I'm a kaleidoscope of desire for her, the most infuriating woman on the planet. She's everything I hate, everything I want, all perfect lips and that perky warrior spirit.

I'll do what it takes to protect, to lift this family. I'll play dirty if needed.

God, she would've hated that pompous conference call speech more than anybody—maybe even more than I hated reading it into that microphone. The high-handedness of it, the hypocrisy, the work interruption.

"Seriously," she says. "If you want to talk."

"Why would I want to talk? Why would I want that?" I breathe in that coconut flower doll scent of hers. I'm drowning in that scent, unmoored.

It's here that it comes to me—this wild notion that flies into my brain from somewhere across the universe and takes hold of me.

I draw in closer to her, lost in her clear hazel gaze. "And by the way, I know who you are."

She lets my arm go. Wariness suffuses her expression—eyes a tad wider than usual, lips parted. I'm onto something. My mind spins. Could it be?

"What do you mean?" she asks.

"You're the butt-dialer," I say.

She covers her shock with a smile. Too late. "Me?"

I'm sure of it, now. Jada's the butt-dialer. I'm reeling with every kind of emotion. Ocean waves churn and roil where my brain once was.

Jada, the woman who torments me, fascinates me, and energizes me—she's the person I came to find and destroy.

"You," I say.

Twenty-Three

Jada

"You," he says.

My belly drops down past my knees. "You think it was *me*?"

He comes closer, stuffing the rolled-up red envelope into his pocket. He fixes me with his villain gaze, wild and wounded. "I *know* it was you."

I study his face. He seems so sure. "Hah," I say.

"Are you denying it?" His rumble connects to something deep inside me. "Because don't bother."

Did somebody tell him? Did he break somebody? "Whoever told you that..." I narrow my eyes. "Who told you that?"

He raises his villain brows.

Yup, I just confirmed it like a fool. "Aren't you so clever," I whisper. "You think you're clever?"

"I do think I'm clever." His eyes burn into mine, kicking up my pulse. He's on fire, this man. Dangerous.

I say, "You'd better not tell anybody."

He smiles, lips full, dark whiskers shimmering in the hallway light.

"Oh my god! You can't be bothered to do any actual helpful work, but you're happy to do the most messed-up thing possible?"

"I find the most messed-up thing possible tends to be the most pleasurable, as a rule."

"I can't even with you," I whisper.

His eyes sparkle. I should hate him.

I go up on my tiptoes, getting right into his face. It's supposed to be threatening, but it turns out anything but. "You're an asshole."

"Oh, I know." His breath is a feather on my lips.

I grab his shirt, move in closer. I should let him go, but my knuckles brush against the hard planes of his chest. I'm mesmerized by this small bit of contact through the fabric of his shirt. It's a physical sensation, coursing through my body, and my brain can't form the command to let go.

Quite the opposite—my fists tighten.

"I mean it. You'd better not tell," I whisper into his maddeningly perfect face, a face so perfect that the stupidest styling can't mess it up. Even with the glasses. Even with the hair. He transcends all of that.

He grins. "What would Don Juan the Entitled Delivery Driver do? What would Don Juan the Entitled Delivery Driver want in exchange for his silence?"

"Excuse me?" I ask in disbelief.

He draws his finger down the side of my cheek, leaving a slow trail of sparkling sensation as he slowly turns my world upside down.

He's wrong and outrageous and I want him like fire.

He gives a wicked smile—not his fake one, not his lopsided dimple one, but his glittering one—the one that's pure dark heat that spears through my core. "If you want to keep your job and your precious family, it'll cost you a kiss."

The breath goes out of me. "You're blackmailing me into doing sexual favors for you?"

"Isn't it awesome? How many demerits do you have? One? Two?"

My pulse whooshes. "You wouldn't."

"It's already happening."

"Do you have no self-respect? Are you just like, hey, I'm a thoroughly corrupted, power-drunk Lothario who enjoys sexually blackmailing people who are simply trying to keep their jobs, and I'm good with that?"

"Flatter me all you want. Those are my terms."

I suck in a breath and close my fists harder over his ridiculous shirt. It's like an out-of-body experience, but not the ghost kind. If anything, I'm too much in my body, too much in my skin.

"I'll take your evil bargain," I hiss, pulse racing. "Your twisted demand."

And then I go up on my tiptoes and I press my lips to his. They're soft and warm, and I push into him, moving against his body like he's got the gravitational force of a moon.

He rumbles into the kiss. The rumble has a direct line to my pelvis where it melts things into a cauldron of want.

He presses his hand to the center of my chest and pushes me roughly against the wall.

"Seriously the worst," I gasp in the split second before he covers my lips with his.

I'm kissing him for real now. I'm pulling him to me, disintegrating under his touch.

I feel like I'm falling, spinning. He snakes a tongue into my mouth, and I groan, kissing him harder—greedy and frantic.

But then some faint voice inside me—some voice of self-preservation—sounds the alarm. What we're doing here, it's practically prostitution! So wrong.

I push him away. "That'll be all," I say.

We stare at each other, panting. There's this strange look on his face. For a moment I think he's as affected as I am.

"That'll be all?" he says. "I'm not so sure. I think you liked your entitled delivery driver."

"Please. And if you think it will ever, ever happen again, you're cracked in the head—cracked. And you'd better keep up your end of the deal," I warn.

He gives me one last villain smile and then he heads back down the hall, ducking back into the design department, leaving me trembling with unfulfilled excitement. That was so outrageous, what just happened.

But so, so, so hot.

Not a good person, not a good person, I chant in my mind as I head back after him.

Also, who told him? Or did he figure it out?

Jack is sitting in his cubicle looking all sparkly. If he was as wowed by the kiss as I was, he's fully recovered himself. He probably kisses women all the time. He probably has so many notches on his bedpost, it's lost structural integrity. Maybe he has blackmail deals with half of them.

I frown, hating that.

My phone lights up as soon as I settle into my cubicle. It's a text from Renata even though she's one row away.

Renata: Well?

Jada: What?

Renata: Did he get
the mole checked out?

Jada: Erp. No clue.

Twenty-Four

JADA

I STOP at a bodega on my way home from work to get the stuff for my signature sharing dish, layered buffalo chicken dip. I'm still vibrating from the kiss—so much so that I nearly forget the chili sauce and have to double back.

He's everything I can't stand in a guy—arrogant, lazy, entitled. And yes, there's more to him. But there's more to everybody, isn't there?

Something happened with that woman who came to visit him with that red envelope. Maybe she's a relative, or family friend or something, and she had devastating news for him. And somehow he knew, because the way the color drained from his face when she appeared—it was dramatic. Whatever it was, a normal person doesn't react to something like that by blackmailing a person into sexual favors.

I'm not a good person, Jada.

At least he's honest. But if you're honest about being an awful person, does that really count in your favor?

And yes, it was the hottest kiss I've ever experienced, but it's probably just because it was so wrong. Because *he's* so wrong.

No way did anybody tell him. He must've figured it out.

I'm walking down Ninth Avenue craving more, more, more of him, which makes me want to scream, because how messed up is that?

I remind myself that a lot of bad things feel good in the moment. Eating a dozen chocolate truffles in one sitting, for example. Hypothermia, at its end stages, reportedly feels good. Riding on a broken roller coaster—that's probably quite the fun experience before that bolt holding the track together comes loose.

I worked my ass off to build a nice life and to create a family here in the city that I can count on and vice versa. And romantically, I'm attracted to men who value hard work and behave like noble, upstanding citizens. That is what's truly sexy to me.

Two hours later, I'm knocking on Kelsey's door on the fifth floor. I've long since traded my drab work clothes for midnight-blue sequined Uggs that go perfectly with faded jeans and a T-shirt featuring my favorite Candy Crush candy, the Coconut Wheel, also in sequins. And in my hot little hands, adorned with many rings and bracelets, is the dip.

Kelsey flings open the door. "Galpal!" Her eyes fall to the dip. "That's what I'm talking about."

I stroll in and set it on the counter next to the homemade jalapeño wontons and the hummus plate. "Mia and Francine, in the house."

Kelsey grins. We can identify each other's presence at a place with a glance at the hors d'oeuvres spread. She pours me a glass of something bubbly and pink. I couldn't be more grateful for a girl's night.

Mia's stretched out on the floor in the living room. "If Rhona gets a rose tonight, I'm gonna dive right out that window—I swear to you. Headfirst, I don't care. It'll show humanity is so close to self-destruction if she gets a rose."

"So close," Francine says.

"She won't get a rose," I assure her.

Mia sighs. She hates Rhona.

"How's life in the castle in the sky?" I ask Francine, who recently moved into her man's place, a veritable castle in the sky complete with the ballet studio of every dancer's dreams.

"Well, it's no 341," she says diplomatically.

"Sooooo...better water pressure and a bedroom bigger than a breadbox?" I tease. "You can dish about the luxury. It's called vicarious enjoyment, and I, for one, am all in."

"I will not hold back on the dishing—promise!" Francine says.

"Jada, the twirlers costumes came in this week, and the kids are freaking!" Kelsey says.

"Oh my god, Jada, they love them!" Francine says.

Phones come out and the four of us moon over photos of Francine and Kelsey's dance troupe in the outfits that I designed. I used SportyGoCo clout to get them an amazing deal from a garment constructor. They're little explosions of shiny pink silk and muslin and sequins with deeply glittering black tulle skirts.

"Lucky for us, we found a designer with a nine-year-old's taste in clothes." Kelsey's gaze falls to my sparkly boots.

"That's right," I say. "Nine-year-old girls have style, that's all I can say. No boring shit. Office attire would be so much cooler if nine-year-old girls had a say."

"Can you not wear your normal clothes, like even on casual Fridays?" Mia asks.

"Hell no. I mean I could, it wouldn't be technically against the rules, but I need people to take me seriously."

"Screw 'em," Mia says.

"You're in a Broadway show, you're supposed to be a little wild, but I need to be taken seriously. Dudes can get away with that stuff, but..." I shake my head. "That new guy I told you about, he's always wearing these bright vintage party boy shirts with pastel shapes and squiggles all over them. He's technically support, so he doesn't have to wear business shit, but seriously. Men can get away with that, though."

"Is that the lazy one?" Kelsey asks, setting down a bowl of rice crackers.

"Lazy? Oh, Jack's not just lazy, he's insolent. He loves to be a problem. If there's some wrong way to go, he finds it. It's like a mania of his to be the worst possible employee and worst possible person," I say as the memory of the kiss takes over my body like a demon possession.

I stare down at my phone, not ready to tell them about the blackmail kiss. I'm still processing it, turning it around in my mind, my body. It was such an intense kiss. It was so wrong and so good. A little bit of a role-play with an edgy reality component.

"You hate dudes who don't pull their weight," Kelsey says. "Like your freeloading brothers."

They all know about my brothers, sitting there playing their video games while I worked my ass off and worst of all, put my dreams aside. Until I realized how completely they were taking advantage of me.

"Well, he is a high achiever in the area of having a lot of confidence for a guy with blond-tipped hair and skinny glasses," I say. "Like this lazy and entitled yet strangely magnetic villain."

"Oooh," Lizzie says, walking in with a box of cookies, followed by her sister-in-law, Willow. "A lazy and entitled yet strangely magnetic villain. Are you sure he isn't so wrong he's right?"

"I'm beyond sure," I say. "And he wants to beat up Bert. Since when does violence solve anything?"

"I've wanted to beat up Bert plenty of times, and I've never even met him," Mia says.

"But you wouldn't actually do it," I say.

"I'd think you want to see Bert get his," Kelsey says. "He's making your life miserable. Firing your favorite people."

"More dialogue is always superior to violence," I say. "We're humans, not honey badgers."

"I need to see a picture of this guy," Mia says, grabbing a cookie. "Is he on Facebook or anything?"

"Yeah, what's his last name?" Willow asks as the phones come out.

"Smith," I say. "Jack Smith. Supposedly he worked upstate, but we're starting to have our doubts. It's possible his experience is fake."

Kelsey raises her brows. "The villain being villainous. I like it."

I grumble.

"What?" Kelsey protests. "Wasn't it just the other day you were complaining that the guys you've been dating only want to listen to boring success podcasts?"

"There are a lot of Jack Smiths," Francine says. "Even Jack Smith New York, you get a lot of them. Any other data?"

"He's maybe thirty-five. He has this kind of...fierce, classic bone structure. Intense brown eyes. A mole right here." I touch my cheek. "His hair would be this rich dark brown if he didn't have the bleached tips. Sometimes he wears glasses, but he doesn't seem to need them. He's clearly American, like he doesn't have any accent...actually, he has a flawless accent, come to think of it—one of those general accents they teach you in acting school. His parents took him from the States when he was a boy and moved them to some sort of rural European village. My assistant Renata quizzed him all about it and she's convinced they live in like... rubble or something."

"Maybe his parents were hippies that wanted to go back to the land or something," Mia suggests.

"But in Europe?" Kelsey says. "There are plenty of places in the US to go back to the land."

"I doubt he's even on Facebook," I say. "I mean, he doesn't know basic office technology. Dave in accounting swears he'd never used a vending machine in his life, like he was super bewildered that food came out of it. And he doesn't know how to act. He nearly got fired the first day from this weird interaction..."

"Do you think he's...challenged in some way?" Francine asks softly.

I shake my head. "He's challenged at giving a shit, combined with zero skills," I say. "And it's like he has no exposure to contemporary style at all. He could be hot, but he's styled himself so weirdly. And he has this rich friend Arnold who calls him sir and plays tricks on him. But I think he lets Jack live with him, so Jack just takes it. The whole thing is bizarre!"

"Could he be one of those wild boys they find in the wilderness?" Francine asks.

"Huh," I say, considering the savage way he kissed me. But then, his driving skills.

"Get Antonio," Mia says. "Maybe he'll know about these sorts of rustic villages. I sort of don't think Europe has those anymore, though."

"Antonio won't know," Kelsey says. "Antonio knows about the sorts of people who party on the French Riviera. He knows about the hoi polloi of the fashion runways of Milan. Not impoverished back-to-the-earther wild boys who are alarmed by vending machines."

"He's not a wild boy," I say.

Francine sighs. "I really want him to be a wild boy."

Mia puts down her phone. "You need to take a picture of him, Jada. Get one at the office when he's not looking. I seriously need a visual."

Francine claps. "Stealth picture! Antonio's having us over for Willow's birthday next week, and you are bringing stealth pictures."

Twenty-Five

Jada

I get in early the next day and Jack is there, surprisingly.

I'm passing right by his cubicle, trying not to look at him, but then I do, and he's so smug and relaxed with that stupid knowing twinkle that I find myself standing over him, clutching the cute messenger bag that I use as a briefcase.

"Look who's early to work," I say. "Just in case anybody needs help from the world's worst worker."

He lowers his voice. "Or if anybody needs another one of the world's hottest kisses."

"That's it, I'm officially changing your name to Don Juan the Deluded Delivery Driver."

Jack, of course, is entirely unperturbed. "And I even punched in."

"Good, when you get your paycheck, you can find the most messed-up thing to purchase."

"I was thinking about upgrading my wardrobe a bit," he says. "I think working here has inspired me on the fashion thing."

"Really?" Is my tone too hopeful?

"I was thinking about a T-shirt that says, 'Jada is the butt-dialer.' What do you think?"

I move in closer and lower my voice. "You better not."

He snorts. "Maybe I'll have them made for the whole shipping team."

I grab the back of his chair and turn him to face me. I'm tempting fate, getting right up close to him. I tell myself I'm immune to him. So immune.

But I'm not immune. Our proximity renders me breathless. Just that.

I say, "You'll never last that long. You'll get fired any day, and it won't be soon enough."

"You so want a repeat of the kiss."

Twenty-Six

JAXON

HER EYES BLAZE. Her scent envelops me. Workaholic Barbie with all of that disdain. I want her so badly, it's criminal.

"It's like there's no end to you," she says. "No limit."

"That's part of why you're so hot for me," I say.

"There will not be a repeat. I prefer to kiss men who have some kind of a moral compass."

"I'm sorry to hear that," I say. "A man with a moral compass will never kiss as well as a thoroughly corrupted and power-drunk Lothario."

"He'll kiss better. Ask me how I know." With that, she walks off.

I watch her, fascinated.

I've kissed princesses, fashion models, socialite hostesses with the mostest. I know a good kiss. That was a great kiss.

Beyond great.

I was stupid for her—stupid for the taste of her lips, obsessed with the feel of her skin with my palm. I couldn't suck in enough of her scent. And Jesus, the way her eyes changed when I pushed her against the wall. The entire feeling of us changed, as if we were trembling and coming alive together. I was a hungry beast, dying of starvation, and she was the feast, and I had to devour her, drown in her, ruin her like she was all I knew. Though "knew" isn't the word. There was no "knowing" happening whatsoever. My brain was being bypassed entirely, there was just my need and my hands and my lips, a mad orchestra directed by my cock and my libido.

It's not like me to lose control like that. Fucking has always been a sport to me. Ninety percent strategy. Ten percent luck. A hundred percent control.

That'll be all.

I grit my teeth.

She dismissed me? In the middle of *that* kiss?

The rest of the employees drift in, and soon the place is its usual hive of activity. A few minutes later, Jada's up at the work-table ripping open packages with the usual garment-making suspects.

I'm trying to focus on making notes for Soto, but then I look back over, and they seem to be struggling, all high drama. Jada reaches up and pushes a bit of hair out of her face.

Of course she had to push me away. She's a good girl, after all. She didn't think I had that level of wrongness in me, and she didn't think she had it in herself, either. Those delicious kissable frowning lips and the grabbable blonde bun.

Her imitation runs through my head. *Quick, bring the servants, I shall need some smelling salts. Where is my cravat? Where is my Foppish Ascot?*

How could I have ever thought it was anybody but her? That imitation was pure Jada—Jada in her noble warrior Joan of Arc mode, sniffing out the hypocrisy and going for it.

Now that I've found her, what will I do? I tell myself I'll decide when I decide. I'm running the show here. In the meantime, there's a problem in shipping: Some software glitch made it so that we lost a lot of inventory data last night, and the guys have been scrambling to catch up before Bert does something drastic.

I ride down the elevator, ready to pitch in. I need to stop pretending to be somebody else at some point. I know who the butt-dialer is, after all, but for now, the shipping guys need my help. They're good guys who don't deserve to have to cancel their weekend fishing trips and football games because of a software glitch.

I grab the tablet and get to work.

My parents truly were amazing. Not only did they have the world convinced that they were parents and philanthropists with big hearts when the complete opposite was true, but they had people believing that they run a good business when even I can see it's being trashed.

We're making good time. The inventory project is a mindless task that requires me to hold a tablet and check stock against numbers in the system—just enough distraction to not think about the kiss with Jada or Jenny showing up with all of those explanations and memories.

It would have been nice for the ten-year-old boy that I was to have gotten one of those cards or to hear her say those things. But for the man I am now, it's an unwanted if not outrightly perverse gift.

Needless to say, I lit into Arnold after work. He had no business sending Jenny into the office. Into my place of business! Arnold protested that she was leaving town for a while and there wouldn't have been another chance, as if that matters. I was harsher with him than I should've been. But seriously, after all these years?

Jenny showing up to explain things at this late date is like showing a man who'd cut his arm off to escape a trap that the key had been hidden within reach all along.

Not. Helpful. At all.

Jada would think she can sew back the arm. She'd give it everything—this is the woman, after all, who thinks she can bring a dead cactus back to life. But no way would she succeed, and I wouldn't want it anyway. The good thing about losing something crucial is that nobody can take it away from you a second time. It's a glorious form of immunity.

The shipping and logistics end of the business is actually kind of interesting. I'm doing inventory with a man named Sammy who's been here for years. Sammy knows everything about ground shipping, about getting pieces of garments moved all over. It's complicated and fascinating, a large system where all the parts need to be functioning at peak efficiency, just like a pit crew.

Sammy is complaining about how much money gets squandered by shipping late or having to ship in separate parcels lately. This seems like intel that I could bring to Soto in my quest to wrest control away from Bert and Bloxburn or however it's all arranged.

Surely I can get rid of them if they're outright screwing it up.

I order twenty-five pizzas for lunch—enough for the entire shipping team. I lie and say the pizza place owes me; not out of any Good Samaritanism, but we're running behind. I add an anchovy pizza and use it to bribe Dave to come down and help; I happen to know he has a light afternoon.

My plan works. Sammy and Dave start tossing out ideas over pizza. They start running numbers and discover that adding one more full-time shipping person would save the company double that expense in rush fees. They tell me about this new kind of order alert system that would help with inventory. Not that I give a shit about the business, but I do think a lot about speed and logistics in motorsport, and we all start geeking out on it.

Clearly this company would've been better off being run entirely by the employees this whole time, not that my parents would have gone for that.

Dave is all about helping with inventory now that he grasps the situation, and he identifies some other employees who'd pitch in for pizza, and soon we have a crowd, and we get back to work.

Being a member of a team racing the clock is invigorating. Not that I'm going to go all in on the charms of honest work, but we finish with two hours to spare, and there are high fives all around, even this sense of camaraderie, like we've been through something together.

When Sammy invites me out for beers after work with the crew, I hear myself telling them that I'll meet them.

I head back up in the elevator, wondering if Varsha has a gopher list.

She doesn't. Instead, I find tension—I can feel it the moment I stroll into the design department. Jada looks up as I pass her. She widens her eyes and shakes her head ominously.

And then I see Bert leaning by the back shelving, looking all smug. He's watching Lacey go from design table to design table. She looks like she's about to collapse, and nobody's helping her, which is strange, considering she's the design department mascot.

What's going on?

I focus back on my spreadsheet—not easy with the silent keening and gnashing of teeth. I can barely concentrate.

What has Bert done now?

I pull out my phone, put it in selfie mode, and study the scene behind me. Bert is more than smug; he's looking like the cat that swallowed the canary.

I text Jada:

Jaxon: what's up?

Jada: Lacey screwed up a promo thing that had to go out. She has to switch a thing around and get it out in the three o'clock Ship2Speed rush overnight or it's too late.

Jaxon: frowny face

Jada: He gave us extra tasks when
we tried to help. Shondrella might
have to miss her kid's soccer game now.

Shitshow.

Jaxon: Lacey has 2 demerits, right?

Jada: CANNOT get another.

I glower at Bert who's twiddling merrily on his phone.

Jaxon: I don't understand why
it can't be rushed.
LA is not on another planet.

Jada: it has to be Ship2Speed.
Approved vendor only.

Jaxon: so this is a setup

Jada: to fire Lacey

Charley was right about meeting people I'd like to hit on this job. I would've gone after Bert so fast in my old life, but of course I keep thinking about Jada. Her distressed expression. And the shipping guys. I can't let myself get booted without knowing for sure that I have control over the operations here.

Is this how poor people have to go through life? Wanting to hit shitheads like Bert but there is too much to lose? And said shitheads control their lives and make thoughtless, asinine decisions that screw things up for them, and there's nothing to be done?

Because it really is intolerable.

I grab my phone and storm out of the office and down the hall to the rooftop patio. It's nearly rush hour; the street down below is fully gridlocked. The sounds of horns and sirens drift up on the breeze along with the diesel fumes and the faint scent of grilled meat from a nearby gyro cart.

I put in a call to Soto. He's gotten a copy of the Bloxburn contract, which he calls "unusually extensive if not draconian." He's pulling in contract lawyers. He tells me that wresting control away from them might not be easy.

"Make it easy," I say, tired of having my hands tied. "Also, there's an employee here who I want moved to minimal part-time hours, but she still keeps her health insurance. Ten hours a week, ideally. Add that to my list of requests."

"Now you want to get involved in individual employee arrangements?"

"That's right," I say.

"That sort of thing can involve modifying entire categories on the human resources level," Soto says. "Why is this person suddenly important?"

"She's not, it's just that everyone is so maudlin about her situation, I can barely concentrate. It's annoying. Figure it out." I hang up, staring out at the scaffolding on the building down the way. I have to get rid of Bert.

Bloxburn. The name still bothers me. I was never in the same location as my parents for long, but I do remember the name. I have this memory of it coming up in angry whispers. Though that might not mean much, being that so much of what my parents said came out in angry whispers.

Jada comes out and frowns. "Oh, *you're* here." Her voice drips with disdain.

A good man would tell her his real identity at this point, but I'm not a good man.

"Three pencils in your bun. Things didn't go well, I'm thinking."

Outrage flares in her eyes. Outrage is scathingly hot on her. I have this sudden and utterly savage urge to haul her little body right up to mine; this sudden, savage urge to take those angry lips in mine. I have this need to provoke her that I can't seem to control.

"Our friend is about to lose her job but *oh-ho-ho* I have three pencils in my bun," she says. "You want a comedy award?"

"Depends on the award."

"Don't you even care? Her life is basically ruined."

"So I'm guessing you missed the last Ship2Speed courier pickup."

She glares up at the clouds.

I don't know much about shipping, but even I know Ship2Speed is a bad, low-rent option for overseas shipping. The carrier everyone makes fun of.

"Do they not have flights from the airport?" I ask.

"Their customer window closes in thirty minutes, and it's at least an hour away at this time of day. Obviously we would've thought of it otherwise."

I look over at her, heart pounding. I wait for her to feel me, to look back at me, because I'm just that evil.

Eventually, she does.

Our eyes lock.

The heat between us spirals.

"What?" she demands

"I can get it on that plane."

"The customer window closes in thirty minutes."

"I could get it there," I say.

Jada narrows her eyes. "Thirty minutes? No way. You'd have to have perfect luck on the road. Parting-of-the-Red-Sea luck."

"A good driver makes his luck."

She's giving me this look like she doesn't believe me. "It sounds reckless."

My eyes fall to her lips. "Well." I lower my voice. "I could get a little reckless out there with the right incentive."

Her lips fall open. Her outrage sparks something deep inside me.

"You wouldn't."

I give her the evilest smile I can. Which, let me just say, is pretty evil. It's a talent of mine.

Her pulse pounds visibly in her throat, and the urge to put my lips there is overwhelming. I wanted her before, but now that I know she's the butt-dialer, she's irresistible.

"God, you are the worst," she bites out. "Lacey is in there crying. Our friend might lose her livelihood, her health insurance, her family. You would literally get pleasure out of making a woman give you sexual favors as payment for things you should do out of the goodness of your heart?"

"If you keep standing there pointing out the obvious, I'll never make it."

"You are an unbelievable jerk!"

"Again with the obvious. Do we have a deal?"

Her lips twitch. The movement is tiny, but it's fucking delicious, because yeah, she loves it a little, and I love her loving it.

I turn to her, go up close to her.

This little game turns her on, and she struggles so hard to pretend it doesn't, it pushes the hotness factor clear off the charts. I'm addicted to her struggle. I'm addicted to her pleasure.

She comes right up close, her mouth near mine. Smudgy eye shadow. Pink cheeks. "You would be so fired for this."

"As we've established, I'm a jerk who doesn't give a shit. And we now have twenty-eight minutes."

Twenty-Seven

Jada

He's so evil! And possibly our only hope.

Worst of all, I want him to do the delivery successfully and bring back the slip—not for Lacey, but because I'd have to kiss him. Maybe even in the supply closet.

My blood races with the image of us. He'd set me up on that table because a maestro knows his tools, and maybe he'd even toss his glasses aside. And we'd have another wrong, combustive kiss.

Yes, please!

As if saving Lacey's job is an afterthought.

As if playing that game again is more important than saving our office family. What is he doing to me?

"Fine. What do I have to lose? Give it a shot."

"I want my payment in advance."

"What?"

A lazy smile spreads across his face. "I'm the one setting the terms here. I'll have my payment now."

"What if you don't deliver?"

"Please," he rumbles. "I have yet to meet a machine that I can't push beyond the specs."

My breath hitches as he traces a finger over my cheekbone, over my lips.

"Internal combustion engines enjoy being handled, and even mishandled. Pushed. Maybe even used a bit wrongly, a bit outrageously. I'm Don Juan the Entitled Delivery Driver, baby."

I grab his wrist and get in his face. "You are the worst!"

"I know." The rumble of his voice shoots down into my pelvis. He presses his hand to the top of my chest, fingers spanning up my throat. Slowly he pushes me into the wall.

Dimly, I think I want all our kisses to start like this—him pushing me into the wall as my pulse bangs under his wicked fingertips.

He presses his lips to my neck. Kisses me once. Again.

"Could you be more of a jerk?" I gasp.

"Is that a request?" He nips my ear and I nearly explode from the shock of it. "We don't have enough time for the hate fuck you've been dreaming of, but we can make do, don't you think?" He's kissing toward my lips, fingers hot on my throat.

I grab his hair, panting shamelessly. I don't want it to stop.

He slides his hand to my breast, down into my shirt. He strokes a thumb over my nipple, movements sure and strong, and the feeling of it arrows down to my sex.

"I would do repugnant, thoroughly corrupted, power-drunk Lothario things right here, and it would be so good," he says.

The breeze blows. Electricity skitters over my skin.

"Do them," I whisper.

With a growl, he presses me harder against the wall, pushing me up against it. His thigh pushes between my legs.

I arch into him. Our kisses turn frantic and ferocious. He's rock hard against me.

He drags his nails over the silk of my bra, zinging my nipple.

I gasp and hold his hair harder. I'm all-out riding him, nearly humping his thigh now. I don't even care.

If we were in the supply closet, I'd go for the full hate fuck. As it is, I could so come right now. So wildly, madly come, and I think he could, too.

He slows. He's coming to his senses.

I blink. I'm coming to my senses.

He pulls away, looking dazed.

I remember Lacey, who I'm supposedly fighting for. "You've got a delivery to do," I say, panting.

"Get me the envelope," he grates out.

I beeline back to the office to get it.

~

JACK TEXTS from LaGuardia an hour later.

Jack: it's on the plane.

Jada: The Ship2Speed plane to LA?

Jack: no, the Fantasy Island plane.

Jada: Srsly

JACK TEXTS a shot of the papers. The timestamp reads 3:59. He made it.

Jada: Thank you so much.
Lacey will be so grateful.

Jack: I'm heading back to the city, but
I doubt I'll make it by 5. You can look
for the delivery truck in the Holland Tunnel.

Jada: I'll get the papers to Bert.

As if he'd abandon the truck.

I download the image of the papers to my photos and text it all to Lacey across the office. I'd told people Jack was trying to race the stuff to the airport, but none of us thought he'd make it.

I stand there grinning, waiting for her head to pop up above the sea of cubicles, which it soon does. Her jaw hangs open.

I put up empty hands as if to say, "Dunno how he did it."

She pumps a fist.

A few more heads pop up. Texts fly around.

"Oh my god, he's a rock star!" Renata says.

I shrug. What is there to say? Yes, Jack is a rockstar who I'm conducting this whole torrid freak roleplay thing with.

So messed up.

But I never felt so wicked and sexy and beautiful. I can still feel his hands on me and hear his sharp inhale, as if he was as overcome with need as I was.

I tell myself that he probably makes sounds like that with all the women even though I hope it's not true.

"He must've gotten ten speeding tickets," Dave says. "I'll find out tonight."

I frown. "What's tonight?"

"Shipping crew's going for beers at Harrigan's."

"Oh," I say. Jack's going out with the shipping crew? It's nice he's going out with the guys. There's no reason to feel jealous of them.

"You can come," Dave says.

"Nah. That's okay."

Lacey comes over. "We decided to knit Jack a team hat. Glenda's getting the yarn. Shondrella's gonna do the star. Can you make one of your poms?"

"Sure," I say. "But I doubt he'll wear it."

"I don't care. He deserves one," Lacey says.

Twenty-Eight

JAXON

EVERYBODY'S TREATING me like I'm some sort of savior the next day. It makes me want to yank off my own fingernails.

As if things can't get worse, Lacey comes up to my cubicle with effusive thanks, and she sets to hugging me before I can move out of position.

"We made you this, Jack." She whips out a crudely knit winter hat like the others have—royal blue. Giant pom. An insignia on the front done in white yarn, which she tells me is a shooting star but which looks like drunkenly interlocking geometries.

It's all I can do to stifle a miserable groan.

I shouldn't have come—we're not family, in spite of the mass delusion happening here.

"I can't take this," I say.

"Of course you can. You saved my ass!" She presses it into my hands. "It's the official winter hat of the design department. We all have one."

"You gave me an excuse to drive like a maniac," I say. "If you'd been one of the cars on the road with me, you would've knit a noose."

"Stop it. We wanted to do something. Come on, try it on."

I clutch the hat, looking at the bulky, wavy lines the yarn makes. I can't believe they knit it for me.

Nobody ever knit a hat for me.

If Jenny saw this, god, she'd be even more stupidly convinced that we're family. Something loosens in my chest. Phlegm, maybe.

Jada's leaning against the side of her cubicle. Renata's there.

Dave has wandered over. "Did he put it on yet?"

I keep holding it, staring at the insignia. I tell myself to snap out of it—it's just a hat! The sooner I can put it on, the sooner I can escape this ridiculous hero's welcome.

"The shooting star is the symbol for our family," Shondrella says. "We're meteoric!"

"You do know a shooting star is just a hunk of rock that's burning to a crisp in our atmosphere," I say.

Jada groans. "Put it on, you freak!"

I grumble and shove it over my head.

Shondrella claps. "It looks great."

I mumble my thanks and get to work at my desk, wondering how long I have to wear it.

A few moments later, Jada's head pops over the side of my cubicle. I smile up at her and adjust it on my head. "What do you think?"

"Nice," she says.

"I was given this hat because I'm a good person who does things out of the goodness of my heart."

"Fuck off," she says. "Lacey wanted you to have one."

I cross my legs and lean back. "Some men need incentives to be generous, but me? That is just the person that I am."

She throws a paperclip at me, and I want to kiss her again. I want to continue where we left off on the patio. I want to know what she sounds like when she comes. I want my face in her tits and her fingernails in my back.

Renata comes up. "Cute, but it doesn't exactly go with the party shirt."

"Really? Are you sure?"

"Jack." Renata gets this serious look on her face. "You know what would look great with that is a nice Henley. Like a waffle-knit Henley shirt—you know that kind with two buttons off the collar?"

I put on a confused face. "Are you not a fan of my shirts? I thought they looked good."

Renata is just laughing. "And now that we're on the subject, why the shaded glasses? Why for god's sake?"

"Because they're awesome," I say. "You don't think they're awesome?"

"No," Renata says.

"How can you not like them?" I complain.

Renata draws her brows together in a look of grave concern. "I don't mean to insult you, they're just...look, they were super fashionable for a while, and an amazing style move at one time, but I do think you should try something new."

I frown. "So you don't like the glasses."

"Shut up." Jada turns to Renata. "He is so full of shit."

Renata gives Jada a stern look now. "Maybe they're fashionable in Europe where he's from?"

Jada is shaking her head.

"Or get contacts. You would look so cute," Renata says. "Wait, you know what? My friend has a before-and-after makeover TikTok channel. She would style you for free and even give you free new glasses. Oh my god, she would seriously love to do that!"

"No, thanks," I say. The last thing I want to do is to be a before-and-after TikTok.

"You should think about it!" Renata exclaims. "My friend would get you really flattering glasses—nice designer ones. Brands always give her things like that. She'd give you a new haircut—she's so good. And you'd get it all for free! You have beautiful bone structure, Jack. Or even contacts—whoa, you could get contacts."

I'm shaking my head. "No, thanks."

"Think about it. And when she's done, let's just say your dating experience would really improve. Like, through the roof—think about *that!*"

I slide a discreet glance in Jada's direction. "I already have to fight off the ladies. I don't think I could take anymore."

"Of course you look great as is," Renata continues, "but who wouldn't want to look even more amazing? You have so much potential, just so much completely unrealized potential—"

"Completely unrealized potential?" I joke.

"I didn't mean it negatively!"

"Stop it, oh my god!" Jada breaks in. "The way he's styled himself, that is a deliberate choice, Renata. Jack *wants* to look like this. He wants to look weird and off-putting. It's how he's comfortable in the world."

I look over, surprised. "Weird and off-putting?"

"Admit it," she says. "You know it's true."

"Uh..." Renata leans in. "Isn't that...harsh? It's just a cultural thing."

"Oh, please!" Jada says. "Because he's from Europe? Europeans usually have better fashion than us. This is not a cultural thing." Jada is talking to Renata but she's looking at me, looking through me, even. "Jack's fashion is a deliberate extension of his personality, his personal keep-out sign. Like a spiny fish that adopts the coloring of a sour-tasting fish so that predators pass him over."

I fix her with a hurt look. "A sour-tasting, spiny fish?"

"You know it's true."

"Did I not just become the office hero yesterday?" I ask her. "Out of the goodness of my heart?"

She snorts.

"Geez, Jada," Renata says. "He did save Lacey's ass."

"In spite of himself," she says. "Look what he's wearing! He's a perfectly capable man, and this is how he dresses himself. He'd wrap himself in barbed wire and keep-out signs if he could."

"Ouch," I say with a lightness that I don't feel. I'm not used to being observed this closely. I'm usually the one who does the observing, and the rest of the world does the scrambling or preening or whatever. "My fashion choices are barbed wire around a spiny, repulsive-looking fish?" I ask. "And why would I want that?"

"Yeah!" Renata turns to Jada. "Why would he want to be a spiny, repulsive-looking fish?"

Jada eyes me. "I wonder."

Twenty-Nine

Jada

It hadn't occurred to me until now that his style is as deliberately obnoxious as some of the things he says. I'm sure he has access to all kinds of nice clothes. His friend Arnold wore a normal outfit the other day. Arnold probably has a closet full of stylish clothes, not a loud print shirt to be found among them. If Arnold's bringing him money, he'd surely be up for giving Jack a few cast-offs.

Jack sits there so suave and cool, but I know I've hit a nerve—I can see it in his sly sideways glance. "I strive to appear repulsive," he says in an amused tone. "Is this some kind of reverse psychology where I insist it's not my goal to look repulsive? And I rush to accept the makeover?"

"No, it's more of an observation. My point is, he doesn't want a makeover," I say to Renata. "Let it go."

Jack gives me a lazy smile, that one dimple in full flare. His phone pings and he shuts it off without even checking to see who it is, eyes fixed on mine the whole time. "Let me offer another theory," he says.

"Oh, this should be good."

"You don't want me to have a makeover because you want me all to yourself."

"Hah!"

"Jada would never do that," Renata assures him. "She cares about others first. If she was in an airplane that was in trouble, she'd make sure everybody else had their oxygen masks on before affixing her own. She would give you the shirt off her back before she'd be selfish like that."

I cross my arms, daring Jack to say whatever bullshit comment he's thinking of.

He just smiles, of course.

Renata glances at her own pinging phone now. "Damn." She goes back to her cubicle, because unlike Jack, she cares about the texts that come in.

"You so want me," Jack says.

I move around the opening of his cubicle and press my finger into his chest. "I so have your number."

He grabs my finger and a whoosh of excitement flows over me. "My number? Meaning that I make myself look repulsive because otherwise predators would surely hunt me for my meat? Which is so delicious that I need two layers of defense, spines *and* camouflage as a sour fish? Is that what you're saying?"

I lean in nearer. "That would be the least plausible of several explanations."

"The truth is, I am quite delicious," he says.

"You think you're delicious? That's interesting that you would know that. With an unfortunate mental image to go with it. Are you an acrobat, Jack?"

He keeps hold of my finger, sitting up now, bringing his face near to mine in the confines of his cubicle walls. "I've been known to create that impression." He angles his gaze in the direction of the supply closet.

I hold my ground. I know he's trying to corrupt me, but it's unbelievably enjoyable. I suppose that's the point.

"You have no idea," he whispers.

"You shouldn't oversell things like that," I say.

"I'm underselling it."

"You are the worst," I say.

"That's part of the fun." He smiles.

Renata's swearing at her screen in the background; usually I'd be involved by now, but the office is a million miles away and this sexy reality with Jack is a respite, a secret oasis in the middle of the dusty, war-torn reality of SportyGoCo.

He comes in closer. I can feel his heat, his strange allure. He's so much more than he seems. "The experience of my spiny protrusions, you have no idea."

"Oh my god!" I yank away my finger. I'm just laughing now. What is he doing to me? I'm trying to save this company, to save my work family, and he's making me forget it all. "Don't you have something to do in shipping?"

He grabs his phone and takes a look. "Apparently so."

"So they've been texting you this whole time and you're ignoring it?"

He sighs. "A hero's day is never done, that's for sure." With that he takes off, still wearing our department hat.

I go over to where Renata is stressing out over the small selection of sample clasps we can get in time to make a Wonderbag prototype. "We could go to MayRay Fashion but look at this price."

I press my palms to my eyes, trying to think of a new option.

"What is up with you two?" Renata asks.

"Other than him being a freak?"

"Yes, other than that," she says. "You guys seemed intense."

"Because he's intensely jerky."

"Check it out." Renata shows me her phone with a stealth shot of Jack. He's leaning against the side of his cubicle, talking to somebody outside the frame. The shot captures everything dorky about his styling, and everything nice about him, too, except that you can't see his eyes through his famous skinny glasses. Then she flips to another picture where he has his glasses off. Then another where he's at the watercooler laughing with Shondrella. "What do you think?" she says. "I bet my friend would literally pay him to appear on her channel. The transformation, if he were to allow it, would be staggering. I'm not giving up. He could be so doable. Maybe I'd even do him."

"You can't!" I say.

"Why not?" she asks.

"He said no," I say. "Hey, can you forward those to me, though?"

"Something for the spank bank?"

I give her a playful glare. "My roommates were asking about him. Deliberate or not, his style is definitely in the you-gotta-see-it-to-believe-it category."

"No shit," she says, staring at the laughing photo.

"Double-lock closure ahoy!" Shondrella says, beelining over to us with a small box. "Three sizes!"

"This has gotta be our answer," I say. "Please let this work."

We race to the back of the table to try this new closure with the design. It's a Velcro alternative.

Shondrella gets one of the prototypes out. Renata lines up the strips to sew.

"Base too big." I fly to my computer to redo the dimensions. We decide to try it in two different ways. Naturally, just as Renata starts cutting, Lacey tells us that the yoga pants fit session got moved up with our size twelve fit model.

"Yoga pants first, then Wonderbag," I say. "We can do this!"

Varsha takes over the cutting while we hop onto the yoga project. We skip lunch, making headway.

And then Bert arrives and announces that everybody needs to do a CPR training.

"What the hell?" Varsha whispers.

"Since when do we need that?" Shondrella whisper-squeaks.

I speak up. "Every one of us? Would there be any exceptions outside of a current CPR certification?" I ask, laying a little trap.

"No exceptions outside current certification," Bert says.

I try to look sad. "Well, my certificate is good for another year. Anybody else?"

"Sorry, I'm shutting off the system," Bert says. "I'm shutting down the office and turning off the intranet and locking up."

"But since I have my certificate and we have our fit model onsite..."

"Nope."

"Maybe I'll just take a half-day," I say. Because I can finish the bag at home, not that I'd say that. I have a lot of days stored up, being that I never take them off.

"Half-days require notice," he says. "If you aren't going to be in the training, I need you to go with Jack on his deliveries for the rest of the day and confirm he's following the company guidebook on customer courtesy. He's also been having challenges filling out the paperwork correctly," he says.

"Shouldn't somebody from shipping do that?" I protest.

"Is that a no?" Bert asks. "You're one of our top people on protocol. And you seem to be interested in his poor work habits."

Jack puts on a face of mock surprise. I grit my teeth. Bert definitely overheard my useless comment from back when Jack started.

People are filing out, heading down to the space we use for trainings, the space we used to use for parties and fitness breaks when this was a great place to work.

"Why would Jack be exempt from the training?"

"So that you can do this errand," Bert says with a completely straight face. "Leave the project here. It'll be there in the morning."

Thirty

JADA

"DID YOU SEE THAT? DID YOU?"

"Yes." Jack pulls out into traffic, shifting deftly.

I want more. I care about Jack's opinion, and I want him on my side.

"Right?" I urge. "Can you tell me that there's any possible chance that he's not trying to destroy the company? What boss actively tries to prevent a capable and motivated employee from working?"

He drives with his usual expertise, flowing in and out of the traffic like it's water, all serene concentration. "He's a very bad boss," Jack says. "He shouldn't be in that position."

"Thank you!" I say, gratified. "He literally is trying to destroy morale. Shutting the system off like that. This stupid training. He doesn't care. And of course he exempted you so that we could do this errand. He knows I think you're a shitty worker."

"Karma's a bitch," Jack says, switching lanes.

"Not helpful."

"We'll get this done so you can get back, how about that?"

"Is that an offer? Without extorting sexual favors?"

The glance he gives me is dark and real and sends shivers into my core. "We could add it in."

"Just drive." I look down at my phone, trying to keep my head. I haven't been able to stop thinking about our game since it started. "Literally shuts down the intranet. He wants us to fail, but you'd think he'd at least be more stealthy about it."

Maybe Jack senses how upset I am, I don't know, but he asks me questions about Wonderbag, and also the history of sequins, which happen to be two of my favorite subjects, and gets us to the first stop—a massive warehouse outside of Newark—in no time.

I linger around, playing supervisor while he unloads the stuff, and then I hover around to watch him do the paperwork.

There's a potential problem with a few backordered items that the customer is getting angry about. I'm about to step in, but Jack handles it like a pro—he's firm, but with just the right degree of humor, providing the perfect amount of assurance—enough to calm him, but not so much that a promise might be construed.

We go on the rest of the deliveries which Jack has reordered for efficiency.

"You're good at this," I say.

"I'm good at a lot of things."

"Screw off," I say, laughing, as if he's being ridic. As if I'm not thinking about how he said there's no machine he can't push beyond the specs. He meant it sexy, of course.

He catches me looking at him. "What?"

"Is this how you made it to LaGuardia so quickly? Extreme concentration?"

"You don't want to know how I made it to LaGuardia."

"Dave thinks you probably got several tickets."

"A gentleman never tells."

"Skills include driving and finding a jerky reply to any sentence," I say.

He shrugs happily.

"Have you had any other jobs besides driving?"

"Nope. Just driving," he says.

"Always in a delivery capacity? Have you done Uber? Taxi?"

"Nope," he says. "Now what? Back to the office?"

"You're all done?" I ask.

"I'm just an overachiever."

"Bert'll just give us other bullshit to do," I say. "Busywork. Can we go pick up some food? I don't care. Just one of the noodle places up here. I missed my lunch doing the yoga pants. Is there some rule about eating in the truck?"

"You haven't eaten yet?"

"Have you?" I ask hopefully.

He does a sudden U-turn.

"Dude!"

"We're getting you a meal."

"Any noodle place. Or Mexican anything." We pass more restaurants. "Look, a parking spot! We could grab a quick burger."

"You picked Holey Icewich; it's my turn now," he says.

~

"I CAN'T EAT HERE!" I say as we head into the ultraposh environs of Café Maximus. Because naturally he finds the most inappropriate everything.

"My treat," he says as we're seated at a luxurious booth in a palm-and-velvet-draped corner.

"You'll blow your whole paycheck!"

"What do you care?"

"Because I'm a responsible person who cares about things?"

"Lucky for you, I'm an irresponsible person who doesn't," he says. "You may as well take advantage of that fact."

"I'm not that kind of person," I say.

"Why not play one for the day? You may as well enjoy my reckless nature." He lowers his voice to a rumble. "Wouldn't I do it if the tables were turned?"

I narrow my eyes. Waters are delivered. A waiter comes and hands us menus. Jack studies his, but I'm studying Jack. All of these big, reckless things without a second thought. What would it be like to live like Jack? Just let the chips fall where they may?

Finally I look down. "There aren't even prices!"

"You like black bean soup?" he asks.

"Not if it doesn't have a price," I say. "I have a limit to how much I'll take advantage."

"Bo-ring," he says. "You love grilled chicken stuff, that we know."

I scan down, stomach growling. Everything looks delicious. "Yeah, but..."

"And we know you like turkey with swiss. This turkey croquette right here comes with a salad. How does that sound?"

"Too expensive!"

"You always take pickles out of your stuff at lunch, so I'm gonna guess dill is out, which nixes the steak salad. You shared that lasagna with Renata the other day, so you might like this puttenesca." He looks up. "Do you like spicy things?"

"Don't you want to know?"

"You like anything Mexican," he says. "I'm going with a yes on that."

Is Arnold supporting him financially? Is that what's going on here? He pretty effectively narrows it down to the three finalists I'd choose, and he gets me to say if he guessed correctly. I tell him he got two out of three, because I would have the raw tuna salad in the running—if I was the kind of person who'd order an entrée at a place like this, which, I inform him, I'm not.

Jack shrugs and orders all three entrees, plus some appetizers and a twenty-one-year-old scotch on the rocks. "And for the lady..." He regards me thoughtfully. "Do you like Manhattans?"

"The drink? We're on work hours!"

"Work is over for the day," he says.

"Training could be unexpectedly done before work hours are over. Renata's supposed to text me."

"So what if it gets over early?"

"I'm not a screw-up, that's what."

He sighs and checks the menu while the waiter waits. "Look—there's a champagne cocktail. You like champagne cocktails, judging from how often you and Renata say, 'Break out the champers!'"

"It's just an expression."

"So, you don't like the champers?"

"Not during work hours!"

"Scotch rocks and a champagne cocktail," he says, handing the menu back to the waiter.

"Don't bring the champagne cocktail. I'm having water." I say this in a hard enough voice to the waiter that it overrides Jack's bullshit. "Fizzy water."

"Tough customer," he says after the waiter leaves.

My napkin has been folded into a strange little sculpture on my plate, and my place setting involves four forks. "You charging this to Arnold or something?"

He sits back, stretching a lazy arm along the seat back. The men here are dressed in Ralph Lauren and Alexander McQueen, but Jack looks perfectly at ease and even at home in his 1990s print shirt—today's is powder blue with black triangles and random yellow squiggle lines. "Maybe I won some more shell games."

"You could be fired for this."

"I don't see Bert around here, do you?"

I smile in spite of myself. Jack is the worst, and I can't stop loving it.

He makes a big show of swirling the dark amber liquid in the glass, inspecting its color. He takes a sip and closes his eyes. I'm drinking him in. He's a fascinating and sometimes wonderful creature, enjoying his cocktail in the middle of the day. Defying Bert. He makes it look fun.

"You have such persuasive powers, and you waste them entirely on being a destructive, corruptive influence."

"Yeah, yeah, yeah. Is this you changing your mind?"

"No!" I sip my water, wishing I'd ordered the champagne cocktail now. What's stopping me? But I can't bring myself to do it. It's the middle of the day! It's just not me.

"So I've heard this is a European thing—drinks at lunch," I say. "And you eat dinner at ten at night or whatever."

"That's about right. And dancing 'til dawn."

The way he looks at life is so different. I try to imagine him dancing around a fire pit in some little village with goats running around like Renata said. Did they live in tents? Were his parents back-to-the-earthers with no place to call home like Mia suggested?

"Is that what they did where you're from? Dances and things? Even in your little village?"

He furrows his brow. "My little village?"

"Renata says you're from this...small rural village. Very...rustic."

He laughs. "We lived in a lot of places, but I wouldn't call them rustic."

"Of all the places you lived, which place would you most consider to be your home?"

He looks down at his scotch. "I don't know if there is a place I'd actually call home."

I stiffen. Have I strayed into embarrassing territory? I grab a piece of warm bread and slather butter over it.

"I suppose that just means everywhere is your home," I say brightly, trying to put a good face on it. "It sounds like you experienced a lot of different places. Do you have a favorite place in Europe, even if it's not your home, to maybe just walk around in?"

He looks thoughtful. "I don't know. I find that being out on the street in any city can be a hassle."

"Of course!" I say, internally scolding myself for not thinking of my privilege. Of course living on the streets would be hard. I'm sure the police hassle the homeless in every city, not just America. "I've always loved the ocean," I say quickly. I feel like this is a safe subject—everybody, rich or poor, has access to the majesty of the ocean. "I don't care where it is. It's about the sound. The power. I didn't see it even until I was in my twenties."

I try the bread and nearly die. It's fresh, with just a hint of rosemary. And the butter seems to have honey in it. What is this witchcraft?

"You didn't see the ocean until your twenties?"

"I grew up in central Illinois, a town you wouldn't know. Even the nearby towns, you wouldn't know them. It was a tractor-parts plant town. If we had money to go anywhere, it would be to the Six Flags. It's the place with rides. Like a fair."

Our appetizers come. Again I feel bad for letting him order all of this stuff, and I find myself wondering if maybe he just never learned proper money management. I came up poor, too, but I was obsessed with saving money—I had to be. A lot of my friends would squander money immediately when they got it.

"Try the calamari," he says, wiping his fingers and settling back into his seat, assuming that relaxed and princely pose of his.

I put a bit on my plate and try it. And nearly go into shock. It's heavenly—perfectly crunchy, perfectly sweet.

"Whoa! Yum," I say.

Jack grins.

I eat some more. I'm starving. I'm fully indulging now.

In the fable of the ant and the grasshopper, I'm the ant, toiling away, storing grain so I have something for winter. I grew up with grasshoppers, always taking advantage. I came to despise the grasshoppers of the world. I swore I'd surround myself with responsible men—dependable men who know how to pull their weight.

Jack is so team grasshopper, just singing and loafing. What would it be like? To just say, "Screw it all! I'm a grasshopper, now!"

"I think you want to change your mind," he says. "About the cocktail."

His lowball glass is cut crystal...is it real Waterford? He rotates it a bit, positioning the napkin to be parallel to the table edge, fingers light on the luxe surface—a light touch that's deft and sure, like in the delivery truck.

"We may get called back, though. There's so much to do."

"Mmm," he rumbles, voice like deep velvet on my skin. "Sounds like an argument *for* the cocktail."

I rotate my own glass, lining my own napkin up with the edge, feeling like I've been in battle forever. They made my fizzy ice water the best they could, with a lemon and two raspberries on a long toothpick thing. It's nice.

"I'm fine," I say.

"Even a non-alcoholic one?"

I flick my gaze to his scotch. What would it be like? "I just can't get behind such a madly expensive drink."

"I love your pondering and debating face."

"Oh, you think I have a pondering and debating face?"

"You always bite the right side of your lip and stare into the middle distance with this sexy half-squint."

I keep hold of the side of my lip and turn my half-squint in his direction. "Maybe I'm pondering you."

"Maybe you should be."

"Uh-huh." I try the other appetizer—a flatbread thing with balsamic-drizzled goat cheese—surprised at how much he notices about me.

I'm used to men monitoring me, paying attention to me, wanting to make a good impression or whatever, but Jack's attention feels different. He's interested and engaged, even affectionate. It feels like the difference between a harsh spotlight and a glow I want to bask in.

Just to tease him, I grab the menu and scan down the cocktail area to the very bottom. That's where I find the lavender gold. "Hmmm, here is a cocktail that has actual gold flecks frozen into the ice cubes along with rare lavender flowers from the remote monastic Mediterranean island of Île Saint-Honorat. What do you think about that one?"

"Get it."

"Just kidding. It has literal gold! It's a ridiculous cocktail."

"Having ridiculous cocktails courtesy of Don Juan the Entitled Delivery Driver while everybody learns some stupid skill? Sounds like a win-win."

It's like he's trying to lead me down this path of ill repute and I find that I'm loving it. I want to have the cocktail. I want to kiss him again, dorkiness and all. I want to have fun with him. I want to have adventures with him.

"I dare you," he says.

Suddenly I'm thinking about what Renata always says—that I'd give the shirt off my back if I could. If a plane was crashing, I'd put on everybody's oxygen masks before my own.

What is that? It's bonkers! Even the flight attendants say to put on your own mask on before assisting others.

Bert has kicked us out of the office for what he no doubt hopes is the rest of the day, and I'm still acting like I'm at work. And Jack is practically begging me to order this thing.

I pick up the menu. "Lavender-infused gin, rhubarb, lemon, and sparkling rose with ice cubes that have rare lavender flowers and gold flakes frozen into the middle of them. Maybe I will."

The light in his eyes makes me feel weirdly happy.

"Are you sure Arnold's not paying?"

"What the hell do you care?"

Something effervesces in my belly. "Yeah, what do I care?"

A waiter comes over and uses a small tool to scrape the crumbs from the tablecloth. I look into Jack's eyes, mirroring his playful attitude. "I've changed my mind. I'll take that lavender gold cocktail."

"Very good." The waiter walks off.

Jack's watching me.

"It feels weird to be this person," I confess.

"It's hot as hell on you," he says.

"Being a reckless libertine is hot? That's what you like?"

"There are people in the world who'd order that without a second thought, but when you do it, it's different. Like you're kicking a door down. You have no idea, Jada."

My cheeks heat. "You'll be kicking the door down to the Café Maximus dishwashing room."

"I won't."

I narrow my eyes.

My cocktail comes and I give it a taste. It's all tangy sweetness like the best, most fragrant sweet tart on the planet, but yummier. It's delicious—wildly delicious. But it's about more than the taste. It's like I snatched gold from the dragon's lair.

"You like it?"

I mirror his relaxed pose, just because he's the picture of fun leisure and suddenly I want some of it for myself. Why is everything so fun with Jack? I give him an evil smile. "Very much!"

He gives me an evil smile back. It's as if we're the only two people in the world. "Excellent," he says.

"I'd still rather be nailing those projects, but as long as we're here..." I swirl the drink, watching the flecks in the ice cube catch the light. It's food-grade gold. Who ever even heard of that?

"So what would your perfect day be?" he asks suddenly. "Let's say if there were no emergencies or demands. You could do whatever you want."

"I walk to work and it's nice out and I see people on the way. The people you met."

"The Jada fan club."

"And Bert's not in the office all day. We do a fitting with a fit model, and everything is right on the first try."

"So your perfect day is you at work?"

"Of course! It's my dream job. It's no Chanel, but I love it. I've always wanted to be head designer at a fashion house."

He nods, watching me. What is he seeing?

"But also, it's a family—it really is," I add. "Maybe you think family's the devil, but it's important to me. I came to New York scared and alone with no people, and Shondrella and Lacey and the former owners of SportyGoCo all took me under their wing. I literally showed up with a suitcase and sewing skills and some dreams about acting and they saved my ass."

"You came to New York to act?"

"Right? I probably don't seem like an actor."

"It's not very practical."

"It's practical if you think you're gonna be a big star," I say. "I can't believe I'm telling you this. It sounds arrogant."

"What actor doesn't go into it thinking that? So it didn't pan out?"

"I landed a decent part in a show right off the bat. That's how I figured out I didn't like being in the theater. I enjoyed the acting part, but the whole world of the theater—it wasn't for me. There's so much waiting around. And you depend on other people to pick you, to react off of, to schmooze."

Another course comes. Exotic nuts and olives and little dishes of paté.

"Acting would be very collaborative," he says. "And you like to hustle. You were probably the kid in school who did all of her assignments ahead of time."

"It's true. And I don't like to wait around for people. My friends are actors, so I'll do it as a fun friend activity now and then, but it's not for me." I sip my drink, pausing to fully appreciate it. "I knew how to make my own clothes, and I parlayed that into Varsha's job, and from there the owners let me start assisting. Though I greased that along by learning everything I could off of

YouTube. They were having problems with an update in their CAD program, and I spent an entire night learning the new program and studying discussion threads so that I could swoop in and save the day. Sometimes I'd try to anticipate problems."

"That is so you."

"What?" I protest.

"You took home homework on a job."

I shrug happily. "It worked, didn't it? My evil plan worked. That first year in the city was so rough, though. I made new friends over the years, like in the building where I live? Best friend group ever. But I still do a lot of holidays with the SportyGoCo gang. Especially Thanksgiving, because who wants to leave Manhattan in the fall? It's like my friends are on Forty-Fifth Street, but SportyGoCo is my family."

He looks up, and right there, I can see he wants to ask about my actual family but stops himself, as if he senses I don't want to discuss them. Jack's more intuitive than he likes to let on. I get the feeling that there are worlds inside of him.

"What about a perfect day that doesn't involve work?" he asks. "What about a perfect day that's doing useless things that are just pleasure?"

I gaze into my drink. "Hmmm."

"Besides being the victim of sexy blackmail."

"So that's off the table, too?" I complain. I say this like I'm unhappy about it, but I secretly love our sexy blackmail game, and I want to tell him so. I want to find the words. It's not the kind of thing I typically say.

"Something I don't know about," he adds.

I stir my drink. "It's a pleasure to watch you struggle to contain your annoyance when we sing the Keith song," I say.

"Do you never do anything useless? A movie marathon? A stupid game that you play on your phone all day?"

I roll my eyes. "Video games. Not likely."

"You hate video games?"

"With a passion. Wait—do you love them?"

"I've played them but..." He shrugs.

I'm hugely relieved. Why should I care if he likes video games? But I do.

"Why do you hate them?" he asks.

I groan. "What's not to hate?"

He looks at me with mischievous affection and something warm flows through my chest.

"Are you getting me drunk and interrogating me?" I ask.

He waits.

I gaze back down at my drink. I've never stopped feeling stupid about not standing up for myself. "Just family bullshit."

"I know about that," he says.

I don't know what it is—maybe because we have this wrong yet totally fun game where he's my sexy blackmailer, maybe because we're playing hooky and having cocktails in the middle of the day. Maybe it's that he's a self-confessed terrible person, or that we have this secret world, or just that I feel happy with him—him and his stupid hair and outlandish mole and bright shirts and fun corruptive influence. Whatever it is, I find myself telling him the whole story. How I'd spent the entirety of my teens caring for my mom when she had cancer. How hard it was. How alone I felt. How I stopped being in sleepovers, dances, gymnastics, school plays. "I wouldn't trade it for the world," I say.

"It was just you two?"

"There was my dad and two brothers, but they coped through World of Warcraft." I try to keep the bitterness out of my voice, but I'm sure Jack hears it. "They couldn't deal. And the more I stepped up, the more helpless they seemed to become. A vicious cycle."

"I'm sorry."

"No, it was a precious time with my mom that I would never trade for anything. Except having her back, of course. Because we said so many real things to each other, and she told me everything she could about being an adult and a woman. She's the one who taught me how to sew. We'd sit for hours in that medicine-smelling room, and I'd make sparkly bright things, dreaming of a different life. I'd make garments for her, too—bright things designed to be comfy to wear in bed. Easy to get on and off."

"It sounds like a gift. That time."

"It was a gift," I say. "Did you not have that...before you lost your parents?"

"No," he says simply.

"Sorry."

He shrugs. "And your dad and brothers..."

"They went deeper into those video games. I hated them for leaving me alone. I mean, my dad worked at the car parts factory, and he'd come home and they'd play those games together, him and my brothers—both younger and older."

"No wonder," he says, meaning my thing about video games.

"Right? And our family sunk into debt because of her illness. Dad was having a hard time paying it off after she died, so I went to work as soon as I could at McDonald's. I kept on working, year after year. My brothers never took jobs, and they could've—they were perfectly capable. I told myself I got that time with her, and they didn't, and that I was the strong one. I liked being the strong one. I was holding down all the jobs and making sure this family survived. Like an idiot."

"It doesn't seem idiotic to me," he says.

I sip my drink, feeling so stupidly grateful for the beauty of it. The perfect flavor. Like a taste of being Cinderella.

I'm also grateful for Jack's solid, steady presence, and how keenly he listens. I have this sense, sitting here, that he's feeding me—not on the food level, but on the human nourishment level. How did I get here? To this place of caring and sharing with Jack of all people? Because I really like it.

"Maybe it wasn't idiotic at first," I continue, "but it was idiotic that I stayed in that role. Then there was this one day where I came home exhausted. I'd graduated high school two years earlier; I should've been out of that town by then, trying for my acting career. Anyway, I walk in, and my brothers and dad are laughing and playing that game and the place is piled high with fast-food containers, and it was as if this lightning bolt struck me. The three of them were playing the entire Saturday while I was working. They didn't even make their own food! I went right into my room and got a plane ticket. I'd had the money saved up. Why did I stay so long? And guess who got jobs the moment I blew town?"

"Your brothers?"

I shake my head. "I was a fool to stay."

"Jada—"

"Don't tell me I wasn't a fool."

His brows are still all dark and slashy and villainy, but there's this soulfulness in his eyes that hits me deep. "Can I *think* that you weren't a fool?"

"Don't try to take it away. It's how I feel. I don't know why I'm telling you this whole sordid thing."

"People tell me secrets all the time. They know I won't judge."

"Being that you're such a wicked person," I say.

"Yes."

I snort. "Except doesn't telling everybody you're a wicked person nullify some of the wickedness? Wouldn't a truly bad person try to come off as good?"

"Too much work," he says. "Being a self-centered Lothario who blackmails women for sexual favors is already hard enough."

"I have to say, Jack, I find that aspect of you..." I pause, soaking in his delicious attention. "I find that aspect of you quite enjoyable, to be honest."

He does his lopsided smile, one dimple firing. "Do you?"

"Very much."

His eyes sparkle. "It *is* an enjoyable aspect of me, isn't it?"

"Hah." I kick him under the table. "It's probably same old, same old for you, huh?"

"You think I go around blackmailing women for kisses?"

"You don't?"

"Only you."

The rush of pleasure that comes over me is intense. "Wellllll," is all I manage.

"The way you refuse to throw yourself at me. What choice do I have?"

I bite back a smile. In spite of all of his get-back, spiny-fish offensiveness, I really *can* imagine women throwing themselves at him. He may not know what to wear, and he may have the dorkiest hairstyle this side of Olive Garden and an almost fake-looking mole, but he's the most alluring person I've ever met. "I feel special that I'm the only one that you would...blackmail for sexual favors?" I say it like it's a joke, but I do feel special now. "I'm gonna go on record here and say that it's...fun. Unusually hot, in fact." Our gazes lock. "It's fun and hot."

I don't have to say anything more. I basically just wrote out a name tag that says, *Hi, I'm Jada and I'd like you to sexually blackmail me a bit more!*

He loops his foot around my ankle and pulls up my leg, setting my foot on his knee under the table. He slides my shoe off. It's so brazen it steals my breath away.

I wiggle my foot in his hand. "You so like to push it."

"Don't change the subject. You still haven't told me your favorite thing to do. Video games are out, I'm guessing." He cradles my foot with surprising gentleness. "Let's have it. One non-goal-oriented thing that you love to do."

This conversation makes me nervous; do I know who I am when I'm not pulling for somebody else? Also, we're outside of work now and Jack Smith has his very capable hand on my foot, and the touch of his clever fingers has the butterflies in my belly doing the Lindy Hop.

Suddenly I hit on it. The most useless thing I do all the time. "I like watching pigeons."

"Pigeons?"

"I know. I can't help it. I like sitting and staring at them. Out my window. At bus stops. The people who grew up here, they think pigeons are the bird version of rats or something, but I think they're beautiful. I love their cooing song—it's so pretty. They have lots of different kinds of cooing, but my favorite is that soft coo they make when they're just hanging out. How could people hate that sound?"

He studies my eyes. "I don't know. Why do you think?"

"Because it's too common, maybe. It's the prettiest sound, but if you have to listen to it all the time, I guess you come to hate it? Do they even hear it? I know that crows are supposedly more badass, but pigeons..."

Our entrees come—all three of them with extra plates. I eat five times my body weight in the most extravagant and delectable gourmet dishes ever. He keeps my foot the whole time, his hand resting on my ankle, fingers grazing my stocking foot as we talk about the people at work. He asks questions about the different departments. He really is interested in the place for somebody who recently suggested we all quit.

We linger over dessert and coffee. Before I know it, it's two hours later and the restaurant is setting up for dinner. I grab my phone. "It's five. We have to get back to the office. I have to meet my friend Willow for yoga at six."

He slides a finger down the tender part of my foot. Shivers flow all over me. "Does that mean that I have to give this back?"

"Feet are a requirement for yoga." I look around nervously, feeling guilty about the bill that's coming. "Are you sure I can't at least pay the tip? I feel weird."

He gives me a hard look.

I raise my hands in defeat. I'm not going to diminish this gesture of his by refusing it anymore. "Thank you very much. It was delicious."

He excuses himself and ambles confidently up to the maître d', presumably to pay. This meal was such a bold, impulsive, too-huge gesture. I am loving how reckless he is. I'm wishing our afternoon didn't have to end. I want his hand on my foot, on my leg. I want for him to blackmail me for a kiss again.

"I'll drop you off," he says when he gets back. "You don't need to go back to the office, right?"

"Yeah, except my office sweater but...right? I suppose I don't have to go back in."

"I don't either. I'll just leave the truck on the side of the road."

AFTER SOME MORE OF the competence porn that is his driving, he stops in front of my building. Our time together felt like the best date ever, and when he turns to me, I know he feels the same.

And I want to kiss him.

But I think of something better. I press a finger to his chest. He looks down at it, then up at me, all stern and sparkly.

"You can't double-park like this, mister. What do I have to do to convince you to not park like an asshole?"

A lazy smile spreads over his face. "Can't I?"

"No!" I bite out, heart pounding.

With rough, sure movements, he slams the vehicle into park. "You're telling me you want me to move this thing?"

"That's right."

He draws one wicked finger up my neck and tips up my chin. My breath hitches. Cars streams past us. "It'll cost you," he says.

My heart races. "You wouldn't."

"Wouldn't I? Come here," he says.

I lean over, ready for my kiss there in the wide, flat front seat of the SportyGoCo delivery van. He's having none of it. He curls a hand around my waist and takes a fistful of my puffer coat and jerks me right up next to him.

I gasp.

He slaps my far leg. “Spread.”

“Excuse me?”

“It’s gonna cost you more this time.”

My lips part. “What?”

“Do you want me not to park like an asshole?”

“Uh, *yeah*!” I breathe.

He reaches down and settles a hand on my right thigh—the one that’s farthest from him—and shoves it away—far enough that the bottom snap of my jacket pops open, far enough that the fabric of my breezy pleat skirt stretches tight, far enough that you could consider my legs to be officially and obscenely spread. “You’re not running this thing; I am.”

“Bossy much?” I gust out, a rhetorical question if ever there was one.

“You think this is a cute little game?” he growls. “Scoot that ass forward.”

I swallow and scoot up. He smooths his hands over the fabric of my skirt like he’s getting the lay of the land of my lower half. The topography, up one thigh to my sex, which he cups briefly, and then down the other thigh to my far knee, which he pushes out more. “Are you wet for me, yet?” he asks. “Thinking what I’m gonna do to you?”

I *am* very wet for him, but that’s not the game, and I want the game. “What do you care?” I whisper all sassy. “You’ll take your pleasure either way.”

“Oh, I will.” He slides his hand under the inside of my skirt now, up my bare thigh. Confident fingers play over the wet crotch of my panties. “What color are they?”

“You’ll never know,” I say.

He grabs my sex and squeezes, putting wicked pressure on my swollen bud. “Wrong answer. Now you’ll show me. Pull up your skirt and show me.”

“What if somebody walks out into the street and sees?”

“You are so hot when you act like a good girl.” He lets me go.

"Show me."

I lift my pelvis and pull up my skirt to show him.

"Blue." He grabs the fabric and yanks with brutish force, ripping the crotch right out of my panties.

"Oh my god, what did you do?"

He tosses the shred of cotton aside and his fingers are back between my legs, exploring roughly—from my clit to my hole, down and up, down and up. "I think you like being out here with the traffic rumbling by, being used."

I'm panting as he finds my nub with his finger, ruthlessly honing in on what I need.

"Hmmm." My senses begin to whirl. My eyes drift closed. My head plops back on the headrest.

"No, no, no. You want to get arrested? Look at me. Look at me like we're talking."

I sit up and look right at him.

There's something shockingly intimate about looking into his eyes while he shamelessly fingers me. I don't know how long I can keep it up.

"That's it."

"You are the worst," I whisper into his lips. His gaze is fully feral, brown eyes flecked with black under villain brows.

"I know. Now grab onto my coat."

I grab on and he inserts one finger into me, right inside. It goes in slow and thick.

Heat spears through me. It's not a cute little game, anymore; it's a wild game that's gone slightly out of control. He's owning me in the middle of traffic.

My breath shudders out of me. "What if a cop comes?"

"They'll see you whoring yourself out. They'll see your pussy being owned by a lazy, filthy-minded roustabout."

He pushes his finger in deeper, and presses his thumb to my clit, and whatever he's doing, I'm gone, coming in a million shattered pieces.

Thirty-One

Jaxon

I flick on the shower and pull off my clothes, still wired from my time with Jada.

It's an unwritten rule that guys who head out for a night or weekend with me can expect a whole range of outcomes, from outrageous bar tabs and gambling debts to being chased by packs of paparazzi to ocean-ruined clothes, transport to other countries, police records, involvement in brawls, and/or unwise sexual escapades.

Women who date me get their own version, minus the bills and the brawling, of course.

I'm the one you hang out with if you want to roughen up your squeaky-clean image. I'm the one you go to when you want to upset the family or make sure the tabloids haven't forgotten about you between films or coronations or whatever it is that gets you in the papers.

Pushing people past their limits and getting them to go against their better judgment has been my thing for as long as I can remember.

But pushing Jada past her boundaries was something different altogether.

It may have looked like I was pushing and corrupting her, but in truth, it was my soul getting taken apart. It was my heart getting twisted into new shapes.

I stumble in under the hot water and press my forehead to the rough stone that forms the mosaic on the shower walls, probably created by a team of artisans flown in from lord knows where.

I grab hold of myself, letting the water rush over the back of my head and stream down my cheeks as I jerk off to the memory of her expression when I took control, and the way she watched me as I fingered her. Just the wild intimacy of it, something I'd normally find cringy.

I come in a torrent of heat and euphoria.

I'm addicted to her pleasure, but it's more than that. It's her. Everything about her.

I let the water rush over me as one single realization dawns: I need to tell her who I am.

It's messed up I've let it go this far. Jada admires honesty and hard work and people who believe in things. She'll hate that I posed as somebody else. Past me would've found it funny. Current me doesn't see anything funny about it at all, because over the course of the weeks, I've come to care about her opinion. I've come to care about her.

Caring and concern. Jesus Christ, no wonder I've avoided it for so long. And now I'm twisted around like a motherfucker.

I'm gonna go on record here and say that it's...fun. Unusually hot, in fact.

Unusually hot. That's how she asked for it. So Jada. No-nonsense, straightforward Jada, blown away by a few bits of gold in some ice cubes. I get this streak of irrational anger for the jackasses she grew up with here, even though I might be the worst jackass of them all.

After my shower I do a punishing workout. Not the best order of activities to go in, but I'm not exactly the picture of mental health at the moment.

Afterwards I place a call to Soto, who's supposedly on the West Coast at this point.

"What do you have? I have a lot of changes to make."

"Yeah, about that..." The way he says it, I know I'm not gonna like it.

"Spill it."

"Your hands are absolutely tied when it comes to Bloxburn. And Bert Johnston is a direct employee of theirs."

"I don't care. I've documented at least four instances where he's directly working against the interests of the company. The only way he's doing a good job is if they've put him there to screw things up."

"Yeah, but here's the problem. Your parents got into some sort of hassle with the owners of SportyGoCo. They bought SportyGoCo specifically to destroy it."

My blood goes cold. "They bought it to destroy it?"

"That's right. I've spoken with a few of the Wycliff executives. Your parents were angry with the owners. I have no idea what about, but they apparently went through a great deal of trouble to force those owners to sell. I gather that SportyGoCo was a labor of love for those ex-owners."

"My parents bought it out of vengeance."

"Yes."

My blood goes cold, thinking about Jada, about how much she loves the company. The whole crew loves that company. They have all of those hopes and dreams for Wonderbag. The shipping team has been working so hard to improve the systems. The people here consider each other to be family, what with the cookies and the hats and all the rest of it.

"Wait—I don't understand," I say. "If they wanted to destroy SportyGoCo, why keep it running? Why not shut down the business once they had control? Why did they bother keeping it running?"

"Vengeance," Soto says. "The owners loved their employees. So part of the idea is to make their people miserable. Also, money. If they can force people to quit or fire them for disciplinary reasons, there's a payroll cost savings associated with that. I've been told that Bert has until the end of this accounting period to make people quit or fire them, and to otherwise destroy the value and reputation of the company. I'm guessing that inflicts maximum pain on those former owners, but it's also better in terms of a loss. For tax purposes."

"Hurt the people, kill the value, get a tax write-off," I say.

"Yeah," Soto says. "What's more, it appears that Bloxburn specializes in that sort of thing."

"So it was their bully company," I say. It makes sense. The whispered name. The sense of anger and grievance swirling around it.

"Exactly," Soto says.

"Well, I don't want them managing SportyGoCo anymore. Can't I pay them and tell them to go away?"

"There's no way. No ability to cancel the contract once signed, no kill fee—trust me we looked. We had a guy back channeling to Bloxburn, even floated a bit of bribery, but it's not something they're interested in. Apparently they've got other accounts watching this account. SportyGoCo is a showcase for them. A case study in how much damage they can do legally. Bottom line, they're very invested in destroying this firm, and that's exactly what your parents hired them to do."

"This is unbelievable. There's nothing I can do. Me. The owner of this entire corporation. A man worth billions. Just nada."

"That's right," Soto says. "They have about a month to run the company into the ground."

"And they'll write it off as a Wycliff loss."

"Technically, a Wycliff sub-brand loss."

"I won't accept this. Give me one way to void the contract."

"Fine. If at the end of this accounting period the company is profitable, they would be in breach."

"When's the end of the accounting period?"

"End of this month. You won't make it. The hole is too deep."

I go to the window and look down at a horse and buggy parked in front of the entrance to the park. It's a misty, foggy night, and the lights have come on, lending things an otherworldly look.

"And what will it take to simply buy these assholes?"

"Buy Bloxburn? I don't see how. This is a very large business—I think it's owned by Major & Bow. I don't see them letting it go. It's too deeply integrated with the rest of their businesses."

"Get me a number."

"And if they don't want to sell?"

"Then I buy Major & Bow."

"Nope. Too big even for you," Soto says.

"Are you sure?"

Soto is silent for a while, probably looking at stock prices or who knows what. "Financing would take too long." There's a pause. I hear his chair creak. "Let me think."

I wait. Papers rustle. He's probably writing on a notepad. Soto thinks on paper. "You could snap it up with a consortium. It's possible with a consortium. If you got Charley on board and maybe one of the Rheingold cousins and a few others. Marina Apondi. Of course Major & Bow would have to accept any offer unless you went in hostile. You could get what you want with a group. It could be a good investment for people."

"So basically, I go begging to everybody who I have a beef with, hat in hand."

"This is business."

"Begging my frenemies, my haters, hat in hand." Does he not

get it? "That sounds worse than plucking out my own eyeballs. More to the point, it wouldn't work. Nobody in their right mind would think it's a good idea to go in with me, and I couldn't agree more. I'm not the kind of man people partner with."

"Are you so sure?"

"Trust me—I'm not." I grab a glass and pour a scotch. "Find another way to break the contract that doesn't involve me asking for favors. I want control, and I want Bert Johnston gone."

"Then we're back to making the company profitable."

"What if I buy all the merchandise?"

"Won't work. There are about five legal problems with that. You can't inflate your own profits by buying your own merchandise."

We go on brainstorming. In the end, we're back to the company having to be profitable—an impossibility, considering that Bert's in charge, merrily sabotaging the operations. It all makes sense now. Jada thought he was trying to throw a monkey wrench into things, and I didn't believe her. But she was right.

"Find another way." I hang up feeling unbelievably annoyed.

I head downstairs and pull on my coat and boots and hat.

"Is that a new hat, sir?" Arnold asks; due to his valet duties, he's familiar with every piece of clothing that I have.

"Somebody at work gave it to me," I mumble. "I should toss it, is what I should do."

"Do you want a different one? We have a selection in the cedar chest."

"It's fine," I bark.

Arnold hovers with a concerned expression.

"What? I can see you have something to say."

"Why not try to save the company, sir?" Because naturally, he heard the whole call.

"I'm trying. Did you not hear what he said? I can't cancel the contract or affect it in any way."

"Except...you are currently an employee there, are you not?"

"What? I should hop onto the hamster wheel and run as fast as I can? That's how you think I can save the company?"

"People do that sort of thing all the time."

"There are actual industry professionals about ten times as qualified as I am who've been trying to make SportyGoCo profitable. The problem is that the man who runs that place, the man who has the power to make all of the operational decisions, is dedicated to destroying the business. It's not feasible." I button up my overcoat.

"Bullshit, sir," Arnold says.

This stops me. "Excuse me?"

"You rose to the top in one of the most grueling sports in existence," Arnold says. "You worked out in the gym and on that track for longer hours than any of your opponents. You were in the garage, shoulder to shoulder with your mechanics. You put together a team that would've killed for you. You kept your cool during that crash in Azerbaijan and you dominated for a good two years. You're telling me you can't take on some man whose main talent is to run companies into the ground?"

"I nearly got thrown in jail for assault, you forgot that part."

"Gundrun cheated and endangered your team," Arnold says. "Give it a shot. This SportyGoCo bit. What do you have to lose?"

I grumble my answer and get out of there. As if that's the answer to my problems—more investment, more involvement. It's not bad enough that I'm obsessed with a woman I can't have in the end—not once she knows the truth—but I should work my ass off for a company I can't save?

A chilly autumn wind blows as I make my way up Seventy-sixth. Shop windows are starting to fill with orange lights and pumpkins, though some shops have skipped right to Christmas. We'll have our first snow in a month or so. What am I still doing here? I got what I came for—the identity of the butt-dialer. I could sell Wycliff and be done with the whole thing. The stock price has long since stabilized. Nobody will be jumping from the rooftops. I have a plane in a hangar out at Teterboro Airport, ready to take me to any beautiful place I choose.

Charley was right; coming here was a bad move.

I wouldn't have gotten involved in all of this.

I wouldn't be wearing this ridiculous hat.

I wouldn't be stumbling across Broadway, confused and alone, trying not to look at the fucking pigeons.

Thirty-Two

Jada

"You're home early," Kelsey says. She's lounging on the couch next to Willow and Antonio, and Lizzie is on the floor. The four of them are watching one of their beloved true crime shows. "We just started. Want me to catch you up?"

"What about yoga?" I ask Willow.

"Blowing it off. There's stuff for cherry Cokes on the counter —I'll make you one," Willow says.

Willow's a techie who is always saying she has no understanding of chemistry unlike her famous chemist brother, Theo—but she makes a brilliant cherry Coke where she uses bitters and actual cherries.

"That's fine." I toe off my shoes and hang up my coat, body still buzzing from the sweet, sweet experience of being in Jack Smith's competence-porn hands.

Jack Smith.

My body is into him; my heart is getting on board, but my brain is all waaaaaaait a moment! You like hardworking men who believe in something, and he's a lazy office gopher who is sometimes an impressive delivery driver.

"You okay?" Willow asks.

"Sure! We, uh, got a half-day. I had to do some deliveries with Jack and be his overseer, so then we grabbed a bite afterward."

"Oh my god, the magnetic yet fashion-challenged wild boy who's alarmed by vending machines?" Kelsey sits up. "Can he even drive in the city traffic?"

"He's an amazing driver. And he's *not* a wild boy."

"When are we getting our picture?" Lizzie asks.

"Oh, right. Actually, my coworker got one." As soon as it's out of my mouth, I wish I hadn't said it. The whole idea of showing them a picture of Jack was to shock and amaze them with the fact that his style is as outlandish as I'd described. I don't want that now.

"A wild boy?" Antonio asks.

"Jada's mysterious new coworker," Kelsey says. "He's a hot guy with the worst fashion ever, raised in a poor, rural village somewhere in Europe."

"And he was all, 'What is this strange thing that you have here called a vending machine that you have here?'" Willow puts in.

"What are you talking about?" Antonio asks. "Vending machines are all over Europe." As an international male model from Italy, Antonio is an expert on all things European.

"Maybe they don't have them in goat cart and mud hut villages," Kelsey says.

"We don't know his village was like that," I say. "All we know is that it's rural, and people live in crumbling medieval homes without proper heating systems."

Antonio furrows his expertly coiffed, male-model brows. "Where exactly is this guy from?"

"He's cagey about where his home is," I explain. "He says he's lived all over. It seems like he might not have a true home. I know he lived at one point in a village in Türenbourg in some sad crumbling structure at one point."

Antonio nearly chokes on his drink. "Türenbourg is one of the wealthiest and most sophisticated nations in the EU. The only place you can find goat carts in Türenbourg is a petting zoo, cara."

"I'm sure they have people without homes in Türenbourg," Lizzie says.

"There are people without homes in New York," Antonio says, "but you don't see them hauling things around in goat carts."

"For the record, he never specifically said goat carts," I say. "That's my coworker's impression."

"So? The picture?" Willow presses.

I clutch my phone. This thing that Jack and I have together, it's new and tender and secret and wild and *good*. My friends will see a dork in an unfashionably loud shirt, but he's so much more. He's clever and fun and sexy...

"Well?" Kelsey's standing now.

"You can't laugh. There's more to him than meets the eye. Once you get to know him, he's clever and interesting, and—"

"We won't laugh, okay?" Kelsey says. "Come on."

"Please?" Lizzie begs.

I find the pictures that Renata sent me. I cue up the one where he's standing next to his cubicle, one arm draped over the top of it, talking to somebody just out of the frame. It's a good picture if you look past his weird hair, too-small glasses, and possibly cancerous mole. But my favorite thing about the image is his playful, swaggery expression, what I think of as his jousting expression, where he's frowning, square jaw set just so, but his eyes are smiling. It's the look he gets when I call him on his shit. I'm smiling, looking at the picture. Even with the silly glasses, you can see the sparkle in his eyes.

It really is a good picture of him, fashion fail and all.

"Hold the presses!" Kelsey's standing in front of me. "You *like* the wild boy?"

"He's not a wild boy!"

"I am looking at you mooning over an image of him!" Kelsey says.

"I'm not mooning! But, I mean, yes, I like him well enough. He's fun and smart—"

"And magnetic and villainous, if I recall."

"He's complex," I say. "He's so much more than he seems. He's not the kind of guy that would wear these clothes. I don't know what to say...being that yes, he is wearing these clothes..."

"Oh my god, show us already! We won't laugh," Willow says. "You have to show us now, though."

I hand my phone to Kelsey, wincing inwardly.

She blinks at the screen. "Damn! You weren't kidding about the nineties hair. Did he steal these glasses from NSYNC?"

"Hey!" I say.

"Sorry!"

I swipe so she can see the other two photos—one of him with his glasses off and one while he was standing at the watercooler with Shondrella. That one's good because his profile is striking—Greek-statue striking—all fierce lines and pleasing symmetry.

She hands the phone to Willow.

"What the hell! Is he, like, being funny? With the glasses?" Willow asks.

"No," I say sadly. "He's been there for weeks. This is how he comes to work every day."

"Not every man can be as fashionable as Antonio," Willow says grinning over at the model himself.

"Many try, few succeed, *stellina*," Antonio replies, scrolling through his own phone. "Can we get back to the show anytime soon?"

Lizzie goes over and grabs the phone. "Wow. Way to go against the tide. This really shows commitment. He just doesn't give a shit!"

"That's his thing," I say. "He truly doesn't give a shit. Outward appearances aren't a value of his. Definitely not a shopper. I had to take him shopping for work boots and it was like he'd never been in a store before."

"There was a wild boy found in France in the nineties," Kelsey says.

"Dude, no!" I say.

"Bleached tips," Kelsey says.

"Okay." Antonio holds out his hand. "I need to see."

"You have to look past the ensemble." I pass it over.

"Maybe it's so uncool that it *actually is* cool and we just don't know it," Willow says. "That does happen."

Antonio furrows his brow at the photo. "What the hell?!"

I say, "He's totally hot if you look past the getup, don't you think? If anything, I think the fact that he can wear such a dorky outfit and still look good shows how hot he actually is. This girl at work wants to give him a makeover but—"

"*Ma che cazzo*!" Antonio sounds outraged. "Are you fucking kidding me?"

A surge of protectiveness wells up in me. "He doesn't look that bad!" I stomp over and hold out my hand. "Give it here."

"You can kind of see his handsomeness, right, Antonio?" Willow nudges Antonio. I hadn't realized they were so chummy.

Antonio swipes through the other two with a stunned expression. "This man works at your office? Since when?"

"A few weeks."

Antonio has the strangest look on his face, like he's offended or something.

I say, "You may not think much of his looks, but he's witty and charming."

"What is this guy's name?" Antonio demands. "Could it be Jaxon, by any chance?"

I frown, surprised, because I hadn't mentioned his name. "Jack," I say. "Jack Smith."

"Uh-huh," Antonio says. He pulls out his own phone with a shit-eating grin. "Jack Smith? *Dai!*"

"What?"

He hands me his phone, which has a picture of a dark-haired man standing next to a low-to-the-ground racing car. He's clutching a helmet in his hand, and the stands behind him are full of people.

Antonio wiggles his thumb and forefinger together. "Enlarge it. Enlarge the man's face. Tell me if he looks familiar."

I enlarge the picture and my belly drops through my feet. It's Jack, or at least somebody who looks an awful lot like Jack, minus the mole and the little glasses. And the bad hair. "I don't understand." I grab my phone and compare the two. "It's him but...what the hell?"

Kelsey comes and stands next to me. "Twin brothers?"

It's the obvious conclusion, but I know those eyes. I know that smile. I know that left-side dimple and that slyly humorous expression. And who names their twins Jack and Jaxon? I look up at Antonio. "What the hell?"

"You've got Jaxon Eadsburg von Henningsly, asshole extraordinaire, working at your office."

"Why..." I can barely breathe. "Jaxon Eadsburg von Henningsly...I've heard that long name."

"Jaxon von Henningsly is notorious," Antonio says. "He's the only son of one of the most admired and wealthy families on the continent. It's a cliché to wonder how such a bad kid came from such fine parents. Some ten years ago he was a promising young Formula One driver, but then he attacked Tybalt Gundrun, everybody's darling. He knocked Tybalt out and completely destroyed the man's career—gave him a detached retina from the fight. Jaxon was barred from ever racing again, but he's never far from the spotlight. Billionaire bad boy and all that. Tabloids love him."

"A billionaire bad boy?" I say.

"Maybe it's not him," Kelsey says softly. "Everybody has a twin."

"No, it's him," I say, mind spinning. "Oh my god! Why would he work at our office in disguise?"

"Nobody knows why Jaxon von Henningsly does anything. Gambling and dancing in nightclubs and attacking paparazzi..." Antonio waves a hand as though the list is too long and wearying to recite. "Jaxon's always good for a stupid brawl or biting commentary on perfectly nice people. Tybalt Gundrun was my favorite driver. I'd like to show Von Henningsly exactly how I feel about that," Antonio growls.

"But to come to New York and work at our company? Why would he do that?"

"Bored and in need of laughs, no doubt," Antonio suggests. "Now that his parents are dead, he's richer than god and the world is his playground."

I gasp as I put it all together. Jack is the new owner. The billionaire racecar-driving son. It was him on that conference call.

Kelsey looks concerned—I'm sure I've gone white as a sheet. "What?"

"Remember back in September when the new SportyGoCo owner did that company-wide call? And I was goofing around and making fun of him afterwards, and it turned out that the phone had butt-dialed him back?"

"Right, and he heard the whole thing," Willow says. "Hilarious."

"And Bert went on that witch hunt." Kelsey's jaw drops. "Your guy's not actually him..."

"Oh yes. Yes indeed. That's him." I wrap my arms around myself. "This would explain his interest in the butt-dialer's identity. What the hell. Is he here for vengeance? On me? Would he be so cruel?"

"He would," Antonio growls.

"Honey." Kelsey grabs my forearm with both hands. "We'll protect you from that asshole."

Too late. My mind races with images of kissing him. The way he touched me in the van. The sparkling intimacy and closeness I felt with him. It's all fake?

"Let me get this straight," Lizzie says. "This Jack guy is the owner of your company, pretending he's one of his own employees to get back at you? Jesus, who does that?"

"The man is depraved," Antonio says.

My pulse whooshes in my ears. I'm shocked. Enraged. Bewildered. Most of all, I'm mortified. I can't stop replaying scenes of us double-parked outside in the truck. The whole thing with our game. Snippets of conversation from our time at the restaurant. The painful things I told him about my family. And what did he really tell me? Almost nothing.

Jack made me feel free and bold and a little bit like a princess. I felt new. Happy. Excited. Sexy.

And he was laughing the whole time.

"How could he?" I whisper hoarsely.

"So he's pretending to be a fellow employee as part of a plan to unmask and punish the butt-dialer?" Willow asks.

"He already knows it's me," I say. "We've been hanging out and having all of this fun—"

"You kissed him," Lizzie guesses.

I throw up my hands. It's impossible to hide anything from my girls. "Yes, I kissed him."

"I will kill him," Antonio growls. "I will rip him apart."

"You can't," I say. Antonio and I dated briefly, but now he's more like a brother—an angry, protective brother. Exactly what I don't need.

"If he knows you're the butt-dialer, why not just fire you?" Kelsey says.

"Too easy. He prefers to toy with his prey," Antonio says.

I'm not a good person. Jack had said that over and over. I should have listened.

Everything falls into place. Like the way he said, "That'll be all, you're dismissed!" to Bert. That's probably how he talks to everyday people! And his ignorance of office operations. His driving chops. Does he know Bert? Is he in cahoots with Bert?

"And I know this is a minor detail, but excuse me, that outfit?" Lizzie says. "That's what he thinks Americans wear? Is there anything not jerky about this guy?"

I put Jaxon Eadsburg von Henningsly in the search bar on my phone and spin through the images. There's Jack in a tuxedo. Jack on a yacht—his own, no doubt. Jack with beautiful models. My belly churns. There are tons of pictures of him out there, and he looks good in all of them. There's him at his parents' funeral, all dressed in black. This picture is from some financial newspaper under the headline: "Wycliff Takes a Hit Over Investor Fears."

"Well, his parents had just died. And I made fun of him."

"So he comes after you?" Kelsey says. "That's a bit much."

My friends are watching, waiting.

"Yeah, it is a bit much. You can go back to your TV show," I say morosely.

"As if." Willow stomps to the kitchen to make me a cherry Coke while Kelsey describes an extended fantasy that involves Smuckers biting Jack in the face. Willow returns and sets down my souped-up Coke. "We are taking care of you."

"Thanks," I say.

"Stop scrolling. Put down the phone and walk away," Lizzie says.

"I can't." I keep spinning through the images. I land on one of him at some kind of fancy restaurant. So this is the real him—wavy dark hair, sexy white suit, arm draped over a booth backrest the way he likes to do.

"We were on this wavelength...it felt real. But he's a billionaire and I'm a nobody to him." I look up at the sweet, concerned faces of my friends. "It couldn't be real, could it?"

"Piece of shit," Kelsey says, holding her hand out for my phone.

I can't give it up just yet. There's another picture where he's a young kid. He's sitting with a man and woman who must be the parents. A smiling family on a brilliant green lawn in front of a majestic castle.

Willow sits on the armrest next to me. "I've seen that before. I think that's a famous picture, like from *TIME Magazine* or something."

"He told my officemate that their family lived for a while in a crumbling and drafty medieval place that leaks. We assumed it was a sad little village ruin. But it's a castle. He was talking about a *castle*."

"Home sweet castle," Lizzie says from behind me. "A happy little family."

"Not really. That's his fake smile," I say.

"He looks pretty happy to me," Willow says.

"He isn't—his eyes give it away," I say. "Also, his real smile has this one dimple."

"What are you going to do?" Kelsey asks. "Are you going to confront him?"

"You must give him hell!" Antonio says.

I stand and toss the phone onto the couch, reeling. I go to the window and gaze down at the gloomy courtyard. "I don't know if I can face him. He was laughing at me the whole time...I feel sick. Maybe I should just quit."

"Screw that!" Kelsey says. "That company needs you! Those people are your second family, and this jackass can't ruin that for you."

"Of course he can ruin it for me. He owns it!" I say. "I'm sure he approves of everything that's going on there. He acted so mad at Bert, but they're probably laughing behind our backs! Good friends, yucking it up while they destroy SportyGoCo. All of our hard work. All our dreams with Wonderbag."

Kelsey says, "I'm so sorry."

"Thank you," I say. "Wait—you know what? Screw it. I'm going into work just like normal. I'm gonna keep going forward, keep trying my best. Be with the people who mean everything to me. He can take away my dignity, and he can close the place down and fire us all after he gets bored of taking vengeance, but he will never take my loyalty to those people there. Maybe our ship is going down, but I'm gonna goddamn go down with it, fighting the whole way!"

Lizzie claps. "You take the high road, girl. Act as if."

"Doing the right thing is always the right thing," Kelsey says.

"I'm kind of surprised anybody bought that mole of his. It looks so totally fake," Willow says.

"Fake as a three-dollar bill," Antonio says.

Willow's been teaching Antonio American idioms, and this one makes her grin.

"No wonder Jack didn't want to see a dermatologist." I sigh. "We talked about getting an office screening going, and he was not enthusiastic. It would've been funny to see him squirm for once."

"That would be funny. Why not pull one together?" Kelsey says.

"He'd just opt out," I say.

Willow gets a mischievous look on her face. "Well...is it possible that we know somebody who might play a dermatologist? Somebody who might be willing to show up and do an office screening? And maybe have a few things to say about the mole?"

All eyes turn to Antonio.

"No. You guys!" I say. "No!"

Antonio sits up. "I am passionate about skin care, my friends," he says. "I have many feelings about a mole such as this. On such a smug face as his."

Willow snorts.

"You can't," I say.

"Your boss is out Thursday afternoons, right?" Kelsey says. "That would be perfect! We need a lab coat and some kind of privacy screen."

"We're not having a fake skin screening tomorrow," I warn.

"Jaxon von Henningsly is plaguing one of my friends?" Antonio growls. "I will play the most passionate dermatologist you can imagine. I will inspect that mole—that, I promise you. I will inspect the stuffing out of his mole."

"You are not coming to my office as a fake dermatologist," I say.

"Why not? What's he gonna do, fire you?" Kelsey says.

I point at Antonio. "Also, do we really want this face to get in a brawl with a notorious brawler?"

"Don't you worry, I know how to handle men like that." There's a gleam in his eye. "I am feeling very animated by my passion for skin care."

"Marni on the first floor has a white coat from when she worked at Saks skincare counter!" Lizzie's fingers are flying over her phone—texting Marni, presumably.

"Seriously. It's a funny idea, but no. This is me officially forbidding it."

Thirty-Three

JADA

RENATA'S at the worktable looking morose the next day. Even her rockabilly polka-dot scarf seems to droop.

She tosses me a Wonderbag prototype. "The new closure sucks."

I try it out. She's right.

"Shondrella tracked down a claw buckle at a warehouse in Brooklyn. She got her man to do a pick-up."

"Nice," I say, trying to sound enthused. Jack doesn't seem to be in yet. Why bother being on time when you're the owner?

Renata half-collapses on the table. "A clasp is not the answer, and we know it," she moans, and I feel this rush of love for her. She's been by my side here for so many years.

I want to tell her what I know about Jack, but this isn't the right time. She'll freak out, and possibly even confront him. Everybody will find out, and there will be tears. Anger. And how would Jack respond? Will he shut down the whole place once he's had his fun? Send us all home? The last day of our SportyGoCo family?

I need to keep it to myself until I figure out what to do.

"What?" she asks.

"We should have a drink after work," I say. "We don't do that enough."

Her face brightens. "I have derby practice all this week, but next Monday?"

"Perf."

We pick back up where we left off when Bert shut things down for CPR training, and Shondrella's excited about the new closure.

Lacey arrives looking extra goth, or maybe it's just fatigue. She asks about my afternoon of babysitting Jack.

"Worst employee ever," I say. "Is he not even in yet?"

"Shipping," Lacey says.

"Hmph," I say, feeling a little stung that he didn't even bother to say hi. And then I'm angry at myself, because seriously? I'm mad because he's not doing a good job of pretending to be my attentive new fling?

I'm eating lunch at my desk when he finally makes his appearance in the design department. I concentrate on my work even though he's making quite the production of his arrival back there, clearing his throat and sliding his chair around.

"You guys get that snafu handled?" Renata asks him.

"Best it'll get for now," he says.

The two of them chat a bit and I get this warm, syrupy feeling inside from hearing his voice.

I close my eyes, hating life. What is wrong with me? I was such a pushover with my brothers, letting them play video games while I spent those crucial years after high school working my ass off on their behalf. It was a big thing to me that I'd sworn off lazy, entitled men after that. An important promise to myself, and who's lazier and more entitled than a billionaire heir who only wants to drive and fight?

I need to re-swear them off, clearly. With a solemn flag ceremony and a ten-gun salute. I like hardworking men who strive for things they believe in. I need to write that a zillion times on a chalkboard, and maybe on the insides of my eyeballs.

"Hey," Jack says. "Catch any double-parkers lately?"

I spin around. He has his feet up on his cubicle desk and he's just sitting there, smiling, hands behind his head. He probably looks like that when he's on his stupid yacht. "No, I have not." I go back to work.

Of course he comes over. "Something wrong?" he asks in a low voice, concern written all over his face.

"Just not a fan of double-parkers at the moment, that's all," I snap.

"Oh my god, right?" Renata says from behind.

I look right at Jack. "They suck," I say.

"Have double-parkers done something to upset you?" Jack asks.

"Umm, I'll take this one for five-hundred, Mayim," Renata puts in. "Utter pieces of shit who sadly exist in this world?"

"And that would be your opinion, too?" Jack asks me.

"Do you not have anything to do?" I ask him. "Because we are trying to make things right here."

"Not until..." He draws his brows together in this face of concern.

"Do I need to assign you a task?"

"Depends," he says, and then he flicks his gaze at the supply closet.

I grit my teeth. "You want a task? I'll give you a task." I jerk open my desk drawer and get out my box of Q-tips. "Hold this."

He complies, standing there holding the box, watching me, all smiling eyes and solo dimple. "A task?" Because naturally he's thinking this'll be a sexy task.

"Follow me." I storm into the breakroom and grab a mug from the cupboard and fill it with a little bit of water. I go around to the dark corner where poor Keith is.

"Keith has gotten dusty. You're going to clean him."

"Come again?" he says.

I ignore his stupid double entendre and kneel next to Keith. I dip a Q-tip into the water and then I roll it against my finger so that it's merely damp. I use the tib to rub the dust off the parts of Keith's fragile cactus skin.

"You'll get every bit of dirt and dust off. See how carefully and gently I'm doing this? You're gonna need to be careful not to press too hard. Avoid the prickers—some of them are fragile, and if you hit them, they can fall out. Especially on the brown parts like this. See? I go around it."

Thirty-Four

Jaxon

She kneels by the ridiculous dead cactus, rubbing off invisible dust.

"What's going on?"

"Keith needs to be cleaned."

"I'm not talking about Keith. Are you angry with me?"

"Not everything is about you, Jack." She continues with her demonstration.

Is she unhappy that I spent the morning in shipping? I'd wanted to get back up here the whole time. All I could think about was her in the truck—how beautiful she looked in the light from the street. The softness of her sigh when I found the spot that spoke to her. The taste of her skin. The feel of her pulse under my tongue.

"A cactus takes in water and sunshine from every part of it. We're going to need to maximize that now that he's so far from the light. You will take care not to be clumsy or assholish."

"Have you ever known me to be clumsy?" I ask.

She scratches her cheek with her middle finger.

I lower my voice. "Are you going to tell me what's wrong?"

She glares at me. She *wants* to tell me, so why won't she? "I have things to do. Are you going to complete this task, or do I need to recommend you for a demerit?"

I give her a mischievous look. Is this some more of our role-playing thing? I lower my voice. "Is the butt-dialer going to recommend me for a demerit?"

"Oh, is that what we're doing?" she bites out. "Really?"

It's official. She's angry.

I'm usually indifferent if not downright amused by people's anger, but everything's different with Jada. Her anger feels threatening, somehow. As though I'm cut off from the source of something warm and good and life-sustaining. "What's going on?"

"So that's a yes on the demerit?" she asks.

Would she do that? I don't think so, but then, I've never seen her in this mood.

I take a Q-tip. "If and when I get my last demerit, it will be far more spectacular than this."

"Like how you're gonna punch Bert?"

"Is that what it'll take?"

"Please. Fighting and brawling, that's for losers. You have twenty minutes." She storms back to her desk.

I rub the damp cotton end on the dirt, just to humor her. I do the whole cactus, even though the thing is never going to survive. The whole office putting their hopes into this dead cactus feels like a metaphor for something incredibly tragic. And no, I won't be calling him Keith.

I proceed to clean the dead husk these people call a cactus. The thing is dusty, it's true, but it's going to need more than the ridiculously painstaking cleaning I'm giving it. When one swab is fully dirty on both sides, I grab another, moistening it like she demonstrated. This is important to her for whatever reason.

Ten minutes later, I toss the box of swabs onto her desk. "All done."

She goes over and inspects the cactus. She points to a section. "You didn't do this part yet," she says. "There's still dust to get off."

"That's not dust; it's the dried and mottled surface of a dead cactus."

"Do better," she says. "Do it over. *Gently*. Also, he's not dead."

"I'm done with this fake task," I inform her. "And he is dead."

"Your performance is sadly lacking, Jack. You'll do it properly or I'll recommend you for a demerit."

"Oh, please," I say, trying for a humorous expression. "I think we both know that my performance in the area of gentle rubbing is unparalleled."

"Unparalleled? You are living in a fantasy world!"

Right then, there's commotion at Varsha's desk. Some kind of doctor is carrying in some sort of privacy screen. His wavy dark hair is stark against his white coat, and he seems to be giving orders to Varsha.

Jada stiffens. Whatever is happening up there, she doesn't like it. She beelines over and I follow.

The doctor, who has an Italian accent, is instructing Varsha to set the privacy screen up near the window where there is ample light.

She carries it over to the window. He hands Renata a clipboard. "Names here. People will sign up and I'll see them one by one."

"We're not supposed to have a screening today," she says. "There must be some mistake."

"But it is authorized," the doctor says. "Fully authorized. I'm Dr. Tonio, here on the authority of a man named Bert. That is your boss, no?"

"The screening was canceled," Jada says to Dr. Tonio. "Therefore, it isn't authorized." She calls to Varsha to bring back the privacy screen.

"Bert instructed me to come this afternoon, and I'm to have whatever assistance I require from..." He pauses and looks down at his clipboard. "Jada Herberger? Is there a Jada here? Bert said that Jada Herberger is to assist me."

A few people drift over, enthusiastic about the idea of a screening.

"I'm sorry," Jada says in a strangely pointed tone. "But you are misinformed. This will not happen."

"Bert insisted," Dr. Tonio says. "My fee is taken care of already. A yearly screening, it's very important, as you know—"

"As long as he's here, we should do it." Renata aims an oddly sharp gaze at Jada. "People here need this for their skin, don't you agree?"

Shondrella's on the scene, hair in a swept-up style that showcases her silver hair streak. "We should do it! As long as he's here, I agree!" She widens her eyes at Jada. "I can't think of any employee who *wouldn't* benefit."

"If Bert says we need a screening," Dave shrugs, "what's the harm? We should all have one of these every year."

These people are really interested in a cancer screening, something I'll definitely be skipping. I text down to shipping, letting them know I'm coming down. The last thing I need is for a dermatologist to be examining my mole.

Jada shakes her head. "Not gonna happen. You'll have to leave." She gestures at the door.

"Screenings save lives," Dr. Tonio warns. "Do you not wish to save lives?"

"No, not if it's unauthorized," Jada says firmly. "And I'm in charge of the department while Bert is offsite." She points again.

"But we all *need* our screenings." Renata's tone has turned foreboding. "*Lives* could be *saved*."

"This is the last time I'm gonna ask you to leave," Jada says.

"I cannot," Dr. Tonio says.

The whole thing seems unprofessional, but then, I don't know much about the American medical system.

"Please." Jada looks frustrated—desperate, even.

I don't like it.

A growl forms in my throat.

Before I can think better of it, I'm in the guy's face. "You have been informed that your services are not needed," I bite out. "You have been asked to leave. Now you will leave."

"But I cannot, I simply—" Dr. Tonio blinks. He's gaping at my face. He's obviously noticed my mole here—more than noticed it. A look of abject horror suffuses his features. "Holy mother of Jesus," he whispers, making the sign of the cross.

Renata gasps. "What is it, Dr. Tonio? What do you see?"

"He doesn't see anything because there is no screening," Jada says.

Dr. Tonio is fixated on my mole. "What monstrosity is this?"

"None of your business," I say, frowning.

"This is very dire! You must let me inspect this...this..." He pauses dramatically, as if at a loss for words.

Renata covers her mouth, looking frightened.

Shondrella clutches Varsha's arm. "Jack," she whispers.

"Maybe he should take a closer look at it, Jack," Lacey says. "In private, maybe. Like behind the screen."

"The screening is over," Jada says.

"You heard the lady," I growl, going nose to nose with Dr. Tonio, pressing a finger to his chest.

Dr. Tonio narrows his eyes, throwing back my menacing energy. He seems almost enraged, as if my mole has whipped him up into an uncontrollable fervor. Have they not heard of bedside manners here?

"There is a nearly carnivorous thing that is consuming you from the face," Dr. Tonio warns. "Like a grotesque plague upon your face, consuming you from the outside in. I cannot leave here without treating it."

"Oh my god!" Renata says. "Jack!"

"I will show this depraved blight no mercy," Dr. Tonio continues. "No mercy."

"Enough!" Jada grabs his arm and tries to drag him away.

"Jada! What are you doing?" Shondrella says. "Can't you see Jack needs a screening?"

I take the doctor's other arm and pull him toward the door.

"An unholy beast is upon your face," Dr. Tonio says as we get him into the hall.

A frightened Varsha follows us with the screen. Half the office crowds into the hall after us.

Dr. Tonio frees himself from us when we reach the elevator. He takes the screen from Varsha and storms into the elevator with it. He spins around and punches several buttons, or maybe he punches one button several times. "A horrible pox is eating your face! Vile and disgusting—"

The doors shut with a squinch.

I stand there, pulse racing, conscious of the entire design department arrayed behind me.

I've heard the American medical system is in trouble, but if this is an example of the care you get here, it's worse than people think.

I turn to find people looking at me, concerned, giving me sympathetic smiles.

"Um...savage," Dave says.

Jada purses her lips as if she's trying not to smile, though I don't see what's funny.

"Maybe it's a sign," Renata says. "To get that checked out by your doctor."

"Right!" Shondrella chimes in. "Forewarned is forearmed, don't you agree, Jack?"

"I've got it under control," I say.

People start filing back into the office.

I look over at Jada, who still looks highly amused.

"What?"

She bites her lip, then she spins around and bolts down the hall to the patio area.

I follow her. "What?"

She bursts out into the late afternoon sunshine.

"What's going on?" I demand, going out after her. "That doctor—what the hell?"

"Oh my god." She's at the rail, covering her face, shoulders shaking.

"What the hell is so funny? You think that was funny?"

"No," she squeaks, face contorted with the effort to suppress her laughter.

"Was that even for real?" I demand.

She spins around. "Was that even for real? I don't know. Are *you* even for real?"

"Excuse me?"

"Don't answer that. Don't bother, Jaxon Harcourt Eadsburg von Henningsly. Has this been entertaining for you? You found out who your butt-dialer was—congratulations. But that wasn't enough, was it? You had to completely mess with me."

I straighten. *She knows.*

She comes to me, expression grim. "Is that what you do when life on the yacht or the racetrack gets too boring? You screw with people who displease Your Highness? Make fools of them?"

"That's not what this is," I say.

"Playing sick games with the nobodies who work at your zillion companies?"

"You have this wrong. And you're not a nobody—far from it."

"Oh wow, I'm not a nobody. Far from it. I'm somebody—somebody you wanted to get back at. Have you been having a good laugh, Jack? Amusing yourself? Was it hard to keep a straight face when you acted like you wanted me?"

"That was no act." I go to her. "God, Jada, you have no idea—"

"No way." She shoves me off. "Excuse me if I don't believe you. You were pretending to be somebody else, and this whole time I'm being real with you. More real than I am with most other people. You know how that feels? And you're like, 'Look at me, playing a joke on the butt-dialer!'"

"That's not how it was."

"Well, you weren't coming to give me an award. You're a billionaire, Jack. Why bother with somebody like me? I know your parents died a few months back, and I'm sorry, but that doesn't explain this—"

"It wasn't about them. I hadn't seen them in years."

"Why, then?"

She deserves the truth. *We* deserve it—the two of us. This new thing between us deserves it. This relationship I screwed up before it got off the ground. This thing that I need to rescue.

I stare at the sky and try to get back to that day. Sitting at the microphone. The company. People all around. Everybody congratulating me on saving the company with that awful speech that felt like chewing glass.

"My parents were monsters that the whole world thought were saints," I say. "Ask anybody and they'll tell you I'm the one who should've gone down in that plane instead of them."

"I'm sorry—"

"No—don't be. Being seen as a saint like them is the last thing I'd want. My point is, they did terrible things under the banner of a bright and shiny family, and I went the other way. I did what I could to drag our name through the mud. The great Von Henningslys. It wasn't something I thought through, and not even the most effective form of rebellion. But then, I was raised by wolves, so what are you going to do? I went with it, and never stopped—"

"So I'm part of your rebellion? Nice." She goes to the railing and looks out over the noisy street.

"No, you are so much more. I need you to understand—it's important to me. You're important." I go to her side. "When they died, all I wanted to do was jettison their precious legacy—especially Wycliff. But people were begging me not to do that. I was warned it would crash the markets, etcetera. So I gave in and did the one thing that I never wanted to do: I stepped into my father's shoes with that ridiculous company-wide call you heard, reading a script written for him to read. I sounded as full of shit as he ever did, and I hated myself for it. I felt like I'd sold my soul."

"I can see how you'd hate that," she says. "Still."

I look out over the buildings, remembering that day. "All of these people congratulating me, thinking I was taking up the Von Henningsly mantle. I felt like I was becoming part of their whole lie, becoming *them*. Like I was the same as them. I wanted to destroy something. I couldn't wreck Wycliff, being that I'd agreed to save it. And then your voice came crackling through. Your speech about mustard and ascots and whatever else. Everybody was so worried about my reaction. Terrified."

She turns to me. Her attention feels different. Jada appreciates honesty, and I love that about her.

"I decided that you'd be the thing I destroy," I confess. "It was the worst activity I could think up in the moment—mean-spirited and despicable."

Her eyes sparkle, diamond-bright. "You came to destroy me."

"I came to destroy the butt-dialer. I followed your voice. But when I discovered it was you, everything changed. Being with you has changed something in me. Whenever I think about you, the world feels new in a way I can't describe. You amaze me all the time, and I want to be near you. I came to destroy you, but instead I found everything I needed."

"But Jack, you *blackmailed* me."

"I know. I've never been in a situation where I give a shit. I didn't know what to do, so I reverted to what I know best because, like I said, I'm...not a good person who does the right thing."

"Oh my god, that's such a shitty excuse!"

"All I have are shitty excuses."

"I don't like shitty excuses. I don't want them," she says.

"I'm shitty at introspection. I'm shitty at change and all that."

"Jack," she says. "That's not good enough. Do better."

My heart pounds in my ears, and all I know is that I'm falling for her, and I always was falling for her.

Thirty-Five

JADA

HE COMES to me and presses his forehead to mine. He's a large beast. A wounded beast. Shitty at introspection. "I don't know how to do better," he says.

I groan. He's everything I never wanted in so many ways. Why do I want to kiss him so badly?

I grab his shirt, look him in the eye. "You should've told me."

"I know," he says. "I know, but—"

"You'd better not be about to say, 'But I'm not a good person!'"

He kisses the tip of my nose. "And you infuriate me and drive me crazy and make me want to do better."

I suck in a breath. I want to believe him. I want to trust him.

"I should've told you—I know that," he gusts out.

"Also, hello, you're the freaking owner of this company! How could you stand by when you see how horribly it's being run? And poor Lacey—she needs to go down to part-time. You know how serious her fatigue is. And Bert...how could you let any of this stand?"

"I know. It's complicated," he says.

"But you're the owner!"

"I'm the owner, but I don't seem to have control of the operations here. I might not even be able to fire Bert."

"How can that be? He's making life miserable for us and trashing our best projects."

"Trashing the company is the task he was hired to do."

"I don't get it," I say.

"I had my guy look into firing Bert after our visit to the shoe store, and it turns out that my parents had some sort of conflict with the couple who owned this place. It looks like my mom and dad bought SportyGoCo specifically to wreck it. Not just shut it down, but run it into the ground—the reputation, the people."

This wave of gratitude fills me. He was trying to fire Bert? He was fighting for us? And then I'm overcome with anger because... "They'd buy a company just to wreck it?"

"Definitely. They worked with a company called Bloxburn to do that sort of thing—Bloxburn is their bully company. Bloxburn installed Bert. For the record, Bert has no idea who I am. He could fire me, too. The contract gives Bloxburn a lot of power."

"But you own the place! Tell them the plan is off."

"It won't work. There's a contract, and Bloxburn's owners don't want to end it. I've got lawyers on it, but my parents gave Bloxburn a lot of control."

Rage heats my face. What kind of people buy a thing just to kill it?

"There's nothing you can do?"

"My people are still looking into it, but it doesn't look good. Bloxburn signed a contract that they'd destroy SportyGoCo, and as long as they're doing it, I can't get out of it. The only way I could break this contract is if SportyGoCo ends this accounting period profitable. But Dave says we're so far down in the red, there's no way."

"Right. Thanks to the Target yoga pants debacle and all of the other projects Bert ruined," I say. "No wonder that asshole's making us put luxury zippers on Wonderbag. Nobody can afford it, and that's how he wants it."

"I even looked into personally ordering inventory, but that won't work."

Gratitude surges through me. "Really?"

"Of course. But my people tell me that it would be considered a form of fraud."

I sigh. "So if we don't get tons of orders in the next few weeks, we're done."

"I'm exploring more options."

I grip the railing, feeling like my world is upside-down. "I've been working my ass off for a company that's already dead and kissing an office gopher who isn't who he says he is." I narrow my eyes at him, half playful, half not. "You should've told me."

"I'm sorry," he says.

I frown and turn away. At least he didn't say he's a bad person, but it's not enough. I want more. I like him so much, yet I know nothing about him. Am I an idiot?

I whirl around. "Tell me something real about yourself. Like really real."

"Like what? Like the way I feel about you—"

"No." I press my fingers to his lips. "Something real about yourself."

"I don't know what that would be."

"Well, how am I supposed to know? How about this—I want you to show me your home. I want to see where you live and who you really are when you're not at work," I say.

"Who I am? You won't get that from where I'm living. There's nothing of me there, nothing to see. It's a place I lived in years ago."

"But you're living there now."

"There's no point."

"So you won't show it to me?"

"There's no point."

"This isn't open for debate," I say. "We will go to your home, and you'll show me where you live."

Jack relents, so after work, we bundle up and head out into the chilly autumn evening: Jack in his overcoat with his blue knit hat, and me in my long, black puffer jacket. The car that picks us up after work looks like the limo Arnold drove up in, and it's super luxurious inside.

"I've never ridden in one of these."

"It's just another car."

"Just another car," I snort. "This old thing?" I open the minifridge, stocked with booze, soda, and candy. "I'm guessing you don't have to pay for these like at a hotel."

"Go for it," he says.

I grab a mini-Almond Joy. "So is Arnold a billionaire, too?"

"He's my assistant," Jack says. "Valet. Head of household."

"Wow," I say. "But why would he order you that fancy lunch service? And then the next day he sends you with a vending machine sandwich?"

"Well, uh, those things weren't his fault," Jack says. "They were requests of mine. Demands, you might say."

"Demands? You?"

I enjoy my candy bar while Jack tells me how the Papaggio lunch happened, and how he took a picture of my sandwich and instructed Arnold to get exactly that sandwich. I'm just laughing, and then he's laughing too. His laugh is friendly and warm and makes me happy all over. How did I never hear him laugh before? I'm trying not to stare too hard or grin too hard lest I chase that laugh back into its cave.

I also take this opportunity to tease him about not knowing his own freaking shoe size.

I'm having fun with this guy. But can I really trust him? He's an international billionaire who will probably flit off to his yacht next week. Isn't that what they do? I'm going to see where he lives, though. It's a start.

I make us drive by the building where I live so I can point it out. I tell him how the building almost got knocked down, but then my friend Noelle posed as the developer's court-ordered emotional IQ coach and made this poor guy watch hours upon hours of footage I'd filmed for this commemorative video project I'd gotten into. "It was hours of people who live there talking about the most minute nonsense," I say. "Footage of painting parties. Tours of potted plants."

"Potted plants? This worked?" Jack asks.

"It was hilarious," I say. "Even more if you know the guy—Malcolm's this total alphahole and Noelle's the shyest person ever." I tell him about my other friends there and some of the goofy things they've done.

Twenty minutes later, the car stops in front of a massive white-stone building with four stories of windows as big as doors. There's stone scrollwork all around them.

"Home sweet home," he says. The driver comes around and lets us out.

"You live here? It looks like the public library," I say.

"Yes, it's a bit much."

"Oh, yes, how tedious. A bit much. A tedious architectural gem!" I poke him in the arm. "Which floor is yours? Let me guess—the top."

"Well...all of them."

"Get out!" I say. "So is it as beautiful on the inside as it is on the outside?"

"It's ostentatious. Like Christie's auction house exploded all over the place." He turns around to face me. "There are better places for us to go."

"You heard my terms."

We get out and climb the very library-like steps. Just the entryway is as large as my studio apartment, with exquisite seating where you can hang your coat and exchange your boots for the plushest slippers ever created by humankind. We shuffle into a mind-blowingly elegant living room. He refers to it as "the parlor and dining room floor."

"Okay, then." I walk around, stunned. Some of the furnishings are so exquisite, it seems like they should be in a museum. The chairs probably have names like King Louis the Fifth. The art is real. The massive fireplace is carved marble.

Jack stands there watching me with his hands in his pockets.

"What does it feel like to live here?" I ask, spinning around.

"I don't live here. This floor is just for guests. Below are staff apartments and the kitchen."

"You know what I mean."

Jack looks around. "Like one of those birds that makes a home in other birds' nests."

I slide my hand along the gold-and-green-patterned velvet of a vintage couch with gold lions-paw feet. "I may not know furniture, but I know fabric. This is silk velvet."

"If you say so," he says.

"I do say so, mister." I sit down and rub my hands all over it. "This might be the most beautiful couch I've ever seen outside of a museum." I lean sideways on it and let my cheek slide against the back of it so that I can feel the fabric more. I close my eyes. "Mmmm. This fabric is just...everything."

"*Everything* might be a stretch."

"So blasé," I whisper.

When I look back up, Jack is standing there, still wearing that blue hat, watching me with a hungry intensity that warms my belly and my cockles and a few other places.

I make him give me the full tour. The upper three floors seem to be where he actually lives, with bedrooms and comfier areas to sit and yet another kitchen. The top floor, which used to be the ballroom, is a large workout studio and library that opens onto a massive patio. It's glorious.

We end up on the third floor in a more relaxed living room area, more *Architectural Digest* than Parisian museum. Jack still says he feels like a bird in somebody else's nest, even up here.

He tosses his glasses and hat onto a delicious boucle chair that probably cost more than an RV, mumbles something about Arnold being out doing the marketing with the housekeeper, and fetches me a ginger ale, my favorite vending machine drink.

"Thanks," I say.

He wanders off again.

I go around looking at stuff and shamelessly touching everything. There's a truckload of art, including a large version of the photo that I saw on my google scroll hanging over the dining room table with its own light sources beaming onto it. Jack as a little boy with his two parents standing together in front of some kind of castle-looking mansion.

When Jack returns, I nearly fall over in shock. He's wearing jeans and a tight, sexy black T-shirt. His hair is combed back, and his mole is gone. I've seen pictures of him looking like his normal self, but I was unprepared for how good he looks when he's not trying to look like a dork. He's so sexy, it hurts my retinas.

I grab my drink and wander over to the famous photograph. "This is you," I say. "Are those your parents?"

"Yeah," he says.

"And that's another one of your homes?" I ask.

"Türenbourg." He studies the photo with a flinty gaze. "We lived there for a good while."

"So where do you really live? If not here or there?"

"Lots of different places."

"Like where? What's your home base?" I ask. Most men I date, you can't get them to shut up about themselves, but Jack is so intensely private. Even now that he's been busted.

He lists off a lot of places. A London apartment. A Paris residence. A small place in Baku. "I meant it when I said I didn't have a home."

"How can none of them be home?" I wonder.

"Home is a different concept when you're me. It's more about convenience and facilitation than anything about roots."

"Did you pick any of them out yourself?"

"Some of them were picked by people who I picked."

"Oh my god, that is such a rich guy thing to say. Also? Totally doesn't count!"

It's as if he doesn't want to lay claim to anything at all. I look back up at the famous picture of him with his parents. "Your side dimple is missing," I say.

Thirty-Six

Jaxon

"My side dimple?"

She's looking up at the famous photo, so beloved by my parents and aficionados of Danbery's late-period photography. When I arrived here, I requested that it be taken down. It's only still up because apparently there's an art installer who needs to get involved when art is rotated. That would be a rich-guy thing to say, too.

"Usually when you smile, you get this cute side dimple." She points at the photo. "You don't have it there."

A dimple? I'd never noticed that before, but it's not as if I smile at myself in the mirror.

"Zero dimples. That's how I can tell it's your fake smile. One of the ways."

Of all the people who looked at the photo, nobody ever noticed my smile was fake. Forced. People bought it, hook, line, and sinker; except for the people who were there that day, of course. Like Jenny.

I study Jada's pert nose in profile as she studies the photo. She sees beyond the obvious with an alarming level of clarity. She cares deeply about things, and she wants other people to care, too. What she brings is rich. What does a man do to deserve a woman like this?

"So fake." She turns to me. She senses more to the story. I want to give her more, but I don't know how. I'm not a man who tells sad-little-rich-boy stories.

"You're absolutely right," I say. "About the fakeness."

She rambles around the room in her Jada way, stroking the different fabrics, letting her fingers glide lightly over random shiny objects, looking impossibly gorgeous, even with her disheveled bun that still has a pencil in it.

"What's your favorite thing in this place?" she asks. "And don't say they're not your things. Because I know they are."

I groan.

She turns to me, her hands on her hips, all grit and spirit in a tiny package. "The alarms are going off. You have one minute to get out. What thing do you save? And you can't say any electronics or a person or somebody else's stuff. You grew up here. Surely there is one thing here you'd want to save."

Of course she wants something real; it's why she's here. I want to give that to her, but what *would* I save?

I'm thinking about the cards from Jenny, but I wouldn't save those—there's just sadness in those cards. I'd help save something of Arnold's, I suppose, but she'd never allow that as an answer.

I look at the inlaid armoire I used to hide in as a boy. The Faberge egg I used to play with. All the paintings I'd stare at, outlines to trace, faraway worlds to imagine myself escaping to. I cared about those things once, but little by little, I learned that if you don't give a shit about people and things, nothing can touch you. It was a kind of safety, and also a massive "fuck you."

My gaze falls on the hat that she and Lacey and Shondrella and whoever else made for me. Aside from my phone, that's the thing I'd save. God, how pathetic is that?

She's waiting. Hopeful. She raises her brows.

I imagine saying it, forcing my lips to form the words—*I'd save the hat that you guys made for me. It means something to me that you made it.*

But I can't say it.

She wouldn't believe me, but that's not why I don't tell her. I don't tell her because telling her feels like telling her too much. It feels like giving her a thread that unravels the whole sweater.

I'm not ready to be unraveled. I'm not so sure there's anything underneath.

I go to her. "They're just things to me." I hear myself say it with a queasy feeling. She knows I'm bullshitting her—I see it in her eyes.

Even worse, I see when she decides to give up on her pursuit of learning something real about me. She's writing me off in her mind—*there is a limit to this man. This is as far as he goes. This is as deep as he goes.*

It feels like acid in my stomach.

"I'll be selling most of the stuff through auction houses," I add.

She goes to the couch and lowers herself down. She's back to admiring the fabric. "This is old and beautiful. You can feel the quality." She runs her hand over it, then leans down and rubs her cheek against it.

"Again with the cheek," I tease.

"That's where the most nerves are," she says. "Well, aside from the hands, but hands can be calloused, whereas cheeks..."

"I thought the most nerves were somewhere else."

She gives me a witchy smile and presses her cheek to another part of the couch. "Nope." She closes her eyes and her face softens with pleasure, just like it did when we were double-parked, when I got her off.

That fucking look—I haven't stopped thinking about it ever since. And here it is again. This strange rush of pleasure fills me. It's such an alien sensation, taking pleasure in somebody else's pleasure, but the way I feel now, I could make a life's goal out of giving her things and watching her enjoy them. It's as if her pleasure has awakened a craving.

She switches to her other cheek and my breath catches in my throat. It's as if she's quietly anchoring herself in this place, laying claim to it, even.

Jada would find things to save.

The urge to go to her is fierce. My cock strains. My palms itch to touch her. I want to consume her in every way—it's an urge so primal, it's a struggle to stay rooted where I am. Sex was always a cool calculation with me, but standing here, I'm feeling positively Neanderthal.

She picks up a quilt that's draped over the back of it and stands up, holding it up, inspecting it. "This pattern. So pretty. Moroccan?" She rolls her eyes. "As if you would know. Why am I even asking?" This, too, she rubs on her cheek.

I can't stand it anymore.

I go to her, wrapping the quilt around her and holding it tight.

Her eyes sparkle. We're face to face. I take an end of the quilt and rub it along her face. This is how she takes in fabric—through the cheek.

She closes her eyes, all pleasure.

I let the quilt go and stroke her cheek with the backs of my fingers, then I stroke along her hairline.

She opens her eyes, slyly gazing up at me.

"What are you thinking right now?" My palm glides over her skin. My other hand traces the curve of her hip. I'm eating her up with my hands, down her thigh and up her sexy ass, pressing my cock into her curves through the fabric.

She whispers, "There's no way that I could ever pay rent in this beautiful place."

I scowl. *Rent?* What?

"I don't have the money," she says. "I have nothing to pay with."

My heart skips a beat. The game. She loves that game. And this is what we do, now, isn't it?

She gazes at the floor, shy and demure, then looks back up. She's getting into her part.

I don't want to be acting out roles. I want to be us.

"I'm not playing right now." I pull her close, pressing kisses along the line of her jaw.

Her breath quickens. She's still cocooned in that fabric, trapped in there, right on the sweet side of edgy.

"I just can't get enough of you," I whisper.

"What are you suggesting, sir?" She pulls back, regarding me with an innocent expression.

Sex has always been about release for me—the more impersonal, the better. Just two people who want to fuck. No questions, no emotions, no games—unless it's the kind where you're playing a role.

God, how ironic. The one woman I'm desperate to know everything about, the one woman I want to be real with, and she wants us to play sexcapade roles. It's my own fault. I started this thing. But I don't want Jada to be an impoverished tenant or a woman willing to trade her body to keep Forty-fifth Street clear of double-parkers.

I want to be with Jada and only Jada. I want her to do Jada things. And I want her to be with *me*—not a landlord or a horny blackmailer—but me, Jaxon.

I may be shit at revealing my innermost self, but I still want it to be me she's with.

She mumbles something more about the rent.

"We're not doing that." I grab hold of her bun and tip her head sideways exposing her neck. I plant a kiss on her neck. "I'm not playing right now. I want us to be real." It's a confession, the best I can make, being that I'm not the confessing kind.

She makes a humming sound. She's warm and soft against me. My hand trails down her belly through the quilt and pushes between her legs. I fumble for the general location of her clit through the fabric.

"Nothing I can give you?" she gasps.

My heart sinks. Serves me right. Why would she want to be real with me when I won't even tell her what I'd save in a fire?

I imagine myself telling her. *The hat,* I'd say. Two words, two syllables. I could expand on it—*I'd save the hat.*

Four simple syllables to show how empty I am.

She's worked her arm out of the quilt down there. She grazes my cock through the fabric of my pants, and just that much contact nearly makes me come. It's about so much more than her touch—it's about the way she's going after what she wants, the way she appreciates beauty, and how she moves so fluidly from stern to playful. It's about the way she says *hmm* to herself as she explores the contours of my cock, as though she's pleased with what she's finding.

Then she grabs it hard.

And suddenly I can't resist any longer. My cock will happily play the game. My cock doesn't give a shit if the game is ten ways of messed up. I push her to the wall and pull the fabric off her, unwrapping her like a candy. "The rent here is exorbitant," I growl.

Her eyes gleam.

This is what I have now—this pleasure of hers. I'll take it.

"How exorbitant?" she asks.

"You'll have to give a lot."

"I don't have a lot," she says, arching into me.

"You'll give me a lot," I say in the harsh tone she wants. "And then you'll give more." I slide a finger down the side of her face. "And I'll do excruciating things."

She squeaks, "Please. Take pity on me."

"Pity," I growl, "is the only thing I won't take."

She takes in a ragged breath.

I hoist her up, carry her across the place to my bedroom, and throw her down on the bed. I back up in the dim light, kicking the door closed behind me. "Off. All of it."

"All of it? This is my price?" She's on her knees, unbuttoning her blouse. She's acting shy about it, hands clumsy.

There's a dim part of me that still knows better—knows that this can't be how we fuck for the first time.

But she's peeling off her shirt and her bra. Her breasts are fucking stunning—and I'm mindless with lust. I'm across the room in a flash, clumsily tearing at the rest of her clothes.

I'm not playing, but she doesn't need to know that. I pull up her skirt, right up to her waist, because she wants it a little bit dirty. That's the game, and I'll give her what she wants.

Her eyes light with shock as I push her back down on the bed. I reach down between her thighs and take the crotch of her panties in my fist, knuckles grazing her sex.

She's breaking character, laughing. "Oh my god, not again!"

I force myself not to smile; I rip apart her panties like I did in the truck.

"Erp!" she exclaims, but then she finds my cock. "It's so huge. Too big. Not this, sir."

There's a response I should probably make, but I'm lost in the scent of her skin. She's totally naked now except the skirt. I pull my shirt off.

She reaches up and grabs the belt of my trousers and pulls me close. I push into her a little, pants pressing up against her silken folds. She seems to like it, so I go a little harder.

She threads her fingers through my hair.

I kiss her, doing her with my thigh while we make out. It's a little bit dirty and wrong that I still have my pants on, but that's the game. I'm the landlord with bad intentions. I move down her body, kissing my way down. I close my teeth over her nipple—just lightly. She sucks in a sharp breath. I lick her nipple and then her other nipple, and then I do the teeth thing.

I can't believe how soft she is.

She groans with pleasure, fumbling faster with my belt. I love her sounds.

I rise up on my knees and shove her legs apart. "Do your nipples," I say.

"What?" she gasps.

I grab her hands and put them on her nipples. "Squeeze them. Do them nice and hard."

She complies. I take a good look at the hotness that is her pleasuring herself, my cock straining against the confining layer of my pants, and then I give her pussy a long, ruthless lick.

She cries out.

I grip her thighs with iron force and lick her mind-blowingly delicious core, growling into her sex like a maniac, which she probably thinks I'm doing for effect when it's actually pure primal hunger. I've never been hungry for a woman like this, never had this urge to claim a woman like this.

Eventually she's writhing under my grip. She's so sexy, I can't stand it. I begin to finger her while I lick her.

"Yes," she breathes.

"You're going to come for me," I growl, "and then you're gonna come again when I fuck you, and after that I'm gonna fuck another orgasm right out of you. I'll take as many as I please, do you understand?"

"That many, huhhh..."

"That many and more."

Her protests turn nonsensical as I zero in on her quivering center. She cries out, coming exuberantly. I consume her to the last drop, and then I kiss her mound, which is covered with perfectly trimmed wisps of damp blonde hair. I undo her skirt and get it off of her.

Her perfectly rounded belly shudders as she pants. I kiss it and slide my hand over it; I'm iron-hard, knowing that I made her come so hard, she can barely catch her breath.

"I love this right here," I say, sliding my palm over her belly.

She grabs my hand. "Come here."

I crawl over her, and she goes back for my belt. I let her undo it. I stand by the bed and pull my trousers all the way off, enjoying her pleased sound when my cock springs free.

She kisses the side of it. A small, gentle kiss. It nearly kills me, just that kiss.

I grab a condom from the drawer. "See this?" I say, holding the little square packet aloft as I loom over her.

"Yes," she says breathlessly. She wants me to say more dirty shit, and I will, because we're this far now, and I want to make it good for her.

"This is the condom I'm going to use to fuck your rent right out of you."

"Is that so," she says, a little bit sassy.

I sit next to her. "Grab onto the headboard."

She grabs onto the wooden slats above her. I set the foil corner on to her tender belly and draw it lightly along her skin. Her whole body shivers at the slight bite of it.

"Close your eyes," I say. "What am I writing?"

I make a J, then an A, and of course she gets it right away.

"Jack."

"That's right, because I own you right now." I finish my name, then I loom over her and let her watch me put the condom on. I'm hard as iron, and she's definitely ready to go again. I crawl over her. "You're going to take me all the way in," I say in a low, rumbly voice. "You are going to let me fuck you nice and hard. This is how you are going to earn your keep." I give the side of her breast a light slap. Her eyes widen, and it makes me think that no one has ever done that before. "You understand?"

"Yes," she pants.

I position myself at her entrance and then I take her wrists and pin them over her head, watching her face as I enter her. She closes her eyes, but I'm watching her. She may be fucking a filthy landlord, but I'm fucking Jada Herberger. I'm right here with her.

We get up a rhythm like we've been fucking for years—it's that natural between us.

Eventually I let her arms go. She's exploring my body, seeming to marvel at my muscles, which stokes me ridiculously high.

I change my angle, speeding up.

She comes with a cry just as I come with a white-hot blast of lightning that melts my brain.

~

JADA TURNS OVER, lids heavy. Sated. "That was...oh my god."

I slide a finger along her cheek. Her skin glows in the moonlight. She smiles, happy. I smile back. It's my fake smile, but she won't notice up close like this. She won't notice I'm broken open.

Is this what it feels like to be with somebody you actually care about? It's messing me up. She's the only thing in the world that I want now. I should probably send her home.

"It's like we have a secret together," she says. "This whole secret world that nobody would ever guess."

She means the game.

"Stay for dinner," I say.

"Is that what that noise is downstairs?"

"Arnold and the chef. Will you stay?" I grab my phone and check the menu. "Grilled salmon and veggies and couscous with a ton of sides." I show her.

"Jesus," she says. "And there would be enough?"

"Please," I say.

"Wow, okay," she says.

I text down to add a guest and then I text Soto for an update and toss the phone aside. "Come here," I say, leading her into the bathroom.

"What the hell!"

I start up the jets and let the tub fill while she explores the place. She runs her hand over the mosaic countertop. Everything here is inlaid with tiny tiles—arranged to replicate the Turkish bath experience or something like that. She pokes her head into the nook full of plants under a massive skylight. She peeks into both the steam room and the sauna.

"You want a glass of wine before dinner?" I ask.

"You don't need to trouble anybody."

"It's right here. White, red, or bubbly?"

"What, you have a wine cellar in your bathroom?"

"I wouldn't call it a cellar," I say, opening the door to the temperature-controlled cabinet.

"Oh my god, seriously?"

I pour us each a nice Bordeaux and we get into the tub.

Jada slides her foot along my leg, grinning. "This bathroom isn't over the top," she teases. "No, no, not at all." She gives me shit for a while. People never give me shit, but I don't mind it with her. We're in each other's corner.

"The wealthy will pay anything for luxury shit they don't need," I say.

"I guess!" She lies back and closes her eyes, and I watch her perfect breasts. In size, they're more soup bowl than coffee mug, and her wide, pink nipples are very Jada in attitude—energetic and cocky and punching above their weight. But they're relaxing now in the water, just like she is.

She swishes her feet and makes a contented noise—not her sexy "hmm" this time; this noise is more of a happy "nngh."

Her contentment does something to my chest. I don't want to stop giving her things. I want to keep her here and spoil her and watch her pleasure and never let it end.

"You meant it when you said your hobby was driving," she says. "Do you want to go back? Will they let you?"

"I'm too old," I say. "I can still work out on tracks and race in lesser organizations, though."

"You're like thirty-six, right?"

"Yup. Too old to jump back into the big leagues. Not that they'd let me."

"Did you like it?"

"So much." Before I know it, I've got my iPad. I play a clip of Baku from ten years ago, and then Azerbaijan, and then the fight. People thought the punch was me being the worst guy ever, and I was happy to let them think it; sometimes I'd even laugh about it. I got a lot of mileage out of doing impersonations of people's self-righteous commentary on yachts that winter.

But now I wish I hadn't let people think the worst. Because I don't want her to think it. And suddenly I'm telling her the real story. The behind-the-scenes story that only my pit crew guys know, how the golden boy I'd punched had sabotaged my pit operation, endangering my guys. The proof we found had conveniently disappeared, and people were quick to assume I was lying.

She believes me, and it means a lot.

Suddenly I care what she thinks. I care about the SportyGoCo crew. I even care about knit hats and a dead cactus.

She's staring at the bathroom wine cabinet. "Rich people will pay anything for luxury shit they don't need," she mumbles.

"It's so true."

"I just got an idea," she says, "and it's pretty wild."

"What is it?" I ask.

"So, there are certain cost parameters we need to stay within in order to make our products viable for the big box stores and discounters that we work with. If it's too expensive for our customers, it doesn't matter if it's the coolest thing ever."

"Wait, are you talking work right now?" I say. "We are enjoying a post-fuck soak with fine wine and you're talking about work?"

"Yeah! Keep up!" She grins. "Okay, so it doesn't matter how cool Unicorn Wonderbag is, because Bert is making us use a luxury zipper, right?"

I nod, loving how her eyes light up when she gets a new idea for Unicorn Wonderbag.

"Our customers can't afford it. We need a shit ton of signed purchase orders in the next two weeks to break the contract with Bert's overlords, and Wonderbag was our last hope."

"Correct," I say.

"We can't get those orders from our regular customers—fashion big box and discount mall brands. They can't do expensive. But what if we made the bag wildly expensive and went after a different customer?"

"I already looked into making the orders myself," I say. "It has to be legit retail."

"No, but that's what I mean. The rich will buy luxury shit they don't need. We could make Unicorn Wonderbag into a luxury bag and sell it high-end."

"But don't you need to be a luxury brand?"

"Maybe we don't give a shit." She floats over and puts her chin on my shoulder. "We're blazing a new brand pathway. Also, maybe somebody we know has connections to a different class of stores. A higher end on the retail spectrum." She's gazing at me, so full of trust and hope, it kills me.

"You think there are luxury shops out there wanting to do things for me?"

"Maybe?"

"Disregarding the fact that I never shop, do you think anybody out there wants to do anything with me? I'm the last person somebody would want to help or partner with."

"I bet that's not true. It's not true for me. It's not true for all the people at work. And you know that world, right? Surely you have one contact."

"I have a lot of contacts. They all hate me."

She sighs.

I get out of the tub.

I dry off and button my shirt, staring at the wall full of squares and triangles in different shades of blue, racking my brain for another solution. Because god, that look of trust. It's going to turn to devastation when her beloved company and beloved family gets disbanded.

I'm a billionaire and I can't save this one company that I *literally own* due to this vindictive contract my parents created. One last nasty move from the grave. And this move is hurting the woman I'm falling for.

It's enraging. Intolerable. I'd burn the world if it made a difference. But it wouldn't.

When did her happiness and her pleasure become so critically important to me? Is this how a relationship feels? What the hell happens if the other person is hurt or in trouble, and you can't help them? How do people do this?

I throw her a towel to dry off, trying to come up with something. And then it occurs to me. "Hey," I say.

"Yeah?"

"I have an idea."

Her eyes gleam with pleasure and it's everything. "What?"

"Let's start a new company. Just leave SportyGoCo behind and make something we like better."

"What?"

"Remake SportyGoCo. Inside a new company."

"You mean cut and run?"

"No! We take everything that's good about it and move it into a new company. A better office space, better management, better neighborhood."

"But it wouldn't be SportyGoCo."

"It would be similar, though," I argue. "We'd make an offer for the current employees to come over. Create great bonus packages."

"But a lot of us have contracts that won't let us work for competitors," she says.

"We'd get around the contracts."

I outline my ideas. She protests that people won't want to do a longer commute, that we'd have to build a new brand with new designs.

"But even more, it would be a different neighborhood, different neighbors, all of our little routines would be gone. It wouldn't have the heart. Our traditions. The things that make it a family would be gone."

"You don't know that."

"I do know." She heads back into the bedroom and starts dressing. "I know you're trying to help—and I do appreciate it—but it wouldn't work."

I follow her, frustrated, pulling on my shirt. "There'd be different things to love."

"It wouldn't be our family."

"Maybe it would be a better family with new people to love." Why won't she let me help her?

She grabs her phone. "You don't upgrade your family like it's a rental car."

"If the car's broken down at the side of the road, you do."

"It's not broken, though. And it's worth fighting for. The SportyGoCo family is worth fighting for."

"Is it, though?"

She stiffens. "I can't believe you just said that! Do you not think it's worth fighting for?"

"I think it's not worth the extreme amount of pain you could be in for when you could simply build something else."

"Simply build something else," she echoes.

"Yes!"

"Jettison my *family*." She pulls on her socks with angry force.

"They're not your family, though—they're paid to be there."

"Seriously? Did you actually just say that?"

This cold feeling goes over me. I shouldn't have said that. But it's true, isn't it? It's factually true.

"Be honest," I say. "Would you know any of them if they weren't paid to be there? There's a difference between people who are paid to be around you and those who are around you because they want to be."

Her gaze blazes hot. I realize only too late that I've gone full idiot.

Her voice sounds gravelly for once. "Maybe my people didn't start out as my family, but they're family now. And maybe you don't think they're worth fighting for, but I *know* they are."

"You need to see that it could be a lost cause." At this point, I'm basically just trying to get her to understand why I said the other stupid things I said, but I'm just adding to the stupid.

"I don't need to see anything." She fastens her skirt. "You go ahead and think it's a lost cause. I never will."

"Some causes are lost."

"And some causes are worth fighting for. All the way to the end. That's what you need to see."

"But some aren't," I say.

"Oh my god. I can't do this if that's your attitude." She heads out the door, down through the day room.

"Jada—"

She stops. Spins. "I don't care if a man is rich or poor, or if he has a mole or weird glasses or is the hottest thing ever. I care if a man believes in things and if he's willing to fight for them. I care if a man gives a shit enough to save a few items from a fire instead of letting it all burn."

With that, she's heading down the stairs, one flight then another.

I follow her.

Arnold is standing at the first-floor landing, looking bewildered.

"Excuse me, Arnold," she says, heading into the entryway. She's putting on her coat, her boots.

"Jada, let's figure this out. Let me help."

"I don't like your help. I hate your help." She puts up her hands. "Let me be. I just want to leave."

With that, she's out the door.

"Sir?" Arnold looks at me quizzically.

"Put her in the car," I say to him. "Make sure Stanley sees her safely home."

I watch Arnold go out after her. She'll let Arnold help her. She doesn't like my help.

I flatten my hand against the cold windowpane.

I need to get out of here. Maybe I could go back to motorsport. Not F-1, but the British Racing & Sports Car Club has something coming up. There are interesting races on the horizon in Australia.

The car comes around. Arnold points to it. He opens the door for her, and she gets in. There's a biting wind out there, and the car will feel warm and nice. She'll go back to SportyGoCo tomorrow. Back to that family of hers. They'll all go down with the ship together, refusing lifeboats like fools.

I watch the taillights disappear.

Arnold comes back, looking doleful. "I'm sorry, sir," he says.

"Nothing to be done," I say.

"Whatever it is, you can't talk to her? Apologize? You like her. I saw it in the park that day. She likes you."

"Liked."

"Oh, come now. You have immense persuasive powers. Talk to her."

"I don't have persuasive powers. I have people who are scared of me. There's a difference. I have people who are wary of what I might do. People who are inspired to do things out of how much they despise me."

"Not everybody despises you. Not the people who know you," he says.

Past me would've made a quip like, *Sounds like I need to work harder at my asshole skills* or some shit.

Current me regards Arnold warmly. This man with his keen eyes and thick shock of white hair who's always been a steady, fair presence.

"Thank you for saying that," I say.

Thirty-Seven

Jaxon

I step off the elevators the next morning nice and early, ready to work. Today's shirt is black with white triangles and lots of neon-pink dots.

The office is nearly empty, though Varsha is there, poised and proper, concentrating on looking at my nose instead of my mole. "How was your night?"

"I made it through," I say. "And I haven't been consumed from the face inward by the carnivorous plague yet, so that's good news."

"Oh! Umm..."

"Like a Venus flytrap, right on my cheek."

Her face is red. "It's not that bad."

"Voracious."

Frantically, she nudges her dish of saltwater taffies toward me.

I grin and take one and head back to my cubicle, passing by the accounting section. I rap on the top edge of Dave's cubicle. "Good morning," I say.

"Dude. Kill me now. Spreadsheet implosion." He holds up a finger. "Not my fault. I think Bert rebooted something."

I wince. "Can I do anything?"

"Thanks, man," he says surprised. "I don't think so, but...I'll let you know. A little wastepaper b-ball later..."

"You're on." I return to my station and busy myself with my spreadsheets, looking at the roster of deliveries and miscellaneous chores I need to do today.

People start to drift in.

I didn't plan to come in. For a long time last night, my mind spun on what to do next. What racetrack, what city, what residence. I spent time angry that Jada didn't want my help. Until I thought through a few things; I even did what I think people call introspection.

Renata arrives, complaining about having wet socks from a slush puddle that didn't look deep and was. She tells me she used to keep an extra pair of socks in her drawer, but she wore them, and she didn't re-up.

A pair of socks sails through the air. Shondrella pops her head up from her cubicle like a groundhog with skunk hair. She smiles and pops back down.

"That works!" Renata whispers. She's on her phone, probably texting her thanks to Shondrella.

"Jack?"

I look up. It's Jada. "Good morning," I say.

She blinks, standing in front of my cubicle. "What are you doing here?"

"I have deliveries to do. The inventory system is still a mess. Dave may need a mental health break from his spreadsheet implosion—ten minutes of wastepaper b-ball, at least. Varsha's gopher list items aren't gonna cross themselves out."

She narrows her eyes. "You know what I mean."

"Look..." I lower my voice. "Last night you said you didn't like my help. You were right—my help sucked. You don't want a replacement family; you want this one. I get it—this family's a good one. We're gonna have to turn this orders situation around."

"What about the whole lost-cause thing?"

"I don't love it," I say. "Not a fan."

"You hate that it's a lost cause, but you still came to help."

Needed—I needed to come fight by her side, all of their sides, with their sad sandwiches and ugly knit hats and dead plants and cookies.

She smiles. It does things to me.

"Also, the idea of leaving you all to your own devices, pathetically trying to rescue this place, it was too—"

"Thank you."

"What's more, there's still that spectacular last demerit on the table. A nice, well-placed left hook? Take a certain somebody out for a little while?"

"Don't! You'll be fired or go to jail. You'll be sent back to Europe. And we really do need you," she says. "Plus, brute force. So idiotic."

"Is that a no?"

"Shut it." She sets her chin on the edge of my cubicle. "I'm glad you're here."

"Me, too."

She gets a playful gleam in her eyes. "Okay, then. And FYI, I'm not gonna say anything about you-know-what. It's your thing to reveal yourself. But just so you know, if you tell one person, everybody will find out."

"Appreciate it. And I don't know if this will work, but I have a new idea," I say.

She narrows her eyes. "It had better not rhyme with *parting a pew pompany.*"

"No! Look, here's the deal—you guys are always talking about getting influencers to wear your yoga stuff. I was thinking about Unicorn Wonderbag, the luxury idea you had."

"Yeah. I was looking into it, too. My friend Tabitha is gonna try to do something, but she's not officially retail herself. She is gonna try to talk to some retailers, though."

"This might help. There are these socialites I know in Europe. One is the princess of a nation state you've never heard of and the other is this duchess that does a lot of skydiving, and they're both named Genevieve. I looked them up last night to see if they have a social media following—"

"Wait, the two Genevieves? They're huge luxury influencers. Oh my god—are you friends with them?"

"Oh, no. They hate me."

Her face falls.

"With a passion," I say. "But I was talking to Arnold after you left, and he helped me remember that sometimes people who despise me are inspired to do things out of how much they despise me. And those two owe me a favor. I got them out of a jam one time—"

"You helped them?"

"Sort of. But it's more like I thought it would be funny for them to owe me a favor. And of course I never cashed in, because why would I when I have the delight of knowing they hate that I can dangle this favor over their heads?"

"What happened?"

"Just a compromising situation I got them out of, and they begged me to stay quiet about it. The point is, they owe me."

"Okay, but let me just say one thing here. If you never cash in on it, what's the difference between that and doing something out of the goodness of your heart?"

"Because it's different," I inform her. "Anyway, I'm thinking I could cash in on that favor. If you have a couple of those bags to overnight to them, I could make sure they carry them at the Monte Carlo Fash Bash."

Her eyes widen. "They would do that? Wait—the Fash Bash is this weekend."

"It would be a hell of a courier bill, but if we could get two bags on a plane by lunch, they could be delivered to their hotel by the time those sloths wake up."

She straightens. "They would *each* carry a Unicorn Wonderbag?"

"People hate being under my thumb."

She blinks, as though barely comprehending. "We'd have to upgrade the fabric. Get beautiful packaging."

"I thought you had prototypes ready."

"Oh my god, these are the two Genevieves! If we're making a luxury version of Wonderbag, a few things have to change."

There's a flurry of activity over the next two hours while the design team sources high-end fabric and sews new prototypes based on the original design. Shondrella and Varsha create gift boxes. Lacey works on the lining. They send out for custom, enamel-resin unicorn zipper pulls. They're all very excited about the zipper pulls.

A Bert alert goes through the office at around ten. They manage to hide the bags just as he storms into the office. He's got some angry words for Dave and the design accounting group, and then he checks in with Renata on something.

I watch Bert strut around. He could really ruin our plans. It's literally his job. He slows near Jada up at the design area.

I grit my teeth. The urge to get up and stand menacingly as a wall of support near Jada is nearly irresistible, but she doesn't want that. I have to respect her wishes to not do brute force things. I can be a hardworking man who lets things slide off his back.

He continues on to Shondrella, then Renata. He seems to be asking her questions.

I wince.

Jada melts back into her cubicle and slips the bags into her drawer. "Dammit," she whispers. "He might see the fabric buy."

But then he leaves. The relief is nearly palpable, so much so that I high-five Jada, and then Dave.

Shondrella brings over the boxes and packs them up.

"I don't understand how you could've even met the two Genevieves," Renata says. "Did you fix their car or something?" Nobody can believe the two Genevieves would owe Jack the office-gopher-slash-delivery-assistant a favor.

"State secret," I say.

"So chivalrous," Lacey says.

"You're going to have to pay cash or credit for the courier," Renata says. "It could be hundreds, but we'll pay you back."

"He'll figure it out," Jada says.

We take the boxes down to the truck. She sets one on the passenger seat and taps it. "Good luck."

"People are going to love them," I say.

"It's like getting a mention in *InStyle*." She turns to me. "Is this going to cost me?"

"Nope," I say. "I'm not playing that."

She frowns and toys with a button on my shirt. "Not even..." She looks up.

I kiss her. "I'll pick you up at seven."

Her face brightens. "Any hints on the dress code?"

"Where we're going, baby, it won't matter. You might as well go with something warm and practical."

She grins ear to ear. "If you insist."

Thirty-Eight

Jada

Jack pulls me close in the back of his limo. Lights flash by as we glide up Amsterdam near the park. It's a windy Friday night; fallen leaves and bits of trash swirl in eddies in building entryways and street corners, mirroring the motion of the butterflies in my belly.

"Where are we going?" I ask.

"You'll see," he says into my hair. His mole and dorky glasses are gone, and he's wearing the hat we made, which covers the bleached tips of his hair, rendering him 99% pure hotness.

It's funny that he thought he needed such an extreme disguise. Antonio says he can't walk around in any large European city without people recognizing him, but I really don't think he needs it in America.

He told me not to worry about what I'm wearing, which suggests I won't be wearing it for long. Will we be going to a romantic hotel? Maybe a sexy club where there will be full-blown costumes for us to wear?

I didn't see Jack much after he delivered the bags to the

airport. Shipping had him for the rest of the day, so I catch him up on our progress, letting him know that we cranked out two additional Wonderbag prototypes while pretending to work on yoga pants. We're still a long way from rescuing the company—a few social media influencer pictures won't sell bags—but it can get our foot in the door to buyers, and that's all we need. The orders.

We turn down a gloomy, tree-lined street and stop at some sort of park. There are empty basketball courts and a dimly lit area behind it that seems to have a kiosk and some trees. Not exactly the type of place where you'd expect a hotel or sex club.

"Soooo…" I say when we get out.

He hands me a large duffel bag sack that seems to be full of fabric and he grabs a picnic basket. Stanley speeds away.

I hoist the thing over my shoulder. "What's the plan?"

"You'll see." Jack leads me down a path behind a basketball court into a pocket park featuring a trio of horseback-riding statues. The main statue rises up from a massive stone slab the size of a small car. A pair of smaller horseback riders trail behind the main rider on either side like a jet-fighter formation of old statues. A few leaf-covered benches are arranged in front of the statues. The noise of jets and cars and horns is subdued here; I'm sure it's pretty in the summer.

"What is this place?"

"Gunther Creek pocket park," he says. "Come on."

He leads me around to the back, to a nook created by the three statues. He swipes his foot, clearing the leaves from the stone surface. He takes the bag from me and unfurls a few picnic blankets, putting one on top of the other, and then he sets out the basket.

"Are we having a fall picnic?" I ask.

"You'll see." He holds out his hand. "I'll show you where to sit."

"Okay." I let him guide me to a spot at the center and I sit down, cross-legged. As soon as I'm settled, I hear it—this gurgling river sound, almost like bells, along with pigeon cooing sounds.

"Whoa!" I whisper. "What is that?"

He grins. "You hear it?"

"Where's it coming from?"

He sits behind me and pulls off my hat and wraps his arms around me. "Turn your head to the right—really slow."

"This is getting kinkier by the second," I say. I turn my head slowly and that's when the volume cranks—like a symphony of gurgles and birds. "Whoa!" I turn my head back forward and it softens. "Where's it coming from?"

"The pigeons roost in that huge fir tree, and the creek has a bend up there—I don't know what it is about the shape, but it makes this bright sound. And the sounds echo off the statue base. Do you like it?"

"I love it. It's so pretty. And so weird. Like a strange duet. More than that. A symphony. Birds with a babbling brook."

"Pigeon cooing is your favorite sound, right?" he says.

"I love that you remembered." I turn in his arms. "How do you know about this place?"

"There's a school for boys a few blocks up that I went to for a while. I'd skip out and come here." He opens the picnic basket and hands me a thermos. "Hot cider," he says. "This insulated bag is full of pizza rolls stuffed with parmesan, sweet potato, and pesto."

"Excuse me? What is this pizza roll madness?"

He hands one to me. "Chef Ursula makes them."

"More wonders from the kitchen of the man who brought a vending machine sandwich to work." I bite into the crunchy, flakey shell and nearly keel over from the flavor explosion. "Dead," I whisper.

He grabs one and stretches out on his back.

"This is our mysterious and torrid date?" I say. "I have to listen to the prettiest secret sound ever while eating gourmet pizza rolls?"

"Don't tell anyone. You'll ruin my reputation."

I grab another and stretch out next to him. I make him tell me more about this place when he was a boy. What his life was like. He'd forgotten about it until I mentioned the pigeons.

I snuggle close. "I thought it was going to be something wild."

"I know," he says.

"It feels weird to do nothing but lie on the ground and listen to a sound together. Like I'm nowhere. Out of time. Is this what it feels like to be a tree?"

"You don't do much relaxing, do you?" he teases.

"No," I say.

"You want some more cider?"

"Yes, but I don't want to sit up," I say.

He tells me to open my mouth and he carefully dribbles some in. Some gets on my cheek. I'm laughing and almost choking. He blots it with a napkin and settles back down next to me.

It's sexy being under the blanket with him in this secret place, listening to the magical sounds.

After a while, I feel like I'm unwinding. Like something is unwinding in my head. I try to describe it to him, and he's just laughing. "Of all the ways I imagined corrupting you, relaxation was not even on the list."

I get on top of him and make him tell me what was on the list.

"Sex-addled debauchery," he whispers.

"Shut it." I press my finger to his sexy lips.

He takes hold of it and kisses my fingertip. "Do you want any grapes or cookies? I have those, too. All of them are foods that you can eat on your back."

"Sounds like the voice of experience."

"Well, you know me," he says. "A loserish and thoroughly decadent Lothario."

"Why do you do that?" I ask.

"What?"

"Why do you make yourself sound worse than you are? You're

the world's worst publicity agent for yourself. If you were my publicity agent, I'd fire you."

He turns me so I'm on my back again. He's leaning over me, feeding me grapes, and the sound is all around me, but all I can see is him. All I can feel is him. I can tell from his expression that he's thinking about my question. I want him to answer it for real. I want to know.

"Seriously, Jack, why not say, 'I've brought you to this amazing place and I thought of everything myself, because I rock.'"

"That's what I'd say if I were my best PR agent?"

"Yeah. Why not?"

He looks at me for a long time, during which he feeds me another grape, sitting up there, careful not to put too much weight on me.

I love the feel of him. I love this magical place with its strange, secret music featuring pigeon sounds. He slides a cool finger down my hot cheek. I think he won't answer my question, and then he says, "I don't know how it goes where I'm not the bad guy."

"Well, you brought me to this place because you thought I'd like it," I say.

He leans down and rumbles into my ear, "Maybe I wanted to feast on your pleasure like a demon."

"Fuck off." I'm trying not to smile, but he really is sexy when he's being like that. I won't encourage it, though—not right now. "Try again."

"I wanted to corrupt the shit out of you. You never relax and do stupid things, so I'm making you do a stupid thing so that I can watch you sink into a life of debauchery."

"Nope."

He twists a strand of my hair. He's quiet for a long time. "I want to give you things and make you happy because you're like nobody I've ever met."

My breath catches in my throat. "Okay."

"And you're beautiful and funny and a fucking warrior, and I can't look at you without thinking about touching you."

"Was that so hard?" I'm keeping it light. "That's how I feel, too. Looking at you."

He says, "And I want you in my bed tonight, but not as part of a transaction where you owe me things as part of some game. I want you to *want* to be there, as yourself. Because the more I get to know you, the more I care about you. And that's just a little bit terrifying, but I don't want it to stop. So I brought you to this amazing place and thought of everything...because I rock."

I snort. "You so rock." I look up at him in the moonlight. He thinks he's this closed-off villain, but he's honest and vulnerable and raw in his own weird way.

"And if anybody ever threatens you or makes you unhappy," he adds, "I'll punch their face off."

"I'll come over," I say.

Thirty-Nine

JAXON

HISTORICALLY, the transition from the place where you agree to fuck to the place where you do the fucking has always felt to me like an awkward holding pattern preceding the main event. And maybe you chat, but you'd just as soon be on your phones until you get inside the hotel room or wherever it is you're going.

With Jada, this transition could be the main event. Picking a leaf out of her hair could be the main event. Her grabbing my hand as we head down the sidewalk could be the main event. It's as good as it can get every moment we're together.

She sits on my lap in the back of the limo and shoves her hands up the sleeves of my overcoat. I grasp her forearms inside the sleeves of her coat, and that's how we ride.

We're under each other's clothes, but my heart is on the outside of my fucking sleeve. It's total high-wire-act shit. No net. No safety. Total danger. Total exhilaration. It might be the most foolhardy thing I've ever done, but I can't stop it now.

I push my arms deeper into her sleeves. Her eyes sparkle.

She's telling me about some echo place at some airport, and then she's giving me shit when I reveal to her that I never set foot inside of a commercial airport in my life. I make her tell me what they're like, and then she's laughing.

"What's so funny?" I demand.

"You never having been in an airport would be more proof to everybody that you're from some village straight out of *Hansel and Gretel*."

"People don't think that," I say.

"Why wouldn't they?" She ticks through the proof, from my lack of office skills to my refusal to drink from water fountains.

"So you're saying the mega-rich are nearly indistinguishable from medieval villagers?"

"You walked into a shoe store and thought somebody should *trace your foot.*"

I growl and tighten my hold on her. "I'll have you know that outlines of my foot are on file with the finest shoemakers in Milan."

"Whatever you say, Grey Poupon."

I kiss every kissable place on her face and neck and ear, finding the sensitive spots. I want to know everything about this woman. I'll never get tired of discovering things about her.

As soon as we arrive, I dismiss the staff for the night and pull her into the elevator.

"That wasn't suspicious," she says.

"Oh, it was very suspicious." I hit the button for the third floor and press her to the marble-paneled wall. "I'm planning on making you scream loud enough to rattle every piece of china in this whole place." I kiss her neck. "Maybe enough to break every bit of china."

She's panting. She likes that. Again with the pleasure.

"And maybe ruin a few priceless objects," I continue.

"Except the silk velvet."

I slide my hand between her legs. "No, I'm gonna make you come all over all the silk velvet."

"You can't," she gusts out.

"I can," I tell her with evil inflection. "On each and every piece. At least once."

The elevator doors slide open. I swoop her up into my arms and carry her to my bedroom. I undo her bun and start unbuttoning her shirt.

The moonlight streaming through the window makes her hair glow golden. She's a lush mirage, sitting in my bed. The cups of her red bra hug her pale, sexy tits snugly.

I kiss a nipple through the satiny fabric. She shudders out a breath.

"You, too," she says, tugging at my sweater.

"You think you get to say how this goes?" I taunt.

"You're not my evil landlord anymore, are you? Careful what you wish for." She takes off her bra with a flourish and throws it—a little striptease like she knows how desperate I am to have her and her perfect tits that are currently wrecking my mind.

"Careful what you wish for" is what you say when somebody might regret something, but I don't regret that we're not doing roles anymore. I'll never regret anything about this.

"I'm definitely not your landlord. I'm the man who's gonna fuck you senseless." I pull off my sweater and T-shirt in one single go and toss it all aside.

I help her strip off her jeans. She's wearing red panties that match her bra. I hold her gaze as I trail my fingers over the smooth fabric, enjoying that she put them on for me. I swipe a thumb between her legs, grazing over the wet spot. Just the feel of her wet for me swells my cock. Slowly, I slide them off of her, kissing my way down her legs.

"The panties get to live?" she asks.

"For now." My progress slows at her thigh, then her knee. I'm lost in the soft, coconut-scented silk of her skin under my lips. "Your scent..." I shudder out. "Like tropical candy."

She closes her fists in my hair. "My wicked plan..."

"You've got more than a little wicked in you," I say.

I stroke a hand over her blonde mound and she groans. I didn't take the time to properly enjoy her before, but now I'm feasting on her with my fingers, letting her feel my utter lust for her.

She looks down at me, chest heaving, gaze unfocused. "You think I have *more* than a little wicked in me?"

"I know you do. A wicked streak in a good girl is too hot."

"Like a good streak in a wicked man?"

"Don't count on it." I grab her ankles and pull her under me, spreading her legs out wide in front of me. I kiss her pussy and she gasps, but I'm the one who's reeling, intoxicated by the perfect pink of her.

I move up on her, pressing kisses to every part of her.

She roams her hands over my chest. Over my belly. Over my cock, caressing it loosely. "How are you so sexy?" she asks.

I have no answer. I'd trained myself out of giving a shit about what anybody thinks of me or my appearance. But with Jada, I really do care. And the idea that she's enjoying me, that she's as mesmerized by me as I am by her, it feels like dark magic, like it defies the laws of the cosmos.

I dislodge her hand from my cock. "Too close," I say. I want to last.

I kiss her palm. I kiss the tender underside of her forearm and then her shoulder and then the little puff of flesh next to her breast. "I could make out with every part of you."

"You want to make out with my boob buddy?" she asks, incredulous. "You sure?"

"I love your boob buddy." I rub my cheek over it, like it's the finest silk velvet.

"Oh my god, you are nuts," she says in her sassy way.

I kiss her quivering belly. I push her legs apart and pet her slick folds, slow and tender.

She takes hold of my hair again and makes the *hmm* sound I

love, rocking into my hand, breath coming faster. We're in perfect sync, as though we've always been here.

"Please, Jack," she gasps.

My name on her lips has me in flames. I roll over and, with shaking hands, I grab my wallet from the bedside table and pull out a condom.

She snatches it from my fingers and nudges me over. I roll onto my back, torn between needing to experience the feeling of her competent hands rolling on a condom and needing to be inside her.

Forty

Jada

He's on his back now, watching me with a heated gaze that makes me ache for him. His whisker stubble glints in the light, the curve of his cheekbone outlined dramatically in shadow.

I brush my hand over the damp, course hair on his belly. He's built like an athlete. His penis jerks as my hand heads southward.

"You have such a beautiful penis."

His nostrils flare. He's all coiled, sexy energy.

I tear the foil package open. "Be happy I'm not tracing my name on your chest." I roll it onto his cock, nice and slow, getting it exactly even.

"Oh, god," he groans. "Such a perfectionist!" Suddenly he's taking charge. He has it on and I'm on my back.

I grin. "Do me," I whisper.

He moves between my legs and presses himself into me, filling my ache, invading me completely and deliciously.

"Mmmm..." I say, loving the feel of him inside me, completing me.

He thrusts into me, rumbling in his sexy tenor. I arch up to him—just enough to feel his chest hair rub on my breasts. I want to feel him in every way possible, on every surface of my body.

We get into a rhythm, mindless and ancient.

He slows, then he stops moving. His gaze invades mine.

My breath catches. I can't look away. It's like time has stopped, like the whole city has stopped to create this space of pure primal truth between us.

"Jada."

"Hey," I say.

"Hey." He grinds slowly now, circling against me, watching me. I feel like he's looking right into my soul and I'm glad. I'm trembling with pleasure, and I want him to see everything. I want him to see me.

I push my hips up to meet his, to somehow take in more of him, to get my clit into the rubbing action. It feels great, so I put my finger on my clit between our bodies.

He shudders out a breath. "Jesus, you gotta warn me before you touch yourself. I nearly lost it."

"Touching alert," I whisper, stroking myself, my finger sandwiched between our bodies, loving how intense we are together.

He grinds my finger into my clit, shoulders rippling with muscles. "Jada, Jada, Jada."

"I'm about to come," I gasp, nearly there. I stop with the finger and grip his hard arms.

A rumble curls from his throat as he shudders into me.

"More," I gasp. He's fucking me with savage force, now, and I just want more.

My skin feels electric.

The air is dark and heavy.

Pleasure blooms up my body and explodes in my brain.

He presses into me one final time; I can feel his cock pulsing inside me. He sucks in a breath, hot and sharp, lost like me.

He cries out and then collapses against me.

We're both panting.

"WE CAN ORDER SOMETHING," he says. "There's nothing to eat here."

It's midnight and we're hanging out in the kitchen. I'm wearing one of his shirts and a pair of his thick socks. His clothes smell like him, a faint spice that is so Jack.

He's watching me across the kitchen island, and there's heat in his sexy eyes, but I'm invested in a late-night meal.

"I'm telling you, I got this. Because I have a superpower—I can make the best meal ever out of just a few ingredients. As long as there's a fat and a starch. The things I can whip up—prepare to be amazed, Jack."

"I'm ready." He pours me some gingerale. Did he get gingerale especially for me? I love how he acts like the world's hugest jerk, but he's so not.

I peruse the produce that's been set out in colorful bowls. "I see tomatoes. Garlic." I check the refrigerator and the cupboards. "Oh, no," I say. "No, no, no."

"What's wrong?"

"Fresh parm, pesto, sundried tomatoes. You even have fresh pine nuts. Whatever!" I throw the bag of pine nuts at him. "How can I demonstrate my superpower in such a ridiculously well-stocked kitchen?"

"Sorry?" He tosses the pine nuts back at me.

"It's too easy! You've got the most well-stocked kitchen this side of the Hudson." I set them aside and put out some parsely. "Start chopping this. We'll do a quick orzo." I open the cupboard and groan again.

"Hey! I believe you," he says. "I believe in your superpower."

"I don't feel that you can unless you see it." I start some water boiling.

I'm acting put out, but I feel...wonderful. Dangerously euphoric. I love being with Jack. I've never had a man act so irrationally obsessed over me. He makes me feel special and wildly beautiful.

I assemble a few things and go over to where he seems to be struggling with cutting the parsley. I soon see the problem: he's sawing at it with a steak knife.

"Jack!" I'm laughing. "You need to chop it!"

"I am chopping it."

"Poor Jack," I tease, circling my arms around him from the back. "So bewildered by the ways of the world. What is this shiny thing? What is this chopping you speak of?"

He puts down the knife and turns around and growls into my hair.

Forty-One

Jaxon

She gives me a chopping knife and shows me how to chop the parsely properly.

We work side by side while she regales me with past feats of creating tasty dinners out of nothing. She wants me to get how resourceful she is, but what I'm also getting is how little she had growing up, and not just on a material level. Her dad and brothers provided the bare minimum while she made a home.

She's at the stove sautéing garlic in butter.

"Did they ever thank you for all that you did? For putting your life on hold?" I ask as I slide the bright green bits into a small bowl.

She stands there concentrating on the pan. "My dad sort of did. I was back there one Christmas and he told me he regrets not being more present for me. Not doing more. My brothers were there. They talked about how they didn't realize how much I was doing until I was gone. They were laughing about how bad things got once I left. I was glad they realized it. I felt vindicated, I suppose. But at the same time, I wanted more."

"That's not much of an apology," I say.

"Maybe it was the best they could do. People are at the level that they're at." She sets a hunk of cheese and a grater in front of me.

"You deserved better," I say, starting to grate.

She shrugs and turns back to her cooking.

I love watching her. I can't believe I ever thought she was a buzzkill. This is a woman who would burn it all down for her people.

We bring our little feast up to the third floor to eat. It's delicious. Mind-blowingly so.

She turns sideways on the couch and settles her legs over mine, holding her bowl in her lap atop a colorful cloth, the fabric of which she naturally had lots to say about. "This is fun, Jack."

"It is fun."

After we're done, I take our bowls to the kitchen and lock the place up; when I return, she's curled up on the couch, asleep. I take the napkin from her lap and set it aside, then I scoop her up and carry her to my bed. I work off her shoes. She snuggles deeply into the covers.

I stretch out next to her and tuck her in just so, and there's that feeling again, like we're connected.

I let it live inside of me, a terrifying companion.

She makes me happy—happier than I've ever felt. And unlike possessions and races and social intrigues and whatever the hell else used to make me happy, this happiness is completely out of my control. I would fight for this woman. I would do anything for this woman and for this work family she's so attached to. It's my family, too, I guess—hat and all.

I'm not sure how to navigate around it yet. I'm not sure if it even works for me. All I know is that she's all I want.

I WAKE up the next morning to find her sitting up, doing things on her phone, wearing my shirt again.

"Oh my goodness, look who's up!" she says, beaming. "The man whose foot tracing is on file with the finest shoemakers in Milan!"

I drag her back under the blanket and cover her with my body. I thread my fingers into her hair and kiss her.

"Hmm," she says into the kiss. Somewhere in the distance, her phone clatters to the floor. She winds her hands around my neck and hooks a leg over my side, arching into me.

"That's right, baby," I say. "You grind into me. Get yourself ready for me. My foot tracings are huge, you know."

"Oh, I know," she says, moving hard against me like a horny teen, and I couldn't love it more. My body is flooded with warmth and lust. My fingers are a blur as I rip my shirt off of her. We're a tangle of limbs, then she's on top of me, sliding on a condom.

She lowers herself onto me slowly, watching my eyes. I grab her hips, shuddering with the relief of being inside her again. We move together, slow and sure. We come so hard, we nearly fall off the edge of the world.

~

JADA'S in the day room when I come out after my shower, all scrubbed and dressed. She's holding a steaming mug of coffee and I kind of can't believe it.

I love her in my home. I need her to stay the weekend. But what the hell do couples do on weekends together? Is that what we are?

More new territory.

"I made a pot," she says, lifting her mug. "I hope that's okay."

"We'll have to hide it before Chef Ursula returns."

She shows me her phone. "Guess what bag got press already?"

I settle in next to her and take a look. The two Genevieves

came through in a major way. Jada's already compiled links and emailed the gang from the office. "And tonight is the gala. If even one of them carries the bag... You have no idea what a coup this is!"

"They'll carry the bags," I say.

"Because you're such a demon who nobody wants to owe."

I shrug.

"The only thing that can go wrong now is if Bert has an alert set up for SportyGoCo. But even if he does, he can't stop people from ordering it. He signed off on the project as long as it had the Ravaldi zipper."

We'll need a lot of orders to get this accounting period profitable so I can break that contract, but this is a start.

We drink our coffee while she tells me the office plans. The salesperson, Mackenzie, is working up a new pitch with the help of Shondrella.

It's here I notice her eyeing the distinctive red envelope that Jenny had brought me that day. Of course Jada would notice and remember. I'd set it on the side table when I'd gotten home, and it's still there. It's like a sign. Here's what couples do—they tell each other things. They show real things.

"I know you wanna ask about it," I say.

"No. Well, a little. But it's more that I was concerned because that woman who visited you at the office...you looked like you saw a ghost when she showed up."

I go grab the thing and sink back down next to her. "That was Jenny who came to visit me that day. She was my nanny for a long time. She traveled with us between continents. She was one of the best things in my life, the closest thing I had to a real mother."

"I'm glad you had somebody like that," she says.

I slide my finger along the edge of the envelope, thinking I owe Jenny an apology for the way I was that day.

"She left our family abruptly, and it really messed me up. She didn't leave of her own volition, but I didn't know that until recently."

I unwind the string from the little disk clasp thing and pull out the picture, still curled from when I rolled it up and shoved it in my pocket. There's me, looking so morose with my smiling parents.

Jada grins. "Oh, Jack."

"What, you like it?"

"Way better than the other. This one is you," she says.

"It's me to look morose?"

"No, but the famous one is fake. Were you morose that day?"

"It started out happy. They flew in special for the photo session. I hadn't seen them in months, and they had presents for me, but I knew they'd leave after they got the nice picture, so I refused to smile. Frowning was all I had for leverage."

"You wanted your parents to stay," she says. "To be a family."

I cringe inwardly, hating that I wanted anything from them. "And then they got the smile," I say. "Not in the traditional way."

She nods. She gets it. She gets me. A warmth blooms in my chest.

"And of course they took off again."

"No wonder you hate that stupid fake smiling picture of yourself."

"I do. It's a picture of me capitulating. I should've held out." I take the photo from her hands and slip it back into the envelope. Jada lies down with her head in my lap, this woman from across the ocean with her fierce powers of observation and her good-girl wicked streak. She knew it was fake.

"Jenny liked this one. It's why she kept it. She told me I was headstrong and full of feeling. 'Such a big heart,' she'd said." I chuckle.

"I think it's true." Jada runs a finger over my jaw. "I think you're still like that."

"Is that a little bit of *pishful pinking*?"

"No." She pokes my chin.

I grab her finger. "I think my new PR agent is blowing smoke up my ass."

"Not at all. You were like, 'Fuck this, I want a real thing or just burn it all down.' That's how you are now. Honestly, you have no concept of yourself. Also, how come you let that smiling picture of you stay up in the dining room? I hate it now, too."

"Yeah, Arnold's got an art installer coming to deal with it soon."

"We should rip it down. I don't ever want to look at it again."

I smooth back her hair, marveling at how hard she fights for people. And this is her fighting for me. The feeling is like nothing else.

Unless... Is this what it feels like to finally find a home?

"What?" she asks, because I'm sure I'm looking sappy.

"I love your warrior streak," I say.

She snorts and sits up. "Seriously—here's a plan for the day. Let's bring the picture Jenny saved and get it blown up onto a large canvas at one of those instant photo places, and then we'll switch the pictures ourselves. Screw the art installer. And then we can have a nice feast in the dining room to celebrate."

"What kind of feast?" I ask, twirling her hair around my finger, something nervous and excited bubbling up in my stomach.

"Any feast you want, baby. Isn't that how it works here?"

I smile.

In the end, it's a feast of curry dishes. Chef Ursula is excited that I have a guest for dinner, and she does it up with several courses. We're both starving by the time we finally eat, having walked all up and down the Upper West Side without a break, unless you count grabbing a quick falafel from a halal guy and eating it on the steps of a city building while we waited for the canvas to get printed and mounted.

After our curry extravaganza, we get Chef Ursula to take a picture of Jada and Arnold and me doing a jokey pose in front of the new version of the photo. I email it to Jenny, thanking her for bringing it. I ask her to let me know her travel plans, and tell her I'd love to get dinner when she's back in town.

Arnold joins Jada and me for dessert. Jada tells him the story the office had worked out about him as my tormenter. She and Arnold think it's a lot funnier than I do.

On Sunday morning we end up at Jada's apartment, which is ridiculously small but big in color, with lots of wild pillows and friend photos. She gives me the tour of the place in a jokey way, because it's only one room with a murphy bed, which we promptly put to use.

Later, we head up to the rooftop deck—it's one of those bright, warm, late autumn afternoons you can only get in Manhattan. She wants me to see the sparkle of the river.

The rooftop deck is actually nice, with umbrellas and trellises and a few seating areas. There's an elderly couple at a wind-protected table in the corner. Naturally, Jada knows them, and has to drag me over and introduce us. I learn that John and Maisey were featured heavily in the apartment building documentary that Jada made some time ago. A couple of her friends pop up—Kelsey and Tabitha. Tabitha is deeply offended by my bleached-tip hair.

"It would take so little to fix that," she says. "Not to insult you, but it would take so little—just the simplest trim—and it would look so much better."

"Not to insult me," I joke.

Everybody here seems to know who I am—from Jada, not the tabloids or anything. We talk about the possibility of my going into work looking like my regular self—without my mole, even.

"Nobody's gonna recognize you," Jada assures me. "Nobody knows Formula One here."

"Is that a shampoo?" Tabitha teases.

The consensus is that people won't recognize me, but they might think it's weird that my mole is completely gone, though Tabitha insists that mole removal techniques are that good these days.

John, the neighbor with gray hair, informs us that Formula One is growing in popularity due to the show, but it's not big in Manhattan, and few of the fans obsess over the history of it. He does, however, seem to know about Mario Andretti.

Over the next hour, the group of them put up holiday lights while Tabitha gives me a trim—right out there on the roof, with a towel pinned around my shoulders.

We chat easily as she snips away.

I used to consider myself to be somebody who had a giant world. But ever since I've crossed paths with Jada, it's as if my world has grown much wider—not in terms of geography, but in terms of people.

I look across the place and catch Jada's eye. She smiles, and I smile back like a fool, but I don't care, because it feels great.

And right then, this strange thought crosses my mind: I'm not alone anymore.

But then this little voice wonders if it can last. The little voice wonders if having people is maybe only for other people. And what happens when this inevitably goes away?

I close my eyes and push the questions out of my mind.

~

STANLEY DROPS us at the bagel place near the office. We phoned in an order for ten dozen mixed bagels and tons of toppings.

"So now suddenly I'm buying all the food," I joke as we head down Eighth Avenue, both carrying boxes.

"That's right," Jada says. "Until you can change things to give raises to your employees, you'll need to feed them."

I roll my eyes, but I'm happy to do it. It's also nice not wearing my itchy fake mole and that bright shirt.

We stop at the security station so that Marv can pick bagels for his team. We drop two boxes off in shipping, and then it's up to the design department.

"Jack bought the office bagels," Jada tells Varsha as we breeze in. "We should put them in the break room. There's a shit ton if you want to alert people."

"Thanks...uh..." Varsha's blinking at me, looking stunned.

"What's up?" I tease, stacking the boxes up on the ledge.

"Nothing!" she says.

"Nothing?" I take off my hat and coat.

"Stop teasing her," Jada scolds, beaming at me. "Jack got his hair cut and his mole removed. I think he looks great."

"Right!" Varsha says, eyes wide. "Wow. Not that you didn't look okay before."

"And no more printed nineties shirts," I say to Varsha with a sigh. "Even the glasses. Gone."

"Hell yeah, the glasses are gone," Jada says.

Renata comes up, looking shocked. "Hold on. What. The. Hell." Renata's pointing at me, and then at Jada, and then back at me. "What is happening? Who..."

I wince—I was afraid of somebody recognizing me.

Renata turns her accusatory gaze to Jada, hands planted on her hips. "Did you give Jack a makeover? Jack, did she give you a makeover?"

"Sort of," I say.

"So much for respecting his right to be weird looking," she says to Jada.

Everybody's gathering around. Shondrella is loving the change. Lacey is blown away by the perfection of the mole removal—she can't believe there's no scar.

Luckily, Dave comes up before everybody gets too obsessed with the no-scar thing. He does a full pantomime of his surprise, complete with a staggering walk and a cartoonish rubbing of the eyes. "Dude! This is some caterpillar-to-butterfly-level shit right here! Caterpillar to butterfly!"

"Does nobody care that warm bagels are growing cold?" Jada asks.

People adjourn to the break room. There's a lot of feasting and scrolling for more links to pictures of Unicorn Wonderbag—they're all over certain corners of the internet.

At around ten, Mackenzie from sales comes up to let us know Sadie Woo wants a meeting.

Jada claps. "Paydirt!"

Sadie Woo is apparently a small group of high-end stores.

This rush of pleasure warms me clear through. I never knew I could feel so good about another person's happiness. It's as uncomplicated as a mountain stream, this pleasure I feel, seeing her excited. She loves this company. These people. And she really fucking loves that bag.

"They called *me*," Mackenzie adds. "Not the other way around. *They* called me! We're set up for three. They want to see the bag and meet the team."

"Wait, what?" This throws Jada for a loop. "The team?"

Mackenzie shrugs. "The designer and, I don't know. They said the team."

Everybody turns to Shondrella, who always seems to know about these things. "Let's give them a team."

Forty-Two

Jada

I'm walking down Fifth Avenue with Mackenzie, Shondrella, and Jack. I'm in a much cuter outfit than before, having whipped home over lunch to change.

It was my last-minute idea to add Jack to the team. I explained to Shondrella and Mackenzie that Jack has driven princesses and socialites, and therefore he gets the world. I think it was a sign of their nervousness that they agreed. The idea is that he'll stay quiet, like the silent, elegant partner.

Mackenzie is the most nervous. She's used to selling products on price, not quality, and certainly not luxury. "My main prop is always spreadsheets!" she says.

Shondrella says we should tell the story of our passion, how we wanted to create something beautiful that could travel easily in a carry-on but is the most elegant bag. "The unicorn zipper pull is probably going to be key," she adds.

"They're gonna love it," Jack says. The way he sounds, it's more like a threat.

I grin at Jack when the others aren't looking, and Jack grins back. He seems so gruff, like he doesn't care; in truth, he's sensitive. Maybe he's gruff *because* he's sensitive. Because things mean so much; that's what I've been thinking ever since this weekend.

And as we stroll through the golden doors off Sadie Woo's flagship store, I know it was the right decision to bring him—he's the only one of the four of us who looks like he belongs here. It's not his clothes or anything outward like that; it's his demeanor. The sense of ease that he exudes.

There are clusters of people sipping champagne in plush seating areas amidst elegant displays. That's how the shopping is done at a place like Sadie Woo—people bring you things while you relax.

A woman in a severe white suit comes up and asks if anybody is helping us. I tell her we're here to see Zanaka Boudon, the buyer.

"This way." She leads us under massive chandeliers and past naked golden statues; I hear snatches of Japanese, Arabic, French.

Zanaka's office features a large marble desk that's completely empty except for an old-fashioned clock. We hand over our business cards—all except Jack—and sit across from her. Jack looks elegant, sitting there with his legs crossed, taking up space in a way that only a rich person does.

Zanaka examines Unicorn Wonderbag. She wants to know how we got it into the hands of the two Genevieves.

"Friends of friends," Shondrella says, because it sounds better than telling her that our delivery driver drove for them once and they owed him. That's the story that the office has gotten, and it's not untrue.

"Wonder Unicorn Brand features a limited number of made-in-America items that are gifted to influencers before they hit the market, and everything is a limited run."

Zanaka looks unconvinced as Mackenzie continues through the speech we developed. She asks a lot of questions about production methods and numbers.

She's not so sure about the bag, I can tell. Or maybe it's us.

I'm starting to get nervous. Also, I can feel Jack looking at me and reading my emotions. He can be so volatile—especially when he senses any kind of threat to my happiness. Was it a mistake to bring him?

I launch into the story of how we came to the idea. I point out the stitching and show how fun it is to roll it into the unicorn horn.

Zanaka turns the bag inside out. She rolls it and unrolls it. She seems unsure, and my heart is starting to sink, because enthusiasm is key to what we're trying to do.

I grip the arm of my chair. Why doesn't she like it?

Jack, for his part, is looking more and more unhappy.

"SportyGoCo is a big box brand," Zanaka says. "You're spinning a luxury brand off of a big box brand with a flagship four-figure bag. Usually one would do everything they can to conceal the connection, but you're up front with it. Can you go into the thought process for me on that pedigree path?"

"This is our confidence," Mackenzie says. "It's bold and new. We're not doing things the old way."

"We don't want to conceal our connection with SportyGoCo," I add, trying for confidence. "That's our love for this beautiful bag."

"Hmmm." Zanaka sets the bag on the desk. It looks...pathetic. And I know she'll say no.

My heart lurches.

Suddenly Jack is standing. "This meeting is officially over."

"Wait, what?" I say, giving Jack a significant look. What the hell is he doing?

"I'm sorry." He snatches the bag off of Zanaka's barren desk. "We cannot sell it to you."

"B-but—" Mackenzie looks baffled, looking between Jack and me.

I turn to Jack, eyes wide. "She's not done with her evaluation."

"I'm done with *my* evaluation," Jack says. "The stitching? The brand pedigree path? Sadie Woo is wrong for the bag. We appreciate your time."

"And you are?" Zanaka says.

"It doesn't matter," Jack says. "This is the wrong fit. That's what matters."

With that, he walks out.

The four of us sit there in dead silence.

"So...is he the decision maker?" Zanaka asks.

I stand, pulse racing, unsure what to do. All I know is that this is over. "I'm sorry to have wasted your time." Shondrella and Mackenzie stand, too, following my lead, and we head out as a unit.

Jack drives us back, the four of us all squished into the cold cab of the delivery truck.

"Well, that went shitty," Shondrella says.

"She wasn't going to place an order anyway," I say, feeling protective of Jack.

"She might have. We could've given her the opportunity to make an order," Mackenzie says to Jack. "You said you'd stay silent, Jack."

"Screw that," Jack grumbles. "Screw her if she can't see how beautiful that bag is. You guys put your heart and soul into that bag, and if she can't see that, she doesn't deserve it."

"Jack..." I don't know what to say. "It's sweet of you, but—"

"She didn't deserve it," he says.

"That's sales, Jack," Mackenzie says. "It's how it works. Some people say no. Some people need time to decide."

Jack concentrates on the road with a thunderous expression. I love how protective he is of me, but we can't take him on any more sales calls, that's for sure.

If there are any more sales calls.

The three of us head up the elevator while Jack drops the truck in shipping.

"God love him," Shondrella says, "but he really blew that. And I don't see any more offers coming down the pike."

Mackenzie sighs. "It was nice to have him there until he started talking."

"No way can we bring him again," Shondrella says. "I know you like him and everything."

"No, I agree," I say. "I'm sure he didn't mean to wreck it. Maybe we'll get other interest. Why not, right?"

The elevator clanks to a stop at our floor and the door opens.

"Dudes!" Dave is standing there like he was waiting for us. Was he? "High five!" he says.

"We didn't get it," I say.

"What are you talking about? The PO just came through."

"When?" Mackenzie says.

"Five minutes ago?" Dave leads us to his cubicle. There it is: the purchase order—a dozen per store with front-of-the-house yacht season merchandising if we can get them out in a specified amount of time.

Shondrella clutches my arm. "What. The. Hell."

Renata runs up and does a happy dance. "I was hoping they'd take a dozen, but whoa!"

"This doesn't compute," I say.

Mackenzie checks the form to make sure it's not a joke. "Well, hell. That's a technique I've never tried. 'You want it? You can't have it, so fuck you!'" She puts her palms to her head. "His trick worked!"

Shondrella explains what happened at the meeting to the gathered group.

"Watch me parlay this order into getting my foot in at Anton's." Mackenzie points at me. "Same team. Jack has to come." She rushes off.

Dave is working with his team to route all Unicorn Wonderbag orders into a special silo so that Bert won't notice until it's too late. Dave doesn't have the inside information that I do. He doesn't know that Bert was hired specifically to drive the company into the ground, but we all know that Bert wrecks everything he touches.

Jack gets a hero's welcome when he gets back up to our floor. He seems mad when he finds out we're going to be fulfilling the order. "They're not good enough for your bag," he growls. "She didn't appreciate it enough."

Everybody laughs, but he just seems grumpy. He sits at his desk, quietly working at his spreadsheets.

"What's going on?" I ask him once people get back to work.

"It's just bullshit."

"What's bullshit?" Renata asks, sitting down at her desk.

"Nothing," Jack says.

"Mackenzie is never going on a sales call without you ever again, I hope you know," Renata says.

Jack just looks stormy. Does he not understand how great he did? I try to catch his eye, but he's ignoring me. I go over and grab his stapler and bang it a few times. "You shouldn't leave this empty," I say to him. "It needs to be *filled*. And now, apparently, I have to do it *myself* in the supply closet."

I stroll off. I know he'll follow. How could he not?

A few moments later, the door creaks open.

I don't know what I expected—his cool, witty self, maybe. Something sardonic about staplers, or him crowing about a jerky attitude saving the day.

That's not what I get.

He comes in looking undone. His gaze skewers me. His nostrils flare.

"What's going on?" I ask.

He just shakes his head.

"That was a coup! You did amazing. You know Mackenzie is gonna get another call off of that order. Maybe two or three." I take a step toward him. "We're really doing it, Jack. We might actually get this accounting period back in the black."

"I guess," he rasps.

"More orders like this and we can save SportyGoCo from Bert and your parents' bully company! Aren't you happy?" I press my hand to his chest. "Hey."

"I'm not doing the hate fuck," he says. "It's not where I'm at."

I reach up and cup his cheek. "Where are you at?"

He grabs my wrist, just holds my wrist and watches me. "People here think it was a trick over there at Sadie Woo, but it wasn't a trick. The way she was acting like your bag was shit? It pissed me off. I hated it."

Shivers skitter over me as I realize what he's saying. It wasn't a ploy. It was Jack feeling deeply. Reeling. "That just makes me feel...honored."

He grunts unintelligibly.

"I am. I love that you're in my corner, Jack."

"I'm not used to this. I'm not used to pulling for things and being invested in things that I have no power over. The way my life is set up, people hate me and I don't give a shit, or they're like Arnold where they get paid to be my people, or they want something from me. That's how it always is with me. But now everything feels out of control."

"But it's turning out okay," I try.

"I have to tell you something." He brushes my hair from my face. "Remember when you asked me what I would save from the fire?"

"Sure."

"It would be the hat."

I squint, unsure what he could possibly mean. "The hat that we made for you?"

His cheeks are rosy, pupils huge. "Yes," he says, breath coming quick.

"That's...really?" I say.

"Yeah."

"I love that."

"Maybe you love that, but to me—I burn bridges, Jada. I punch people. I crash cars. People don't knit hats for me."

"People here knit hats for you," I say.

Wildly, he looks around the small, dim space. "I don't know how to do this. I'm not used to all this fucking harmony."

"All this fucking harmony?"

"Yes! And Keith the cactus. And Bert sticks him in the breakroom corner? Every time I look at him, I want to tear Bert's fucking face off, even though it's only ten percent Bert's fault, being that Keith was already dead. It's the principle of the thing." He swallows, brows drawn. "I don't know how people do any of this."

"Any of what?"

"I don't know..." He gestures in the direction of the office. "Any of this. Without going crazy and trashing things."

"They do it together," I say. "If the next buyer hates the bag, we'll figure it out, because we're in it together. If things go wrong, we'll figure it out together. We have each other's backs."

His gaze is hard and deep. There's something of King Kong in him at the moment, a cornered beast batting at planes. Batting at feelings.

He says, "Life is easier when you pay people to do what you want, and everyone else hates you."

Not easier for that little boy in the picture, I think, but I don't say that, because his hand is in my hair.

He's so raw. I've never seen a man so raw or so beautiful, and I'm starting to get it about him—Jack doesn't have too little feeling; he has too goddamn much.

I grab his shirt and pull him to me, kissing him full on. Our kiss turns hungry, greedy. Suddenly we're tearing at each other's clothes. I'm unclasping his pants. He's forcing up my skirt. I'm thumbing down my panties, stomping out of them. We're in a mad, all-out sprint for a full-on sexytimes show and tell.

My knees feel shaky. I grip his shoulders as he fights his pants free of his feet. Need courses through my heated veins.

He's kissing me, breath ragged. He fumbles around, and then there's a condom in his fingers.

He tears at the package, swearing under his breath as he rolls it on. With barely a huff of breath he lifts me. I wrap my legs around his waist. His cock is a hot iron bar against my sex. I grind on him.

"Jada, Jada, Jada." He sets me on the table, mumbling nonsensical things into my hair.

"Hurry." My sex aches for him, excruciatingly empty in the cool chill of the closet.

"I've got you." I feel the blunt tip of him at my entrance. He presses into me, filling me. My body blooms with pleasure.

I clamp my legs around him more tightly. He pumps into me, urgent and savage. My hands clamp onto his shoulders, holding on with everything I have. My breath saws in and out.

"I've got you, baby," he says again. Strong hands grip my ass cheeks, pry them apart, pry me apart from the inside out.

"Harder," I whisper, though there's a sob on the tail end. "More."

He goes harder. He gives me more. I give him more, though it almost hurts the way I scrape myself raw for him, and then I'm coming in a blaze of white-hot sensation. I'm vaguely aware of his breath stuttering, of his movements going feral, of him joining me as he presses deep.

I open my eyes at the end and find him staring at me with something I can't quite understand, though it looks a lot like the shock coursing through me.

Forty-Three

JAXON

PEOPLE MIGHT BE GETTING suspicious about my buying so many treats for the office over the next week. They sometimes act surprised as they thank me effusively, and I know they're wondering how I do it on my gopher's salary.

That Thursday, I instruct Soto to have the legal team check to see if there's a way that Wycliff can supply office treats. We can't supply treats, but one enterprising lawyer noticed that one of the few things that the contract didn't give Bloxburn sway over is celebrations.

I direct somebody in Wycliff PR to do a monthlong sportswear maker celebration that involves elaborate company lunches being sent into every department, and a generous happy hour celebration budget that includes unlimited food. When Bloxburn complains, they are referred to my spokespeople, who tell them I'm on extended leave but they can leave a voicemail, which they do, reminding me that these celebrations undermine the spirit of the contract my parents created with them.

Good.

We continue to pull as a team, going through the motions of being a company with no orders or decent products on the horizon while furiously producing Wonderbag prototypes and sales materials.

Jada and I get into a routine of taking long walks after work. We sleep mostly at my place, but occasionally we stay at hers. This involves one evening visit to her friend Kelsey's apartment to watch *The Bachelor* and eat pizza.

Jada and I are on the couch drinking some kind of awful pink drink that Tabitha made when Dr. Tonio himself comes in.

I frown and turn to Jada. "What's Dr. Tonio doing here?"

She puts her hand over her mouth.

"What's going on?"

He comes up to me. "I see you got rid of it."

I stand. "You're not my doctor."

Kelsey stands and links arms with him. "He's nobody's doctor! This is just our friend." She introduces him as Antonio, an Italian fashion model here to break into acting.

And even though this was billed as galpal *Bachelor* night, Antonio is apparently an honorary galpal, as is a dog named Smuckers.

Antonio comes right up to where we're sitting on the couch. "I'm cool with you for Jada's sake, but the way you went after Tybalt Gundrun? Not forgiven."

I stand. "Best decision I ever made."

Antonio glowers.

Jada stands up and pokes me. "Tell him what happened!"

I narrow my eyes. "His face needed a fist." Because I grovel to no man.

"Stop it!" She turns to Antonio. "Tybalt Gundrun sabotaged Jack's pit crew and endangered his team. And he can prove it, but he's too stubborn."

"Why wouldn't you prove it?" Antonio asks.

"Why would I bother? The jury was out, and I pander to nobody."

Jada groans. "Come onnnnnn."

I sigh. Annoying as it is, I do suddenly care what Jada's friends think, so I explain the whole thing. How my pit crew guy had brought me the little chunk of plastic that was shaped like a bolt, designed to melt at high speeds. How the press was instantly against me, how it felt like begging, hat in hand, to try to prove my innocence when my career was done anyway.

"Was that so hard?" Jada teases. "He likes being the villain. He hates harmony, but I'm trying to break him of that."

"I don't trust harmony," I say, thinking about it. "I don't actually mind it."

Antonio regards me strangely for a beat, and then he just laughs. "That is so you."

"Grazie," I say.

"You need to tell everybody," Jada says. "You need to tell the press your story."

"Screw that," I say. "A man has his limits."

"Such an uber-villain," Jada teases.

"You're dismissed," I say to her.

"No, you are!"

I wrap my arms around her and pick her up. "You are," I growl.

She's laughing. I've never wanted to kiss her more, but suddenly the little dog is barking. I come to my senses and realize we're in somebody's living room, and that her friends are all beaming at us.

That night in her tiny little apartment among all of her sparkly things, we make love—I suppose that's the phrase for sleeping with a woman you feel close to. It's a new experience for me, that's for sure.

Later on, we lie in her bed and look up at the tiny sliver of stars and sky you can see between buildings. It seems too good to be true.

But what if it isn't?

MORE WONDERBAG PICTURES appear on social media over the following days. The team gets three more out to influencers—a good sign, apparently. Shondrella says the influencers are influencing each other.

We're in bed at my place Friday morning, drinking coffee and trying to figure out the day's Wordle when Mackenzie texts Jada about an important sales call she just accepted that she wants me to go on.

Mackenzie: Have him wear something elegant.
But not trying too hard.

"SO SHE JUST ASSUMES WE'RE together this morning," I say.

Jada puts on a fake confused face. "How did she know? Could it be that we show up together every freaking morning? Could it be that I wore your shirt as a cute shirtdress on Wednesday? Could it be the office PDA? Our mysterious disappearance into the supply closet?"

"She better not be hoping for a repeat of that last meeting," I say. "Because that is not happening, and I can't imagine it's good for business to bring along a guy who loses his mind."

"It was good having you there, even before you said anything," she says. "All you have to do is sit there. You add a certain gravity."

"Gravity, huh." I pull her onto my lap, loving the weight of her, the feel of her tight little curves in my arms.

"Only you would manage to make that sound weirdly sexy." She climbs off the bed and pulls me with her into my closet. That's how I end up walking into the office wearing a classic tweed blazer with a black polo shirt and gray pants, an ensemble Jada pronounced as killer.

Renata scowls playfully at Jada when we walk in. "You're just trolling me now, aren't you?"

"What?" Jada protests.

"It wasn't enough to get him off the hair and ridiculous shirts," she complains. "Now you've got him dressed up like a hot-English-professor-slash-country-squire. But please, let's respect his right to look weird."

"What?" Jada laughs. "He has a right to look hot if he wants."

"She wanted me for herself," I tease. "And once she had me, the makeovers began."

"Clearly," Renata says.

Dave comes by. "Bert alert."

"Shit!" Renata says. "I put Keith in the sun!"

We all look over at spindly Keith, now basking in the sun right out in the open.

"Bert's gonna freak out," Jada says.

"I'm so sorry," Renata says. "I'll move him."

"No! Not enough time," Jada says. "You'll just draw attention. We have to leave him."

"Maybe Bert won't notice," I say.

Shondrella pops her head up above the cubicle walls. "You guys!" She points at Keith and makes a horror face.

But it's too late. Bert is strolling in. Keyboard sounds start up. I'm at my desk with my spreadsheet program open, updating stuff from yesterday, but I can barely concentrate, because Bert could destroy everything we've done with the bag. He could fire these people at any minute. He could banish Keith to one of the shipping bays.

Not my circus, I think.

But that feels like a lie.

It *is* a lie.

This is my circus. My people, my family, my life.

How does anyone do this?

The tension ratchets up as Bert strolls along the perimeter toward the window. You never let your enemies know what's important to you—that's rule number one. If he sees Keith has been moved, if he sees he's been cared for, he'll know it's a vulnerability.

And what if he's gotten wind of our sales push for Wonderbag? He'd find a way to shut that down.

Bert's footsteps turn back down the other way—away from the window. He stops by Dave's cubicle, and they have a low discussion. He moves on to the resources group. Maybe he'll keep going—that's my hope.

Renata should never have moved Keith.

I tap a few more keys.

Bert's on the move again. This time he slows near our area. He comes and stands next to my cubicle.

I look up. "Something I can help you with, sir?" I ask. That's how Dave always addresses him.

"What's the occasion?" Bert asks.

"What do you mean?"

"You're awfully dressed up for doing office gopher stuff."

I grin. "The ladies like it."

"You think that's funny?" he asks.

I cross my legs and lean back. It's a casual pose, but inside, I'm wired as hell.

Letting a guy like Bert talk to me like this upends years of habit and everything I've ever thought about myself. Someday I'll fire this guy, I tell myself. For now, I have to protect the office. I have to protect this family. I have to hold it together.

I rack my brains for something conciliatory and non-threatening to say. "I was told my bright shirts are unfashionable."

Bert frowns. "Where are your work boots?"

"They're here if I need them."

Bert gives me a hard look. Does he want to get into it with me? I'm thinking that if I can get him to throw a punch at me, then I can kick his ass without making Jada disgusted at me. My mind races with scenarios, but then he moves on to confront somebody else.

Eventually, he leaves.

Jada pops her head over my cubicle wall. "Fact: You rock."

"Fact: I rock," I say back.

She makes a silly disgusted face and pops back down.

Varsha leans in the doorway, monitoring the hall, while Renata and Lacey carefully slide Keith back to the dark and sunless breakroom.

"Keith is a scrapper," Dave says. "He's looking stronger every day. He wants to live."

"He really does have so much more green," Shondrella says. Jada agrees.

A cry goes up from the break room. It's Renata. "You guys! Come quick!"

We all rush in.

"Keith has a bud!"

Everybody crowds into the breakroom, ooh-ing and aah-ing over Keith's supposed bud. The photo apps start firing. I heave myself up and go over to see.

Keith's bud turns out to be a little nodule on one of the half-shriveled arms. Is it truly a bud? I'm skeptical. But I'm the only one. Lacey informs us that only a happy plant produces a flower.

"You're gonna be okay, Keith," Jada says.

All this for a dead plant with a small dingleberry. They may as well pin their hopes and dreams to a can of baked beans and throw it off the Empire State Building.

Somebody starts up the Keith song. Dave is doing his Keith dance.

I groan. I'm trying to sound humorous, but my pulse is racing.

This is just all a bit much. "I hate to break it to you all about Keith..."

"Don't you dare say it!" Jada says.

"Shut it!" Shondrella squeaks.

"Garbage bin cactus!" I whisper.

"Dude," Dave says.

I give them a comical sigh and go back to my desk, feeling anything but comical.

Our sales call—at a store called Bonobo—goes great. There's this feeling of boldness on our side of the table that wasn't there before. Bonobo's buyer is up on the buzz, and she's heard about the large order that Sadie Woo made. She wants to hear the Miracle Unicorn origin story, and for us to talk a little about the brand.

They're all sneaking looks at me, wondering if I'm going to do that thing again.

I'm not.

In the end, there's no need; the team does great. The buyer makes the order right then and there, and it's all the three of them can do not to run out onto the sidewalk screaming.

I'm not the screaming type, but I get it. This feeling of working with a team and pulling together on a project is addictive.

~

"Not going up there," I say to Jada as Lacey belts out a karaoke version of Lizzo's "About Damn Time" on a little stage in Chelsea.

Jada makes a big pouty frown. "Pleeeeeease?"

"I draw the line at being on stage."

"Because you're so famous...in Europe."

"That's the least of the reasons."

She sighs and stirs her drink. She and I are sitting at the end of a big, long table at the karaoke bar that's a few blocks down from SportyGoCo. Every department got to pick the location for their

Wycliff paid-for happy hour, and the design department went for the drama. We all have our knit hats on. Like we're a club.

Dave and some of the other guys from design accounts have been playing a dice game at the other end.

Earlier, Dave informed us all that this Friday's appointment with Nobella could put us in the black for this accounting period. "We're selling them for such a ridic amount of money, we don't need that many orders," he says. "This luxury shit is sick."

Dave's still holding all Wonderbag orders back from central accounting until the day before the period ends. Bert still thinks it's all dead in the water, and we're planning on ambushing him with our mad success when it's too late for him to ruin it.

Shondrella comes by and raises an obnoxiously expensive cocktail. "Here's to Wycliff! They don't know how to run a company, but at least they're supplying booze!"

I raise my cocktail and so does Jada.

Shondrella sits across from us and takes out her phone to film Lacey's song. We were all really happy to see her come out.

Jada puts her lips to my ear. "Do you think we can sneak away yet?"

"Maybe," I say.

Mackenzie comes by. "We're gonna kill it on Friday."

Renata flops down on the seat on the other side of me.

"Are you sure you can't handle it without me?" I say. "Shipping needs me this week."

"You're our secret weapon!" Shondrella squeaks.

"The bag is selling itself," I say.

"We need to keep our lucky formula going," Mackenzie says. "You have to be there. Wear another suit."

Jada snuggles nearer, laying her head on my shoulder.

Dave goes up to the stage and starts belting out Metallica.

Lacey comes back to the table and sits next to Shondrella. "Done!"

Renata leans so that her back is against my shoulder and she's yelling at Dave. And Jada's sleepy at my side, ready to go home—with me, because that's how we've been rolling these past two weeks.

She's all I think about when we're apart, and she wants to be with me. It's like a miracle.

And these people think I'm their secret weapon. They think we're this family, and to look at us from the outside, we are a family.

I feel this sudden wave of happiness and wonder. I'd never thought this was for me. Even now, it doesn't seem like something that's for me. As though it's too good. As though it's too much. I'm a man who burns bridges, not someone who builds them.

Jada kisses me on the cheek and then pulls back. "What's wrong?"

What am I supposed to say to that? *I'm falling in love with you so hard, I'm losing my mind?*

I've never had a family before and now I can see that it's the best thing in the world?

I'm loving all of this too much, and you most of all?

I smile at her and tell her that nothing's wrong. She snuggles back against me.

Nothing's wrong. But that's the problem.

Nobody ever warned me that happiness is a kind of hell, because it could vanish in an instant.

How do normal people endure this? How does a normal person let their heart be out there, unprotected? How does a person bear loving when it could all be lost?

Forty-Four

Jada

I adjust the collar of Jack's black wool blazer in the elevator on the way up to the office the following Friday. "Suit porn take two!" I tease.

He's in Prada today; underneath the jacket, he wears a gray sweater vest over a pinstripe cotton shirt and wool trousers.

He yanks me to him and kisses me deep. "Did you dress me in this just to taunt Renata?" he mumbles into my mouth before moving onto my neck.

"Thirty-percent to taunt Renata, thirty-percent for our meeting and forty-percent for me," I say.

"I want a hundred," he whispers. "I need a hundred percent of you right now, in the supply closet."

I push him away, laughing. "First of all, that doesn't make sense, and second, we almost ruined this suit once this morning. This is the big sale, Jack. If we make this, we're home free. They can't close us next week." I fix his tie. "We got this."

The door opens. He grabs my hand. We always have to be

touching lately. I've never experienced this feeling of being so happy with somebody that I want to be touching him all the time. Some nights we stay up way too late talking. There's always something more to say, a new topic we haven't covered.

Or else sex.

Or else talking about how great the sex was after the sex. Or just how lucky we are to have found each other.

In short, we're disgustingly into each other.

He actually asked me the other day if things were going too well. Like if things were *suspiciously* too good. "Don't you worry?" he asked.

He was serious. It's the messed-up way he was brought up. Happiness as part of a transaction. Good things always came with a cost for Jack.

I'd climbed into his lap—a place I spend an inordinate amount of time these days. "I believe in us," I'd said. "We're in it together, no matter what."

He'd tucked my hair back behind my ear like he does, looking intense. He was so aloof when I first met him. Nothing mattered to him. Nothing touched him. I didn't realize there were worlds inside him.

They say a cynic is a wounded idealist. I've come to think that maybe a villain is just a wounded saint.

"Fuck. You," Renata says when she catches sight of Jack. "Fuck the fuck out of both of you. That's what I have to say."

Jack chuckles and I make a pouty face. Renata sticks out her tongue at us and we all get to work. Fridays tend to be lighter, even with the chronic understaffing we're facing. Our appointment at Nobella is at four. We haven't figured out an excuse to tell Bert yet. Lacey thinks he'll be out of the office by then, and people can pretend we stayed and punch us out in absentia.

Bert leaves even earlier than we hoped. Renata sees him pull out of his usual space out front. "Bert just left," she says. It's two in the afternoon, and she's by the window that overlooks the VIP parking area. "Bye, asshole," she says.

The whole office relaxes. Renata and Dave push Keith to the window.

"Keith needs to be soaking up sunshine for two now," Dave says.

"Don't forget to move him back at the end of the day," I say. "We won't be here to help you remember."

"We won't forget," Renata says.

Mackenzie wanders over. "We are so nailing this." She leans in and lowers her voice. "I talked to my friend at Hilfiger and she said Nobella's nailing down their spring line right now. We got in just under the wire. If they seem hesitant, I might offer a discount."

"Don't do it," Jack says, coming over. "They're not buying on price."

"Right," she says. "I keep reverting back to the discount shit."

"If they don't love the bag, they're assholes who don't deserve the bag," he reminds us. "They're lucky we're even considering them."

"Thank god you're coming," Mackenzie says. "You're our secret sauce."

"I didn't even do anything at the last meeting," he says. "I'm just telling how it is."

"You're our secret sauce," Mackenzie insists. "These buyers are like horses. They sense confidence. By sitting there being how you are, you help us get in the right mindset. The mindset of: This bag is too good for you!"

Everybody's excited. We are going to have a whale of a celebration once we save the company. One more week to go.

As far as Renata and Dave and the rest of my co-workers know, we're only saving the company to fight another day, or the next accounting period, as it were.

Jack and I know the truth—if we can pull this off, he'll be able to void the contract with Bloxburn and kick them—and Bert—to the curb.

We're debating taking a cab over and when to leave.

That's when Bert walks in. He strolls around, wearing an expression of smug suspicion.

A dead hush falls over the place. People creep back to their assigned places.

Where did he come from? He was supposed to be gone! Did he move his car to fool us? Did he sense we're hiding something? We're hiding a lot of somethings.

Bert's walking up the row of cubicles, away from the project area. "Where's Lacey?" he asks.

Is that why he's here? Did he figure out that we're protecting Lacey? Letting her nap or even possibly leave early sometimes?

He turns and stands in the front of the room. "I asked a question. Where the hell is Lacey?" He's scanning all of our faces.

Nobody speaks.

"A funny thing about people who are keeping secrets," he continues. "They always give themselves away. For example, I've noticed a few of you glancing over at the small meeting room. What might I find in there?"

I grimace as he strolls over to the small meeting room. Out the corner of my eye, I see Jack standing up. I look over and catch his eye. I shake my head. This is no time to be a hothead.

Bert flings open the door to the small meeting room. "Rise and shine!" he barks.

A few minutes later, a weeping Lacey is cleaning out her desk. "Sleeping on the job. Not permitted," he crows. "Does anybody else want to help me reduce payroll expenses?" He's walking around again.

My heart breaks for Lacey. I can't believe he fired her. I try to catch her eye, to somehow assure her she's not alone.

Bert slows, and then he turns toward the window. That's when he sees Keith.

I hear Renata inhale sharply.

Bert takes his time walking over to where Keith basks in his little sunbeam, listing slightly in his sad clay pot.

We all rise from our cubicles, watching.

"Did I or did I not instruct you to put this thing in the break room?" Bert turns around, addressing us all. "My directive was clear, was it not? There is not to be anything obstructing this window." He turns back around. "So why is this thing here?"

My heart beats like a bongo. Keith just got that little bud. Is Bert gonna banish him to an even worse place than the break-room? Like a janitorial closet where he'll never see the sun?

He's still too fragile for us to pick up and move across the city in the cold, blustery weather. Jack's glowering at Bert.

Slowly, Bert walks up to Keith. He stands right in front of him. "Why's this piece of shit even in the office?"

I stiffen. Why is Bert so down on Keith? It's not like Keith takes up that much room.

And then, all in a blur of speed, Bert swings his leg and gives Keith a ruthlessly hard kick.

The blow lands on Keith's lower third with a sickening *thwick*. Keith practically explodes. I gasp. Bits of cactus fly across the room, landing on the carpet.

Keith, or what's left of him, is just a little stub sticking out of a pot.

I clap my hand over my mouth.

"His bud!" Shondrella squeaks.

Bert turns, smirking. "That was incredibly satisfying, I have to say." His smirk quickly turns to alarm, however, when he sees Jack beelining toward him.

"Jack, no!" I run over and get between them and set my hands on Jack's chest. "No."

Jack's face is pure fury. "Out of my way."

"Forget it!" I say. "Ignore him. Don't do this."

"He fucking kicks him?" Jack growls.

"What's the problem, prettyboy?" Bert says. "You sad about your *widdle pwant*?"

Jack surges at Bert, but I hold him back with the help of Dave. "Don't wreck this," I say.

Bert's smiling. He's doing it on purpose—that much is clear.

"You'll ruin everything, Jack," I say. "It's the wrong move."

"It's the only move I've got," Jack says.

"What about us? We need you, Jack!" I say. "We're a family!"

Bert's laughing. "Did somebody say something about a bud?" He crunches a section under his boot. "Oops."

There's no more holding Jack. He surges at Bert. His fist flashes powerfully, almost too fast to see.

There's a weird, suspended moment when Bert's face shows nothing but surprise. For that split second, I can almost trick myself into thinking that everything's just fine.

Then, in the next moment, Bert stumbles back and falls to the ground, almost in slo-mo.

"Come on, you bully prick, get up!" Jack says. "You beat up on a poor, defenseless cactus, but you won't fight me? Come on. I'll give you two free ones!"

"Jack, no!" I scream. "Stop it!"

Suddenly, everything goes into fast-forward. Bert's on his feet, going at Jack, throwing punches, one after another. Jack bobs and weaves. Bert's fist never connects.

Jack dives in and tackles him low at the hips. In a flash, Bert's on his back, and Jack is on his chest, one knee on either side, drawing back his fist, about to pound Bert's face.

Dave rushes in and grabs Jack's arm.

"Stop it, Jack!" I plead, even though I can see he's gone fully feral. "Please! You're ruining everything!"

"Good," Jack growls, lost in fury, struggling to get loose from Dave and get back to Bert.

I rush in and help Dave. Renata helps, too. Somehow, we get him off Bert.

Bert's face is bloody and angry. He has his phone out. "Nobody is leaving! I'm calling the police, and you're all witnesses."

"What have you done?" I breathe.

Jack's nostrils flare. "What I've wanted to do for a long time." It's like a switch flipped.

"This isn't you!" Even as I say it, I can see that there's something different about Jack. Something cold and calm. Like he's gotten a dose of some drug. He's expressionless, his eyes blank, his body tense and angry. In an instant I don't recognize the man I've grown so close to.

"That was very me," he says.

Security rushes up. Bert instructs them to subdue Jack. They're clearly confused, because Jack is just standing there, acting all weary and unperturbed. And blank. Totally blank.

He offers to sit in a chair by the door, and he plays on his phone, unruffled. I keep trying to make eye contact with him, but it's as if he's beyond reach.

Lacey is sobbing, cleaning up her stuff with Varsha's help.

Mackenzie comes up to me. "We have to slip out of here or we'll miss Nobella. No way will they let us reschedule."

"Go with Shondrella," I whisper. Shondrella is already putting on her coat.

Renata comes and grabs my arm.

"Nobody goes anywhere until this is finished," Bert barks.

"Damn," she whispers.

Forty-Five

Jaxon

I'm locked up in a large, sterile holding cell in the Manhattan Detention Complex, aka The Tombs. I'm stuck in here with five other guys who've been picked up for various offenses. None of them bother me or even try to talk to me. I can hold my own in groups like this.

Being a foreboding island is kind of my thing.

It's where I should've stayed.

I lean my forehead on a cool metal bar, trying not to think about what I did. Trying not to think about Jada and how I messed it all up.

It was inevitable–excruciatingly inevitable—that this thing with her was going to crash and burn. It's good that it's over, and it's good that it ended so badly; it's cleaner and faster this way. There's no sense in prolonging the death of something doomed.

I look up at the clock. I called Arnold to arrange to have him get me out. It's been one very long hour. They even take your phones in here.

Not that I need a phone when I've got Jada in my brain.

I'll stop thinking about her, though. It can be done. Five minutes here, ten minutes there. String together an hour, and then a day, and then a life.

My chest hurts. I can't breathe.

It was nice being in the office group for the time that I was. It meant something, but that, too, was always doomed. Who did I think I was? Jack from upstate?

God, no. I was never him. I'll never be him, the guy who wears whatever the hell he wants and helps out with cookie errands and tears his way through spreadsheets like they don't scare him.

Though it was satisfying as hell to hit Bert. I'm not sorry about that, even though it's going to lead to a world of trouble. I didn't decide to hit him in any conscious way. It's more that once I got the impulse to go at him, I didn't stop myself.

The old me was back in the driver's seat.

The timing was regretful. If I was any kind of a good man, a man who'd give a thought to anything but his own satisfaction, we might have made that last sales call, and they could've saved the company they love. But it turns out I'm not a man who gives a thought to anything but his own satisfaction, a fact that people everywhere from Milan to Dubai could've told the SportyGoCo crew.

My jaw goes hard as stone.

I'm sorry that SportyGoCo won't survive. That was bad form. I've never claimed to be a savior, though.

And anyway, it's done.

I probably won't see them again. I certainly won't see Jada.

I sigh and turn around, eyeing the other inmates. There's a particularly pungent man in the corner, and I enjoy a moment of silent, shared annoyance about him with a chop shop driver who's taking up most of the bench. Sitting in here with my fellow public enemies, I feel more like myself than I have in weeks. It's as if I've returned to solid ground after months at sea.

It feels very bad in a good way.

Bloxburn will drive the final stake into the heart of SportyGoCo next week; there's no getting around it now. They'll pulverize the company once the people are gone. My parents wanted vengeance on the owners, and they wouldn't have hired a second-rate firm to do the job. The destruction will be complete. They'll probably lock up the intellectual property forever and find a way to tarnish the name. My parents were highly competent in the awfulness department.

I'll have Soto see that the staffers all get good severance pay and that their health insurance is extended. If Jada and the others want to start something, they can have seed money. Wycliff has a venture capital arm that can handle it. One of the great things about being rich like me is that I can direct that it be done and not have to be personally involved with it.

Fall is a good time on the Mediterranean.

I bend forward, breathing hard, pain splitting my side.

The door opens. I expect to see Arnold.

Instead, I see blonde hair sprouting pencils, a purple skirt suit, bright hazel eyes piercing through the gloom. I breathe in, starting to stand, make it halfway up and sink down to the bench seat again, out of air.

For a second, I don't believe what my eyes are telling me. No. Not Jada, with her hands on her hips and her chin held high.

"Jack!" she says, rushing toward me. And it's her—not the bossy version, not the version showing me nothing but disdain for the way I acted—but the woman who's been in my corner.

"No contact," the guard reminds her.

"Are you okay?" She grips the bars, brow furrowed. Her overcoat is buttoned wrong and of course she has a smear of ink on her cheek.

"What are you doing here?" I ask, hardening my face, making my eyes go dead.

"Hello? Where else would I be? I came over as soon as they

finished taking our statements. We missed the sales call, but it's okay. The important thing is that we get you out. Lacey's been contacting the DA. They're being obstinate because it's a Friday after business hours, but one of my friends is dating a man who is very influential in this city, and she thinks that he can maybe pull some strings—"

"Hold up," I say. "No, no, no. I've got this. I'm fine."

"You don't look like you're fine. You're in jail, mister. But don't worry—"

"You think I need your help?"

She looks surprised. "Well, yes. I mean…obviously."

I lower my voice. "I'm a billionaire. It's under control."

"Jack, why are you being like this? It's me. Jada."

"And this is me," I say. "I'm not Jack the delivery driver. I'm not office Jack in a stupid knit hat. I'm Jaxon Harcourt Eadsburg von Henningsly. I came to find the identity of the butt-dialer and I did it. I can manage to get sprung out of jail on my own."

Jada blinks, lips moving soundlessly.

Don't cry, I think. *Don't you fucking cry.*

"No," she says finally. "I don't accept it. You're doing something out of feeling bad, or I don't know what, but I don't accept it. Whatever this is, we're in it together."

Why is she making it hard? I straighten and look her head on. "All this togetherness. It's a bit overrated, frankly."

She looks shocked for a moment, staring at me. And then she smiles. Her smile is like the sun coming out.

It hurts. God, why does it hurt so much?

"Oh, Jack. Don't act like you don't care about anything. It's too late—the jig is up. And I'm not mad at you. You had a lapse in judgment, but I get that your heart was in the right place. I mean, one could argue Bert deserved it. Maybe it wasn't the best option punching him and all, but we all make mistakes and revert to old habits. It doesn't change how I feel about you."

Why is she prolonging this? I'd hoped to avoid a scene. "Do

you not see what's happening here? We're done," I bite out. I've gone someplace dark and far away. "I'm bored of this. Your feelings about me? No thanks."

"Well..." She sucks in a breath, her jaw going tight the way it does every time she gets some wild new idea. "You can't stop me from how I feel."

I go back and sit on the bench next to my fellow detainee with the stolen car parts.

"I know you don't mean it," she says.

"You believe in a lot of things. Doesn't make them real." I give her my weariest sigh. "I'll see that the Wycliff Group makes it right for everyone, but beyond that, we're done here. That's just how it is."

"It's not how it is," she says. "This isn't you."

"It's very me."

"Come on. Let's work this out."

"Not likely," I say. "After I get out of here, I'm relocating to Bahrain. The Bahrain International Circuit has some of the best night racing there is." Something heavy lodges itself in my chest.

"You can't just leave!"

I wave at the guard, forcing my hand to go loose and languid. "This one's not welcome to visit anymore."

Jada looks at me, horrified. The how-could-you glare. Good people angry and disgusted with me.

This feels familiar. I'm definitely home.

The guard pushes off the wall. "Let's go. Time's up."

When she gets to the door, she turns.

I give her an academy-award-winning look of boredom. "Rhymes with frost maws." She turns and heads out the door.

"Harsh, man," the chop shop guy says.

"It's no favor to hang a person slowly," I say.

ARNOLD SHOWS up at around seven. He's got lawyers on the project of getting me out, but it's not so easy, considering the judges have all gone home for the weekend. Apparently, even my expensive lawyers are having trouble with that one.

"The good news is that Charley has connections across the city," he says. "It's three in the morning in London—"

"No," I say. "No way. We don't need Charley. I won't go begging to Charley, hat in hand. I'd rather spend the night in lockup."

Arnold says, "He'd want to help you. Charley has always admired you."

"I've always done my best to break him of that. Sometimes dreams do come true, you know." I wipe an invisible speck off the suit jacket Jada helped me choose this morning. A lifetime ago.

"Jaxon, you were just getting a new lease on life. You were with that lovely girl, and working together on a project that was close to your heart with the work family of yours—"

"Quite the tale of tragedy, I know. As a matter of fact, Jada stopped by earlier. God knows why, but it won't be happening again. Turns out the new lease on life had a few loopholes. Like the loophole that I didn't want it."

"What have you done?" he asks.

"What have *I* done? She doesn't understand how I am." *How I've always been. How I have to be.* "I set the record straight, and she walked away." Even as I say it, I feel this twist in my gut. I wish I'd never come to America. Why did I come? The siren song of the butt-dialer, I suppose.

Arnold presses me for details. The guard is busy with other people and I'm bored, so I fill him in. Arnold and I have been talking more recently, relating more on a human level than an employer-employee level, and I'm not sure how to put that particular genie back in the bottle. He probably thinks I've changed or something. Jada's not the only one who could do with a better grasp on the reality of the situation, I suppose.

"That girl believes in you," he says. "She does—I saw it. She's smitten with you, and if you forgive me for speaking bluntly, you need to pull your head out of your ass."

I blink. "This new tough love bit. Not a fan." Turning away from him, I go back and sit down. "I don't want to stay the weekend. Let's get the lawyers believing in that one."

As it turns out, I do end up staying for a good part of the weekend. It's not until Sunday afternoon that Soto manages to place the right amount of money in the right hands to get me in front of a judge who releases me on my own recognizance.

Forty-Six

Jada

I'm squeezed between Willow and Kelsey in our usual booth at the Wilder Club. Tabitha, who's on the other side with Francine, catches the attention of the server and orders a basket of tater tots and a large order of nachos.

"Yes, please," I say, trying not to cry, though it's hard with the constant lump in my throat.

Vicky's over at the old jukebox—not her first visit. Joan Jett blares from the speakers. Again.

Kelsey slams down her empty tequila shot glass. "Emotionally unavailable man-boys need not apply!"

I do my shot and my friends all clap. "Another!"

"No way," I say. "If you get me drunk, I might call him."

"You can't call him," Willow says.

"The ball is firmly in his court," Francine says. "He needs to step up. Not that he will."

My galpals are all really mad at Jack. And yes, I'm mad at him, too, but I'm mostly sad. I know his heart. I know he's hurting. I know he doesn't want to be alone.

Neither do I. I used to not care, but that was before I met Jack. My heart lurches sickeningly when I think of his eyes during that fight. How he seemed so far away from me.

"He wants to be with me," I say. "He really, really does. He wants to cross this bridge to me, but he can't stop himself from burning it."

"You deserve better than that," Tabitha says.

I sigh. I don't want better; I want Jack, or at least the version of Jack that I had for a few weeks there. I want open and vulnerable Jack, telling me real things in bed at night. I want witty, protective Jack who was in my corner. I want brave Jack who let his heart have big feelings.

I want the Jack who cared about a dying cactus like it was his own damn child.

I fight back the tears, thinking about long, lazy mornings in bed. His dry sense of humor. Him in that hat with the lone dimple.

Vicky comes back. She's decked out in a fabulous black jumpsuit with white piping. She's heading to Paris to do an event for the Smuck U line of jewelry. I aggressively question her about every aspect of the trip as a way to get my mind off of Jack.

She pulls out her phone and shows us pictures of the hotel where she'll be staying, and we all help her plan her itinerary, right down to looking at the menus of fabulous restaurants on the Left Bank and some hole-in-the-wall place in Marais. But then Lizzie arrives with a box of heart-shaped cookies that have jagged cracks frosted down the middle, and on one side of the broken heart is the letter 'F' and on the other is 'U' in pink frosting.

"Nice," I say, doing my best to swallow the lump back. "Stay positive."

"And they're lemon flavored." Lizzie shoves the box toward me.

How can I resist?

We all stuff our faces while Francine and Kelsey seat-dance to Heart.

"I still think you should take some time off after SportyGoCo closes," Tabitha says. "November is your favorite month in the city. Kick back, girlfriend!"

It's true—November is my favorite month in the city. I love the crisp, cool sunshine. I love the crunch of leaves and the fall coats and the excitement in the air. If I last out next week at work, they'll have to give me two week's severance pay, so it'll be like a paid vacation. I won't have the stress of finding a new job, because Tabitha's offered me a position doing merchandising for her style storefronts while I look for another design job.

"You can take your time and find something perfect," she'd told me.

I'm grateful, of course, but what I want is to keep my Sporty-GoCo job. I want to keep building the Wonderbag line. I want to stay working with my people. I want our routines and our dreams and our family.

Our food comes. I scoop a heaping helping of tots onto my little plate and squeeze thick, deep red lines of ketchup over them in a crisscross pattern.

"You're better off without him," Kelsey says, passing the salt. "He can fuck himself."

"I don't hate him," I say. "But maybe some causes really are lost."

I'M STILL HOLDING onto a shred of hope when I get into work Monday. Yes, we missed the Nobella cutoff, but maybe we can get into other stores. It's a longshot, but we still have the week.

The place is still in disarray from the chaos of Friday—I can't even look at the area near the window. I duck right into my cubicle and text Mackenzie to stop by when she gets in.

Shondrella looks over my cubicle wall. "Did you hear?" The way she says it, it's not good news.

"What now?"

Renata comes up. "Did you tell her?"

"Tell me what?" I say.

"Bert earmarked Wonderbag as summer season only," Renata says.

"What?" I hiss.

They nod in unison.

"But if we don't get our spring season orders up, there will be no summer season," I say.

"Yup," Shondrella says.

I hang my head and stare blankly at my keyboard. "In other words, SportyGoCo's toast."

Renata comes around and squeezes my shoulder. "At least we know we have to look for jobs now."

"He is such an unbelievable asshole," Shondrella says. "But I'll tell you one thing—I'm lasting this week out. Hell if he's screwing me out of my severance pay. I swear to god."

Renata and I pack up the Wonderbag prototypes. My heart does a sad little bleat when we put the lid on the box and set it on a shelf.

We act busy. We work hard to be polite to Bert, determined not to be more notches on his fire-your-ass belt.

One week. That's the end of the accounting period. The end of SportyGoCo.

Jack's cubicle stays empty. I'm sure he's out of jail by now. Maybe he's in Bahrain. I check my phone. Late afternoon in New York is late night in Bahrain.

The idea that I might not ever see him again is a steak knife in my gut.

Forty-Seven

Jaxon

I go up to my bedroom to check on the packing progress.

I'd wanted to get out of town last night, only to discover that there are more decisions to be made in advance of putting this property on the market, including some paperwork to handle.

Arnold calls me up to the third floor so that I can take a look at the clothes he's recommending I take. They're all laid out on the bed—a lightweight white suit, swimming trunks, polo shirts, jeans, belts, and so forth.

"Looks fine," I say. What the hell do I care? "The crew's filed a plan for a midnight take off. We'll sleep on the plane and be in Manama in the morning. Our morning, anyway."

"Very good, sir," he says.

"Anything else?" I ask.

He looks at his watch.

"What is it?"

"Somebody who wants to see you."

My heart lurches. It can't be Jada.

"Jenny, sir. She'll be here any minute."

"She's in the Catskills."

"Not anymore."

"Arnold, why? You didn't call her, did you?"

"She wants to see you."

I groan. "We're leaving in a few hours."

"She asked to say goodbye."

I groan. "I did want to grab a meal with her. This will have to do."

"She loves you, Jaxon."

"Yeah, yeah, yeah," I say.

"I strived to be carefully neutral in matters of family drama," Arnold continues. "I told myself it was my place, and I regret that, now. Jenny never shrank from a fight. She was a woman to admire."

"This isn't necessary, Arnold."

"I beg to differ, Jaxon. I should've stepped up."

I clap a hand onto his shoulder and look at him—really look at him. It comes to me that he's been there for me in his quiet way all along, a steady, comforting presence. Somebody who modeled what it is to be a calm, fair man who gets things done. A father figure in all the ways that counted. "You did step up. You've always been there for me. Always."

He gives me a quick nod.

I meet Jenny in the parlor room. She's in a powder-blue cardigan, the kind she always used to wear. Chef Ursula brings us small sandwiches and tea.

"I'm sorry we can't grab that dinner," I say. "How was the Catskills? You didn't leave early just to see me off, I hope."

"What the hell are you doing?"

"Um, what?"

"You heard me."

"I'm, uh, heading to my favorite wintertime track?" Why did that sound like a question? Why do I feel like I'm being chastised?

"Arnold tells me that sweet girl was smitten with you, that you were smitten with each other," she says.

"Wishful thinking—"

"Oh, stop. I saw it with my own eyes back there in that office. The way you looked at each other. And this group of yours. You were making your way, you were finding your people. You have no idea how I loved seeing it, after all this time!" She shakes her head, clearly angry. "You looked so…happy. Like the Jaxon I caught glimpses of as a child. Like the boy his father tried to…" She swallows and looks away, her jaw going tense, as if to hold the truth in. "Then I find out you got into a fist fight and ended up in jail? And now you're leaving?"

"I was never going to stay."

She blinks, dead-eying me in a way that hits me viscerally. Something from early childhood that I feel more than remember. "What about that girl?"

"It wasn't going to work, Jenny. I don't do relationships, and even if I wanted to, even if I was the type, I burned that bridge."

"So fix the bridge," she says, as if it's that easy.

"Did you hear the part about me not being the type? Anyway, it's too late," I say. "That life there, it wasn't for me. It can never be for me."

Jenny folds her arms and gives me her famous look of disapproval.

"That stopped working three decades ago," I say.

"Nothing to risk if you're sure you don't want it, if you're sure it's going to fail, is there?" Jenny says.

I snort. "Sounds like another vote for Bahrain."

Jenny frowns. "I don't remember you being a coward. Taking the coward's way out."

"But the coward's way out features a few days at Jarada Island Beach, night racing at the track, and some serious foodie action versus selling handbags and acting like I give a shit about a whole lot of people who I didn't know two months ago."

"Bullshit." I blink at the curse word. "That boy in the photo I gave you, he'd risk anything for love."

It's the dead certainty in her voice that sends a cold chill up my back.

But I ignore it, the way my parents would have, the way they taught me. I cross my legs and sip my tea, beyond ready for this tête-à-tête to be over.

IT'S nine at night and I'm alone in the limo, heading back from a flurry of signing legal documents in Midtown—an annoying way to spend an hour that ensures I won't have to come back anytime soon.

I'm looking out at the dark, rainy streets, gearing myself up for the trip, when I realize we're near the SportyGoCo offices, or at least near the turn that would get us there. I'd left a few things in my desk drawer, most notably my favorite watch; years of experience have taught me to always remove my watch before hitting a man. I decide I should have Stanley swing by so I can run up and pick up my things while nobody's there. Otherwise, somebody's sure to turn up at my door one of these days with a plastic shopping bag of my last belongings and a doleful expression. And that person's name will rhyme with *Made-a*.

I'll need to stop doing that.

Marv is at the security desk. The place is empty and quiet, and he's not so sure about letting me in, but I make him an offer that he can't refuse in terms of a tidy stack of Benjamins, and he relents.

He accompanies me up to the design department. "Five minutes. And I never saw you."

The office is a sea of cubicles, dimly lit by scores of colorful balls bouncing on computer screens.

I go over to my cubicle. My fucking cubicle. It was an experience, I suppose. I sit down, thinking about my unfinished spreadsheets. The program wasn't that hard once I got the hang of it. Even those stupid formulas.

I run my hands lightly over the keyboard, touching every key, but not hard enough to wake up the machine. I open the drawer and take out my watch and a few other things. I spin around in my chair and that's when my eyes fall on the knit hat. I'd hung it up on the rigid plastic thumb that goes with the cubicle, a coat hanger that's constructed so poorly you can't even put a jacket on it, but it works for a hat.

I pull the hat and hold it, squeezing it. I shouldn't have come back here.

I put the hat back on the hook and head back, pausing briefly to slide my hand over the smooth strip of plastic at the top of the wall of Jada's cubicle. The brown plastic strip where I put my hands so often, and sometimes even my chin when I'd talk to her. Jada utilizes her shoddy coat hook for a hedgehog calendar that her friend Noelle gave her. Next to that is a picture of her gang of girlfriends and Antonio, all standing outside of the shabby apartment building where they live. Next to that is a group photo of the office gang, limbs draped over each other, everybody making goofy faces.

A flash of red on her desk catches my eye just as I'm about to continue on out. A spot of red, very small and bright, in a tiny bowl of dirt and gravel.

I go in close.

The red bit seems to be attached to a shriveled husk-type thing.

I blink. With a lurch in my chest, I recognize what I'm looking at, though it doesn't seem possible.

It's part of Keith's shriveled little arm. And the red bit is Keith's bud—opening. Blooming. Becoming a flower.

I lean in closer. Yes, it really is happening. This stupid bloom growing off a shriveled little arm of a garbage bin cactus. This stupid doomed cactus, making a ridiculous flower for no reason at all.

It's so Keith. Because honestly, why bother? And of course Jada is cheering it on. Nurturing it.

Caring.

I stand up, trying to pull myself back together, to remember what I was doing, why I'd even come.

Fucking dead Keith with his fucking flower.

Suddenly I can't breathe.

I'm choked up like an idiot because a garbage cactus made a cactus flower. I sink to the floor next to her desk, face hot. The wheels of her chair blur. My breath comes in shudders.

I tell myself to get up. Eventually, I do.

I go back over to my cubicle and grab my hat and leave. Somehow I get out of the building. I get into the back of my car. I shove earbuds into my ears to signal that I'm not in the mood to talk.

But I'm not listening to anything. I'm not even thinking.

I'm riding in the back of a car, speeding down the rainy street, and my dead, shriveled heart is bleeding red.

Forty-Eight

Jaxon

Charley is dressed in tennis whites, the picture of leisure life with a tennis racket in his lap. He reclines in the plush seating on the veranda of his Amalfi Coast villa, surrounded by potted palms and hanging plants that explode with flowers.

Everything feels too bright.

There's a pitcher on a side table with something fizzy inside, and edible flowers floating in it. Charley's staffers love putting edible flowers in things.

I take a seat and he pours us each a glass. He wants to know why I've come. He's still wary after our last interaction, and I hardly blame him.

It takes me a minute to untwist my insides and open up, but once I have, I let it all out. First, I tell him about my job and then Jada. *Everything* about Jada. Not just the part where I fell madly in love with her, but the other bits—the way she feels things with her cheek, the way she cares about every single being, the way even a measly cactus is good enough to merit her attention.

I love her. I do. Oh, god.

It only took me this long to see it. Because I'm the world's biggest bonehead. I tell him how amazing she is. I attempt to describe how fiercely she believes in things, and how small and mighty she is with her puffed up stance and diamond bright eyes and secret sense of humor. And she thinks no cause is lost, walking around with pencils stuck into her messy blonde bun.

No cause. Not even mine.

Charley pushes his thumbs against the strings of his tennis racket as if to test the tension, but I know that he's listening.

I tell him how much I care about the whole family at Sporty-GoCo. They had no idea who I was, and they let me be one of them. We worked together on goals at the company. I learned all kinds of new skills. "It turns out that you were right about my being unfit to hold a job. The people there thought I was—"

"What?"

"Nothing."

"Seriously. What did they—"

"They thought I was from some backwards, impoverished village."

"You? An impoverished..." He's laughing full-out, though when he catches the look on my face, it's quickly suppressed. "I wish I'd seen you in the costume, though. Would you just put it on?"

"No."

"Just once?"

"No!" Like a fool, I lift up the hat they made for me; of course I had to grab it that night. I grabbed the hat, canceled Bahrain, and then I called Soto to brainstorm about his plan. Now I'm here.

"We all have hats like this," I say to Charley. "It's cold in Manhattan, and we wear these matching hats they made."

"They knit it? For you?" His brow's beetled.

"Yeah. And then, of course, I screwed it up." I turn it over in my hands. "I don't have any kind of excuse for myself. I loved being there, and I loved her, but I trashed it all like an idiot. I couldn't bear the idea that it could all be lost. Or the knowledge that it could all be taken from me, or that it was doomed. I don't know how to explain it..."

Charley looks up. "You couldn't stand the fact that you were vulnerable? Could that be it?"

I start to shake my head in denial and then stop, Jada's face bright in my mind. Jada who has hope and faith, who thinks I'm more than my parents' child.

"I suppose...that could be it," I say, my voice a little shaky under the weight of the truth. "I've been a real jackass for a long time, Charley. I've been a particular jackass to you." I meet his gaze, head-on, owning my faults instead of hiding behind them. "You stood by me when I didn't deserve it. You were always there with a kind word and a generous interpretation of things, but I rejected you again and again. It must've been awful for you. I want you to know that I'm sorry."

He looks out over the sparkling sea, probably to hide the surprise on his face. After a moment, he says, "She affected you."

"She believed in me." Sudden pain slices me deep. "I shredded the life that I was starting to build there. That belief that Jada had in me—I *ruined* it." I stare out for long minutes, waiting for that hurt to ease. It doesn't. "I may not be capable of what she needs in terms of a life partner, but I can give her something she desperately wants: the company she loves. That work family being able to stay together. It's all that I have for her."

"Oh, please. You're capable of immense love," he says, turning to me now. "I saw it. You loved your parents too much, and they never deserved it."

I'm stunned. "Since when do you think that?"

"I've always known it. I know you. I saw the way they trampled your feelings. You were a good friend to me, though, always. Don't you remember the way you held off the Bramster-Stoke twins? The way you hid me when it was time to leave for school? The way you lied to your parents when you were questioned, despite the punishment you knew you'd receive?"

I barely remember those things, and I don't know what to say. I didn't know I had people in my corner. I didn't know.

He asks me about what it means that I want to rescue the company. I tell him about my parents' vendetta against SportyGoCo that continues from the grave, and how Bloxburn has a contract to run it into the ground, and they won't let me buy that contract out.

"What are you going to do?"

"I've got this plan."

Charley squints up at me. "What kind of a plan?"

"Well," I begin, "Bloxburn is the company with the SportyGoCo contract, and they won't let me buy out that contract, and they won't sell the firm itself to me. Bloxburn is owned by Major & Bow. I'm sure you've heard of them."

"Of course." Charley sips his water.

"I want to buy it."

Charley chokes on his drink. "Major & Bow? How do you expect to do that?"

"A consortium."

Charley is laughing.

"What?" I say. "It's a strong company with a lot of upside potential."

"No doubt about that. But you know you're going to have to hit up half the people you have vendettas with."

"How is that funny?" I say. "I'd rather get a root canal."

"That's what's so funny! It's just so fucking ironic. To undo your parents' vendetta, you have to end a bunch of yours."

"I don't think it's funny," I say.

"I find it hilarious. And I accept your apology, Jaxon. It really wasn't necessary—I've always been here waiting for you, you know. You've always been one of my favorite people in spite of it all. Now, who else do you have in mind? Let's put together a consortium."

"You're in?"

"Of course. I'd love to do this with you. We could move on them in a day. At least enough to get them to cancel contracts that could compromise the deal. That's what you want, right? Cancel this business with SportyGoCo?"

"That is what I'd want."

"You should look into Hugh Jacobsen—he just came into something big. Maybe even Marina Apondi."

"Those two hate me," I say.

"Those two only hate you because they think you hate them. They'd love to have you on their side. People want somebody like you on their side—you're brilliant and charismatic and completely fearless. A brawler with a heart...and a conscience. Everyone saw how you built your Formula One team. You built a real organization, and you would have been on top if you hadn't screwed it up. I'm glad you're going for it with this one."

"I really fucked it up. You have no idea."

"You go big." He shrugs. "It's one of the best things about you."

"Thank you." I pick up my glass and watch the bubbles in the sun, rising to the surface and popping one after another. "I don't know what I'm doing."

"None of us do," he says. "None of us have any goddamn idea."

Forty-Nine

Jada

It's amazing what can change in a week.

Just one short week ago, I was deliriously happy.

Because of Jack.

I couldn't believe I could be that happy. I couldn't believe I could enjoy even the most mundane activities.

Standing in an endless line for coffee? Fun if Jack's there. Crossing the street to avoid heavy construction? Magical when Jack has my hand. Shoe shopping? The best.

Playing hooky? Day drinking? Lying on the ground listening to birds? It's like I'd never really relaxed until Jack came around. And I can't remember ever laughing like I did with Jack. I'd never savored things. Especially not sex.

I had so much.

Now I've lost it all. Not just Jack, but it's Wednesday of our last week at SportyGoCo. Dave says we don't have enough sales to show a profit, and without Wonderbag, there's just nothing we can do. For a while, Mackenzie, and Shondrella and I were busting our asses to try to get more orders on yoga pants, but it's a losing battle.

Renata comes over and leans her chin on the top of my cubicle wall. "We're gathering lunch orders. We're thinking of ordering from a little place called Sushi Station."

Sushi Station is a ridiculously expensive sushi restaurant a few blocks up. Wycliff is still footing the lunchtime bills for whatever reason.

I still haven't told the gang about Jack's identity. There's so much fuss being made about our breakup and his punch and his disappearance, I don't want to talk about him anymore. I just want to move on.

People have been ducking out to interview for new jobs. There was a time when having SportyGoCo on your resume was a major plus, but thanks to Bloxburn's work to ruin SportyGoCo's reputation, it's becoming the equivalent of doing fashion design for the Hee-Haw Dollar Mart. We're sharing leads, and my friend Tabitha has offered a few people interim positions.

I scroll through the Sushi Station menu. "I'm not that hungry," I say.

"We're ordering extra in any case. Sammy down in shipping is going to drive a sushi care package over to Lacey."

I nod. Sammy down in shipping has taken over Jack's driving duties.

"You're gonna feel good again," Renata says. "Actually, I have a smokin' hot cousin moving here from Omaha. I should fix you two up."

"That's okay," I say.

"We can double!"

"Not there yet, sister."

Renata points at my desk. "Look!"

I looked down at Keith's bloom. It's almost a proper flower now.

"So pretty," Renata says.

"I might try to take it home. Keep up the Instagram, you know." No post ever got so many comments as the sad one in the aftermath of Bert's attack on Keith. Now everyone's excited about the bloom.

Dave comes by with a Bert alert. Shondrella groans from her cubicle. Bert has been everywhere lately, picking on people and generally striving to give out some last demerits, hoping to do a little more firing; all the better to reduce liabilities.

We're all on impeccable behavior, determined to hang on until the end of the week in order to get our severance packages. It's unbelievably sad, though. This family that we love. And also, we can never sell Wonderbag, being that it belongs to SportyGoCo, and Bloxburn will kill it with fire just like it's killing everything else here. Which also really hurts. Wonderbag is my baby. Lord knows what our old owners did to Jack's parents. Must've been a doozy of a thing.

I tap a few keys and bring my computer back to life, trying not to think about Jack.

Easier said than done.

I've dated my share of men, but this thing that Jack and I had was in another stratosphere. And yes, he could be challenging. He didn't know how to do emotions or family, but that was part of his amazingness—that he was venturing into new territory, bravely trying these things that are second nature to other people. He made me feel alive.

Bert comes through being his mean, petty self. He has cruel words for Dave to start things off as usual, and then he's deriding the rest of us. He pauses at Varsha's desk and plucks a saltwater taffy from her little bowl without even asking. He unwraps it and shoves it in his mouth, then he makes a face and spits it out. "Yuck."

Seriously want to kill him.

Right at that moment, the door opens. A woman with pink hair and big red glasses strolls onto the design floor and introduces herself as Maya. "I'm to report to the design department," she says. "I'm the assistant to the new CEO."

"Wrong company." Bert points at the door. "Out."

Clarence and Marv from security have wandered in.

"I'm to report to a Jada Herberger," she says to Bert. "Are you Jada?"

I go up, praying that whatever this is doesn't lead to a demerit. "I'm Jada, but I'm senior designer here, not the CEO. There must be some mistake."

"I've been told you're the new CEO of SportyGoCo. I've been assigned to execute your vision in all things SportyGoCo." She rattles off a few names—Wycliff executives, it seems.

"She's not the CEO," Bert says. "I am." He points at the door and addresses Marv and Clarence. "Make yourselves useful and escort this one out."

"You're Bert Johnston?" Maya asks.

Bert nods.

Around us, nobody moves. Nobody breathes.

Maya smiles, a quick, curt movement. "The company that holds your contract, the company that hired you, has been acquired in an aggressive takeover. Your contract has been terminated." Another tight smile. "Effective immediately."

Bert straightens indignantly. "Bullshit."

"You're being terminated," Clarence says. "You have ten minutes to clear out your desk, and after that we're to take you out of the building." Obviously, neither Clarence nor Marv is all that sad to see him go.

Bert's well-scrubbed cheeks puff out ever so slightly. "How about this instead—You're fired," he says to Clarence. "You and Marv. Go get your things and clear out. Now."

"Yeah, no." Marv looks at the clock. "Nine minutes."

"You don't have that power anymore, Bert," Maya says.

Bert's expression turns thunderous. He gets on his phone and has a quick, hushed conversation that turns his expression grim.

Maya comes over to me. “I’m here to get you up to speed and to manage all of the operational details so that you can apply yourself to the creative end of things. That’s my mission here.”

“I don’t understand. This company was closing. Now it’s not? And Bert’s fired?”

“Yup. And I was hired by the head of Wycliff HR. I promise you, I’ve done this at quite a few companies, including one other design firm. Have you ever heard of Zoozy Mayhem?”

“I love Zoozy Mayhem!”

“I love them, too.” She explains to me how she works, though I’m still pretty confused about everything. Is this some kind of joke?

A woman in a white coat wanders in. “I’m here to see Jada. I’m from the Plant Genomics Research program at NYU. I understand there’s a cactus that we’re going to root and regrow?”

“Exsqueeze me?” Renata says. “Are you here because of Keith’s Instagram?”

“Oh my god,” I say, falling back into my chair, mouth slack. “It’s Jack.”

“What about Jack?” Renata asks.

My pulse races. “Jack did this.”

People are looking at me with deep concern. They know how heartbroken I’ve been.

Suddenly I’m up and stomping to the door. I fling it open and head down the hallway. “Where is he?” I turn a corner, prepared to search every nook of this building if I have to and hunt him down like the—

And then he’s just...there. Jack. My Jack. The Jack who smiles and spoils me and secretly cares. His face goes bright—exactly the way I feel inside—and he sets off running. I do the same, my arms and legs pumping not nearly fast enough.

When we crash, he catches me, pulling me into his big, strong arms. “I’m so sorry,” he whispers into my hair. “I’ve been such an idiot.”

"What are... What's... What did you do?" I ask. I should probably be more shocked, but I realize here that I always knew he'd come. Deep down.

"What I had to do. What I was meant to do. I bought Bloxburn. Well, actually, we bought their parent company. SportyGoCo is not closing."

"I thought you couldn't," I say.

"I couldn't do it alone. But I learned from a very special person that being a part of things isn't so bad and that working with a team is its own kind of magic. So, you know. I asked for help. Mended a few fences. Made some groveling apologies."

"You did?"

His warm eyes get smile crinkles on each side. "Groveling apologies. People seemed to enjoy it, too. I'm trying to turn over a new leaf—and keep it turned over. I was such an asshole."

"Jack—you don't have to—"

He tightens his hold on me. "Please, let me say this. You believed in me, and I pushed you away like you didn't matter, and I said some really shitty things, too. I can't stop imagining how terrible it must have felt to grow close to a person and then have them do that. I want to be with you, Jada, and I'm not really sure how to do that. All I can promise you is that I'm gonna keep working on being the kind of guy who deserves you. But no matter what happens, the company is back, and I'm putting you in charge. We sent somebody to do the managerial part, but you can direct things—"

"So it really is real."

"Yes. The old owners want to stay retired. You can run this thing how you want, no matter what you decide about us."

I press a hand to his chest. "Jack—" He claps his hand over mine, warm and solid. My heart feels like it's expanding in ten different directions.

"I want to work on being the man that you deserve. I want to win you back."

"Silly Jack," I say. "You never lost me," I say, gazing into his eyes. I have the sudden sense that I can feel his heart, right through his eyes.

"I'm shitty at togetherness. I'm shitty at harmony."

"I know." I go up on tiptoes to kiss him. The instant our lips meet, he yanks me to his chest. I fling my arms around him.

"You!" A hoarse, agitated-sounding voice barks out. It's Bert. He's down the hall between Clarence and Marv, pointing at Jack. "He's the one you should be escorting out of here."

"Are you going to go up and clean out your desk, or are you leaving with just that shirt?" Clarence steers him to the elevators.

"Sorry, Bert, looks like you got your last demerit," Dave says, strolling out into the hall.

Bert stomps into the elevator. "This is not over!" he says just as the doors close on him and the guards.

"Hey, Jack, nice to see you!" Dave says.

Renata and Shondrella come out.

"Jack! You're out of jail!" Shondrella squeaks. "You got sprung!"

Mackenzie and Varsha and a few others crowd out behind them.

"What's going on?" Varsha asks.

"Jack owns SportyGoCo," I say. "Well, he owned it all along—"

"Wait, what?" Mackenzie says. "You own Wycliff? As in the massive international company?"

"Since a few months ago, yes. My parents passed it on to me. But I didn't actually control SportyGoCo due to contractual issues."

"What the hell?" Renata says.

Varsha squints in disbelief. "You're the owner? Why were you pretending to be the office gopher?"

"It's kind of a long story, but we're not closing, that's the point," Jack says, looking a little skittish. "And Bert and all his policies are outta here."

"Dude, you are like, this corporate titan?" Dave blinks in disbelief. He puts his fists up by his ears and then opens his hands while making an explosion sound. "Mind. Blown."

Meanwhile, Shondrella is doing a happy dance. "We're not closing! We don't have to get new jobs! Yay!" She hugs Dave.

Varsha asks if our old owners are coming back. I tell her what Jack said.

"So, just to get this straight," Renata says, raising her hands. "Jack, *you* were the voice on the speakerphone?"

"Yeah, but those weren't my words. It was just this idiotic script that I shouldn't have agreed to read. Though in retrospect..." He knits his fingers in mine. "I'm glad I did."

Renata turns to me. "You forbid me to give Jack a makeover. You told me it would be wrong to change his doofus style and jump his bones. And I backed off of him."

I wince and knit my fingers into Jack's.

"And the next thing I know, you have given him a makeover, and he has turned out like so." With a look of mock outrage, Renata waves her hands at him. "Like so. And you take him for yourself, lording him over the office in his stylish outfits. Yet that is not enough, is it?" she says. "Noooooo. He now turns out to be a billionaire? Is that what you're trying to tell me here?"

"Umm...that's what I'm trying to tell you."

She snorts. "That's one hell of a makeover."

Jack looks over at me. "Yeah, it is."

~

WE SPEND the following weeks resurrecting Wonderbag and putting the pieces of SportyGoCo back the way they were before Bert wrecked things. We even develop new sustainability initiatives and better work-life balance policies. We also hire back most of the people who left, including Lacey, who gets a flexible schedule; Sammy gets control of shipping. It's a new day at the office, and everybody's jazzed.

Jack and I fly to Italy one weekend to stay at the very lavish villa owned by his cousin Charley. Jack and Charley tell me stories of their boyhood over red wine and *Scialatielli ai frutti di mare*—a traditional seafood pasta dish that might be the best thing I've ever tasted.

Jack and I splash around in the sparkling blue sea during the day, and we have frequent sex on our private veranda overlooking the coast. We mostly have hot sex as ourselves, though now and then I find myself unable to pay for a meal and a torrid price must be paid.

Jack puts a lot of fierce energy into his new consortium. We have dinner with the group of his new co-owners one night. Apparently they were enemies, but they all seem thrilled to be on Team Jack. He's a charismatic, brilliant, fearless man of action.

I could not be happier to be on Team Jack.

Back at SportyGoCo, I turn decisions over to the former senior designer—I'm more interested in concentrating on my Wonderbag spin-off. We do a luxury version and a big-box version.

On the last nice day of the year, an unusually warm Saturday in November, Jack and I have another picnic at the pigeon sound park. It's our place now. We are bundled up, sitting on blankets in the little nook of statues. The leaves are almost all off the trees and we're lying there, looking up at the jagged, black lines of the tree branches against the dazzling blue sky.

"Working in the office was one of the most important experiences of my life," he says.

I'm surprised. I go up on my elbow next to him. I trace my finger down his forehead and over his nose, landing on his lips. He grabs my finger and kisses it.

"What brought this on?" I ask. "Because you finally learned Excel?"

"No, because I used to imagine it was a fate worse than death to have to work at a job, but I was happy being there. Doing something side by side with other people was incredibly satisfying. How did I not know about that?"

I grin. "It is, right? Well, not in every job, but yeah."

Jack tells me he's thinking about turning over ownership to the workers long-term—at SportyGoCo as a test, but eventually at more of Wycliff's holdings, too. "People who work at a place should have some real control and some real power, and get some of the benefit from their work."

"Is this you sticking it to your parents?

"A little bit, but I would want to do it either way, knowing what I do, having actually worked there—that's what really got me thinking. I don't want my life to be a reaction to who my parents were; that's as bad as following in their footsteps."

I grab a grape and pop it into my mouth.

I slide a finger over his scruffy cheek. "I think I've sometimes lived in reaction to my lazy brothers. However, it turns out loafing around has its charms. Playing hooky. Day drinking. Goofing off."

"My corruption plan is complete," he says.

"I hope not," I say.

A villainous glint comes into his eyes. "Well, maybe I can find a few more ways to corrupt you."

Epilogue

Jaxon

Thanksgiving is a holiday I usually spend feeling thankful that it's not celebrated in Europe. But now my dining room is filled with members of the SportyGoCo family, talking and laughing and indulging in the massive feast that Chef Ursula prepared before leaving for her own family—turkey, stuffing, all the works, plus copious amounts of wine and pumpkin pie. And people have brought things, too. It's mayhem—unruly, festive, messy mayhem. I love it.

Arnold comes and joins us at one point. He'd gotten a bit of notoriety as my cruel tormentor, and people are having a lot of fun with that. They also seem to just enjoy his company, which warms my chest in ways I'm still not able to express.

I didn't know that a family like this was an option. I didn't know what a family was at all, I suppose.

Jada takes my hand under the table and I'm feeling like the luckiest guy in the world, even after everybody piles on me during an argument about whether Formula One is a real sport or not. (It is.) I know they're just saying it to annoy me, but still.

"You guys have no idea what you're talking about!" I protest. "We work out, we have quick, rapid-fire reaction time and we—"

"You're dismissed," Renata says.

We set to dismissing each other, and then we chat and laugh late into the night. At one point I look up at that photo on the wall, the one that Jada and I put up there. There's unhappy me, wanting so badly to have a family. Fighting for a family the only way he knew how. "You won't always be alone," I imagine saying to him. "You'll find your people."

Later, after everybody's gone home, Jada and I head out to the Wilder Club. We meet up with her huge gang of friends—*our* friends, now—who've rolled in from various Thanksgiving dinners with families and found families, and we talk about what we've eaten and groan about how full we feel.

I already met Kelsey and Tabitha that day on the roof, as well as Dr. Tonio, aka Antonio, who comes in and gives me a big bearhug and immediately wants to talk racing.

I've met Max Hilton, Mia's significant other, before—we were both at a lot of the same parties during one notorious season on the French Riviera.

Jada looks beautiful. Her outfit is all sparkles. She's like a magpie with the sparkles when she's not at work, and she's wearing a bun with a pencil in it—not the writing kind, but a glitter-encrusted pencil I saw in a shop on Fifth Avenue. She looks beautiful and relaxed, and my heart swells ten sizes to think she picked me.

The mayhem is at its peak around one in the morning.

Jada snuggles into my side and tugs at my knit hat. "Are you ever going to take this off?" she asks.

"Is that a request? For me to go back to my other outfits?"

"No."

"Are you sure?" I tease.

"You're dismissed," she says.

"Dismiss me all you want," I whisper in the split second before I kiss her. "But I'm never leaving."

I HOPE you enjoyed the tale of Jaxon and Jada! Thank you for reading! xoxox

Also by Annika Martin

Stand-alone romantic comedy (read in any order)

Most Eligible Billionaire

The Billionaire's Wake-up-call Girl

Breaking The Billionaire's Rules

The Billionaire's Fake Fiancée

Return Billionaire to Sender

Just Not That Into Billionaires

Butt-dialing the Billionaire

Find a complete list of books and audiobooks at www.annikamartinbooks.com

Acknowledgments

I love my readers so much! Thank you for cheering me on and leaving reviews and reaching out and most of all just for READING! You make me smile and you give my characters a reason to exist and do all the wacky things.

Major huge adoration to my bookish friends, also; I could not have written Butt-dial without your help! In the order of their appearance as utter angels in the development of this story, I want to thank my dear friend Jess Lourey for always being willing to hear new iterations of the idea on neighborhood walks. And Zoe York and Molly Fader for helping me find the yummy parts of this idea on the windy coast of Lake Erie one day, and also, OMG Molly thanks for the read and the amazing ideas, including some serious chef's kiss kissing scenes. Joanna Chambers, you gave me so much important clarity around Jaxon—you saw what he was up to before I did! And luckily informed me of it. LOL. Brighton Walsh, thank you for being a sounding board, and for the check-ins that kept me focused. Major love to my husband Mark for the careful read and the awesome ideas for adding air and gravity to scenes, and also not letting me do a wimpy fight scene. Finally, massive gratitude to Adriana Anders for the eleventh-hour read and for adding brilliant emotional gold that lifted this book to the next level.

Big thanks also to my team who helped with other aspects of this endeavor. Nina Grinstead and Kim Cermak and the rest of the team at Valentine PR—you rock! And Melissa Gaston, I'm so eternally grateful you are in my corner with your storehouse of wisdom. And Kelly Reynolds, thank you for your social media brilliance and sassy talents! And Sandy Waters, thank you for always giving Antonio the right Italian things to say. And Brooke of Brooke's Editing Services and Judy Zweifel, thank you for the Herculean effort of proofing this book. Naturally I changed it right up to the last minute, so any mistakes are sadly mine.

About the Author

Annika Martin is a New York Times bestselling author who sometimes writes as RITA®-award-winning Carolyn Crane. She lives in Minneapolis with her husband. In her spare time she enjoys taking pictures of her cats, consuming boatloads of chocolate suckers, and tending her wild, bee-friendly garden.

newsletter:
http://annikamartinbooks.com/newletter

Facebook:
www.facebook.com/AnnikaMartinBooks

Instagram:
instagram.com/annikamartinauthor

website:
www.annikamartinbooks.com

email:
annika@annikamartinbooks.com

Made in United States
Orlando, FL
19 April 2023

32260761R00221